In Little Stars

Also by Linda Green

In Little Stars

LINDA GREEN

QUERCUS

First published in Great Britain in 2022 by

QUERCUS

Quercus Editions Ltd
Carmelite House
50 Victoria Embankment
London EC4Y 0DZ

An Hachette UK company

A CIP catalogue record for this book is available
from the British Library

HB ISBN 978 1 52941 226 0
TPB ISBN 978 1 52941 809 5

10 9 8 7 6 5 4 3 2 1

Typeset by CC Book Production
Printed and bound in Great Britain by Clays Ltd, Elcograf S.p.A

Papers used by Quercus are from well-managed forests and other responsible sources.

For Vie and K
And all those who have been made to feel unwelcome
in our country

We are far more united and have far more in common than that which divides us.

Jo Cox MP (1974–2016)

PART ONE
3 September 2019

1

SYLVIE

Peace reigned in our house for approximately fifteen minutes. It was fragile, and as soon as I heard Rachid descending the stairs two at a time, I knew it was only a matter of time before it shattered.

'Not a word,' I said to Bilal, as he drank the last dregs of coffee from his cup.

'I can't bear to see him making such a huge mistake.'

'I know, and I understand how hard this is for you. But we let him make his choice and it's happening. That's the end of it. Let's try to have breakfast without another row.'

Bilal shrugged and rubbed his beard, which was now more grey than black. Rachid strode into the kitchen; he didn't have to crow about having won the battle, his whole demeanour declared it.

'Morning,' he said, with a broad grin.

'I hope you'll be as bright and cheery as this every morning and not just on the first day,' I said, resisting the temptation to ruffle his hair as I could see he'd already put gel on.

'I will,' he replied with a smile as he picked up a croissant from the table without bothering to sit down. 'Because for the first time in my life, I'm doing what I want to be doing, instead of having people tell me what to do.' He looked pointedly at Bilal as he said it. For a second, I thought that he would not take the bait. I even poured him a fresh cup of coffee, in the hope that might appease him. But my hope was misplaced.

'Well, make the most of it,' said Bilal, folding his copy of the *Guardian*. 'Once you've finished this music production thing and get out into the real world, someone will be telling you what to do for the rest of your life.'

Rachid shook his head. 'You don't get it, do you? I'll work for myself at the end of this, I won't be a slave to anyone. Unlike you, when the NHS is sold off to the highest bidder.'

Bilal's lower jaw visibly tensed. Bringing the future of the NHS into it was akin to waving a red flag. The principle of a national health service free at the point of delivery was, like his family, something he would lay down his life to defend. I asked Alexa to switch from Radio 4 to Absolute 80s, in the hope that the distraction might break the moment, or at least make Bilal, who always insisted on listening to the *Today* programme in the mornings, direct his ire at me, instead of Rachid. 'Club Tropicana' by Wham! was playing. I thought for a second it would be impossible for them to continue their argument with that as the background soundtrack. It did cause a momentary pause in hostilities, but it turned out Bilal was only using George Michael as cover while he loaded another round of ammunition.

'And you think this college course will equip you to support yourself? That you'll be able to buy a nice car and a home of your own and have enough left over to raise a family? Because if you do, you're even more of a fool than I took you for.'

Rachid laughed. Always the worst thing you could do to Bilal.

'Why do you think I want to end up like you?' he said. 'I can't think of anything worse.'

You could almost hear the sting of those words as they landed. Faced with the prospect of a full-blown war breaking out across the kitchen table, I did the only thing I could think of. I started to sing along with George about the fun and sunshine, complete with obligatory shaking of the black pepper grinder on the kitchen counter. Bilal and Rachid both stared at me as if I had lost the plot.

'Don't look at me like I'm the crazy person here,' I said. 'You're the ones having the same argument for the one hundred and twenty-seventh time. Rachid, sit down and eat your breakfast properly and will you both try to be civil to each other? I'm going to see where Amina's got to, and when I come back, I don't expect to find that you've come to blows. Do you understand?'

They both nodded, although neither of them appeared the least bit remorseful. I headed for the kitchen door, only stopping to issue one further command. 'And please don't change the radio station. "Club Tropicana" may not be the finest from their *oeuvre*, but any song by Wham! lifts your soul.'

I knocked on Amina's door. I knew she was awake because my children were morning people like their father and never had to be dragged out of bed.

'Yeah,' she called, her voice sounding unusually flat. I went in to find her sitting on the bed, already in her school uniform, brushing her mane of dark, curly hair.

'Morning, gorgeous girl,' I said. 'Are you coming down for some breakfast before I leave for work?'

She shrugged. 'I don't know. Are they arguing again?'

'They were but I shut them up by singing to Wham!'

Amina managed a smile.

'Everything OK?' I asked, stroking her head.

'I hate going back to school. Every year it feels like being the new girl all over again.'

'Are you meeting Becky and Jasmine on the way?'

I was aware they hadn't seen much of each other over the summer holidays. A couple of meet-ups and a handful of WhatsApp video calls, but that was about it.

'No. I think they're walking down from Becky's house together – with their boyfriends.'

I nodded slowly.

'It'll be fine once you get there. You'll soon slip back into how things were.'

'We won't. They're treating me like I'm some little kid, just because I've never been out with anyone.'

I sat down next to her and gave her a hug. I'd been waiting for this to happen. Aware that her best friends were from different families to ours. Families where a daughter going out with a boy at fourteen was considered the norm.

'For what it's worth, they'll probably have split up with them by half-term. It won't last, it rarely does at that age. Anyway, you've got other friends, haven't you?'

'I guess so.' She didn't sound too sure.

'Why don't you call Leila when you get home later? Maybe arrange to go for a hot chocolate after your mosque group on Saturday. I've got a hair appointment, but I'll come and collect you afterwards.'

'OK,' she replied. 'If you're paying.'

'Cheeky,' I said, smiling at her. 'Think of it as a back-to-school treat for the two of you. Now, get yourself downstairs so I can get to work.'

Rachid had left the kitchen when I returned. Bilal was sitting alone, staring into his empty coffee cup. I gave his shoulder a squeeze, aware that I needed to show I wasn't taking sides, that I merely wanted an *entente cordiale*.

'I meant what I said, love, the fighting needs to stop. Amina's sick of it and so am I. We've got to let him make his own way in the world, make his own mistakes if necessary. Who knows, he may even surprise you.'

Bilal looked up. 'You think he's right, don't you?'

'I think he's doing something he's passionate about, the same way you did. He's not as different to you as he makes out.'

'So why does he hate me so much?'

I hesitated. I'd never told Bilal about Rachid's little face appearing in the bedroom doorway that day. The fear about what he might have heard before he ran away clutching his toy zebra. But I knew now was not the time to bring that up. The last thing I wanted to do was drive a further wedge between them.

'He doesn't hate you,' I said, stroking his arm. 'He's simply trying to be his own person. And this is his way of doing that. He's seventeen, almost a man. It's like he's marking his territory.'

Bilal snorted. 'I think I'd rather he pissed all over the house than not do A levels.'

I laughed. 'I wouldn't,' I said. 'Because I'd be the one who had to clean it up.'

Bilal stood up and took his cup over to the sink while I got my things together.

'Rachid's getting the train after mine,' I told him. 'He won't need telling to go, so leave him to it. Just make sure Amina's OK before she leaves for school; she's a bit wobbly.'

'Why?' Bilal turned to face me.

'The whole social thing at school is starting to get difficult for her.'

'She's not being bullied, is she?'

'No. She's feeling squeezed out because her best friends have both got boyfriends.'

He raised his eyebrows. His little girl was growing up, probably a bit too fast for his liking. 'She's fourteen.'

'I know. And at that age feeling different from your peers is the worst possible thing.'

'Well, I hope it's not going to affect her studies. I'd hate her to fall behind with her GCSEs.'

I sighed, aware that Amina was now his last hope for medical school.

'I'm sure she won't let that happen. But the last thing she needs is any pressure from you, OK?'

Having fired the warning shot, I gave Bilal a quick kiss, picked up my briefcase and headed for the door.

There was a nip in the air. Across the road, in the park, a handful of leaves were already starting to turn yellow. I loved this time of year. Not just the colours and the bright, clear mornings but the sense of new beginnings. I would never admit it to Bilal, but I was excited for Rachid to be following his dreams. His world was opening up, full of hope and possibilities without, at this stage, any responsibilities. I could still remember how good that felt.

I hoped Bilal had listened and would let it go now. While he'd never proudly tell people that his son was doing a BTEC in music technology, perhaps some kind of grudging acceptance would be reached. He'd simply focus on Amina instead. Discuss the differing merits of Oxford, Cambridge or Keele with her. But I was aware that the distance between him and Rachid had opened into such a chasm that it was difficult to see any way to bridge it. Particularly as the one thing they had in common was a stubborn sense of pride.

I checked my watch as I headed towards the station and quickened my step, seeing I was cutting it fine but knowing I could still make it without breaking into a jog. Five years of doing this journey meant I had it timed to perfection. I arrived on the platform as the train came in. I smiled at a few people I recognised as we waited for the doors to open: the older woman who always wore a mac, whatever the weather; the young man with floppy, dark hair who I'd have flirted with if I'd been thirty years younger. It felt good to be back on the morning commute. Out of the house, away from everything that had dominated my thoughts all summer. As much as I loved being with my family, I needed this time away from them too.

The carriage was busy. I sat down at the only window seat available in the far corner, opposite two teenage boys, both with heads bowed, looking at their phones. I got my phone out to send my usual message, which started, '*Bonjour Maman*'. My predictive text knew the rest of it now. Maman replied pretty much instantly. Her response was the same every day, too. She was no doubt aware that I was essentially checking she hadn't had a fall, or any other medical emergency, and simply went along with the pretence to spare my feelings. She knew that not getting back to Paris to see Papa in time had left me racked with guilt for the past two years. And that this was my way of minimising the risk of it happening again.

'You're such a fucking dickhead.' I looked up with a start. The teenage boys were doing a video call on one of their phones. They were not being quiet about it. Other people in the carriage were looking over disapprovingly without saying anything.

The laughing from the other end was followed by, 'Suck it, you twat.' I caught the eye of the older lady in the mac. She appeared uncomfortable. I raised my eyebrows at her and gave her my best 'Yes, it is appalling but what can you do?' look. If you lived in a country long enough, you started behaving like they do. And while I wanted to tell them to lower their voices and mind their language, I was aware that doing so in a somewhat muted but still undeniably French accent was asking for trouble these days. And on my first Monday back at work after the summer break, I did not want to risk that. So, I sat there, pursing my lips, trying to pretend it wasn't happening like everyone else, and hating myself for being complicit in the process.

I took my book out and tried to start reading. But I was now worried that the boys might be on their way to the same college as Rachid. Perhaps they were even on his course. The thought that Bilal might be right after all was disconcerting. Because as difficult as he was when he was wrong, he was pretty much unbearable when he was proved right.

2

DONNA

'Tibs is hurt. He's been fighting again,' Jodie rushed into the kitchen, the ball of matted fur, mud and blood in her arms unrecognisable as the beautiful white creature who had been preening himself by the radiator only yesterday.

'Jesus, what is it about males in this house that they can't keep out of trouble for five bloody minutes?'

'I found him lying under Dad's van. He must have been there all night. I can't believe you didn't hear him fighting.'

'What, above your dad's snores? World War Three could break out in street and I wouldn't know.'

'It's not funny,' said Jodie. 'Tibs could have died.'

'Don't be daft. He could scrap for England, that one. He were probably just lying low and licking his wounds. Bit like your dad after United take a pasting.'

Jodie didn't seem convinced.

'He's still bleeding, Mum. And it's probably been hours. I think we need to take him to see Pete,' she said, her voice high and imploring.

Pete was our vet. We were on first-name terms with him as we seemed to be in there that often.

'Let me have a look,' I said, taking Tibs from her and depositing him in the cat bed he never used while I prised apart his fur at various points to reveal a couple of nasty-looking wounds, deeper than I had expected.

'He'll be fine, love,' I said, seeing Jodie's face, 'probably nowt worse than he's had before, but I'll get your dad to take him to be checked over, just to be on safe side.'

'What am I being volunteered for now?' asked Neil, entering the kitchen still doing up his flies, a habit that had grown no more appealing to me over the years.

'Tibs has been fighting again,' I said. 'He's in a bit of a mess. You'd better run him down to Pete's after breakfast to get him checked over.'

'Let's have a look at him,' said Neil, coming straight over. He was as soft as Jodie was when it came to that cat. He reached into the basket and parted Tibs's fur, at which point Tibs hissed and went for him.

'Oh my God, he bit you,' said Jodie. 'Look, he's drawn blood.'

'It were only a nip,' he said, pulling his hand back and inspecting the damage to his thumb. 'Poor fella must be in pain, though, he's never done that before. I'd better warn Pete he might need his gauntlets on.'

Jodie was clearly still too worried about Tibs to be consoled by her dad's attempt at humour.

'Is he gonna be OK?' she asked, looking between us.

'He'll be fine, sweetheart,' Neil replied. 'I hope other one came off worse, mind. I don't want anyone saying us Cuthberts don't give as good as we get.'

I rolled my eyes as I went over to the kitchen counter to pick up my mug of tea, the honour of our family name following a cat fight not being my major concern right now.

'It'll be that ginger tom from number eight, again,' Neil continued. 'Mangy old thing.'

'And Tibs is completely blameless, is he?' I asked.

'Course he is, he's better-looking for a start. That got me off the hook a few times back when I were in my prime.'

I shook my head as I plonked a stack of bowls down onto the kitchen table, but I didn't have a chance to respond before Sam shouted from the landing.

'Mum, I can't find my PE kit.'

'Maybe check wherever you dumped it in July. Follow your nose, it'll be stinking to high heaven by now,' I shouted back.

'I've looked. It's not there.'

'Bloody hell, then that PE kit washing fairy must have been during holidays. Someone ought to give her a pay rise.'

It took a moment for the penny to drop before Sam lumbered downstairs and arrived in the kitchen.

'Thanks,' he grunted, still not grateful enough to give me a smile, let alone a hug. 'Where is it?'

'In your PE bag by front door. Bit of luck one of us is

organised. Now, can everyone sit down, shut up and eat their breakfast, or we'll all be late.'

To my surprise, everyone did as they were told. Cereal was poured without squabbles. For a few minutes, peace descended on the kitchen before the doorbell rang.

'I'll go,' said Neil, standing up. 'And if it's owner of that ginger tom complaining about state of him, I'll tell her she can pay our vet's bill.'

I heard the door open. A few moments later there were raised voices. Neil's and another man's. I tried to ignore them in the hope it was someone complaining about a dodgy bit of joinery, but when I heard Neil say, 'You're having a laugh, aren't you?' I sighed, put down my half-drunk mug of tea and hurried out to the hall.

Jakub, the oldest of Pawel and Eva's two sons from next door, was standing outside. He didn't look happy.

'What's going on?' I asked.

Before Jakub could answer, Neil spun around and said, 'Flash Harry here reckons I owe him for a few little scratches on his precious car.'

Jakub turned to me, presumably having realised he would get no sense out of Neil.

'I'm sorry, Mrs Cuthbert, I didn't want to cause a fuss, but I looked out when I heard the noise last night and saw your cat fighting another one on the bonnet of my car. And there are quite a few scratch marks there this morning.'

'Let's have a look, then,' I said, stepping outside. Jakub's Mercedes was parked on their drive, only a couple of yards from Neil's van. A trail of blood ran from the bonnet of the car to the rear of the van.

'Looks like Tibs has been caught red-pawed to me,' I said.

'Don't take his side,' hissed Neil.

'I'm simply telling truth.'

Jakub pointed out the scratches on his bonnet. A clump of white fur was still attached to the windscreen wipers.

I turned to look at Neil and raised an eyebrow.

'It's only a few little scratches, you can't hold me legally responsible for what our cat did.'

Jakub shrugged. 'I thought you'd want to do the neighbourly thing.'

'That's rich. Being lectured on how to be a good neighbour by immigrants my taxes provide for.'

Jakub looked stunned. I turned to stare at Neil.

'Have you not noticed Polish supermarket and second-hand car dealership in town? Only I think you'll find our neighbours don't get a penny from us.'

'Yeah, well. Rest of them do.'

'Get back inside,' I said to Neil. 'Now.'

For a moment I thought he was going to protest, but he'd been with me long enough to know when it was futile. He shook his head and went in.

'I'm so sorry,' I said to Jakub, feeling the heat rush to my face. I wasn't sure if it was a hot flush or embarrassment, probably both. 'He shouldn't have said that.'

'I know. I hear it from plenty of people, but you don't expect that from your neighbours.'

'We'll pay for damage, just let us know what it costs. Will you be able to get it done at work?'

'Yeah. I'll only charge you for materials, not labour.'

'Thanks, pet. And if you hear cats fighting again, chuck a bloody bucket of water over them, would you?'

Jakub managed a glimmer of a smile, but the damage was clearly done. I imagined him telling his parents. I'd never be able to look them in the eye again. I went back inside, aware I needed to be leaving for the station in five minutes and I still hadn't finished my breakfast.

'Pleased with yoursen?' I said to Neil.

'He were one in wrong,' he replied, still visibly bristling.

'Yeah, right. I'm sure you'd see it like that if it were other way around.'

'What did Dad do?' asked Jodie.

'Only refused to pay for damage Tibs has done to Jakub's car because "my taxes support enough immigrants."'

Sam struggled to disguise a snort.

'It's not funny, Sam,' I said.

'See, this is where he gets it from,' said Jodie. 'Dad and Grandad set him a bad example.'

'I still think he were a right cheeky bugger, asking us to pay for damage,' said Neil. 'You didn't agree to it, did you?'

'Course I bloody did. You'd expect him to do same if he trashed your van.'

'It were only a few little scratches. It's his fault for having a flash car. Asking for trouble round here, it is.'

'Drop it and give vets a ring, will you?'

I put my phone into my bag. 'Now, Jodie, make sure you're on next train for college, and Sam, get that smirk off your face and your arse in gear for school. And if I get a call from them about your behaviour today, I shouldn't bother coming home.'

I stomped through the hall, pulled on my jacket and slammed the door shut behind me.

The relief of leaving the house flooded through me. Sometimes I had to fight the urge to go off somewhere, like Shirley bloody Valentine. No one would plan a life that ended up like mine. It was hardly the stuff of Disney fairy tales. But when your boyfriend dumps you after years together, and suddenly you're on the scrapheap at thirty, you don't stop to complain that the person who comes along and 'rescues' you isn't quite the Prince Charming you'd been hoping for.

Mam had brought me up with a heavy dose of realism. If he wasn't an alcoholic or in debt and was capable of keeping his pants on when around other women, then he was a keeper, according to her. And Disney could go and do one.

I had to run the last fifty yards to the station. Though the word 'run' probably suggested something more impressive than the sight of me lumbering down the zigzagging ramp towards the platform. I knew it was there for the disabled, but it was a pain in the arse when you were legging it for the train and had to run a hundred yards when the platform was only ten away.

I arrived just as the train pulled in. I got on and sat down heavily on a seat near the end of the carriage, while I tried to get my breath back. The teenage lads behind me were on a video call with someone, only they weren't being quiet about it.

'You ought to ask her out,' one of them said. 'She's a complete minger but she'd probably suck your cock.'

'Piss off,' said their mate.

I looked around at the other passengers. An older woman in a mac was shaking her head. Everyone else was trying to pretend they hadn't noticed. I turned around in my seat and tapped the mouthy one on the shoulder. He looked up at me, startled.

'No one on here wants to listen to what you're saying, so I'd keep it down if I were you.'

'It's a free country. No laws against talking on trains.'

'No, but I could take your phone, find your mum in your contacts and tell her what you just said, for starters.'

For a second, I thought he was going to gob in my face, but I was saved by the lad on the other end of the phone shouting 'Burn,' and the laughter that followed before they fell quiet.

The woman in the mac gave me a little smile of gratitude. I turned back around, feeling rather proud of myself. Sometimes, the raging hormones came in bloody useful.

3

RACHID

I see her as soon as she gets on the train. It's her hair that I notice first; long, shiny and auburn, it catches the sunlight streaming through the window and gives off an amazing glow. Her skin is pale and flawless. She's wearing black patent laced boots, a short black skirt, and a green velvet jacket. Not that I am staring weirdly at her or anything. I take it all in within seconds. I can't help but notice because she's so different from all the other girls I know. And I like different.

She sits down facing me at the table opposite mine, perching on the edge of her aisle seat like she is afraid of catching something from the man next to her. Which isn't surprising given that I'm pretty sure I can smell him from here. She puts earbuds in. I can't hear what she's listening to, but there's a good vibe about her.

I look back down at my phone, but I can't stop thinking

about her. I decide not to fight it, as it beats thinking about all the grief from Dad, so I try to work out what music she might be listening to. She looks arty and she clearly likes standing out from the crowd. So, maybe Amy Winehouse. I'd be well happy with that. Not that it would matter to her whether I like what she's listening to. Jeez, she hasn't even given me a second glance. And when she gets off, I'll probably never see her again. Unless she catches this train every day, of course. In which case, I'm gonna have a problem concentrating for the next two years.

At Bradford, a middle-aged woman in a business suit gets on and sits down across the table from me. I pull my legs in, so I don't accidentally touch hers. Mum is always going on about my long legs getting in the way.

She has an overnight case with her and puts it on the table between us, rather than in the overhead storage rack. I'm about to offer to put it up there for her, but before I can ask, she unzips the case and starts rooting through it, looking for something, piling things up on the open cover as she goes. A moment later, the pile topples and a large pair of black, lacy knickers lands in front of me. I stare at them, unsure what to do. I glance up and see the red-haired girl across the aisle desperately trying to stop laughing. Our eyes meet for a second before I look away quickly and bite my bottom lip hard.

The woman reaches out, picks up the knickers and stuffs them back in the case without a word. I'm pretty sure I can feel the warmth of her cheeks from here, so I spare her the further embarrassment of making eye contact and stare down at my phone. But for the rest of the journey, I am conscious that the girl with the red hair is, like me, trying to hold herself together.

The girl gets up as we start to pull into Leeds station and moves towards the doors. I stand and make my way over towards her, relieved to be able to make my escape and finally allow a smile to spread across my face.

As the train slows, other passengers gather behind me and push forward, edging me nearer to her. She has her phone out and is messaging someone, her slim fingers flashing back and forth across the screen. Her lilac nail varnish matches the colour of her lipstick. I don't know how I notice, but I do. And her lips are so perfect, they are unreal. The train comes to a halt. I hesitate for a second. She's nearest the button, but she seems too busy on her phone to bother. I reach out to press it, but at that exact second, she moves her hand to it without even looking. My finger hits the button first; her hand presses mine. She looks up with a start as she realises, and turns to me.

'Sorry,' she says.

I open my mouth to say something, but nothing comes out. The doors open and the moment has gone. I'm such a dickhead. At least I'm on my own rather than with any of my mates, who would be pissing themselves laughing now.

The girl steps onto the platform and heads towards the ticket barriers. I follow a few steps behind. Other passengers are surging around me, but I try not to lose sight of her. The station is being refurbished. Some people still haven't got the hang of the new barriers. I see her go straight through. The man behind her hesitates as he tries to work out how to scan his ticket. I move to the next barrier along, where the queue seems shorter, but someone in front of me gets stuck. Eventually, I'm through. But when I look around, she's slipped away into the crowd. That's it. She's gone now. I'm such an utter loser.

I hurry out of the foyer and head for the traffic lights. When they change, I'm the first to make it across the road. I weave in and out between other people on the pavement, hoping I can catch up with her. She might work in one of the shops, Urban Outfitters or Mango perhaps. I pass the entrance to Trinity shopping centre, but I can't see her going up the steps. I carry on and turn left into Briggate. And that is when I see her. Striding ahead of me, her green jacket swinging and red hair blowing back behind her as she walks.

A surge of excitement pulses through me. I haven't lost her. She's heading in the same direction as me. This makes me ridiculously happy, which in turn suggests I'm properly losing it. I hadn't even seen this girl an hour ago and yet, for some reason, the idea that we could be at the same college suddenly seems like the best thing in the world.

She crosses over at the traffic lights and continues along the side of the market. I'm only a few paces behind her now, hanging back a bit because I don't want her to think I'm some crazy stalker dude. She walks past the bus station, another possible destination crossed off the list, and heads over to the main traffic lights, narrowing the options still further.

I stand next to her at the crossing, trying not to look at her or even breathe too loudly. I know that if I say, 'Don't worry, I'm not following you,' that will make me sound like I definitely am. Smiling inanely at her would also be seriously creepy. I do the only thing I can think of and turn the music on my phone up louder. Just at that moment, 'When Doves Cry' finishes and 'The Most Beautiful Girl in the World' comes on. Prince is fucking with me from beyond the grave. I know she can hear the words. I don't dare look up because my face is burning. But I'm pretty sure that out of the corner of my eye I can see her smiling.

The lights change. I decide to go first, striding across the road and up the steps to the main entrance of the college two at a time. A lot of people are hanging around outside, but I go straight in. I remember from the induction day that music technology is on the second floor, so I head up the staircase. Once I get there, I go halfway along the nearest corridor, but it all looks the same as the other floors did and I'm not sure I'm in the right place. I take my AirPods out and turn to see if I can find someone to ask but everyone seems to be in big groups talking and laughing and I don't want to seem like the dumb-arse new kid.

Someone stops next to me. I look across. It's her. She's smiling at me.

'Do women always do that?' she asks. 'Throw their underwear at you, I mean. Or are you a famous member of a boy band who I don't recognise?'

I smile at her.

'No to both of them,' I reply. 'I'm just having a bad morning. Can't even find my room.'

'What course?'

'Music production.'

'You need the next corridor, second door on your right.'

'Thanks,' I say. She smiles but doesn't go to walk away. I know I've got to say something to her, ideally something that doesn't make me sound like a complete prick.

'What course you on?'

'Fashion and textiles,' she replies. 'Which is through the door you're standing in front of.'

'Sorry,' I say, stepping aside.

'It's OK,' she says. 'I know you're having a bad morning. Hope your day gets better.'

She smiles again before going into her classroom. I knew I was right to come here. And now I feel surer about my decision than ever. I've met her. The girl I've been waiting for. I walk back along the corridor, a swagger in my stride and a huge grin across my face.

4

SYLVIE

I wondered if one year I would arrive on campus and not get a thrill out of seeing the Gothic, red-brick building with its tower and turrets that housed the School of Health Care. Clearly, it wasn't going to be this year. I still remembered the very first time I'd seen it, the slate roof covered in snow, and had been taken aback by how wonderfully English and incredibly foreboding it was. At least I no longer walked the corridors feeling like a student on their first day. The imposter syndrome, which had stayed for several years after I started working here, had left me at some point, and been replaced by a sense of belonging, of coming home.

I stepped inside, the coolness of the building welcoming after the brisk walk from the station. To be honest, at my age, it was welcome at any time. I would be the only one comfortable with the temperature as the students donned extra layers in November.

The corridors were quiet today but would be filled with students soon enough. Ours were the first ones to return to campus, as they needed some intensive time in the classroom before we let them out on community placements.

I looked through the window of our room and saw Johanna sitting at her laptop, her hair pinned elegantly on top of her head as always, in stark contrast to my chaotic curls.

'Hello Sylvie,' she said, looking up as I entered. 'It's good to have our ray of sunshine back!' She stood up and embraced me warmly. I hoped she couldn't tell that although my rays of sunshine were attempting to emerge, they didn't feel particularly bright today.

'It's lovely to see you too,' I said. 'How are you?'

She looked down at her feet.

'I've got some news,' she said.

I knew immediately what she was going to say.

'You're going back, aren't you?'

She nodded.

'I've been offered a position teaching a midwifery masters in Maastricht.'

'That's wonderful, congratulations,' I said, trying to hide my disappointment. 'I'll miss you so much, but I know it's the right thing for you.'

'Thank you. I'm here till we break up for Christmas, and then we'll be off.'

'How have the children taken it?'

'Better than I expected. I know they'll miss their friends, but they're excited about their new school.'

'And Marc?'

'He can't wait to leave. He cried when I accepted the job. I hadn't realised the toll the last four years has taken on him, on all of us, to be honest.'

I nodded, remembering her telling me how a colleague had offered Marc, a Dutch national, a slice of the 'Leave' celebration cake she had brought in the day after the EU referendum, Johanna's tears when her application for permanent residence had been rejected last year. It wasn't just her family it had taken a toll on, of course. I thought back to the hours Bilal and I had spent filling out our own permanent residence forms, searching for every payslip, every Eurostar receipt from trips back to Paris. Resenting the need to prove we had a right to be here.

'I understand that. And I wish you hadn't had to go through it.'

Johanna shrugged.

'What's done is done. Staying here simply isn't an option for us. What about you?'

'It's different because the children are older,' I replied. 'They were born here. It's all they've ever known.'

'They'd adapt. They'd also have lots of new opportunities. And besides, I didn't ask about them, I asked about you.'

It only occurred to me as she said it. How I always interpreted 'you' as my family. I rarely answered on behalf of myself.

'If they're happy, I'm happy.'

'Well, you must come and visit us, all of you.'

'Thank you,' I said, although I wasn't convinced that would happen, as our family holidays were usually spent visiting Maman in Paris.

'Coffee to start the day off?' asked Johanna.

'That would be wonderful, thanks. And then I'd better start sorting everything out. Because before we know it the students will be back, and I'll be trying to remember where I put the model of a uterus.'

She laughed, being ten years younger than me and having no idea that I genuinely couldn't remember where I'd put it. Or where my mug was, for that matter. The perimenopausal brain fog had descended to such an extent that I was surprised I'd even made it to the right department.

Johanna came back a few minutes later and handed me my mug.

'Where was it?' I asked.

'Next to the model of the uterus,' she replied with a smile.

As soon as I got on the train home, I texted Maman; the middle of my three daily check-ins. All was as usual for a Monday. She'd been to her art class, got a lift home with Bernard, the nice gentleman she'd met on the course who lived nearby. I'd teased her about the possibility of a burgeoning romance the first couple of times she mentioned him, but we both knew nothing would come of it because she wouldn't let it. Her devotion to Papa hadn't ended with his death. The art class had been my idea; an effort to get her out of the apartment and meeting new people. She'd gone along with it somewhat reluctantly, but I got the impression she was at least glad she had now.

She reported that the sun was shining in Paris. That seemed to happen a lot more frequently than I could report from here. I'd grown to love many things about my adopted country, but not its weather. And the thought of a walk along the Seine in the sunshine was still guaranteed to make me a little homesick.

I sighed and told Maman I would arrange a FaceTime call later in the week, in the hope that Amina and Rachid would be in the right mood to chat to their grandmother. The last thing I wanted was for Maman to pick up on the tensions in the house. I had already disappointed her on so many levels, I wanted to maintain some level of pretence that everything was fine at home.

As I got to the end of our street, I caught sight of our neighbour Edwina coming out of the corner shop. I hurried to catch up.

'Hello Edwina. How are you?'

She turned and looked up at me, her mouth crinkling into a smile and her eyes still able to dazzle at eighty-five years old.

'Hello, Sylvie sweetheart,' she said, clutching my hand. 'I'm just plodding along but I'm fine, thank you. How are you?'

'All good, thanks,' I replied. 'Rachid's started college in Leeds today and Amina's doing her GCSE subjects now.'

'Goodness, they grow up so fast, don't they?' she said, as we walked along together, my arm through hers. 'My youngest great-grandchild Evie started school this week. Doesn't seem a minute since she was born.'

'Well, I hope she enjoys it. Will they be coming to visit soon?' Edwina's family were split between London and Dublin. She didn't see a great deal of any of them.

Her smile faded a little.

'I expect I'll see them at Christmas as usual. They lead busy lives, I understand that. Although September is always a difficult month for me.'

I gave her arm a squeeze, realising it must be coming up to two years since Feodor had died.

'You must come round to ours that evening, or I can come to visit you. I wouldn't want you being on your own.'

'That's very sweet of you, dear. It doesn't get any easier, does it?'

Edwina had been there for me when Papa had died, just a few months after Feodor. Grief had brought us closer together, and even now, I still found it easier to talk to her about it than anyone else.

'No,' I replied. 'It doesn't.'

'How is your mother coping on her own? She must miss him terribly.'

'She does. She gets by the best she can. Tries to keep busy. I worry about her, though.'

'My family worry about me,' said Edwina. 'But we're tough, my generation. We've been through such a lot, you see.'

We stopped outside Edwina's gate. 'Can I help you inside? Make you a cup of tea?'

'No, thank you. I'll be fine. You go and see those gorgeous children of yours,' she said, patting my hand.

'They're not gorgeous all the time, you know. Rachid can be rather headstrong, he takes after his father. It's a wonder you didn't hear them arguing this morning.'

'He's spirited, that's what they called it in my day. It's what you miss when they're gone, you know, those arguments at the breakfast table. You spend years longing for a moment's silence but when there are days full of it, it isn't welcome at all.'

I nodded, watched her go up the path and waved back to her as she headed inside.

Somewhat surprisingly, a freshly brewed cafetière was waiting for me on the kitchen table. My first thought was that Amina had made it for me, but it was Rachid who came bounding down the stairs to push the plunger down before pouring me a cup.

'What are you after?' I asked, daring to ruffle his hair now he was home.

'Nothing. Just looking after my mother,' he said, giving me a peck on the cheek. He could turn on the charm when he wanted to. I knew where he got that from too.

'I take it you had a good first day?'

'Awesome.'

'What was? The course, the tutor?'

'Everything. I feel alive.'

'I wasn't aware I'd been living with the walking dead.'

'You know what I mean,' he replied. 'When something feels perfect.'

'Yes,' I said. 'I can just about remember that far back.'

He rolled his eyes and smiled.

'Anyway, it's good, I'm good, everything's good.'

'And that's all that matters,' I replied.

'But not to Dad.'

'He'll need time to come around,' I said. 'You enjoy it and leave that bit to me.'

Rachid nodded and headed back upstairs.

I sat for a few minutes, enjoying that rare moment of silence as I drank my coffee. I suspected Edwina was right, though. I'd miss them terribly when they were gone. And all I was left with was the empty shell of a relationship that had once been perfect.

I pushed back my chair and went upstairs, keen to check on Amina.

'So, how did it go?' I asked, as I stuck my head around her door. She was lying on her bed staring up at the ceiling.

'OK,' she replied.

'That bad, eh?' I said, going in and perching on the corner of the bed. She turned to look at me.

'They don't want to know me now.'

'Then leave them to it,' I replied. 'Girls who drop their friends as soon as they get a boyfriend always end up regretting it when they need someone to talk to after they break up.'

She frowned at me.

'Wow, romance really is dead.'

I reached out and took her hand.

'I'm a realist, sweetheart. Lots of girls your age have a

romantic notion that "he's the one" and "it's forever", but it's simply not like that for most people.'

'But you and Dad are still together and still happy.'

The rising inflection at the end of this sentence suggested it might be more of a question than a statement. I had always been so conscious of protecting Amina from what had gone on between me and Bilal, but I also knew how intuitive she was. Maybe she had picked up on some of the body language between us.

'Yes, but that's down to hard work over years,' I replied, keen to reassure her. 'All the give and take that happens in a long-term relationship. Not all that so-called romantic stuff young women dream about.'

She was quiet for a moment.

'But it must have been romantic in the early days when you started going out? Don't they say Paris is the city of love?'

I smiled at her.

'Of course. All I'm saying is you need more than that initial romance to sustain a relationship for years. And you need your friends too.'

'What did he do?' asked Amina. 'What was the most romantic thing Dad did?'

'Goodness,' I said, realising I had never talked about those early days with her, probably because of how painful it was for me to even think about how happy we were back then. 'There were some candlelit meals in restaurants, walks at sunset along the river, all the usual things, I suppose.'

She nodded. Gave a little smile. She was disappointed, I

knew. Disappointed that I had been vague. Hadn't pulled out one specific example and talked about it in a way that lit up my face. I could have done that, but I'd been too scared to in case I broke down as I did so.

'I want that someday,' she said quietly.

I leant over and gave her a hug.

'And you'll have it when the time is right. You're truly beautiful inside and out.'

'No one at school seems to think that.'

'Then more fool them. Concentrate on your studies and you'll have the last laugh when you get into your first-choice university because you weren't distracted by the boys who ended up breaking their hearts.'

'Now you sound like Dad,' she said.

'Well, maybe he's got a point. Just don't tell him that, OK? And remember to text Leila about that hot chocolate after mosque on Saturday.'

'OK,' she said, pulling out a book from her school bag. I kissed her on the top of her head and left her to it, painfully aware that it would probably get harder for her before it became easier.

'Did Grand-mère mind?' she asked as I stood up. 'That Papa was older than you, I mean?'

I smiled. She'd stopped calling Bilal 'Papa' a couple of years ago, at the same time she'd stopped speaking French at home. I'd suspected at the time it was an attempt to be more like her friends. It was nice to hear her use it again.

'Grand-mère was concerned about me, that's all. In the

same way I would be about you. But age is not important, really. What matters is how well he treats you.'

Amina nodded. I left the room, shutting my eyes and taking a few deep breaths before I was ready to descend the stairs.

Later that evening, after we'd eaten and Rachid and Amina had retreated to their rooms, I sat opposite Bilal at the dining-room table, the 'Life in the UK' test questions open on my laptop in front of me.

'I still find this utterly ridiculous,' said Bilal, stretching back in his chair.

'I know. But if we're going to do it, we may as well make sure we only have to do it once.'

I read out the question at the top of my screen, 'What palace was a cast-iron and plate-glass building originally erected in Hyde Park, London, England, to house the Great Exhibition of 1851?'

'Alexandra Palace,' replied Bilal.

'That's not on the list of options.'

'Isn't it? I thought that was built for an exhibition.'

'The options are Crystal Palace, Dream Palace, the Green Palace and Gold Palace.'

'Well, I've only heard of one of them. The rest sound made up to me.'

'So, which one is it?'

'I don't know because the one I've heard of is Crystal Palace but that's in south London.'

'Well, you need to choose one of them.'

Bilal sighed.

'Gold Palace. Although that's clearly made up.'

I scrolled down to the answers.

'It was Crystal Palace.'

'But that's in south London.'

Bilal took out his phone and googled it. 'There, look at the map,' he said, holding up the screen.

'I'm not disputing that's where it is now, but I think they moved it.'

'What?'

'In the question it says it was originally erected in Hyde Park. That suggests they moved it.'

'Moved it? What is wrong with these people? Why didn't they build things where they were supposed to be in the first place? The Bahia Palace was built in Marrakesh because that's where we wanted it.'

I smiled, finding Bilal's indignation endearing.

'No one promised the answers would make any sense.'

Bilal shook his head. 'The whole thing is ridiculous. I don't know why we're going through with it.'

'Because it's the only way we can get British citizenship. Do I get a point for that answer?'

Bilal groaned.

'Seriously, Sylvie. I refuse to spend another evening going through these stupid questions.'

'OK. But if you fail the test, you'll have to tell the children that our future here is uncertain.'

'They were born here. That should be good enough.'

'But you know it isn't.'

Bilal got to his feet.

'Where are you off to?' I asked.

'To listen to music. It's one of my few remaining pleasures.'

It was a dig at me for insisting he stopped smoking before the children were born. It may have been seventeen years, but he was not about to let it go. He turned to leave.

'But that's not going to help, is it? We both need to put in the work.'

Bilal spun around to face me.

'I put in the work. Three vitrectomies and two cataract operations today. And if that's not good enough for them, then screw them, we'll move back to Paris. At least I won't be treated like a child there.'

He stormed out; a roomful of seething resentment remained in his wake. He was right, of course. The whole thing was ridiculous. But I was desperate for all the uncertainty to be over. It had been hanging over us for too long. And I was the one who would have to deal with the fallout if we didn't get things sorted.

The sound of Joni Mitchell singing 'Free Man in Paris' drifted down from our bedroom above. Bilal wasn't a fan of headphones or earbuds. He liked music to fill a room. Fortunately, his choice of artist this evening was one who Rachid approved of. I knew Bilal hadn't chosen it because of the artist, though. It was the name of the track he was trying to make a point with.

5

DONNA

I'd never known that people queued to complain until I'd started working at the council's one-stop shop. The good people of Leeds seemed to think that name meant they could do all their complaining about every council service they had an issue with to the first person they saw when they got there. Which was invariably me.

It didn't matter how many times I told them that a customer care officer was just a jumped-up title for a receptionist with lots of useful phone extension numbers, I still copped it as soon as the doors opened – and today was no exception.

The first person who made it to my counter, presumably having been queuing since at least seven thirty, didn't even sit down before he started his rant.

'They didn't come for me bins again.'

'Good morning,' I replied, 'I'm sorry to hear that. If you

give me your address, I can contact cleansing services on your behalf.'

'I don't want owt cleansed, I want me bloody bins emptied.'

'It's what they call it now, pet. Hang on a sec.'

'And someone's dumped a mattress at bottom of our road.'

'That'll be environmental services you need.'

'It's nowt to do with them environment folk. I don't want some Greta Thunberg lass who should be in school coming round to tell me to recycle stuff when it's not me who's left an eyesore on road.'

'I tell you what,' I said. 'We'll do cleansing services first and we'll take it from there.'

My brain was practically fried by lunchtime. That many people sounding off about that many things. I barely had the energy to open my sandwich box.

'You all right, love?' asked Carole, sitting down on the chair next to me.

'I would be if I didn't have another three hours of ear-bashing to go.'

'One of those mornings?'

'Yep. I wouldn't mind but I've had enough of dealing with it at home past few days.'

'Neil or kids?'

'All of them. Permanently at each other's throats and me having to sort it out. What with all this as well, I ought to be UN bloody peacekeeper or summat.'

Carole laughed.

'At least you'd get paid a damn sight more than we do here.'

'Aye, but I'd still have to go home and sort my lot out at end of day.'

I had only taken two bites of my sandwich when my mobile rang. It was school. My heart sank as soon as I saw the screen but I knew I had to answer.

'Hello.'

'Mrs Cuthbert?'

'Yes, speaking.'

'It's Julie Philips, Mr Hill's PA at Moor Park Academy. He'd like to speak to you about your son.'

'What's Sam done now?'

'Mr Hill said to tell you that it was an extremely serious matter, and he wishes to see you or Mr Cuthbert in person this afternoon. Would you be able to make it for two o'clock?'

I thought for a moment about saying Neil would go but I knew he wouldn't be finished till at least five today and he'd lose pay if he left early, whereas I could wangle some flexitime. Besides, Neil would probably leap to Sam's defence and end up having a barney with the head teacher.

'I'm at work in Leeds, I can't make it for two. Would it be possible to come in a bit later, please?'

'Just a moment and I'll check.' The line clicked and went quiet.

'Do you reckon I could leave a couple of hours early?' I whispered to Carole. 'Head teacher wants to see me urgently. Sounds like Sam's in trouble again.'

'Fine by me, but I'll have to clear it with boss,' Carole replied.

'Thanks. Tell him I'll make time up tomorrow.'

Julie came back on the line.

'Mr Hill says the latest he can make it is three o'clock. He also asked me to give you notice that your son is being excluded from school for three days from tomorrow, therefore you need to ensure he is supervised at home.'

I shut my eyes and let out a long sigh, having no idea how she expected us to do that when we were working.

'Right,' I said. 'I'll be there for three. Thank you.'

I put the phone down and started running through everything that Sam might have been caught doing; swearing at a teacher or fighting with another lad were my best bets. I didn't want to think about anything worse than that.

'Little sod's been excluded,' I told Carole.

'Jesus. That's not good.'

'No. Second day of term as well. It's like he's incapable of behaving for two minutes.'

'You going to give him what for?'

'Oh, he'll be hearing from me, all right. Actually . . .'

I picked up my mobile and texted, *'Whatever you've done, you'd better be ready to apologise'*, and sent it to Sam.

'Right,' I said, stuffing my half-eaten sandwich in the box and turning to Carole. 'I'll get straight back to work.'

I rang Neil as soon as I got on the train.

'Sam's been excluded from school for three days,' I told him.

'Fucking hell. What's he done now?'

'I don't know. Head wanted to see one of us. I'm on my way.'

'Thanks, love. I don't know what gets into him.'

'He's always hated school. Remember when he were little, he used to get so frustrated with having to sit at a desk and write all day.'

'They're not all cut out for this academic crap. I know I wasn't.'

'Yeah, but you never got yourself kicked out.'

'Cos I knew there were a job down pit for me at end of it. What's he got to look forward to?'

'I know. I worry about that too. But right now, I'm more worried about whether he's going to get kicked out for good and not even get to sit his exams.'

'He'll be OK. Just tell head teacher he'll keep his nose clean from now on.'

'Yeah,' I replied. 'Only trouble is I said that last time.'

I hung up and sat staring out of the window, wondering how the hell I'd managed to screw up so badly. My phone pinged with a message. It was Lorraine, saying she'd had a call from school and was going in to see the head teacher. I rang her straight back.

'Hi. That makes two of us. Has Tyler been excluded too?'

'Yep, for three days. I've been told to make other arrangements for him. Like that's easy when you're a single mum working shifts in A&E. They were lucky today's my day off.'

'I'm so sorry Sam's got him into trouble again.'

'We don't know that yet, it could be other way around. Anyway, it's not as if Tyler needs much encouragement.'

'Yeah, but it's always Sam who gives it to him. He's what were called a bad influence in our day. Anyway, send Tyler around to ours while they're off. We'll try and keep them under house arrest between two of us.'

'Thanks Don, and good luck with that.'

'I'll see you there, ready for family shaming. We mustn't let Mam get wind of this. I can't do with all her, "your father would be turning in his grave" stuff right now.'

'OK. Brace yoursen for whatever they've done and apologise for England. That way we might make it out alive.'

It was the same school me and Lorraine had gone to, though it hadn't been called an academy in our day. I still hated going inside, and the fact that I was about to be bawled out for Sam's behaviour didn't make it any easier. Jodie had been a breeze in comparison. She had always been headstrong and mouthy and had been far more interested in art and textiles than any other subjects, but I'd never been called to the head's office once for her. Sam was clearly intent on making up for that.

I climbed the steps to the main entrance and took a few moments at the top to get my breath back before going in. Lorraine was already waiting on the blue seats opposite reception. I gave her what I could muster of a smile before going up to the desk and giving my name. I signed the form and waited while the receptionist tore it off and popped it into a plastic wallet on a visitor lanyard. To be honest, I was surprised they didn't take a mug shot of me and stick it on a 'Parents of Pains in the Arse' board.

I sat down next to Lorraine.

'It'll be OK,' she whispered. I nodded, though I wasn't so sure. They were in Year 11; we could hardly claim they would grow out of it. To be honest, I was surprised school hadn't given up on Sam a long time ago. They'd have had every right to. And yet somehow, teachers were still telling him he had time to turn it around. I wasn't sure I believed them, even if they believed it themselves.

The head teacher's PA, Julie, arrived in reception and asked us to follow her upstairs. I was blowing again by the time I got to the top and into the head's office. Sam and Tyler were already in there, looking, for once, pretty shamefaced, which made me worry even more about what the hell they'd done.

Mr Hill stood up, shook our hands, and told us to take a seat next to our sons. Sam wouldn't even make eye contact with me.

'Thank you for coming,' said Mr Hill, as if we'd had any choice in the matter. 'I'll cut straight to it. I called you in today because Sam and Tyler racially abused a younger pupil yesterday. We've conducted a thorough investigation after receiving a complaint from the boy's mother. Your sons have admitted that they called him racist names relating to his family heritage and told him that the football pitch used at break times was for "whites only".'

The gasp I let out made Sam finally look up. It was a moment or two before I could get any words out.

'I'm so sorry,' I said. 'I can't believe they actually said that.'

I looked hard at Sam. His continued silence confirmed his guilt.

'Me too,' said Lorraine. 'That's not how Tyler's been brought up. Not at all.'

Mr Hill nodded slowly. I wasn't sure if he believed us or not.

'I hope that bearing in mind the severity of the situation, you will understand why I felt it necessary to exclude both boys for three days.'

'Yes,' I replied. 'Of course.'

'And when they return,' continued Mr Hill, 'they will both be taking part in an anti-racism education programme.'

Lorraine nodded and bit her bottom lip, clearly trying to hold herself together.

'Now, boys,' said Mr Hill, turning to them. 'What do you have to say for yourselves?'

'Sorry,' they both mumbled, still looking down.

'Look at Mr Hill when he's speaking to you,' I said to Sam.

'Sorry, sir,' he said, looking up.

'I do not expect to ever have to speak to either of you about incidents of this nature again,' Mr Hill continued. 'Do you understand?'

They both nodded.

'You should consider yourselves fortunate not to have been excluded for longer and if there is any repeat of this, we will be looking at the possibility of a managed move to another school within the Trust. Is that clear to everyone?'

He looked at me and Lorraine in turn.

'You won't have to do that,' I said. 'Because this will not happen again. You have my word on that.'

'I'm glad to hear it. I'll see you boys next week and you are all free to leave.'

I stood up. My legs felt unsteady. It was all I could do to hold it together until we got outside the doors of the main entrance.

'What is wrong with you?' I shouted at Sam.

'Keep your voice down,' he hissed, looking around to see if any other kids were still about.

'I don't care who hears me. You are in so much trouble.'

'I said I'm sorry. It were only a bit of banter.'

'Banter? You call some poor little lad racist names, and you call that banter?'

'He's a Year Ten.'

'Oh, well that's OK then. Because it's fine to be racist to anyone over thirteen.'

Sam rolled his eyes and scuffed his shoe on the concrete. Lorraine turned to Tyler.

'And what have you got to say for yoursen?'

'Sorry. I didn't mean to upset him. It's like Sam said, it were just banter.'

'No. It wasn't,' said Lorraine. 'Not to him. You're grounded for a week, and you can hand over your phone till you're back in school.'

'You can't do that,' said Tyler.

'I can do whatever I like because I'm your mum and you need to be taught a lesson.'

Sam looked at me expectantly.

'Don't think you've got off lightly,' I said. 'I'll decide what's happening to you when I've spoken to your dad. If it's down to me, your phone will be chucked in wheelie bin, and you'll not be going out rest of year.'

I stomped down the steps, wondering what the hell they must think of us at that school. And what the mother of that poor lad must think of us as parents.

We got back home at the same time as Pawel from next door. He smiled and raised his hat to me as he always did, like someone from a bygone era. And all I could think of was how he did this despite what Jakub must have told him about what Neil had said. And that he would probably still do it even if he knew what Sam had been excluded for.

'Afternoon,' I said, in the brightest voice I could muster, before opening the front door and telling Sam to go straight to his room.

I was cleaning the kitchen when Jodie got home from college. I was dreading telling her because I knew what her reaction would be, but it would be better coming from me than her finding out elsewhere.

'What's up?' she asked, as I banged a pan down on the hob.

'Your brother's been excluded from school for three days.'

'Oh great. What's he done now?'

'Promise you won't go and kick his door down?'

'Just tell me.'

'He called a lad at school racist names and said footie pitch were for whites only.'

Jodie's face screwed up.

'What the fuck is wrong with him?'

She turned and headed for the stairs. I followed her out into the hall.

'Jodie, leave him. I've already read him riot act.'

'I don't care. He's out of order.'

I grabbed hold of her arm just as Neil arrived home.

'What's going on?' he said, looking at us both in turn.

'Sam's been excluded for racially abusing a kid at school,' said Jodie. 'Proud of him, are you?'

'What's that supposed to mean?'

'Where do you think he gets it from?'

'I've never racially abused anyone.'

'Says same person who offended Jakub yesterday.'

'That's completely different.'

Jodie snorted and started going upstairs. Before she made it past the third step, Sam came out of his room and called out.

'I can hear you all, you know.'

'You little shit,' said Jodie.

'Oi,' said Neil. 'We'll have less of that.'

'So, swearing's out of order but he gets away with being racist?'

'He hasn't got away with owt,' I said. 'He's been excluded from school and he's going to be grounded and have his phone taken away.'

'You said you'd speak to Dad first,' complained Sam.

'I don't think your father's going to disagree with me.'

I looked pointedly at Neil. He shook his head.

'It were banter, that's all,' said Sam.

'Were this lad giving you grief?' asked Neil.

'Jeez, Dad, it doesn't matter what other lad did or said,' said Jodie. 'That's no excuse.'

'I'm just trying to get full picture,' said Neil.

Sam came halfway down the stairs. 'And they're making me and Tyler do some stupid anti-racism course when we go back.'

'Have you agreed to this?' Neil said, turning to me.

'Yes. Head said if there were any repeat of it, he'd be shipped off to another school.'

'I doubt any other school would have him,' said Jodie. 'If I could exclude him from being in our family I would.'

'Jodie,' Neil called, but it was too late. She pushed past Sam and went straight up to her room, slamming the door shut behind her.

'Fantastic,' I said, turning to Neil. 'Happy families again, eh?'

I sighed as I got ready for bed. I didn't have the energy to be dealing with all this crap. To be honest, I didn't have the energy for pretty much anything these days. It was one of the things they didn't tell you about the menopause; all the jokes about hot flushes are just a cover for the other stuff, which is far worse. I reached into the bedside cabinet and took out my 'flue cream'. I called it that because that's where it got squirted up twice a week. Doctor reckoned it might help to stop me feeling as dry as the bloody Sahara down there and needing to pee three times a night. I always made sure I inserted it when Neil was in the bathroom. I was aware it was a passion killer; not that there'd been anything in the way of passion between us for almost a year now. He'd been good about it. I wouldn't go as far as saying supportive, but he understood I was suffering and didn't whinge or try it on, which, for a bloke from Wakey, was about as good as you could hope for. But I still felt like I was failing as a wife, just as I was failing as a parent.

Neil got in bed and fussed with the duvet for a moment. He went to slip his arm around me and then seemingly thought better of it. I lay there, staring at the ceiling, wondering how the hell things had got this bad.

'What are we going to do with him?' I asked.

'He just needs to learn when to keep his mouth shut so he doesn't get in trouble.'

I turned to look at him.

'Aren't you worried about what he said? That he even thinks things like that, let alone would say them to someone's face?'

Neil shrugged.

'Like he said, maybe it were just banter that got out of hand.'

I rolled my eyes.

'No. Jodie were right. It were racist.'

'According to her, everything's racist. I got called every name under sun at school for colour of my hair. No kids ever got excluded for that.'

'That's different.'

'Not to me, it wasn't. It's still banter. Piss-taking, whatever you want to call it. They'll always find summat to have a go at you about. You just need to learn to give as good as you get. It's survival of fittest out there.'

I propped myself up on one elbow.

'And you'd say that to mum of lad he had a go at, would you?'

'Course not. I just don't think it's summat we need to worry too much about. As long as he keeps his nose clean when he goes back to school, pulls his finger out and does some work so he can get grades he needs to get on that plumbing course at college, he'll be OK.'

I sighed, worried that if word got out about this we'd be known as racists at No. 32.

'You could still make it clearer to him that you don't approve,' I said.

'What good would that do? He's been excluded from school, he's got Jodie practically disowning him, you on his back; if I pile in, it'll seem like everyone thinks he's a worthless piece of shit, and then he'll stop trying altogether.'

I said nothing for a moment. Maybe Neil had a point. I couldn't remember the last time anyone had a good word to say about Sam, whether at home or school. Perhaps he was simply living up to low expectations.

'I could talk to his head of year at school.'

'What for?'

'Maybe ask if they can give him a bit more support. Try to find summat positive he could aim for.'

'Won't do any harm, I suppose.'

'And what about Jodie?' I asked.

'Nothing I can do about her, is there? She won't listen to a word I say. Thinks I'm bloody Antichrist.'

I started to laugh but stopped myself when I saw the expression on Neil's face.

'Hey, she's a teenager, rebelling against everything, including us.'

'Nah,' said Neil. 'She's disowned me as well as Sam. Opposite sides of every argument, we are.'

'Doesn't mean she doesn't love you,' I said, reaching out for his hand.

'I'm not sure about that. Nowt I say is ever right.'

'Maybe if you took a tougher line with Sam it would help?'

'And then both of my kids would hate me. Anyway, she doesn't need me now. She's got all her fancy friends at college.'

I squeezed his hand. He had doted on her from the moment she was born. And she'd been very much a Daddy's girl in those early years, which explained why this was so hard for him.

'Remember when you made her that snowman and she cried her heart out when it melted?'

I looked at Neil. He turned his head away from me, reluctant as ever to let me see him hurting.

'Come here, you daft bugger,' I said, leaning over and giving him a kiss.

'Steady,' he replied. 'I might think my luck's in.'

'I wouldn't get too excited,' I said. 'A quick snog in dark's about as good as it gets these days.'

'Never mind,' he replied. 'Owt else would be too much excitement at my age.'

He said it to make me feel better, I knew that. But it only made it worse. I switched off the lamp and lay there for a long time afterwards, listening until his breathing turned into a snore.

6

JODIE

I see him before the train comes to a halt. Maybe I was looking for him. Perhaps I'm not even embarrassed about that. The truth is, I haven't been able to stop thinking about him. Hundreds of lads go to my college, yet I barely give any of them a second look. Then he rocks up and it's like I have this sudden, intense connection with him. Like no other guy in the world exists.

The train stops. I missed him yesterday because I got on the wrong carriage. I'm not going to make the same mistake again. I'm between two sets of doors, but I go to the ones nearest him. I get on, turn to my left, and feign slight surprise when I see him. Not too much, mind; we are travelling on the same train each day after all. But just enough to make it look like it wasn't planned.

'Hey,' I say, sitting down opposite him. 'How's it going?'

He takes his AirPods out.

'Yeah, good,' he says with a smile. He has a ridiculously sexy smile. And yet, unlike most lads, he doesn't seem to realise it.

'What's your course like?'

'Awesome. I'm so relieved I didn't stay on at school. It would have done my head in.'

'Is that what your parents wanted you to do?'

'Big time. My dad still thinks I'm making a massive mistake not doing A levels. Like that's somehow going to ruin my life.'

'My dad were other way,' I say. 'Couldn't understand why I wanted to go to college to better myself when I had a good summer job at Greggs.'

'He's got a point. You could have got free vegan sausage rolls for life.'

I laugh.

'Yeah. Guess I messed up there.'

'Has he come around yet?' he asks.

'Not really. He'll kick off again when I start applying to uni.'

'Where do you want to go?'

'Leeds, they've got a good fashion design course. Which is a bit of luck because I'll have to live at home, what with cost of accommodation and that.'

'It's a good uni, my mum lectures there,' he says.

'Really? What course?'

'Midwifery. She used to be a midwife.'

'Jeez. Rather her than me. I can't think of anything worse than dealing with screaming women giving birth and all that blood and crap.'

He smiles.

'She's pretty chilled out and good at calming other people down too. Maybe that helps.'

'Well, I'm glad you decided not to follow her career path. I've always thought men who choose to look at women's bits all day are well creepy.'

'My dad's a gynaecologist actually,' he says.

I shut my eyes and momentarily consider jumping off the train.

'Shit. I'm so sorry. I really should learn to keep my mouth shut.'

His face is deadpan, but he gives a little nod in acknowledgement. I've blown it. Utterly blown it. I look down at my boots and start fiddling with the button on my jacket.

'Sorry,' I hear him say. I look up. He's smiling broadly. 'Couldn't resist it.'

'You bastard,' I say. 'What does he do really?'

'He's an eye consultant at St James's Hospital. I suppose staring into women's eyes isn't quite so creepy.'

I start to laugh. Other people nearby in the carriage are smiling, obviously enjoying the joke at my expense.

'You're never going to sit with me on the train again, are you?' he says.

'Absolutely not.'

'Joke's on me, then, I guess. Big mistake. Huge.'

He smiles again as he looks at me. Drop-dead gorgeous, sense of humour and *Pretty Woman* references. It is all I can do not to jump on him.

'Anyway,' I say, deciding to get back to the conversation we were having, 'is that why your dad's mad at you? Because you don't want to be a doctor?'

'Yeah. His father was a doctor too, so he reckons I should uphold the family tradition of going into medicine instead of mucking around with music.'

'Wow, by that score I should follow my dad and grandad down the coal mine. Bit of luck there's none left in Yorkshire.'

'What does your dad do now?' he asks.

'He's a shopfitter and my mum works at one-stop council shop in Leeds. Which is why Greggs looked like a good opportunity to them.'

'Sounds like you're the odd one out in your family, too.'

'Yep. I reckon I were swapped at birth. My dad voted Brexit and my brother's just been excluded from school for racist abuse.'

He raises his eyebrows and looks down at his phone for a moment. I realise he probably thinks he should steer well clear of a girl with family like that.

'I told my brother I've disowned him,' I continue quickly. 'And I'm going on that Stop Brexit march in Leeds on Saturday. That'll piss them both off.'

'I didn't know there was one,' he says.

'Yeah. You should come. It's gonna be massive. It starts at ten, line-up from nine, if you fancy it.'

'Sorry. I'll be at the mosque,' he says. 'Family day out. Me and my dad go to prayers, my sister goes to the education group and my mum usually goes shopping or has her hair done.'

'Oh, is she not . . .' My voice trails off as I realise I don't know quite how to finish the question. He steps in to cover my embarrassment.

'She's French. And she didn't convert to Islam when she married my dad. He's from Morocco. They met when they were both working at the same hospital in Paris.'

'Wow,' I reply. 'I'd love to go to Paris. Were you born there?'

'No. They moved to Leeds eighteen months before. Just my luck, eh?'

'Don't worry, it's still better than being born in Halifax.'

'At Calderdale Royal? That's where my mum used to work. She could have delivered you. When were you born?'

'September 2001.'

'I'm sure she was working there then. I'll have to ask her.'

I get a little buzz inside. I like that he wants to ask his mum about me. He looks out of the window for a moment before he realises.

'So, you're eighteen this month?'

'Yep. On the eighteenth.'

'Excellent. What are you doing to celebrate?'

'Dunno. I haven't made any plans, but I'm worried my mum's organised some surprise family party, which would be well embarrassing.'

'I know what you mean,' he says. 'I was going to get taken to Pizza Express for my birthday last weekend until I pointed out I wasn't ten years old.'

'Hey, happy birthday. What date?'

'The first. I think it was my dad's way of trying to ensure I got a head start in school.'

I laugh.

'I bet you got A-stars in your GCSEs.'

'A few,' he says with a smile. 'I went to a grammar school where anything less than A or A-star is considered a massive failure.'

'Bit of luck I didn't go there, then,' I reply. 'I would have been such a disappointment to them.'

I look up as we pull into Bramley station. I hadn't realised how far we'd got. A few more people get on and I have to move over towards the window. My knee touches his leg. He looks at me intently. Neither of us says anything. We don't have to. I pretend to look at my phone, but I can't concentrate because all I can think of is him.

When the train stops at Leeds we stand up at the same time. He gestures for me to go first. I realise we're going to walk up to college together and I feel stupidly excited and a little bit sick in the stomach about it.

We walk side by side along the platform. When we get to the barriers, I let him go first while I get out my ticket. Though it is also a chance to check him out without him seeing. I like his boots and suede jacket. The way his hair is cut at the sides and his neatly trimmed beard. The smell of him. I like everything about him, and I'm in so much trouble. Because although he might enjoy a little harmless flirting, in the real world, guys like him don't end up with girls like me.

We don't speak again until we've crossed the road outside and got halfway up Boar Lane.

'Do you know anyone else at college?' I ask.

'Not many. There's a handful of guys I see around who I know from the mosque but that's it.'

'What are rest of people on your course like?'

'They seem a good crew. They're music geeks like me, which at least means you're not stuck for anything to talk about. There's a guy called Marcus I'm getting on well with. Lives in Harehills. Massively into rap and grime.'

'Is that what you like?'

'Some of it. I like Stormzy and Missy Elliott but most of the rest doesn't do much for me.'

'So, who do you like?'

'Prince,' he says.

'The eighties dude who wore some great boots and seriously out-there jackets?'

He smiles.

'Also known as the musical genius behind "Purple Rain", "Sign O' the Times" and "When Doves Cry". Please tell me you've heard those?'

'Don't think so. But I've heard "Kiss" because Julia Roberts sings to it in the bath in *Pretty Woman*.'

He stops and stares at me as we turn off onto the pedestrianised area.

'What?' I ask. 'It's one of my mum's favourite films.'

'It's not that,' he says, stopping by a bench and taking out his phone. 'I can't believe that's the only Prince song you know. We need to sort this. Let me send you a link to his stuff on Spotify.'

'Are you signing me up to your secret cult?' I ask. 'Or is it just a sneaky way of trying to get my number?'

He looks down at the ground for a second.

'Don't worry,' I say. 'I'm still going to give it to you.'

His finger hovers over his phone screen.

'I don't know your name,' he says.

'Jodie.'

'Great. I'm Rachid by the way.'

He takes a moment to find what he wants. A few seconds later, my phone pings with a WhatsApp message. He's sent me a link to an album called *Sign O' the Times*.

'Thanks,' I say. 'I'll listen to it later.'

'You better had,' he replies. 'I'll be asking you questions about it tomorrow morning on the train.'

I start laughing.

'Maybe I'll get on a different carriage to avoid you.'

He smiles and nods in acknowledgement of my line.

'And maybe you won't.'

He's right, of course. I put my phone back in my pocket and we walk on together. As soon as I get to my classroom, I add him to my contacts on my phone. I'm not sure how to spell his name and I don't want to guess and get it wrong. So I put him in as 'R'.

7

SYLVIE

Amina was the only one in when I got home from work on Friday evening. I could hear music coming from her room. I stopped outside the door to listen, as what was playing was usually a good gauge of her mood. It was Taylor Swift's 'Love Story'. I groaned inwardly; clearly the being-the-only-one-without-a-boyfriend thing was still getting to her. I knocked on her door. The music stopped. She said I could come in.

'Hi,' I said, sitting down on the end of her bed. 'Tough first week back?'

She nodded. I reached over and stroked her hair.

'Not only are you beautiful but you're intelligent and kind and all sorts of amazing.'

She pulled a face that made it clear she didn't believe it.

'You're my mum,' she replied. 'You have to say stuff like that.'

I smiled at her, knowing that compliments from your mother really didn't cut it at her age.

'Your time will come,' I said. 'And I know it must seem forever away, but when it does, that person will be very lucky to have you.'

'Yeah, and I'll probably be ancient by then.'

'By ancient, do you mean my age?'

She almost managed a smile.

'Becky's having a party for her fifteenth birthday,' she announced after a slight pause. 'I might not even be invited yet, but it doesn't really matter whether I am or not, does it?'

I thought carefully before replying.

'What sort of party is it?'

'At her house. With boys. Her parents are going to be out.'

I nodded slowly, knowing we'd never get that past Bilal.

'I think when you're at uni, that's when things will really open up for you.'

'But that's ages away.'

'It just seems that way now.'

She turned her face away from me. I hated to disappoint her like this.

'I'll be the only one who doesn't go.'

'Come on, I'm sure there'll be others—'

'There won't. They haven't got any other Muslim friends. Even if I make up an excuse, they'll know the real reason. And in the end people will just stop asking me and they'll all be out with their boyfriends having fun and I'll be stuck here listening to Taylor Swift on repeat like some sad loser.'

I leant over and pulled her to me.

'I'm sorry this is so hard for you,' I said.

'It's because I don't fit in. None of us fit in. Nobody wants us here any more.'

'Hey,' I said. 'That's not true. Has someone said something at school?'

'They don't have to. There's like this massive divide. All the older Muslim girls hang out together. That's how it works.'

I tried to process what she had just said. Instinctively, I wanted to argue against it, but I also knew it might be true.

'All of them?'

'Yeah. You only have to look at the tables at lunchtimes. And then you hear people saying stuff on the news and see the headlines on the newspapers and I still remember that stupid Leave advert by the bus stop when I was in Year Six, and I hate it. I hate being hated.'

I tried to give her a hug, but she wouldn't let me.

'You're not hated.'

'Yes, I am. We all are. You and Dad are foreigners and me and Rachid are Muslim and we get blamed for everything.'

'I know it's tough, but you have to try to ignore these people,' I said.

'That's easy for you to say, isn't it? You're not Muslim. You don't know what it's like to grow up having to live by all these rules, but you still go along with Dad insisting that we do.'

The words slapped me around the face. I had dreaded this moment, mainly because I knew I still didn't have a good enough answer for her. Before I had a chance to say anything, however inadequate, in response, she put Taylor Swift back on, making it very clear I was no longer wanted. I stood up and walked out of the room, shutting the door softly behind me and closing my eyes as I thought about what she'd said. I wasn't sure what the right response was. All I did know was that I had to try to find it.

The atmosphere between Amina and me at the dining table was not good. Fortunately, Rachid was still buzzing enough from his first week at college to cover the silences, while the lamb tagine did a good job of distracting Bilal.

'When did you start working at Calderdale Royal?' Rachid asked me, in between mouthfuls.

'Um, January 2001. Why do you ask?'

'Someone at college said she was born there in September that year. I wondered if you might have delivered her.'

'Maybe, not that I'd have any way of checking. Is she on your course?'

'No. But she gets on my train in the morning.'

'Well, it's nice to see you're making friends,' I said.

I looked across at Bilal, but he didn't comment or even nod in agreement. Amina was still staring into her lap, not making eye contact with me.

'How was the clinic?' I asked Bilal.

'Somewhat chaotic,' he replied. 'We have a new nurse, only just qualified. She spent most of the day squirting dilating fluid all over patients' faces. At one point I heard her tell one of them "they had to let me loose at some point, I suppose".'

'Poor thing. She was probably terrified. I hope you were nice to her. You need to remember you can come across as a bit intimidating at times.'

'Charming,' he replied. 'I was very understanding and told her not to worry. Though if she does it again tomorrow, I'll have her transferred.'

There was a glint in his eye as he said it. Although as neither of the children were looking at him, it was probably only me who realised he was joking. I decided to try to divert the topic of conversation back to college.

'What course is your friend on?' I asked Rachid.

'Which friend?'

'The girl on the train you were telling me about.'

'Fashion and textiles,' he said. 'She's going to be applying to Leeds Uni soon. She's in her second year.'

Bilal looked up. I wondered if he could detect the same note in Rachid's voice I could.

'Is she a Muslim girl?' he asked. 'Do I know her father?'

'What does it matter?'

'I simply want to make sure the young women you're fraternising with are suitable.' Bilal said it with a playful look on his face but again Rachid didn't look up to see it.

'Suitable for who?' The tone of Rachid's voice was decidedly hostile. I shot Bilal a reproachful look.

'Come on,' replied Bilal. 'You know I'm only joking.'

'I hope so, because if the Muslim man who married a white non-Muslim thinks he's got the right to dictate who his children should hang out with, he's going to be in for a shock.'

Bilal put down his cutlery with a sharp clank.

'That's enough,' he said. 'You need to learn to show some respect to your parents.'

Before Rachid could respond, Amina pushed her plate away.

'Why?' she said. 'Because you don't respect us. You impose things on us and expect us to go along with them without complaint.'

Bilal stared at her.

'What's brought this on?' he said.

'You won't let me do anything. You have no idea what it's like. How hard you make it to fit in.'

She stood up, pushed her chair back and left the room. Bilal and Rachid turned to look at me, both seemingly as surprised by her outburst as each other.

'Her best friends at school are going out with boys and there's a party all her friends are going to. She's feeling left out.'

Bilal shook his head.

'I thought she understood that her studies come first.'

'Jeez,' said Rachid, standing up and scowling at Bilal. 'You really don't get it, do you?'

I lay in bed later that night, sure I could still hear Amina crying in her room. My attempts to comfort her had been rebutted. All I could do was let her know I cared and would be there if she wanted to let me in. But the sense of our family relationships being fractured ran deep. It was always me in the middle, scrabbling desperately to repair the damage, in the hope that I could somehow hold the whole thing together.

Damage limitation was my secondary occupation. Had been for so long now. Maybe I should have asked Bilal to leave ten years ago when I'd found out. But even then, my primary concern had been not hurting the children. Of course, the truth is you always hurt the children, whatever you decide to do. I suspected Rachid was still hurting from what he'd seen and heard from our bedroom doorway, which he had always refused to talk about. And me? I'd put a huge sticking plaster over it. Made a good enough job of holding things together. Certainly, few people outside our family seemed to have noticed. But underneath the wound had festered and still seemed no nearer to healing now than it had back then. I should do something about it, I knew that. But it was hard when you still loved the person who had caused all the hurt.

Bilal came into the room and got into bed next to me. We'd both slept naked during those early Paris years together. These days, he wore pyjama bottoms (a grudging concession to the Yorkshire chill), but still went bare-chested. Perhaps because, being one of those men who saw gym club membership as a commitment for life, he didn't have to worry about what ageing had done to his body. Whereas I, on the other hand, now wore a modest nightdress from M&S that covered both the stretch marks and the area where my waist used to be. I had a pile of such garments in the chest of drawers next to our bed, so I could change quickly when I woke in the night covered in my own sweat. Bilal had put his hand on me in the early hours once and removed it quickly when he'd felt the moisture. He hadn't said anything, of course, but he didn't need to. He was clearly repelled by my body.

He'd insisted a thousand times after I'd discovered his 'indiscretion' that he still loved me, but it was just that: an insistence, not a spontaneous declaration. What he probably felt for me was affection, as the woman he'd married and the mother of his children. The feelings he'd had for Sylvie Roux, the trainee midwife who'd dared to flirt with him in the hospital canteen and who he'd fucked against the door of his consulting room, had been a different thing entirely. Presumably, the young consultant he'd fucked in a hotel room at various conferences had known exactly what that felt like too.

'I feel like we're losing Amina,' Bilal said, bringing me back to more pressing matters.

'She's growing up fast, pushing boundaries, trying to find her place in the world,' I replied.

'But why is she so angry with us?'

I turned to look at him.

'She made a fair point. And teenagers are highly skilled at sniffing out hypocrisy.'

'But it was different for us.'

'Yes, it was. And that's why she thinks it's unfair.'

'But the circumstances were different. We were adults. Two professionals working in the same field. And my father had died before we got together. No one at the mosque had an issue with it.'

'Because you were a respected professional man. It would have been completely different if you'd been a young woman. Amina knows that and she hates the injustice.'

Bilal ran his hand over his receding hairline.

'So, what do we do?'

'I don't know. I can't help much because I can only guess at what she's going through. She made that very clear to me earlier.'

Bilal turned to me and frowned.

'She said I couldn't understand,' I explained. 'Because I wasn't Muslim.'

Bilal was silent for a few moments before speaking. He'd been so supportive of my decision not to convert to Islam when we'd married, but I wondered if he was now regretting that.

'I'm sorry,' he said, stroking my arm. 'That must have been tough to hear.'

'It was,' I said, my voice wobbling. 'But I can see that it's so hard for her. She's trying to navigate her way through what's a difficult time for any teenage girl, in a country and society that is not making her feel welcome, with a mum who can't truly understand what she's going through. I'm going to have a chat with Leila's mum, to see how she handles things. But in the meantime, perhaps you should consider giving Amina a little more freedom.'

'What, let her go out with some boy from school who'll have only one thing on his mind?' asked Bilal, reverting to protective-father mode.

'No. I'm not saying that. Just give her room to breathe. And Rachid too. He doesn't need an inquisition from you about who he talks to on a train.'

'If he'd stayed on at school, we wouldn't have this problem. We would have known all the parents there. We have no idea of the sort of families his college friends come from.'

I smiled and shook my head.

'What?'

'Have you any idea how bigoted you sound?'

'Don't you want him to find someone from the right background?'

'I want him to find someone he loves and who will love him back for who he is.'

'Listen to yourself, ever the romantic.'

He smiled as he said it. I felt myself soften. It was almost as if there was a hint of tenderness there.

'Try telling that to Amina. She accused me of having a rather jaded view of romance earlier.'

Bilal raised one eyebrow.

'I'd told her to sit tight and simply wait for her friends' relationships to break up,' I explained.

'I'd call that pragmatism.'

'Well, she wasn't impressed and demanded to know what romantic things we'd done together when we first met.'

'What did you tell her?'

'I kept it vague. Candlelit meals, walks along the river, that sort of thing.'

'So you didn't mention the afternoon we spent in the

bath in my apartment feeding each other strawberries and chocolates?'

There was a twinkle in his eyes as he said it. I couldn't help being glad he remembered too.

'I was hardly going to mention that, was I? Anyway, it seems a very long time ago now.'

Bilal kissed me on the forehead. I used to like it when he did that but not now. Now it just reeked of affection. I didn't want that. I wanted to be desired. I kissed him back. Hard, on the lips. Telling myself I had to do this: push past the pain if I had any chance of rekindling what we once had.

He rolled over on top of me. Our bodies did at least still respond to each other, even if not with the same level of intensity as they used to. I reached out and turned off my bedside lamp. I didn't want to see the lack of desire on his face. Get any sense that he was simply going through the motions. He slid my nightdress up to my waist. I groaned as he moved his hand between my legs. And we did that thing we'd become so good at, having sex on autopilot. Physically, everything was still in good working order. But there was so little connection emotionally that it felt like a transaction where you should shake hands when you had finished and thank the other person for coming.

I lay there perfectly still afterwards, willing Bilal to fall asleep, glad it was too dark to see the expression on his face. Because it wouldn't be one of bliss or contentment. A flicker of satisfaction was, perhaps, the best I could have hoped for.

It cut me deep, but I couldn't let it show. Tomorrow I would need to play my part in our public charade of happy families. Because Sylvie could always be relied upon to smile through the pain. To spread a little sunshine everywhere she went. And not to let out the silent scream that was still stuck in my throat.

The Saturday morning routine was an established one that, somewhat surprisingly, everyone adopted without complaint. Bilal rose early and, after prayers, took his BMW to the car wash. There was apparently only one in Halifax where the staff were up to the job. He always requested the most expensive option and I suspected he paid the men a substantial bonus to ensure they met his exacting standards. I imagined they probably called him 'sir', too. He'd like that. However, it did at least keep him out of our hair for a while and allowed for a stress-free start to the day.

Amina got ready in her room while listening to music. Today, Taylor Swift had been replaced with Billie Eilish. I wasn't sure what that said about her state of mind, but I knew that she enjoyed seeing her friends at the girls' youth group at the mosque. And I was glad she would be with people who, unlike me, could understand what she was going through.

Rachid never offered any resistance to his weekly trip to the mosque. I was under no illusions that it was because he enjoyed spending time with his father, although I did think he enjoyed the respect Bilal's standing at the mosque conferred on him. He also liked being treated as a grown-up and being able to mix, as an equal, with all the other men.

He adopted his usual practice over breakfast of asking Alexa to play his own music – something that was only allowed when Bilal was out. Although today Prince was subjected to constant interruptions from the ping of his phone.

'Someone's popular,' I said as he replied to one. He gave me a quick smile, said nothing, and returned to his two-thumbed messaging. He did keep in touch with a few of his friends from the mosque via WhatsApp, and a couple of his old school friends, although something told me they were not the ones he was messaging this morning.

I finished my breakfast and got myself ready, deciding not to attempt any further conversation with Amina. At the allotted time, we trooped out of the house in age order, rather like the von Trapp family, and made our way to Bilal's gleaming BMW, which was waiting outside.

It was rare for us to walk past my car, an ageing yellow Renault, without Rachid making a disparaging comment, but today his mind seemed to be elsewhere. He and Amina got silently into the back of the BMW, I slid into the front seat next to Bilal.

'Ready?' he asked with a smile. His mood always improved when his car was clean. It was as if they'd given his spirits and ego a polish at the same time.

'Yes. If you could drop me near the bus station, that would be great, thanks. I don't want to keep Nat waiting.'

I was going to the hairdresser's. My own version of a visit to the car wash. I would feel better afterwards. At least, I hoped so. I turned to Amina.

'I've arranged everything with Leila's mum. She'll walk you both down to the café after mosque group and I'll join you when I'm done.'

Amina pulled a face.

'Don't worry, we'll sit well away from you two. We wouldn't want to cramp your style.'

'Glad to hear it,' she replied.

'And you've got the money I gave you?'

'Yes, thanks.'

'How come she gets money, and I don't?' asked Rachid.

'Because we spent yours and most of ours on all that tech stuff in your room,' I replied.

'Nice burn,' said Rachid. Although he was sitting behind me, I could tell he was smiling. We drove on in silence apart from the faint sound of Classic FM, which Bilal knew to keep at a volume that didn't disturb anyone else. Rachid had his AirPods in. Amina was reading on her Kindle, and I was left alone with the contents of my head. Were all families as disjointed as ours? Existing in separate worlds and simply coming together occasionally in a pretence of normality? Maybe I was overthinking. Maybe the happy families I saw around me were all pretending too. Or perhaps I was right, and the cracks were widening before my eyes. In which case it was down to me to do something about it, as the one thing that was certain was that no one else would.

Bilal grimaced as he pulled into a lay-by near the bus station. He had given up asking why I didn't go to a swish salon in one of the arcades in the nice part of town. My explanation that Nat was a curly-hair specialist was lost on him, but clearly he still resented having to park in the vicinity of someone sitting on a bench eating a pasty while waiting for a bus.

From out of the bus station came a young woman with long auburn hair carrying a Greggs bag in one hand and a large placard reading BOLLOCKS TO BREXIT in the other. She walked with a sense of confidence and defiance, her long lace-up boots striding forward purposefully, her green jacket swishing as she moved. I saw her smile in our direction. A second later she was waving and brandishing her placard excitedly.

'What on earth?' asked Bilal.

I turned around. Rachid was grinning back at her.

'I know her from college,' he said.

'Well, she's not exactly a good advert for them,' replied Bilal.

'She's trying to stop Brexit,' Rachid said. 'There's a big march in town today. A lot of people from college are going.'

'That's still no excuse for what she's got written on her banner.'

'I thought you liked young people to be politically engaged?' Rachid said.

'It's the expletive I have an issue with, not the sentiment. And as much as I agree with that, marching across Leeds is not going to change anything now. The battle has been fought and lost.'

Rachid muttered something under his breath that I didn't catch. I suspected it was a good thing that Bilal wouldn't have caught it either.

I glanced out of the window and saw the girl stop for a second on the corner. A moment later Rachid's phone pinged. Whatever the message was, it made Rachid laugh out loud. I willed Bilal not to say anything more. The last thing I wanted was an escalation of tensions as I was about to leave.

'Right,' I said, checking in the mirror for any further placard-waving protestors, before opening the door, 'I'll see you all later. Please be nice to each other.'

Nobody replied. I got out, careful as ever not to slam the door behind me. The placard girl walked on down the road. I had a feeling that Rachid was walking with her, in spirit at least.

I watched as Bilal's car pulled away. My family heading off somewhere I wasn't really a part of. It was my choice, and I'd never wavered from it. I had always been made welcome when I'd dropped off or collected the children. And on more than one occasion, a well-meaning individual had told me it was not too late to join them. But I liked being answerable only to myself. Even though I couldn't imagine any god being as hard on me as I was. Besides, I had been raised under France's secular constitution by a mother who believed fiercely in 'laïcité'. She'd raised an eyebrow when I'd told her the children were going to be following their father's faith. I'd had to explain that it mattered a great deal to Bilal, and I was happy to support that, just as he'd supported my decision not to convert to Islam. It was an arrangement that had always worked for us. But now, with Amina starting to question everything more vocally, and Rachid making new friends at college, I was wondering if it was going to cause further fractures in our family. And with our status and future in this country under threat, I couldn't help feeling our family was in a very precarious situation indeed.

Le cul entre deux chaises, the French called it. Which translated as, 'the bottom is between two chairs'. We'd fought incredibly hard to make this our home over the past twenty years. Doing everything we could to 'fit in', ensuring the children were raised speaking English, although thanks to also speaking French at home until they were both at secondary school, and Arabic at the mosque, they were fluent in all three languages. I didn't want to think that had been in vain. But nor could I deny that the feeling of no longer being wanted here was hard to dismiss. There were only so many times you could be asked to prove you had a right to be here, before you started wondering if that was really what you wanted.

I jumped as a bus driver with a snarling expression leant out of his window and shouted 'traitor' at a protestor. She responded by sticking her middle finger up at him. Yet again, I was caught in the crossfire of other people's conflicts. Having just about weathered the political landscape shifting around us, the sticking plasters over our family's fractures were now in danger of coming off. I wasn't sure how much longer I'd be able to hold things together.

I hurried across the road and entered the hairdresser's. Nat looked up from her customer and gave me her usual cheery greeting.

'Hi, Sylvie, park yourself on sofa. I won't keep you a minute.'

A few minutes later, I popped the cape on and took a seat in front of the mirror. And I realised, as I looked at her, that the woman who stared back at me was unrecognisable as the Sylvie Roux who Bilal had fallen for and who once had the whole world at her feet. She was no longer desirable or desired. Not by her husband or the country she now called home.

'So,' said Nat, smiling at me in the mirror. 'How are you doing?'

I opened my mouth to say my usual 'fine', but the word didn't come. Instead, I watched as the first fat tear rolled down my cheek, swiftly followed by all the others that had been queuing patiently behind, waiting for this moment of release.

The haircut perked me up. Nat not only brought me over a cup of strong coffee and a box of tissues, but also somehow managed to style my curls in such a way that they gave a confident bounce as I walked to the café afterwards. A confidence that, though it belied how I felt inside, at least meant I could fake it enough to meet Leila's mum without appearing to be a complete emotional wreck.

Fatima was sitting in the window. She looked up from her phone and smiled at me as I passed by outside. I took a moment to gather myself before stepping inside. Amina and Leila were in the far corner of the café, huddled together over two hot chocolates and giggling. I smiled, knowing better than to try to interact with them, and walked over to Fatima. She was wearing an aubergine-coloured hijab that framed her stunning features perfectly, and a black dress that accentuated her slim frame. As usual, I felt decidedly frumpy in her presence. I tried to reassure myself that I did at least have good hair today.

'Hi. Those two seem to be having a good time,' I said, gesturing towards Amina and Leila.

'Yes, I don't think they've stopped talking once.'

I sat down opposite Fatima.

'It's such a relief to see Amina like that,' I said. 'She's had a tough first week back at school. I'm so glad she's got Leila's friendship.'

'What's been going on?' asked Fatima, as a waitress came over and I ordered an espresso.

'She's being frozen out by her best friends. They've both got boyfriends and are going out to parties. She feels like they're leaving her behind.'

Fatima nodded knowingly. Leila was a year older than Amina. I imagined she would already have had similar issues.

'It's hard at that age,' she said. 'I've noticed Leila seems to be closer to her Muslim friends now. It's a shame because they were much more integrated when they were younger.'

I nodded and hesitated before I asked her.

'Does Leila ever seem resentful? Because Amina made it very clear to me yesterday that she is.'

The waitress returned with my coffee. Fatima seemed to be considering her reply very carefully.

'I think with Leila, it's simply the usual worries teenage girls have around friendships and boys. She's never complained about missing out, or anything like that.'

Fatima was French Moroccan. Her husband was Moroccan-born like Bilal. It seemed the only thing different about our families was that Fatima was Muslim too.

'To be honest, I'm finding it difficult to know how best to support Amina,' I said. 'She says I can't possibly understand because I'm not Muslim.'

'All teenage girls think their mothers can't possibly understand,' said Fatima with a smile. 'I wouldn't take it personally.'

'But she has a point. How can I understand when I'm not Muslim or British like her? I'm no help at all really.'

Fatima reached out her hand to squeeze mine as she heard the catch in my voice.

'You're her mum and you love her, that's all that she needs.'

'She accused me of being a hypocrite.'

Fatima winced. 'I'm sorry. That must have hurt.'

'It did.'

'Perhaps what you need to hear is that, as a Muslim woman, I think you're a marvellous role model for Amina. And I don't think you converting to Islam would make you a better mother to her in any way, nor would it have if you'd done it when you married Bilal. Just keep talking to her, let her know how much she's loved and respected. Make sure her voice is heard and that she knows you'll be with her all the way through this.'

'Thank you,' I said. 'That's what I needed to hear.'

R & J

WhatsApp

Hey, how was the march? 12:27

Good lots of shouting and chanting. How was mosque 12:27

OK. Lots of talking and praying 12:27

😂 12:27

Are you heading home now? 12:27

No we're off to my grandad's. He's Wakefield's answer to Nigel Farage 12:27

😬 12:27

I know. See you Monday 12:28

Yeah. First carriage. I'll save you a seat 12:28

8

DONNA

Tibs was sitting on the bonnet of Neil's van as we left the house, licking his wounds while announcing to the neighbourhood cats that he had survived a knockout blow and was ready for a rematch if there were any takers. He jumped down, miaowing as he saw us, and I shepherded him into the house before shutting the door.

When I turned back, Neil was scowling at Jakub as he reversed into the driveway next door. The fact that his work van had to double as the family car was a constant source of resentment for my husband. The fact that Jakub was half his age, yet drove a Mercedes, only added to that.

To be honest, I would have liked a nice car too. Or at least something where I didn't have to hop three times to gain the momentum to haul myself up into it. It might have been funny when I was a bit younger with legs up to my armpits. It wasn't such a laugh now my arse was the size of a cow's and I was worried I was going to wet myself during the process.

It didn't help when it wasn't even a journey I wanted to be making. I often thought Lorraine had got the best deal with getting knocked up by a guy who legged it out of her life at pretty much the first sight of a dirty nappy. I would never tell her that, of course. But there had been plenty of times during our visits to Neil's parents when I cursed him for having stuck around so long. Sandra may have been bearable in short bursts, but Reggie was hard to stomach for even a few minutes. Throw a mouthy, hormonal teenage girl who hated everything about him into the mix, and a family visit was like running at high speed towards a fork in the full knowledge it was going to poke your eye out.

Sam slid back the side door of the van and got in the back as I manoeuvred myself into the front passenger seat.

'I still don't see why she had to go to this bloody protest,' said Neil, pulling his seat belt across.

'I told you. She's almost eighteen and entitled to do what she wants with her free time. And as we're picking her up and she's three-quarters of way to your parents, it means she can't get out of it.'

'Well, I won't be held responsible for what Dad says to her when he finds out where she's been.'

'That's why you're not going to say owt.'

'What if I tell him?' asked Sam from the back.

'I'll ground you for rest of year and send your phone to charity for kids who haven't got one instead of giving it back to you next week.'

'What am I even supposed to do on way there without it?'

'You can spend time reflecting on your behaviour, like Mr Hill said. And if you can't manage that, you can count grains in pile of wood in front of you.'

There were various grunting sounds. The good thing was that once we got going, I wouldn't be able to hear him in the back.

'Right,' I said, turning to Neil. 'Let's get this over with.'

Jodie was easy enough to spot amongst the crowd still milling about. The combination of her hair, green jacket, and the huge placard she was holding that read, BOLLOCKS TO BREXIT, made sure of that.

'She never was subtle, was she?' said Neil, shaking his head as he pulled into the lay-by next to the bus station.

Jodie opened the side door and climbed in the back, throwing the placard onto the floor of the van.

'I'm not sitting near that,' said Sam.

'I'll stick it up your arse, if you'd rather,' replied Jodie.

'Come on, you two,' I said. 'Don't start. I'm not having this for rest of journey.'

'It's OK,' said Jodie. 'I can handle a bit of verbal from him. I got called a traitor about ten times today and had loads of pissheads standing outside pubs shouting abuse as I went past.'

'Sounds like an average Friday night out in Leeds,' I replied.

'And some twat of a bus driver who put his head out and told us to piss off to Europe if we all loved it so much.'

'It's always an option,' muttered Neil. 'Especially if you're such sore losers you can't accept result.'

'Bring it on,' said Jodie. 'I can give as good as I get, remember.'

'Shut it, all of you,' I said. 'I get one Saturday off a month, and I do not want to spend it listening to you lot bickering. Not another word about it and when we get to Grandma and Grandad's, you will all behave, do you understand?'

No one said anything. Which I took for a grudging agreement.

Sandra and Reggie lived in a former council house, much like ours. Only they were the generation who held the keys to their own home in their hands after years of renting. Although, according to Neil, their enthusiasm for Maggie Thatcher's land of opportunity had collapsed pretty sharpish when she'd turned her attention to the miners.

The scars of that conflict were still there. Visible both on their faces and in the neglect of their estate thirty-five years on. It was the sort of place TV crews came when they wanted to film one of those 'Whatever happened to the mining communities after the pits shut?' pieces. Except few of them even bothered to do that these days.

We climbed out of the van. Sam kicked Jodie's banner as he did so, and I had to separate them before we even made it to the front door. Neil walked straight in and called out to announce our arrival, Reggie and Sandra presumably thinking that burglars would do the same.

The house smelt of fish and chips, as it always did on a Saturday. It probably smelt the same on other days too, but we were always too busy to come and find out. Sandra and Reggie had never offered to visit us, even when the kids were little. Not that I was complaining; their reluctance to leave their little patch of West Yorkshire at least meant we never had to put up with them at our house.

'Hello, pet,' said Sandra, kissing Neil. She did the same to Jodie and almost landed a kiss on Sam's face, but he turned away just in time.

'Hello, love,' she said to me, 'you look shattered. Had a tough week at work?'

I managed to resist the temptation of telling her that it was her precious son and grandson who were the main cause of all the stress in my life.

'Yeah, summat like that.'

'I'll get kettle on for a brew, then. Grab a pew and don't mind him,' she said, pointing at Reggie, who hadn't yet removed his gaze from the giant TV screen in the corner. I remembered Neil telling me how his dad had once broken an armchair by getting overenthusiastic, leaping up and down while watching a wrestling bout on *World of Sport*. I doubted he was capable of moving his arse from the armchair at all these days; certainly, I'd never seen him do it. I had visions of Sandra having to winch him out of it at the end of each day to get him up to bed.

'You OK, then, Dad?' said Neil, as the four of us squeezed onto the sofa.

'Aye. Though I still can't pronounce names of most of United's players.'

Jodie looked at me. I shook my head. He complained about this every single time we came, and I knew it was best to ignore it.

'Well, as long as they start winning again soon,' replied Neil.

'Half their midfield were European last weekend,' said Reggie.

I wasn't quick enough to stop Jodie jumping in.

'They were all European actually, Grandad. England's still a part of Europe.'

'We should build a wall, like Trump's doing. That'll keep them all out.'

'Yeah, that'll work well on an island,' said Jodie, snorting with laughter.

I gestured to Neil to change the subject quickly.

'I've been busy at work this week,' he told Reggie. 'Contract fitting out a shop in Bradford.'

'Are there Romanians on site?' Reggie asked. 'Or are they all Muslims there?'

Jodie stood up before I had a chance to dig Neil in the ribs, which was my usual tactic when Reggie went too far.

'Seriously, I am not going to sit here and listen to this crap,' she said.

'Turn TV over if you want summat else on, love,' said Sandra, coming in with the tea tray.

Jodie rolled her eyes. Sam started to laugh.

'Maybe we can change subject,' I said, trying my best to be diplomatic. 'You could ask your grandkids how they are for a start.'

'How's school going, young man?' Sandra asked, turning to Sam. He looked at me. I shook my head. It was one of those occasions when lying was the best option.

'All right,' he said.

'Not that he's been in much this week,' Jodie said as she sat back down again. I gave her my warning look.

'Oh, you been poorly, pet?' Sandra asked. Sam turned to me again. He was struggling now. Thinking on his feet had never been his strong point.

'Just a tummy bug,' I said quickly. 'He's feeling better now.'

'I hope so. Don't want him passing it on to rest of you. Not with our Jodie's party coming up.'

I groaned inside. I'd told Neil to remind her it was supposed to be a surprise.

'What party?' said Jodie, looking at me.

'Ooh, have I put my foot in it?' asked Sandra. I took a deep breath before replying.

'Never mind,' I said. 'I expect she'd have found out anyway.'

'Well, it sounds right lovely. Expect they'll do a nice spread at social club.'

'What?' said Jodie, louder this time.

I looked at Neil. Making it clear it was his turn to sort out the mess.

'Yeah, we thought it would be nice to have it local, like.'

'What, so you can get drunk on cheap booze without worrying about driving or forking out for a cab home?'

'Jodie,' I said.

'Well, it's true. I don't want my eighteenth birthday party at that bloody place. The carpets smell of piss, for a start.'

'Oi, missy, watch what you're saying in front of your grandparents,' said Neil.

'So, I have to listen to him coming out with all that racist crap,' she said, jabbing her finger towards Reggie, 'but I can't say a word about you booking a party for me at a dive no girls my age would be seen dead in.'

'She's an ungrateful little madam when she's wound up, isn't she?' said Sandra.

Jodie turned to her.

'At least I didn't get myself excluded from school like your precious grandson.'

Sandra looked at Neil.

'Is that true?'

'Just a little bit of aggro with another lad,' said Neil. 'You know what it's like at their age.'

'Well, I hope he gave other one as good as he got,' said Reggie. 'What were he, a poof or summat?'

Jodie stood up.

'Give me the keys,' she said to Neil. 'I'm going to sit in van.'

'You'll do no such thing,' he replied.

'Fine. Then I'll stay here and tell them what he said to that lad, shall I? And we'll have a nice little family chat about it.'

Neil reached into his pocket and threw her the keys. She took them and walked out without so much as a goodbye.

'Time of month, is it?' Sandra whispered to me.

The journey home involved five minutes of everybody shouting, followed by furious silence the rest of the way, apart from constant pings on Jodie's phone as she messaged back and forth. When we got home, Jodie and Sam both went straight to their rooms.

'That went well,' I said to Neil.

'She were bang out of order.'

'Oh, and your dad wasn't, you mean? How many times have I asked you to talk to him about it?'

'He doesn't mean no harm. He's set in his ways, that's all.'

'Maybe you could try explaining that to Jodie.'

'Like she's going to let me anywhere near her now.'

'What did I say about booking social?'

'I were trying to do summat nice for her. Surprise her. I can't do owt right these days.'

He sat down heavily at the kitchen table, his head in his hands. I felt myself soften a little.

'She's a bit old for surprises, Neil. You should have asked her first, like I said.'

'Whatever. It's too late for that now.'

'No, it's not. I want you to cancel.'

'You what?'

'She doesn't want it there and she'll be too embarrassed

to invite any of her mates. Which means it'll end up being a disaster.'

'I won't get deposit back.'

'I don't care. I'll do overtime at work.'

'No, you won't. It were my balls-up, I should be one doing overtime. Anyway, where else can we get at such short notice?'

'Don't worry, I'll sort it. You go and get a takeout. And make sure you get summat they'll both like.'

Neil sighed and walked out. I called Lorraine. I always lost track of her shifts, but if she answered, it generally meant she wasn't at work.

'Hiya. Have fun at in-laws?' she asked.

'Bloody nightmare. Reggie spouting racist crap as usual, and Sandra let slip about Jodie's party at social club, at which point Jodie went ballistic and said she wouldn't go.'

'Oof. I did warn you.'

'I know. And I told Neil same, but you know what he's like. Anyway, I've told him to cancel it and I'm going to find somewhere else. You know that Italian place your old school friend works at?'

'La Luna?'

'That's it. You said they've got a function room upstairs.'

'They do. Right nice it is, Connie showed me once.'

'Could you give her a call and see if it's available?'

'What, for next Saturday?'

'Or one after. That would be better, actually. Give us more time to get it organised.'

'Yeah, course. It's a long shot because they'll probably be booked up, but I'll do owt for our Jodie, you know that.'

'I do, and I reckon it would be much more her sort of place.'

'It's dead nice. Got its own entrance at back. Private bar, and they do a lovely Italian spread.'

'Is it going to break bank?'

'Connie'll do mates' rates for me. I asked Danny Freeman out for her in fourth year. She owes me big time.'

'Thanks, love. Couldn't try her now, could you? I just want to put Jodie out of her misery.'

'Yep. I'll call you straight back.'

I knocked softly on Jodie's door twenty minutes later.

'What?' she asked.

I went in. She was slumped on her bed listening to music on her phone.

'Is that Prince?' I asked. 'Since when have you been into Prince?'

She turned it off straight away, looking embarrassed.

'He's class,' she said. 'Better than that Bon Jovi crap you listen to.'

'Cheers. Anyway, I want to talk to you.'

'I'm not going to apologise. I know I went off on one but he were bang out of order.'

'I know, but I want to tell you there's been a change of plan.'

'What?' asked Jodie, still not looking up.

'Your dad's cancelling do at social. He were only trying to do best for you, mind, so don't be hard on him. Anyway,

Lorraine's found you a new venue. We were dead lucky to get it, they'd had a cancellation.'

Jodie looked up. I was aware it was Lorraine's involvement that had sparked the interest. Favourite auntie status didn't even begin to go there.

'It's function room at La Luna, that Italian restaurant in Halifax. Two weeks from today. They're going to do you fancy Italian canapés, there's a private bar and you can bring in your own DJ and decorate it yoursen if you want.'

'Really?'

The sound of hope in her voice and the expression on her face made my own voice catch as I replied.

'Yeah. It's all booked. And you can invite who you like. Nowt to do with us, then we can't screw it up for you.'

She came over and threw her arms around me.

'Thanks, Mum,' she said. 'I really didn't mean to be ungrateful about social.'

'I know, love,' I said, stroking her hair. 'And you were right. Their carpet does smell of piss.'

9

RACHID

We're pulling into the station at Low Moor and she's on the platform, waiting. The gap from Friday evening till Monday morning has never seemed as long in my life. If I hadn't seen her from the car on Saturday, I'm not sure I'd have made it through the weekend. But even that wasn't the same as being able to be next to her. Hear her, smell her, touch her, even.

The train stops and she gets on. The ache inside me gets worse for a moment before she walks straight over and sits down opposite me smiling.

'Hey,' she says. And with that one word, I can breathe again. My body can function. My head can decide not to explode.

'Hey. Recovered from seeing your grandad yet?'

'Not really. I'm seriously considering divorcing my family and I need your help.'

'Sorry, I'm not a lawyer.'

She smiles, bats at me with her hand.

'No, I need your help on music front.'

'Now you're talking.'

'I'm having an eighteenth party at La Luna in Halifax. But I need to find someone to do music and I wondered if you knew anyone?'

I'm not sure if she's angling for me to do it, but I'm worried that if I suggest that, she'll think I'm desperate.

'I can ask Marcus at college. He's got all the gear. And I could give him a hand with getting it in and setting up, if you don't mind me tagging along.'

'What do you mean? You're on guest list.'

'Am I?'

'Yeah. You just squeaked in to make up numbers.'

She's smiling at me. She wants me at her party, and I'm seriously made up about this.

'Excellent,' I say. 'I'll ask Marcus then. When is it?'

'Saturday twenty-second. We'll pay proper rates, obviously. And I apologise in advance for my family. I'm hoping they'll hide in corner, and no one will notice they're there, let alone speak to them.'

'Is Grandad Farage coming?'

'No, fortunately he doesn't leave Wakefield. But rest of them aren't much better. Anyway, I'm going to decorate room to try to make it dead classy. We've been designing Venetian masks at college, and I were thinking of asking everyone to wear masks, if you don't think that's too lame?'

'Sounds good to me. Do we have to make our own or can we cheat and buy one off eBay?'

'As long as you wear it with style, eBay is fine.'

Her phone pings. I watch as she checks her message. Maybe she's got a boyfriend. *Of course* she's got a boyfriend. I am such a fucking idiot. I guess I'll find out for sure at the party.

She smiles and holds her phone screen out to show me.

'My mate Zoe from college sent me a photo of mask she's started on,' she says.

It wasn't her boyfriend. Maybe I'm OK. Either way, I don't think I can wait till the party. I need to know now, but I don't want to be too obvious about it.

'Will it be mainly people from college going?' I ask.

'Yeah. A couple of old friends from school but mainly our fashionistas.'

'Are there any guys on your course?'

She has a hint of a smile on her face. So much for being subtle.

'Three. One gay, one bi and one straight. We've got all bases covered.'

I'm relieved that one of them is definitely out of the running. Then it occurs to me that she might not be straight herself. Maybe I've got this all wrong and she's just being friendly.

'They're all going to turn up in incredible outfits and make me feel dull and boring, aren't they?'

'Probably, because they're raving exhibitionists. Which is why I will be paying them no attention whatsoever.'

'Is that not your thing, then?'

'Nope. I have zero interest in going out with someone who would take longer getting ready than I do.'

'Two minutes, tops,' I say, pointing to my hair.

'I can tell.'

She's laughing as she says it. Her eyes are shining so brightly. I'm not imagining this. It's real. She's real. And I can't believe my luck.

We walk up to college together. I keep edging away from her because I seriously think my hair might stand on end like I'm some cartoon figure getting an electric shock if I were to accidentally touch her. That's how strong this thing between us feels.

I'm done for. I know that. She's not the 'nice Muslim girl' I am supposed to bring home to my parents at some point. She would forever be the 'Bollocks to Brexit' girl from the bus station in my father's eyes. It's a non-starter. Except it's too late to say that now, because it's already started. And I never want it to end.

10

SYLVIE

'Miss, sorry, I mean Sylvie.' The student, who I thought was called Jess – though my memory could not be relied upon these days – looked down, embarrassed, as she said it. I smiled at her and walked over. Being on first-name terms with your lecturer was a novelty in the first few days at university, but by the end of the week it was easy to slip back into old habits from school.

'It's OK,' I said to her. 'I'm of an age where being called Miss is very much a compliment. My husband says it was not a coincidence that I left Paris as soon as people had a chance to call me madame instead of mademoiselle.'

'Wow, is that where you're from in France?' asked Jess. 'It must be such a cool place to live.'

'It's a beautiful city,' I replied. 'I was very lucky to have thirty wonderful years there.'

'So why did you leave?' Jess asked.

'To move to Leeds,' I replied.

'But why did you want to do that?' asked Abbie, who was sitting next to her. 'Only Leeds is a bit of a dump if you ask me.'

I smiled at her.

'My husband was offered a senior position at the hospital here,' I replied. 'It was too good a career move for him to turn down.'

'What about your job?' asked Jess.

'I handed my notice in,' I said with a shrug. 'I knew I'd be able to find something else here.'

'Didn't you have equal rights for women in those days?' asked Abbie. 'Only that sounds like a pretty crap deal for you.'

A few of the other students laughed. Not mean laughter. Just because they thought it was funny. On one level, I was glad they saw equality as such a fundamental thing, but I was also aware that the nerve it hit still felt a little raw.

'It was a head of department role,' I explained. 'He would have done the same for me if our positions had been reversed.' Even as I said it, I knew it probably wasn't true. Presumably, my students suspected this too because they said nothing in response.

'Anyway,' I said, looking back at Jess. 'What were you going to ask me? I'm sure it was much more interesting than my life.'

'Oh, yeah,' she said, 'what's the name of that first poo babies have again? I didn't catch what you said.'

I realised as soon as I opened my mouth to reply that the

brain fog had descended again, and the word had gone from my head. I froze, unsure how to proceed. In desperation, I did the only thing I could think of.

'OK, can anyone help Jess out with this one?'

I waited, still racking my brain, and praying someone would answer.

'Yes, Thomas,' I said, as soon as his hand went up. He was the only male on the course and seemed incredibly keen and committed, which gave me hope.

'Meconium,' he replied. A wave of relief ran through me.

'Excellent. Thank you.'

They went back to their notes. I went back to wondering exactly when the confidence and self-assurance of youth had deserted me. And whether I would ever regain it.

I texted Maman from the train. Her reply was bright enough, but I always worried it was simply what predictive text told her to write. I couldn't help wondering what she would have thought of my students' comments today. She hadn't wanted me to leave Paris either, of course. Although she had been good at hiding it. She also knew that, having just married Bilal, I would have followed him pretty much anywhere in the world, which made England not such a bad choice. At least when Isabelle had announced she was off to Brussels four years later, it had been to further her own career, not a man's. For a mother who had been determined to raise strong, independent daughters, that must have been easier to take.

I put my phone away in my bag. It was strange how you could

still be fretting about disappointing your mother at a point when you were also worrying about letting down your own daughter. I tried to remind myself of Fatima's kind words but I was still concerned that Amina felt she couldn't turn to me for support because we had no shared experiences. For someone whose job was to prepare students to help women bring new lives into the world, it was somewhat embarrassing that I was still struggling with being both a mother and a daughter.

Rachid was in an unfeasibly good mood when we sat down to eat that evening. While I was glad he was enjoying college so much, I was aware that his bright demeanour was rubbing salt into Bilal's wounds.

'I've got my first paid gig next Saturday,' Rachid announced as he spooned rice onto his plate.

'Oh, is this something you have to do for your course?' I asked.

'No, just helping out my friend Marcus. It's an eighteenth birthday party for a girl at college. She asked us to do the music.'

'Right,' I said, attempting to give Bilal a discreet look that suggested he stay out of this. 'So, where's the party?'

'The function room at La Luna, that Italian restaurant in town.'

'Who is this boy Marcus?' asked Bilal. 'I haven't heard of him before.'

'He's my main man at college. He's got all the gear and he's done loads of gigs before. I'm just helping him out.'

I picked up the rice bowl and passed it to Amina, hoping that would be the end of the matter, although I also knew it was unlikely.

'And will the girl's family be supervising proceedings?'

'Dad, she's eighteen, she hardly needs supervising. But yeah, they're going to be there.'

'Good, I hope it goes well,' I said. 'And we can drop you off and pick you up afterwards.'

'How come he gets to go out to a party on a Saturday night?' asked Amina.

'He's seventeen and at college now.'

'And I'll be allowed to do that when I'm his age, will I?'

Bilal and I exchanged glances.

'No, I thought not,' she said. 'Because it's different for girls, isn't it?'

She banged her glass of water down hard on the table.

'Let's eat now, before our food goes cold,' I said. 'We can discuss this afterwards.'

We didn't, of course. As soon as Rachid and Amina had finished, they both went straight to their rooms without a word. Bilal followed me out to the kitchen and started loading the dishwasher.

'He'll be fine,' I said. 'We need to let him do things like this. It will be a good experience for him.'

Bilal sighed. 'Maybe. I feel like I'm losing them both.'

'They're teenagers. They're simply pushing boundaries. It's what they do.'

'Have you seen the young people coming out of pubs and

clubs on a Saturday night? The absolute state of them. Girls, as well as boys.'

'Neither of them are going to end up like that.'

'But that's the world they want to be part of. That's the cultural experience this country has to offer them.'

'Come on, it has far more than that to offer them. This is our home.'

'Is it?' he asked. 'So why have we got to sit an exam tomorrow to try to prove we belong here?'

Edwina always answered the door promptly. She was still sprightly, despite her age, having been on her feet as a teacher for years and taken daily walks with Feodor during their retirement.

'Hello, Sylvie,' she said, 'it's so lovely of you to come.'

'I brought these,' I said, handing her a bunch of yellow tulips.

'Thank you, dear,' she said, taking them. 'Feo always loved tulips.'

I followed Edwina through into her living room. The walls and mantelpiece were full of pictures of Feodor and her family. Wonderful black-and-white photos of them when they had first met, in a Leeds I barely recognised. And later colour ones with their children and grandchildren. It was like wandering through a museum of their lives.

'Can I get you a drink of anything, dear?' she asked.

'What are you having?'

'A little whisky, in honour of Feo.'

I smiled. I didn't want to disappoint her, although as I drank so rarely, I was concerned it would go straight to my head.

'Then I'll have the same.'

She opened a cabinet and took out the bottle and two glasses, poured a small amount into each and handed one to me.

'To Feo,' I said, holding mine aloft.

'And all our absent loved ones,' said Edwina, her voice slightly shaky.

We clinked glasses before sitting down. The first time I'd come into this room after Feodor had died, I'd avoided sitting in his armchair, but Edwina had insisted I did so. Said she didn't want it to become a memorial to him and that Feodor would have hated it to go to waste.

'Did you go to the cemetery earlier?' I asked.

'I did,' she replied. 'I always feel close to him there and I'm grateful he was buried in such a beautiful spot. He did like to feel the sun on his face.'

Feo had spent many years tending an allotment. We would regularly find vegetables he'd grown himself on the doorstep when we returned from work.

'He loved to be outdoors, didn't he?'

'It was where he felt truly free. No walls, no barriers, no gates slammed shut behind him.'

We sat in silence for a moment.

'I wish I'd talked with him more about his childhood in Germany,' I said. 'There must have been so many stories, but I was always afraid they might be too painful to tell.'

Edwina nodded slowly.

'He found it difficult. The memories of his parents, particularly. He preferred to think about the future, not dwell in the past.'

I took a sip of whisky, feeling the warmth travel down my throat. When I glanced up at Edwina, she was looking intently at me.

'This must be a difficult time for you all,' she said. 'What's happening with your citizenship application?'

'Well, we passed the verbal English test. Hardly a surprise after living and working here for twenty years, but these are the hoops they make us jump through. We've got the Life in the UK test tomorrow.'

Edwina shook her head. 'I'm embarrassed about how this country has treated you, I really am.'

'Please don't be. It's people like you who make us want to stay. But I can't deny the whole thing has made Bilal unsettled. I hadn't realised just how much it's upset Amina either.'

'I used to think this was a welcoming country,' said Edwina. 'I was born and raised here and had never seen or heard any unkindness. But then Feo told me stories of things that were said and done to him after he arrived. We like to think it was such a wonderful thing Britain did, taking the children from Kindertransport. But not everyone was nice to them, you know. Some people took advantage of the fact they were in no position to complain. When you're on your own, when you have left everyone you love behind, it leaves you very vulnerable.'

'Poor Feo,' I said. 'It's so sad to hear that.'

'And it makes me cross to see what's happened here over the last few years. Sometimes, I'm almost glad Feo is not around to witness it. It would have upset him very much.'

'Did he ever feel like he belonged here?' I asked.

Edwina paused for a moment before answering.

'Mostly, he felt accepted. Sometimes even valued. I'm not sure he ever felt he belonged.'

R & J

WhatsApp

We're on our way   18:16

Great. We're just finishing decorating. Looks pretty good   18:16

Excellent. I'll have my mask on so you may not recognise me   18:16

😂 Yeah right. Like I wouldn't spot you a mile off   18:16

You haven't seen the mask yet   18:16

You haven't got a Nigel Farage one have you   18:16

Fucking hell. Rumbled   18:16

Are you trying to impress my dad?   18:16

And why would I want to do that?   18:16

I don't know. Cos it's actually me you should be trying to impress   18:16

OK. What if I said I'd got you diamonds and pearls for your birthday? 18:17

I'd know you meant Prince album 18:17

Shit. Can't get anything past you. Have you listened to everything I've sent you now? 18:17

Pretty much 18:17

Favourite track? 18:17

If I Was Your Girlfriend 18:17

Am I supposed to read anything into that? 18:17

That's up to you. See you soon 18:17

11

DONNA

'I am not wearing this crappy mask,' said Sam, throwing the black and red Venetian creation Jodie had made him down on the kitchen table.

'You can wear purple one if you'd prefer,' I said.

'Very funny. I'm still not wearing it.'

'Do you know what?' I said. 'Your sister has gone to trouble of making these. All she asked us to do, were to turn up wearing them.'

'I'll look like a twat.'

'And only person from school there to see you will be Tyler, and he'll be looking like a twat too, because Lorraine texted to say she's had same grief from him about it and she gave him same answer I've given you.'

Sam kicked the leg of the table.

'Why can't she have a normal party? It's going to be full of her arty college friends, isn't it?'

'Yeah, and believe me, her arty college friends won't be slightest bit bothered about what you look like. You and Tyler can sit in corner and be on your phones all night for all I care, but you're going to be there and you're going to walk in with her mask on.'

Sam pulled a face, muttered something under his breath and turned to leave.

'What's up with you?' Neil asked, coming into the kitchen.

'I don't want to wear this stupid thing,' he said, holding up the mask.

'Listen, mate. I don't want to wear it any more than you do but it's your sister's night and you're doing nowt to spoil it for her.'

'I'll look like a twat.'

'You and me both,' he replied. 'Now go and get ready.'

Sam slunk off upstairs.

'Thanks,' I said.

'As long as she doesn't expect me to walk her down aisle wearing one.'

'I wouldn't worry. I don't think marriage is on her agenda.'

'Why do you say that?'

'I don't think she's marrying type. And that's even if she finds a lad who'd stand a chance with her. I think she'd give anyone who showed any interest a pretty hard time. And if they overstepped mark, she'd probably knee them in balls.'

'She'd be saving me a job then.'

I smiled as I put the milk away and caught sight of the photo of her at her eleventh birthday party in her Merida from *Brave* costume, which was still stuck to the fridge.

'Your little princess, all grown up now.'

'Yeah. She doesn't need her old dad any more.'

'Come on,' I said, 'that's not true. She still needs you to pay for this party tonight, for a start.'

Neil managed a rueful smile.

'Will I do?' he said, straightening his tie in the kitchen mirror.

'Yeah,' I replied. 'You'll do.'

The taxi dropped us off at the restaurant a quarter of an hour before the party was due to start. I thought I had more chance of getting Sam to wear the mask if we were the first ones there.

We went up the stairs at the back of the restaurant, as Jodie had instructed. Once outside the room, I turned to Sam.

'Mask on. Now. And behave.'

He did as he was told, although not without much grunting and groaning. I liked wearing mine. Jodie had made it in purple to match my dress and it hopefully distracted from the fact that I'd put on a couple of pounds since I'd last worn it.

I could hear music coming from the room: a song I didn't recognise. As we stepped inside, we were greeted with a painted sign that read, 'Welcome to Jodie's Masquerade Ball' in beautifully drawn blue and gold lettering. Tiny strings of star lights dangled from the ceiling, blue fabric bunting printed with golden masks were hanging from the beams. And in the middle of it all was Jodie, wearing a floaty, full-length midnight-blue dress with gold thread running through it and the lace-up boots we'd given her for her birthday – only she'd taken the blue laces out and substituted gold ones. Her red hair was curled over her shoulders, her lips were painted dark blue and she was wearing a sparkling blue mask with gold feathers sprouting from the sides. Behind it, her eyes were shining as brightly as I had ever seen them as she talked to a tall, dark-skinned lad with a neat beard and moustache, who was wearing a black and gold mask.

She was so engrossed she didn't even notice us at first. I didn't want to risk embarrassing her by interrupting. It was her mate Zoe from college who spotted us and nudged Jodie. She turned, her eyes seemed to lose their sparkle a little, and she headed over to us.

'Jodie, you look stunning, and this,' I said, waving my arms around the room, 'this is amazing.' I was probably as surprised to hear my voice catching as she was. But it was hitting me square between the eyes. My little girl had grown into a beautiful young woman with so much style and flair that I swore she must have been swapped at birth.

'Thanks,' she said. 'Me and Zoe have been hard at it all afternoon.'

'Where did you get that dress?'

'I made it. I bought material from indoor market in Leeds and I ran it up at college with help of our textiles tutor.'

'Wow, that's incredible. I'm dead proud of you.'

Jodie smiled.

'Anyway,' she said. 'Bar's open. I'd better get back to it. Got a few last-minute jobs to do before everyone arrives.'

'Sure,' I said. 'Give us a shout if there's owt we can do to help.'

She nodded but there wouldn't be, I knew that. This was her night; she was with her people, and we were only here because we were her family. Neil was right. She really didn't need us any more.

'OK, you heard her,' I said, turning to Neil. 'Go and get a round in.'

'Can I have a lager?' asked Sam.

'No,' I replied. 'You're enough trouble without alcohol. You can have a Coke and be grateful for it.'

'Can I take this off now?' he asked, pointing at his mask.

I sighed but didn't stop him. He slumped over the table in the corner and immediately got his phone out. Neil came back with the drinks.

'Bloody cost an arm and a leg,' he said. 'Twice price of what I pay at social.'

'Yeah. And it's our daughter's eighteenth birthday party and she's in her element and as you said, nowt's going to spoil it, OK?'

Neil shrugged and took a sip of his pint. Fortunately, Lorraine arrived with Mam and Tyler a few minutes later. Lorraine looked the business in a black and gold jumpsuit, which she could carry off, being a couple of stone lighter than me, as well as a few years younger. Mam looked sweet, her little pink mask perched on the end of her nose, and Tyler did indeed look like a twat.

Jodie spotted them and ran over to throw her arms around Lorraine. I was used to the fact that she never greeted me like that, but it didn't mean I was immune to how it made me feel.

'Oh my God, you look gorgeous,' said Lorraine.

'Thanks,' said Jodie. 'And you're a star for getting this place, it's perfect.'

'Aahh, glad I could help, anything for my favourite niece.'

'She made her own frock,' I said.

'Bloody hell,' said Lorraine, 'you got talent and looks for whole family, you did.'

'What about me?' said Tyler.

'You've got mush for brains and appetite for us all,' said Lorraine. 'Go and sit with your cousin and stay out of trouble.'

Jodie gave Mam a hug.

'You look like one of those models on catwalk,' said Mam. 'I'm glad I got all tarted up now.'

Jodie laughed.

'They're bringing canapés out at half eight,' she said. 'Get in quick before all my friends scoff them.'

'It's all right,' said Mam, tapping her handbag. 'Your mam said it were fancy foreign food that don't fill you up, so I brought a ham sarnie.'

Jodie shook her head and went off to hug a couple of girls in elaborate red and black outfits, who had just arrived.

'Come on,' I said to the others. 'We've got table in corner, cos we know our place. Neil, will you get some more drinks in.'

I got out my handbag and gave him a twenty. He opened his mouth to protest.

'Not one word,' I said.

'Wow,' said Lorraine when Neil had gone up to the bar. 'Proper stunner, our Jodie is.'

'That's what worries Neil.'

'She won't take any crap from lads.'

'I know,' I said, watching as she went back to talking to the lad in the black and gold mask. 'But it's her heart getting broken that I worry about.'

The room filled with beautiful young people, all of them dressed as if they were at a Paris fashion show. Mam sat eating her ham sandwich and looking suspiciously at the canapés Lorraine had put on her plate. As I took a bite of something fishy that I couldn't fully identify, I realised Sam and Tyler were no longer sitting in the corner. I scanned the room quickly and spotted them standing near the bar with what looked like bottles of lager in their hands, presumably bought with money Neil had given them. I deliberated as to whether to go and have a word, but decided against it; the last thing Jodie would want was her family creating a scene.

The music seemed to get progressively louder as the night wore on. I did at least recognise 'I Bet You Look Good on the Dancefloor' by the Arctic Monkeys. It was one of the few tracks that both Jodie and Sam liked, but I knew the last thing Sam would do was dance with his sister.

The DJ was a young black guy with a seriously cool line

in haircuts. He was doing everything on a laptop, although I had a feeling he would have been just as adept at spinning vinyl like they did in my day. He was being helped by the lad in the black and gold mask Jodie had been talking to when we'd come in. He'd barely taken his eyes off her all night. He watched as she went up to the DJ, cupped her hand to her mouth and said something into his ear. When the Arctic Monkeys finished, 'Kiss' by Prince came on. Jodie took to the dance floor and a moment later the black-and-gold-masked lad joined her. They didn't touch. They didn't have to. Every step, every turn, they were so close together you could practically hear them crackle with electricity. Jodie wasn't laughing or smiling like she'd been when I'd watched her dancing with her friends earlier. Her face was intense, her lips mouthing along, as she stared into the eyes behind the mask.

'Wow,' said Lorraine, her gaze following mine, 'who's the lucky guy?'

'Someone from college, I think.'

'Since when does she know every word of a Prince song?'

'I have a feeling he's responsible for that.'

'I wouldn't say no, if I were her age.'

'Lorraine.'

'Well, would you?'

'That's not the point.'

Out of the corner of my eye, I noticed Sam and Tyler making their way through the crowds on the dance floor. Sam's eyes were fixed on Jodie and her friend. The expression on his face suggested he was not happy. Before I could do anything, he walked up to the DJ and said something in his ear. Whatever it was, it didn't go down well. Tyler tried to pull Sam back, but he wasn't having any of it.

'Fucking hell,' I said, getting to my feet.

'He's not going to lamp him, is he?' asked Lorraine.

'I don't know. But I'm not waiting to find out.'

I barged my way across the dance floor, scattering people in my wake.

'Sam,' I hollered as a scuffle broke out between him and the DJ. Jodie turned, saw what was happening and screamed. The lad she was dancing with broke away and rushed over to try to pull them apart.

I grabbed hold of Sam's arm and yanked him away. And then Neil was next to me, squaring up to the DJ.

'What's your problem?' he shouted at him.

'He said my fam shouldn't be dancing with his sister because he's the wrong colour.'

There was an audible gasp from the other partygoers. I had a sinking feeling in my stomach as I dragged Neil back.

'Get Sam out of here before he starts a riot.'

'Don't be daft, there's no need to spoil things,' protested Neil.

'He's already spoilt everything. Get him home. Now.'

'You heard,' shouted Jodie. 'I want him out. And I told you before, he is not my brother.'

She started crying. The lad she was dancing with put his arm around her. Neil looked at me. I shook my head. He turned and walked out, Sam following behind. I turned back to face the DJ.

'I'm so sorry,' I said. 'He were bang out of order. Are you OK?'

He nodded. I looked around for Jodie, but she was still being comforted by her friend.

'Come on,' said Lorraine, taking my hand and leading me back over to the table. 'I think we all need a drink.'

'Where's Tyler?' I asked.

'I sent him home with Sam.'

'Bloody hell,' I said, sitting down heavily on the chair. 'Jodie's never going to forgive us for this.'

'Was that DJ causing bother?' asked Mam, whose view had presumably been blocked.

'No,' I replied. 'Just your grandson being a complete arse as usual.'

Lorraine handed me my drink. I took a few deep breaths before I had a gulp. When I looked around a few moments later for Jodie, both she and her friend had disappeared.

12

JODIE

I run down the steps of the fire escape at the back of the building, hot tears trapped under my mask. The air is cold against the rest of my face. I hate him. I hate Sam so much. He's ruined everything. I was having the best night of my life. When I was dancing with Rachid, it felt like we were the only two people in the world. I wanted him so badly it was making me ache all over. And I really think he wanted me. The look in his eyes, the way he couldn't stop staring at me while we danced.

And now he won't want to know me. Why should he? The girl with a racist twat of a brother and a father who isn't much better. She's hardly a catch, is she?

I lean against the railing at the bottom of the fire escape. I hear my name being called from above.

'Jodie. Jodie, let me talk to you.'

I look up. Rachid's at the top of the steps, standing under the sign for La Luna.

I shake my head. I don't deserve him. He needs to understand that.

'I'm sorry,' I say. 'You've seen what they're like. I should never have asked you and Marcus to come.'

He starts coming down the stairs, talking as he does so. His voice calm and warm and even.

'It doesn't matter,' he says. 'None of it matters.'

'It does, though,' I say. 'You don't want to waste your time with me. You can do so much better.'

He arrives at the bottom of the steps and takes his mask off. He reaches his hand out and gently removes mine, putting them down on the wall next to us.

'Listen,' he says. 'I don't care about them. It's not your family I'm interested in. It's you.'

I look up at him. I want to believe him, but I'm scared I'll end up hurting him and myself.

'But how can it work?' I ask. 'You've seen what they're like.'

'I told you, I only care about you. And I'm not about to give up on you because your brother has a problem with the colour of my skin.'

My eyes are blinking back the tears as a smile breaks across my face.

'Do you mean that?'

'Of course I do. I haven't been able to take my eyes off you all night. You're the most beautiful girl in the world.'

'Are you just referencing Prince songs now?'

He smiles.

'I can't listen to it without thinking about you.'

'I'm lucky he didn't write something called "Mouthy Yorkshire cow and her family of racist twats" then, aren't I?'

He laughs and pulls me towards him, his eyes burning into me. I've never wanted anyone more. He leans in and kisses me. Softly and gently, like he is afraid I might break. I shut my eyes and don't dare open them again in case this isn't happening to me. Our lips part for the briefest of moments. In the light from above, I see he has blue lipstick on his face.

'Sorry,' I say, as I try to wipe it off. 'I forgot about that.'

'I don't care,' he says. 'I just kissed you and you didn't run away.'

'I'm not going anywhere.'

'Good. Because neither am I.'

He kisses me again. Harder and deeper this time. His hands are pulling me in tighter to him. I wish to God we weren't in a restaurant car park in Halifax.

'I knew,' he whispers. 'I knew the very first time I saw you.'

'I didn't,' I reply. 'I thought you were a fucking stalker.'

He starts laughing. We're laughing together. For the first time I think maybe we can do this.

'If this is going to work,' I say, 'I want to keep it a secret. From my family, at least. And I don't suppose your dad would approve either.'

He glances down a second and shakes his head.

'OK,' he says. 'We don't need the grief, so we don't tell them.'

'Agreed.'

'And we keep it secret at college too,' he adds. 'Because a few of them go to my mosque and people talk and it could get back to my dad.'

'That's fine,' I reply. 'I kind of like it being a secret.'

He smiles and kisses me again. I hear a noise above and look up as a shadow moves across the doorway at the top of the fire escape. I see a flash of gold in the darkness.

'Who was that?' Rachid asks.

'I'm not sure,' I say. 'But I think it might have been my auntie.'

'Will she say anything?'

'I don't think so. Not Lorraine. She looks out for me. Always has. I'm closer to her than my mum. I sometimes wish she was my mum.'

'We should probably go back inside,' he says. 'I don't want to cause you any more trouble.' He picks up his mask and reaches out his hand for mine.

'You go first,' I say. 'It'll seem less suspicious. If anyone asks, say I'm OK but I need a moment to sort my head out.'

He nods. Leans forward and kisses me. When our lips do finally part, he's still holding my hand.

'Please apologise again to Marcus for me,' I say.

'He's cool about it. He's had a lot worse.'

'That doesn't make it OK.'

I watch Rachid climb to the top of the stairs and go inside before I pick up my mask. As I put it on, I realise my tears from earlier have dried. I like the anonymity the mask gives me. The sense that I can be anyone I want and do anything I want. I wish that I could hold onto that feeling forever.

I climb back up the steps. I pause under the sign for La Luna, trying to wipe the smile from my face before I step back inside. I head straight for the ladies' loos, thinking it will look better if I emerge from there in a few minutes. I push open the door. Lorraine is standing at the washbasin.

'You OK, pet?' she asks, shaking her hands and reaching for a paper towel. 'I wondered where you'd got to.'

She saw us. I'm sure she did.

'I just needed a bit of fresh air.'

She nods slowly, scrunches up the towel and puts it in the bin.

'I only ever want what's best for you, Jodie, you know that, don't you?'

I hesitate, unsure what to say.

'Yeah.'

'Just make sure he treats you right and keep out of trouble.'

My lower lip starts to tremble. She leans over and gives me a hug.

'No more tears now,' she says. 'I wouldn't be crying if I had someone like him look at me the way he looks at you.'

I manage a smile. I can trust her. I'm sure of it. But I still need to say it.

'You won't tell Mum? I don't want any more family grief.'

'I'll keep shtum as long as you promise that if you're worried about owt, you come to me. I don't want you to think you're on your own.'

'Deal.'

'Great. And if he's got a single uncle, you might want to slip me his number.'

She grins at me before walking out, leaving me standing there, smiling, knowing our secret is safe.

PART TWO

23 September 2019

13

SYLVIE

I woke up with a knot in my stomach the like of which I hadn't experienced since my PhD. To an outsider, it would have seemed ridiculous to feel like this when I had a doctorate under my belt, but to me, being tested on whether I was 'British' was far more daunting than writing a dissertation. Because this time it was personal. This time, our family's future might depend on the results. We didn't trust the idea of Settled Status. The Windrush generation had been told they had the right to live here, until another government had decided they didn't have the correct papers after all. We didn't want to risk that, which was why we were applying for British citizenship. And maybe if we could call ourselves British, we would start to feel as if we belonged again.

I stretched and rolled over. Bilal's side of the bed was empty. He would be downstairs in his study. If I was lucky, there might be some coffee waiting for me. Even that made me worry that we should have started the day of the 'Britishness test' with tea. Perhaps we had failed already.

There was coffee waiting for me. And a husband who seemed intent on avoiding the subject of what was happening today. I decided not to push it and busied myself preparing breakfast as Amina deposited herself at the kitchen table and Rachid breezed in with a cheery, 'Morning'. I still wasn't used to his college demeanour. It was like his default button had been reset to 'bright and pleasant'. My instinct was to suspect that he was up to something or was about to ask us for money, but I was too tired of fighting at the breakfast table to be anything other than grateful.

'I'll be late home from college from tonight,' he said, matter-of-factly.

'Oh, why's that?'

'I'm doing the music tech for the performing arts course's production,' he said. 'They're rehearsing after college pretty much every night until Christmas.'

'Great,' I said. 'It's good you're getting involved with things like that.'

'Yeah,' he replied before picking up a croissant from the table.

'Are they paying you for your expertise?' asked Bilal.

'No, but it will be good experience. Look impressive on my CV.'

Bilal appeared floored by this sudden display of maturity

and nodded approvingly before taking another sip of his coffee.

'What show are they doing?' I asked.

'*Hairspray*,' Rachid replied. 'Could have been worse. They did *Legally Blonde* last year.'

I smiled. 'We'll have to come and see it.'

'You really don't,' Rachid replied quickly. 'It's not like I've composed the music, I'm just programming all the tracks, doing the cues and that.'

'Right,' I said, realising we were now firmly in the embarrassing parents category, and he wouldn't want us cramping his style.

'What happens to us if you fail the test?' asked Amina, who had been silent until this point.

I turned to her, and immediately felt bad that I hadn't noticed how anxious she looked.

'Nothing will happen,' I said. 'We'll simply resit.'

'So, they won't deport us?'

'Of course not, sweetheart,' I replied.

She nodded and stared down at her plate. I glanced across at Bilal, gesturing with my eyes that he should say something.

'They're not going to deport a doctor, are they? Or a lecturer, for that matter,' he added, seeing my raised eyebrow. 'This is simply something we're doing to make it all official.'

'So, isn't it official at the moment?' asked Amina. 'Only they deported all those Windrush people because they said they weren't here officially.'

I looked at her, realising I'd been foolish not to realise that you couldn't listen to all those stories, see the headlines, hear every comment, without it seeping into your consciousness.

'Honestly, you've got nothing to worry about,' I said. 'We'll sail through this test, and we simply want to get citizenship to formalise everything, that's all.'

'Can we come to the citizenship ceremony?' asked Amina.

'Yes, of course,' I said. 'If it's not in school time, that is. We'll see if we can get an evening or weekend one.'

'I'm already busy,' said Rachid.

'Wise move,' said Bilal with half a smile. 'Although you don't know the date yet.'

'I'm busy all the days,' replied Rachid. 'I've got a show to do.'

'Anyway,' I said. 'Some of us need to get to work. Bilal, I'll see you outside the centre at twelve.'

He grunted in reply.

'Good luck,' said Amina.

'Thank you,' I said, bending down and kissing the top of her head. 'But you really don't need to worry, OK?'

It was a lie, of course. Because that's what mothers do when their children are worried about something. They reassure them and tell them it will be OK, even if they're not sure it will be. And I wanted to shield Amina and Rachid from the seething resentment that Bilal felt, and which I shared. Which was why I hadn't told them that our applications for citizenship had cost almost three thousand pounds, and that had come on top of the two thousand pounds it had cost to secure permanent residence. Or that this Life in the UK test cost another fifty pounds each, while the verbal English test we'd had to sit – twenty years working in the NHS and academia apparently not being a valid indicator of our ability to communicate in our adopted country – had set us back another three hundred pounds. I hadn't told them any of that because I didn't want them to feel negatively about the country of their birth.

Johanna was already busy when I arrived at work. I knew she was on a mission to keep on top of everything this term so she could leave knowing that her students were ahead of schedule, and everything had been left in perfect order for her successor.

'Morning,' I said as I put my briefcase down by my desk.

She looked up and smiled at me.

'I wasn't expecting you,' she said. 'I thought you had your test today?'

'I do, but it's at lunchtime. I'm trying to miss as little lecturing time as possible.'

Johanna shook her head.

'It's ridiculous,' she said, 'that they should even put you through this.'

I shrugged.

'At least once this is over, everything should settle down a bit.'

'I don't know,' she replied. 'There's a chance the whole thing could come crashing down around their ears if they don't get it through parliament soon.'

'Would that make you change your mind?' I asked.

She shook her head.

'Too much water under the bridge, as the English like to say. Anyway, I've handed in my notice and the children's places at the international school have been confirmed. There's no going back.'

I nodded, wishing for some of that certainty in my life.

'It really is this country's loss,' I said. 'And the university's. They'll struggle to get someone of your calibre.'

'Thank you,' she said. 'But I'm sure they'll have lots of excellent applicants. This time next year, you'll have forgotten all about me.'

'Nonsense. I'll still be complaining about how you were so effortlessly glamorous and annoyingly efficient at the same time.'

Johanna stood up and gave me a hug.

'And I shall remember how I always found your coffee mug, even when you left it in the fridge or the toilet.'

'I do hope they put that on the application form for the key skills your successor needs,' I said with a smile. 'Because both me and the mug will be lost without you.'

I could see Bilal standing outside the large modern building as soon as I turned the corner. He already looked aggrieved, and we hadn't even started yet. It probably didn't help that the test centre was opposite the courthouse and next door to a solicitors'. There was a distinct feeling that you would only come here if you'd done something wrong.

'Let's go in and get this over with,' I said.

We went up in the lift to the floor we'd been told to go to.

I didn't make eye contact with Bilal, not even in the mirror, perhaps for fear I would relent and press the button for the ground floor, so we could forget the whole thing and go for a nice lunch instead. We used to do it quite regularly when I'd first started working in Leeds. But I couldn't remember the last time it had happened.

We got out of the lift and went up to the reception desk. The woman behind it asked to see our ID documents and spent a long time checking them against the scans we'd previously had to send in.

'Right, if you could go through to the waiting area, we need to take your fingerprints next,' she said, very matter-of-factly.

'Why?' asked Bilal.

'It's part of the procedure. We'll need to do eye scans of you both as well and take your photographs. It was all in the email you received when you booked your test online. Under the "what to expect on the day" heading.'

'Is that entirely necessary?' asked Bilal.

'We wouldn't ask you to do anything that wasn't required,' she said. 'If you could go through to the next room, they'll get it all done for you.'

Bilal opened his mouth to say something, then appeared to think better of it. He shook his head to register his protest and followed the signs to the waiting room. Once there, we were greeted by a man in a security-type uniform who told Bilal to stand on a cross while his photo was taken. He was then asked to remove his glasses and ushered in front of a computer screen, from where an eye scan was carried out.

'If you can hand me your glasses a moment, sir,' the official said.

'Whatever for?' asked Bilal.

'It's part of our security checks,' he replied. 'To ensure they are regular glasses and haven't been tampered with.'

'You think I'd try to cheat?'

'As I said, sir, it's one of the things we're asked to check. If you could hand them over, please.'

Bilal shook his head before doing as he was told.

'Thank you. And if you could remove your jacket and roll up your trouser legs and shirtsleeves for me to check before you enter the exam room.'

Bilal stared at him.

'Is this some kind of joke?'

'No, sir.'

For a moment, I wasn't sure whether Bilal was going to laugh or cry. He opted for the former.

'This is a tin-pot test asking multiple-choice questions and you're treating me as if I'm a national security risk.'

'I'm following the official Home Office guidance, sir. If you could do as I ask without any further delays, as there is a queue building up behind you.'

'Well, that's good, isn't it?' said Bilal. 'Because the British love to queue, don't they? See, I know that without cheating. Do I get an extra point? I know what night the bins go out too. And the recycling. Oh, and I've worked as a consultant in your precious National Health Service for twenty years, does that count for anything? Apparently not.'

The security man squirmed and stood with his head down, avoiding eye contact as Bilal removed his jacket, rolled up his sleeves, then bent to pull up his trouser legs. His pride and dignity lay on the floor beside him. His shoulders, usually so straight, were hunched.

I swallowed hard as the security man asked Bilal to empty his pockets, then stepped forward and started to pat him down.

'That's enough.'

For a second, I thought it was Bilal who had shouted the words. It was only when I saw the security guard and Bilal turn to look in my direction that I realised they had come from me.

'Well, that was a triumph, wasn't it?' said Bilal, as we stepped outside onto the pavement afterwards. 'Presumably,' he continued, 'the whole point of that exercise was to ensure we wanted nothing more to do with this country afterwards, so you have to commend them on executing the plan so well.'

'I'm sorry,' I said. 'I didn't know it would be that bad.'

'Please, don't apologise. You have done us a favour by bringing us here today. It has made everything crystal clear.'

My stomach clenched.

'Come on. It was one silly test. One over-officious man.'

'No,' said Bilal, his voice deeper now. 'You heard him, "following Home Office guidance", he said. That came from the top. They don't want us here, Sylvie. They're simply too embarrassed to say it to our faces so they let some pathetic little man do their dirty work for them and charge us for the privilege.'

I looked down at my feet. He was right, I knew that. But I still didn't like where this conversation was leading.

'Yes, they treated us appallingly. But it's over now. We've jumped through every hoop they've put in front of us. It would be crazy to quit at this point.'

Bilal jabbed his finger in the air, his face animated. 'The only crazy thing is that we went along with them until now. This isn't the country I moved to twenty years ago. The country I loved. I don't like what it's become, and I don't like who we have become by staying here. You saw them in there. You saw what they reduced us to.'

'Come on. We'll hear if we've passed by this time tomorrow, and we'll get the stupid certificate and go to their ceremony and that will be the end of it.'

Bilal shook his head.

'We're not staying here. We're not going to be relieved or grateful that they let our family remain. We're going to be proud of who we are, hold our heads up high and go back to Paris, where we belong.'

R & J

WhatsApp

They totally went for the working on the college production line 07:29

Excellent. My parents are way dumber than yours so I should have no probs 07:29

Only trouble is my mum wants to come and see the show 😂 07:30

Shit. We'll have to tell them tickets have sold out 07:30

The other downside is that I've got the Hairspray music as an earworm now 07:30

I said we should have made it something decent 07:30

But there is no Prince musical 🙁 07:30

Devise one then. I'll do costumes 07:30

OK. When Doves Cry it is 07:30

Top title. I hope you'll walk me up the red carpet at the premiere. I'll be wearing a raspberry beret 07:30

Is that all? 07:30

I'll see you soon. Can. Not. Wait. 07:30

14

DONNA

'I'm gonna be late home from college tonight,' said Jodie as she breezed into the kitchen. 'And every night for a bit.'

'Why's that?' I asked as I put some bread in the toaster.

'I'm doing costumes for college production. It's a lot of extra work.'

'And you can't do it in lesson time?'

'Nah. They asked for volunteers. I thought it would look good on my uni application.'

'I can't believe you're still planning to get saddled with debt for rest of your life,' said Neil.

'You won't have to pay it off, so I don't see what your problem is.'

'You'll be living under our roof, for a start.'

'I won't be. I'll be long shot of this place. Do you honestly think I'd want to stay here after what happened at my party?'

I sighed, knowing she meant it. She had barely spoken to us since, and I couldn't say I blamed her. I'd made Neil apologise to her for his reaction. And got him to talk to Sam after I'd torn a strip off him. But I knew there was nothing we could do to make it right.

'We're trying to sort it,' Neil said.

'Well, you need to try harder. Otherwise, he's gonna end up properly hurting someone.'

'He apologised to you,' Neil said.

'Yeah, only because Mum made him. He still had a stupid smirk on his face when he did it.'

'So, what more do you want us to do?' I asked.

'You could tell school he needs to go on that anti-racism programme straight away, not in a month's time. The rate he's going, he'll have got arrested by then.'

'I think you're being a bit overdramatic,' replied Neil.

'And I think you're not taking this seriously enough. So maybe next time Grandad comes out with all that racist crap, you could tell him that it's unacceptable. Instead of letting him set such a bad example.'

'He doesn't mean any harm by it,' Neil said. 'Different generation, that's all.'

'Yeah, try telling that to Marcus from college. Only if you don't call people out about it, guys like him end up on receiving end.'

Sam walked in as she said it and sat down at the table. Jodie glared at him.

'Before I leave for college, just checking if I need to ask

your permission to speak to people who aren't white, or is it just me dancing with them you object to?'

Sam stuck his middle finger up at her.

'Oi, that's enough,' I said. I looked at Neil, indicating that this would be a good time for him to show some support.

'You heard your mother,' he said. 'Cut it out.'

I sighed, aware it was probably as good as I was going to get.

'Sam, remember I'm talking to your head of year later, so try to make sure you stay out of trouble, at least till lunchtime,' I said.

'What you speaking to her for?' asked Jodie.

'To find out if there's owt school can do to help him.'

'What, like shoot him?'

Sam gave her the finger again. Neil gave them both a look.

'To see if he might need some extra support with his work,' I said.

Jodie laughed.

'Don't try to make excuses for him. He does badly at school cos he spends all his time pissing about and being a lazy twat.'

Sam stood up.

'Are you gonna let her talk to me like that?' he said, looking between me and Neil.

'Well, if that's true, I'll find out later, won't I?' I replied. 'And if it's not, she can apologise.'

'Yeah, dream on,' said Jodie, with a mouthful of toast.

I finished my tea and stood up, determined to make one last attempt to smooth things over.

'What time are you leaving work tonight?' I asked Neil.

'About six. Got a job in Leeds.'

'Do you want your dad to pick you up when you're finished at college?' I asked Jodie.

'No, thanks. I'm good. I'll get train home as usual.'

'Too embarrassed to be seen with your old man?' asked Neil.

'Funnily enough, after Saturday, I don't want any of my college friends to see me with any of you ever again.'

Neil looked away. His jaw was set firm, and I could tell he was trying not to show how much that hurt.

'Right, I'm off. Behave. All of you.'

It was the usual Monday morning nightmare at work. By the time I sat down in a quiet spot for my lunch break I was almost looking forward to speaking to Sam's head of year as a welcome break from dealing with the punters. I wasn't going to tell her about what Sam had done on Saturday. I didn't want her to think any worse of my family than she already did. We'd been given a date after half-term for his anti-racism course to start. We'd grounded him till then, so I didn't see the point in kicking off about bringing it forward. Better to try to get school onside and help him.

My phone rang dead on time.

'Hello, is that Mrs Cuthbert?' she asked.

'Yes, but please call me Donna.'

'OK, and I'm Sally. That's a lot less formal than Mrs Hurd.'

I breathed a sigh of relief. It felt like for once I wasn't about to get a bollocking for Sam's behaviour.

'Thanks. Like I said in my email, I know Sam's behaviour's

been bad and we're working on that at home, but as he's never done right well at school, I wondered if there's owt you think we can do to help him.'

I could picture her rolling her eyes on the other end of the phone, probably realising she was talking to someone who only had a couple of C grades at O level and a few CSEs to her name. I always hated the way teachers made me feel insignificant and stupid. Or maybe I felt like that anyway and teachers simply reminded me why.

'Well,' she said, 'I've been talking to Sam's teachers and his new English teacher said she's noticed he seems to find writing anything by hand difficult. That, coupled with his handwriting, spelling and presentation of his written work, suggest it may be worth getting him tested for dysgraphia.'

I hesitated, not wanting to admit that I didn't know what that was.

'Sorry,' she continued. 'It's a learning disability where the child struggles with the physical act of writing, from holding a pen to actually getting their thoughts down on the page.'

'Right,' I said. 'So, he might not be a lazy sod like we thought.'

I had a feeling Mrs Hurd was smiling on the other end of the phone.

'No,' she said. 'A couple of Sam's teachers have told me he sometimes gets teased about his handwriting and how long he takes to write anything, I don't know if he's mentioned that?'

He hadn't, of course. Although now I thought about it, he'd

never really talked about any problems at school, anything he found difficult. If you asked him, he'd always said he hated it and I'd simply accepted that he wasn't academic.

'Not really,' I said. 'Though that does sort of make sense.'

'Well, I've spoken to our special educational needs co-ordinator, and he suggested you could get Sam tested by an occupational therapist. Unfortunately, it's something you'd have to do privately. He may need to see a paediatrician as well, to get a full diagnosis. If dysgraphia is confirmed, he'll be able to use a laptop for written work in class and his exams, and get extra time to complete them, which will hopefully make things easier for him and perhaps help him to get better grades.'

I liked the better grades idea. Not that I thought he would suddenly turn into Einstein, but perhaps it would be enough to get him into college.

'OK,' I said. 'Let me talk to Sam about it and I'll get back to you.'

I put the phone down feeling more positive than I had in a long time. Maybe I wasn't a crap parent after all. Perhaps none of this was my fault and his bad behaviour stemmed from frustration. It was something to cling on to, at least.

As soon as I got home, I went up to Sam's room. Usually, we only saw him after school when he emerged to feed his face. Sometimes I even forgot he was there. I was pretty sure he spent most of his time on his phone or laptop but if he was in his room, it meant he wasn't arguing with Jodie and it was a lot better than him hanging out on street corners every night, which is what I used to do at his age.

I knocked on the door. A grunt came from inside. I went in. He was lying on his bed with his laptop in front of him. I tried to remember the last time I'd had a proper conversation with him about anything, as opposed to me giving him a bollocking about something.

'Hi, I spoke to Mrs Hurd today.'

He frowned at me for a second and then his face broke into a smile.

'What?' I asked.

'I didn't know who you meant because everyone calls her Mrs Turd.'

'Right,' I said, 'glad we got that one out of way. Anyway, she seemed right nice. Said she'd been talking to your English teacher who reckons you might have summat called dysgraphia, which means you have trouble writing. They can give you some support for that, if you like?'

Sam frowned.

'I'm not having anyone sitting next to me in lessons like I'm a retard.'

'Don't use that word. It's horrible. Anyway, she wasn't saying that. She said if you did have it, you'd be able to use laptop in lessons and exams, and you'd get extra time to finish your work.'

He didn't say anything to that, but his expression suggested it was appealing to him.

'We can get you tested if you want. You'll get an afternoon off school.'

I threw the last bit in because I knew it would probably hold most sway with him.

'All right,' he replied.

'Good. I'll ask her to get it sorted.'

'Will other kids at school know where I'm going?'

For the first time in ages, I saw a tiny chink in his armour.

'Not if you don't want them to. You can say you're going to dentist.'

He nodded, went back to staring at his computer screen.

'It doesn't matter what other kids think or say, you know. Try not to let them get to you.'

'I don't,' he replied.

'Right.' I hovered in the doorway, unsure whether to drop it or not. As I went to leave, I turned back to him. 'Just remember that we can't all be good at everything and sometimes there are reasons why we find things difficult.'

'For fuck's sake, Mum, I'm not a retard, so don't start treating me like one.'

I walked out and shut the door behind me. I stood for a second on the landing, wondering, as I had many times, why anyone would want to be a parent. Jodie still wasn't home. Maybe she was making costumes for the college production. And maybe she wasn't. All I knew for sure was that she wouldn't want me asking questions. I opened the door of her room and went in. Various presents from her party and torn wrapping paper were still strewn across the floor. She'd told me about some of them, shown me a few. But my eye was drawn immediately to a framed picture standing up on her bedside table. I went closer and bent to see it properly, deciding against picking it up. Across the bottom, the words 'The Most Beautiful Girl in the World', and above it, a heart, made from the lyrics to the song.

It wasn't hard to guess who had given it to her.

Lorraine sat and listened patiently while I described it later. She didn't look surprised, although, to be fair, few things seemed to surprise Lorraine.

'You saw them dancing together,' she said with a shrug.

'Yeah, but this makes it look serious.'

'They're teenagers, sis. You know what it's like at their age. Hormones out of control. Fancying the first person you clap eyes on at school or college. Whatever it is, it'll probably be over by Christmas.'

'So, you don't think I should say owt?'

'Not if you've got any sense. She'll do her nut, won't she? And you don't even know owt's happened between them.'

'But can you imagine how Neil and Sam would react if it had?'

'The one sure way to push them together is to tell her that she can't see him. Stay cool. Keep your nose out of it and let it fizzle out.'

I nodded, suspecting she was right and trying not to feel aggrieved that she always seemed to know the right thing to do when it came to Jodie.

'OK. I'll give it a go. I only hope she's got enough sense to be careful.'

'She has. And she's got me as an anti-role model, hasn't she?'

I smiled and squeezed her arm.

'Don't be daft. She loves you to bits. I'm one she doesn't want to end up like.'

'Not true. You're her mam. Remember how we did Mam's head in at that age?'

'I guess so. You will tell me, though, if she talks to you about what's going on?'

Lorraine nodded and gave a little smile as she stood up.

'Think it's time to crack open wine,' she said, disappearing into the kitchen.

15

RACHID

I check my watch every few minutes in the hope that will somehow make the time go faster. Being with her is the only thing that matters to me now. I love this course and my new friends, but what I love most about college is that Jodie is here. Not in the same room as me, but in the same building. I'm aware of her presence even when I can't see her. I feel that she's near me. But I need to be actually with her, next to her. To see the light reflecting from her eyes. This morning on the train seems like a lifetime ago already. I need another fix.

Someone kicks me under the table. I glance sideways, Ben is mouthing something at me. I realise that the tutor has asked me a question. I haven't been paying attention for the last five minutes, so I say the first thing I think of.

'Sorry, can you repeat the question, please, I got distracted thinking about how brave Prince was not to put a bass line in "When Doves Cry".'

Everybody, including the tutor, laughs. It's only after the lesson is over and I'm packing my stuff away as quickly as possible that Ben asks, 'So, what was really distracting you?'

'I told you, Prince not having a bass line.'

'Take no notice of the shit that comes out his mouth,' says Marcus. 'Our main man is in lurve.'

He cracks up laughing as he says it. Ben turns to me.

'Is this true? Who is she? Presuming it's a "she" we're talking about.'

'Oh, it's a "she" all right,' says Marcus. 'He practically humped her on the dance floor on Saturday night.'

'Piss off,' I reply.

'Do I know her?' asks Ben.

'No. You don't know her or need to know her name.'

'She's the flame-haired temptress from fashion,' Marcus whispers, before engaging in some groin-thrusting.

I smile and push him away.

'Enough. You're only jealous because you can't score.'

'She's fit, sure. But when I find myself some action, I'm gonna make sure she doesn't have an unhinged brother.'

He does a rendition of the music from the shower scene in *Psycho*.

'What did he do?' asks Ben.

'Tried to have a pop at me because he didn't like her dancing with our brown friend here,' says Marcus.

Ben turns to face me.

'Jeez. Sounds like grief you don't need.'

'He's fifteen. It's nothing I can't handle.'

I pull my backpack on and turn to leave the classroom.

'I'll see you guys later.'

'Hey,' says Marcus. 'Now I get what the rush is. You're going to meet her, aren't you? You getting some action tonight, bro?'

'Fuck off,' I say.

'And off you fuck,' he replies, continuing with his best thrusting moves.

I don't stick around to respond, just shake my head as I leave the room and hurry down the stairs.

I get my phone out and click on the link Jodie sent. It's not far from college, a ten-minute Google walk, which means I'll probably do it in seven. She understands why I don't want people at college to see us together. I can't risk it getting back to my dad via the mosque. She suggested the location because she'd been once before. A café in a former church run by an old people's charity, so no one we know will be there.

I cross at the lights and hurry along the Headrow, slip down a couple of back roads, turn the corner and there it is. The archway of the church that used to stand on this site, and her standing underneath it, smiling at me.

My heart feels close to exploding. I walk straight up to her, and we kiss. It's less than forty-eight hours since we last did this, but it feels like forever, and I promise myself that we'll never go that long again.

'Hey,' she says. 'I was worried you were going to stand me up and some old guy who smelt of piss would hit on me.'

I laugh and shake my head.

'What?'

'Just you. Being you.'

'Is that a good thing?'

'It's an excellent thing.'

We kiss again. It is a long time before we stop, and I'm in danger of breaking out in a sweat by the time we do.

'We'd better order summat and sit down,' she says. 'Else we might get told to get a room.'

I look around. There are a few tables outside and I can see more through the glass entrance to the café beyond.

'Inside or out?'

She thinks for a moment.

'Inside. I want to see what they've got before I order.'

I take her hand; it feels strange and perfectly normal at the same time, and we walk through the entrance into the cool, stone building beyond. There's a counter on one side and she peers into the display case at the end.

'Look,' she says, 'they do proper old-lady cakes.'

'Have one if you want,' I say. 'I'm treating you on my gig proceeds.'

'So, actually, my parents are paying.'

'I guess so.'

An elderly man with white hair, glasses with sticky tape around one corner and a badge saying, 'Your server today is Larry' comes up and smiles at us.

'What can I get for the young lady?' he asks.

'I'll have a Viennese whirl and a mug of tea please,' Jodie replies, before looking at me.

'Er, just a coffee, please.'

Larry gets a tray out, before turning around to make our drinks.

'This is my new favourite place,' she whispers. 'We can be together and not stress about anyone seeing us and I can get fat eating cake and you won't notice because you'll be gazing lovingly into my eyes.'

I smile and shake my head. She digs me playfully in the ribs, I brush a stray piece of hair from her face and allow my fingers to stroke her cheek as I do so. There's a sound from behind us and I realise Larry is waiting.

'Sorry,' I say.

'Don't apologise. I were your age once, you know,' he says, winking at me. I pay for our things and carry our tray over to a table for two in the far corner with a single red rose in a slim vase on it.

'Nice touch,' Jodie says, nodding at it. 'Almost like a proper date.'

'Hey, I bought you cake, and you've got a rose, what do you mean "almost"?'

'Soz. You spoil me.'

'I wouldn't go that far. Anyway, I'm not even sure what a "proper" date is.'

'Have you never been out with anyone?'

I shake my head.

'You're not supposed to have an arranged marriage or owt, are you?'

'No. But Dad keeps banging on about me finding a "nice Muslim girl" one day.'

'But you said your mum's not Muslim.'

'I know. He's a fucking hypocrite.'

'So, he'd really do his nut if he knew about me?'

'He's already warned me to stay away from you.'

'What do you mean?'

She's frowning and her voice is urgent. I wish I hadn't freaked her out now.

'No. He doesn't know about us. I mean that time he saw you with the "Bollocks to Brexit" placard.'

'Jeez. What did he say?'

'Some crap about what sort of unsuitable young women I was mixing with at college.'

She laughs.

'So, what sort of young women *are* you mixing with?' she asks, leaning forward.

I reach out across the table and take her hand.

'The sort who makes me feel glad to be alive. The sort who has the confidence to take the piss out of me. The sort who Larry over there would be chasing after if he were fifty years younger.'

She smiles and looks down, a slight colour rising to her cheeks.

'How are we going to do this?' she whispers.

'We'll find a way,' I say with a shrug. 'Because nothing and no one is going to come between us.'

She fiddles with the cutlery on the table.

'You make it sound like a big deal,' she says.

'Because it is. To me, anyway.'

'And me,' she says quickly. 'I just didn't want to scare you off by going all serious on you so quickly.'

'You won't scare me off. Your family won't scare me off. This is for real. I've never felt like this about anyone before.'

'Me neither,' she replies, tucking a strand of her hair behind her ear.

'So can you do one thing for me?'

'What's that?'

'Eat your cake so I can gaze lovingly into your eyes without it seeming too weird.'

She smiles and picks the Viennese whirl up off the plate.

'Actually,' she says, 'I think it's a biscuit, not a cake.'

'Does it matter?' I ask.

'No,' she replies, taking a bite and chewing for a moment. 'It still tastes good, whatever it is.'

We sit there for ages. Laughing, talking, doing the gazing thing. I don't even notice that everyone else has gone until I see Larry sweeping up and making his way over to us.

'Sorry, folks,' he says. 'It's our closing time now.'

Jodie gets to her feet.

'Sorry, we hadn't realised. Your Viennese whirls are lovely, by the way.'

Larry looks at me with a smile on his face.

'Would you like to take rose for young lady?'

Before I can answer, Jodie does.

'Thank you,' she says, 'but we're going to be back tomorrow. It will last till then, won't it?'

'Of course,' says Larry. 'And I'll put a reserved sign on table for you. Same time, is it?'

Jodie nods.

'Consider it booked.'

We walk away, hand in hand. It's a stupid thing, having a rose and a table reserved for us, but somehow, for the first time, it makes me dare to think this might actually work.

When I get home, I go straight upstairs. I have my AirPods in. I'm listening to 'U Got the Look', singing and smiling at the same time. Amina opens the door of her bedroom as I pass it on the landing. She takes one look at me and raises her eyebrow.

'What you so happy about?' she asks.

I shrug and continue walking towards my room.

'Dad'll go mad if he finds out,' she says.

I turn around. Nothing gets past her.

'That's why I'll make sure he won't,' I reply.

16

SYLVIE

I woke early the next morning with a Bilal-sized space next to me in the bed. Neither of us had slept much, I knew that from all the tossing and turning. What happened at the test centre had got to both of us. Which was why I decided to get up and go downstairs to find him. Bilal hadn't wanted to talk about what he'd said last night but I was determined to discuss it now, before the children were up.

I picked up my phone and quickly checked the messages. There was an email to say I'd passed the Life in the UK test. I felt a surge of relief, before the churning sensation returned.

The door to Bilal's study was open, which meant he had already finished his prayers. He was sitting at his computer scrolling through a French hospital vacancies website.

'Morning,' I said, going in and placing my hand on his shoulder. 'I think we need to talk.'

Bilal looked up at me. Put his hand on mine.

'I want a fresh start, Sylvie. I don't ever want to be treated like that again.'

'I passed the test. Did you?'

'Yes, but that doesn't matter now, does it?'

'We can't uproot our whole family simply because of one incident.'

'It's more than that. We've had nearly four years of this and it's only going to get worse when it finally happens.'

'It might fail yet,' I said. 'If he doesn't get it through parliament soon, the whole government could fall. They were saying so on Radio 4.'

Bilal shook his head.

'Even if that happens – and I don't think for a moment it will – people won't unlearn their beliefs and prejudices, will they? They think it's acceptable to voice their hate out loud now. You can't put that back in a box.'

He was right, I knew that. But I also knew that France wasn't without its own problems.

'Yes, but it isn't as if France is some idyll. You know how unwelcome Muslims are in some places.'

'It's different in Paris. The people are more educated, cosmopolitan. And we'll move to the 18th arrondissement. Be with like-minded people. We know we'll be fine there.'

'And you're happy to live in a secular state again?'

He threw his hands up in exasperation.

'It will be better than this. I'm not looking for perfect, Sylvie. Simply somewhere I can reclaim my dignity.'

'It's not just about you, though,' I replied. 'If we didn't have the children, or even if they were much younger, it would be different. But this is their home. They belong here.'

For the first time, there was a flash of steel in his eyes.

'Please don't make it sound like I'm putting my own wishes in front of theirs. I'm doing this for them. I don't want them growing up in a country where they don't feel welcome. I don't ever want them to experience what happened to me yesterday.'

'But they won't want to go.'

'We don't know that. We haven't asked them yet. You might be surprised by their response. They've always enjoyed their visits to Paris.'

I sighed and looked at Bilal for a sign that he was about to say something else. Something that suggested I had a choice in this. There was nothing.

'And what about me? Do I get a say in any of this or am I simply supposed to follow you again?'

Bilal stood up and turned to face me. He went to put one hand on my shoulder but seemed to think better of it.

'I thought you'd be glad. We'll be close to your mother. I know how worried you've been about her since she's been on her own.'

'Yes, but there's no point in easing my guilt about Maman, if I simply swap that for feeling guilty about uprooting our children, is there? And I have a job. One that I love, at a great university.'

'I'm sure you'll find something equally good in Paris.'

'Are you? Or are you simply saying that to get me on board? Because sometimes I feel you take my support for granted. I may have given up everything and followed you once, but why should I be expected to do that again? Especially after . . .'

My voice trailed off. I hadn't meant to bring it up, but I was also tired of us always tiptoeing around the subject.

Bilal pulled away from me and lowered his head so I couldn't see his face. It was a few moments before he looked up and spoke.

'I want it to be a fresh start for us too, Sylvie. I know things haven't been good between us for a long time, and I know that's mostly my fault.'

'Mostly?'

Bilal sighed.

'How long are you going to punish me for my mistake, Sylvie? Because there are only so many times you can say you're sorry. At some point the other person must either forgive you or move on. And you don't seem to want to do either of those things.'

I stared at him, then turned and left his study without another word.

I sat on the train, looking blankly out of the window. At first, I'd been furious at the very idea that it was me who was at fault for not forgiving him. How could you forgive someone for breaking your heart? For betraying you in the worst possible way? But somehow, by the time I got to Bradford, I'd started to doubt myself. What if he was right? If I was being unreasonable for not letting go of the hurt? Is that what you were expected to do in these circumstances? Perhaps I had missed the article on this in those glossy women's magazines that pored over relationship dilemmas. I might have committed the ultimate marital faux pas by bearing a grudge for longer than was expected. By the time I got to Leeds, I'd almost convinced myself of it. But when I reached the university and stood in front of my students, I found myself reverting to anger.

It was the fact that my support for his idea had simply been assumed. That my role as a dutiful and guilt-ridden daughter would trump any concerns about walking away from my career. Lecturing positions in Paris would be keenly contested and someone who had not lived in the country for twenty years would hardly be top of the list. I would probably end up working as a midwife again, at least for the time being. Looking at the young women in front of me, all full of ideals and the possibilities of the 'have-it-all' world they had inherited, I wondered how long it would be before they discovered that real life was more complicated than that.

It was at lunchtime that my phone rang. I knew straight away that something was wrong, because Maman would never normally call while I was at work.

'Est-ce que tu vas bien, Maman?' I asked.

Her reply was faint. I had to listen carefully as she spoke quickly but quietly in French. She was in hospital, just for observation, she added. She'd fallen down the steep steps outside the apartment. Several people had come to her aid. One had called an ambulance despite her protesting that she was fine. Nothing was broken, the doctor had confirmed that. It was just bumps and bruises.

I nodded repeatedly as she ran through what had happened, unable to speak for a few moments. When she finally fell quiet, I told her I would get on a train that afternoon.

Her voice became louder and more animated as she said I would do no such thing. The doctor had been clear she would not need to spend the night in hospital. A neighbour had offered to drive her home when she was ready. Another was already cooking her an evening meal, with enough to last her for the next couple of days. She had plenty of food and supplies in. She would be perfectly fine after a night's rest. I was to stay where I was needed.

I shut my eyes and sighed. She was probably right, but that did nothing to stop me feeling so wretched. Because it wasn't only this evening I was worried about, it was the next time she fell, or was taken ill in the night. The time when no one was around to help her. And there was no passer-by to call an ambulance. That was what I was worried about, and the feeling would only get worse as she grew older. Bilal was right. The young women at college were wrong. It would be guilt that would be the driver in their lives. The thing that would ultimately be responsible for all the big decisions they made.

I texted Bilal. It was a one-line message, but I needed to send it before I changed my mind again.

'OK. You can start looking.'

PART THREE
27 September 2019

R & J

WhatsApp

I'm clear for tomorrow. I've told them
I'm needed for a rehearsal after mosque
20:45

Great. We're all set, then. How's your
grandma?
20:45

She seems fine but Mum's still freaking
out about us not being there for her
20:45

Must be weird being in a different country
from your mum. Don't think either of my
grandmas have ever left West Yorkshire

20:45

We're probably going over at October
half-term to see her
20:46

20:46

I'll be messaging all the time. We'll make
up for it when I get back
20:46

Wish I could go with you. I've always wanted to go to Paris   20:46

I'll take you one day   20:46

And you must come to Low Moor   20:46

One day, we can go somewhere together. Just the two of us   20:46

I'd love that 🤍   20:46

I'll see you tomorrow at two. Usual place   20:46

          20:46

17

DONNA

Jodie was in an unreasonably good mood when she came home from college, as she had been all week. I suspected this had something to do with the lad who had given her the picture, but I valued the improved atmosphere in the house since the weekend too much to confront her about it. Besides, Lorraine was probably right: it would have fizzled out by Christmas, in which case Jodie would return to being a seething mass of hormones, resentment and fury. I decided to make the most of any respite that came my way.

'How are costumes for show going?' I asked.

'Yeah, good,' she said as she dumped her bag in the hall.

'Sounds like it'll be good for your portfolio.'

'Mmm,' she replied, going through to the kitchen, filling the kettle and flicking it on without me having to ask her to do so.

'When do you have to do uni applications?'

'I'll start sorting it all out next month.'

'If there's somewhere else you want to go apart from Leeds, you will tell us, won't you? We can look at getting a loan for your accommodation too.'

She turned to face me and gave the sort of smile she hadn't given me for a long time.

'You don't have to do that. Leeds has a great course. I don't want to go anywhere else.'

I nodded.

'That's good. We only want what's best for you; as long as you know that.'

'But Dad still thinks it's a waste of time and money.'

'It's a different world from what we're used to, that's all. We've only got three O levels between us, and his were in woodwork. But he'll be dead proud when you graduate.'

Jodie shrugged and gave a little smile. I couldn't help hoping the warmer, happy-to-talk-things-over Jodie might last a bit longer than Christmas.

'Have you got any work on next Thursday afternoon?' I asked Neil, as I started clearing up after tea that evening.

'Depends what I'm being volunteered for,' Neil replied.

I swiped at him with the tea towel.

'Assessment appointment's come through for Sam for two thirty in Elland. Lasts a couple of hours, apparently. Only I really can't take any more time off work.'

Neil groaned.

'Go on, then. I've got nowt on. Though, to be honest, I still don't see what good it'll do. Not for amount it's costing.'

'It'll mean he gets some extra support at school. And it might give him a bit more confidence if he knows there's a reason why he struggles with his writing.'

'He might also get picked on for having summat wrong with him. You know what kids are like.'

'His head of year says he gets teased about being slow anyway. Teachers will put a stop to that if he's diagnosed with summat.'

Neil shrugged.

'Half of kids at our school would probably have been diagnosed with summat if it had been like this in our day.'

'Well, let's be glad times have changed. If you can pick Sam up from school after lunch Thursday. He's happy enough to have afternoon off, but play it low-key. If he starts kicking off, tell him you'll take him for a Maccy D's after for a treat.'

'Do I get one too?'

'If you're paying for it.'

He smiled. I wondered if maybe we were turning a corner, what with Jodie seeming happy for the first time since I could remember, and Sam possibly about to get more support at school. It felt like we were owed a break or two. Although I was old and ugly enough to know that life didn't work like that if you were from wrong side of the tracks.

I woke at 2 a.m. I was used to it by now. The multiple night-time toilet visits. Another one of the joys no one tells you about the menopause. I turned back the duvet and swung my feet out onto the carpet, sitting there for a moment before I stood up.

Neil was snoring, there was no risk of me waking him. He'd slept through both Jodie and Sam crying in this room as babies, so my nocturnal loo breaks were unlikely to disturb his sleep.

The urgency increased and I hurried through to the bathroom, getting there just in time. I briefly caught my face in the mirror as I washed my hands afterwards. I looked like shit at the best of times, but I looked particularly like shit at 2 a.m.

As I headed back out onto the landing, I noticed the light under the door of Sam's bedroom. I stopped and listened for a moment. I couldn't hear anything. Maybe he'd fallen asleep with the light on. I approached the door, unsure whether to knock or go straight in. It crossed my mind that he could be watching porn, in which case I might regret not knocking, but equally, if he was, I didn't want to give him the chance to hide it. Besides, he was probably gaming, in which case catching him red-handed would give me the perfect opportunity to take his console away for a few weeks and get him to do some bloody homework.

I opened the door. His laptop screen was facing me, so I saw what he was looking at before he snapped the lid shut.

'What the hell are you doing?' I asked.

Sam turned, his face reddened.

'Why didn't you knock?'

'It's two o'clock in bloody morning, Sam.'

'Is it? I didn't realise.'

'What chatroom were that?'

'Just me and Tyler and some lads from school. Talking about gaming and stuff.'

'Jesus. No wonder you're in bottom set. I'm surprised you can keep your eyes open at school.'

'I don't need much sleep.'

'Well, you're going to get some now. I'll have that, thank you.' I held out my hand. Sam muttered something under his breath and passed the laptop to me.

'You can have it back tomorrow night if you behave. After you've finished your homework. Same with your phone.'

'That's not fair.'

'Life isn't, Sam. Get used to it.'

I turned the light out and shut the door behind me, shaking my head. Maybe it was him being up half the night on his laptop that was making him slow at school. In which case the visit to the therapist might be a complete waste of time and money. I climbed back into bed. I'd talk to Neil about it in the morning. What I needed in the meantime was a few hours' uninterrupted sleep.

The sound of screeching brakes, followed by the crunch of metal on metal, woke me with a start just before seven. For a moment I thought I might have dreamed it, but when I heard raised voices, I rushed to the window and saw Jakub and his brother Daniel standing in the street, Daniel looking under his car, and Jakub surveying the damage to his. My first reaction was one of relief that no one had hit Neil's van, but I thought I ought to go down and check everything was OK.

I pulled on my dressing gown. Neil was still asleep, and I decided not to wake him, as whatever was going on down there, it was likely he would only make it worse. When I opened the front door, both Jakub and Daniel were on their knees peering under Daniel's Alfa Romeo.

As soon as he saw me, Daniel stood up and came over to me, his head bowed.

'Mrs Cuthbert, I'm so sorry. It was a complete accident.'

'What was?' I asked.

'Your cat,' he replied, gesturing towards the car.

'Oh God,' I said. 'Is he dead?'

'I'm afraid so. He ran out across the road, I swerved to avoid him, which is how that happened.' He turned and gestured towards his brother's Mercedes. It was a hell of a lot more than a few scratches this time. I wasn't even sure if they'd be able to repair the damage.

'I'm so sorry,' he said again, glancing across to his house where Pawel and Eva were standing at the window, clearly concerned.

'It's OK,' I replied, 'it wasn't your fault.'

'What wasn't?' asked Neil. I turned to see him standing behind me. I hadn't even heard him come downstairs.

'Tibs has been run over. He's dead. It were an accident. Nothing Daniel could have done about it.'

'I'll be judge of that,' said Neil. Jakub came over to join us.

'We're really sorry.'

'And I'm supposed to believe that, am I? That your brother accidentally killed cat that scratched your car?'

'Don't be ridiculous,' I said. 'He swerved to avoid Tibs. Look at damage to Jakub's car.'

Neil glanced over to the Mercedes.

'I'd never hurt an animal on purpose,' said Daniel. 'What sort of person do you think I am?'

I heard footsteps coming down the stairs behind me. I groaned, knowing it would be Jodie and having a good idea of how she would react. I stepped back from the doorway and put my arm around her.

'Don't come out, love. I'm really sorry but Tibs has been run over.'

'Is he—?'

'Yes,' I said quickly. 'I'm so sorry, love.'

'No,' screamed Jodie, bursting into tears. Daniel looked as if he was about to start crying too.

'See what you've done?' shouted Neil. 'You've upset my little girl now.'

Jakub put his hand on Daniel's shoulder.

'We're so sorry,' he said again. 'Would you like us to put him in a box for you?'

'No. I don't want you anywhere near my family, do you hear me?'

Jodie was sobbing uncontrollably.

'Leave them alone,' I said. 'You're only making things worse.'

'I'll move the car for you,' Daniel said, 'so you can get to him more easily.'

'Thanks,' I said. 'Don't worry. We know it wasn't your fault.'

'I hope your Merc's a write-off,' said Neil, before slamming the door in their faces.

'Jesus,' I said, 'why did you have to be like that? You could see they were cut up.'

'Yeah, only about damage to their cars. I still think it were revenge.'

'Then you're a bigger fool than I had you down for,' I said. 'Which is saying summat.'

Jodie looked up and finally managed to speak.

'Tibs is dead,' she said, glaring at Neil. 'That's all that matters. Why do you have to blame someone else for everything? No one runs over a cat out of spite, do they?'

'We don't but their sort might.'

She threw up her arms.

'What is wrong with you?' she shouted, before turning and running upstairs, slamming the bedroom door behind her. I knew better than to go after her. Sam finally emerged from his room and came halfway down the stairs.

'What's happened?' he asked.

'Tibs is dead,' I said quietly. 'He ran out in road and got hit by Daniel's car.'

'They reckon it were an accident,' said Neil.

'Yeah, likely story,' Sam replied. 'Their sort always make out they're blameless. Nothing's ever their fault.'

I stared at him, wondering if I knew my own son at all.

'You're bang out of order,' I said. 'Get back in your room.'

'What?' Sam said, frowning at me. 'What have I done?'

'If you don't know, you're even worse than I thought.'

Sam swore and stomped back upstairs.

'What was that in aid of?' asked Neil.

'Didn't you hear him?' I asked. 'He used exact same phrase as you. "Their sort." Where do you think he gets that from?'

'I didn't mean any harm,' replied Neil.

I stared at him. It wasn't just my son I didn't know.

'So, what your dad says is just a generational thing. You didn't mean any harm. And yet somehow, our son's turned into a racist out of nowhere.'

'What you getting at?' asked Neil, his eyes blazing.

'He hears you say "their sort" about Daniel and Jakub and he thinks it's OK to act like they're scum. He takes his lead from you and goes a bit further because he's trying to impress you. Can't you see that?'

Neil's face crumpled. He turned and walked into the kitchen. I followed him. Watched as he sat down at the table with his head in his hands.

'I didn't mean to sound off like that,' Neil said, eventually. 'I were mad at them because Jodie were so upset. You know how much she loves that cat.'

'Not everything is someone's fault,' I said. 'Shit happens. You know that.'

'Yeah, but she's my little girl, isn't she? I can't bear to see her hurt.'

I sat down opposite him at the table.

'But that doesn't make it OK to lash out at other people. You can't stop her getting hurt but you can do summat practical to help her.'

'Like what?'

'Go and fetch a cardboard box from shed and bury Tibs in back garden.'

'Don't you think I should wait for Jodie?'

'No,' I replied. 'She's inconsolable at moment. I'll tell her she can make a little headstone thing for him if she wants. Get Tibs buried and you can bury your grudge against next door at same time.'

Neil nodded without saying anything and went out of the back door.

18

JODIE

Dad's digging a hole for Tibs in the back garden. I turn away from the window as he starts to lower the box in. We got him as a kitten when I was seven years old. I can't really remember a time before we had him. It wasn't Daniel's fault. I understand that. It's the fact that Dad and Sam don't that I have a problem with.

When I'm sure no one else is around upstairs, I slip into the bathroom to shower. I'm still going to meet Rachid. He's the only one who can comfort me because he's the only one who understands me. Rachid is my family now. The only family I need.

I listen to Prince while I get ready. It's pretty much all I listen to now, because when I can't be with Rachid, it's the thing that makes me feel closest to him. 'Take Me With U' is playing. I wish he would. I'd go anywhere with him. Anywhere in the world, as long as we were together. Sometimes I scare myself by daring to think about the future: next week, next month, next year. The scary bit is imagining a future that he's not in. Without him, there's nothing. I never want to go back to the life I had before. Because it wasn't really living, just breathing in and out to stay alive.

I want to message him now, but I know he'll be at the mosque. He'll have his phone turned off or on silent. He certainly won't be able to reply. I've never been to a mosque, which makes it hard for me to picture him there. I wish I could, though, because it's part of who he is, and I want to know everything about him. Maybe one day he'll take me there, if they allow that. I want to prove to him that I'm not like my family. That I don't see only differences when I look at him, or reasons for us not to be together. I simply see someone who I love more than I've ever loved anyone in my life.

I try five tops on before I make up my mind what to wear. I want everything to be right for him. He's seen my family at their worst, so I need to be at my best. When I'm ready, I creep downstairs, hoping to leave without anyone seeing me, but Mum comes out of the kitchen.

'Where are you going, love?'

'College,' I say quickly. 'We're working on costumes this afternoon.'

'On a Saturday?'

'We're a bit behind schedule.'

'Are you sure you're OK to go?'

'Yeah. It'll take my mind off stuff.'

Mum nods. I feel bad lying to her, but I know I can't tell her the truth.

'I'll do summat nice for tea, eh?'

'Yeah,' I reply. 'See you later.'

I open the door to leave before she can say anything else. On the doorstep is a huge bouquet of flowers. For a stupid second, I think that they're from Rachid, and our cover is about to be blown. Then I realise who would have left them. I bend down and take the card tucked inside.

We are so sorry for your loss, please accept our deepest condolences and apologies, Daniel and Jakub.

I hand it to Mum, who is still standing in the hall behind me. She reads it and nods.

'They're good lads,' she says, her voice shaky.

'Yeah,' I say, picking up the flowers and passing them to her. 'Better than ones in our family, that's for sure.'

Rachid is waiting for me outside the church café. I messaged him while I was on the train to tell him about Tibs. I knew I'd start crying when I saw him, and I didn't want him to think it was something to do with us. The tears start to prick, and I practically run the last few steps towards him. He folds his arms around me and rests his chin on top of my head and although I'm crying, I'm trying to breathe him in too, because he's like oxygen to me, and I can't get enough of it.

He kisses the top of my head as he smooths my hair.

'I'm so sorry,' he whispers. 'It's OK, I've got you. Everything's going to be OK.' And it is. I know that. Because I have him and how could I ever want anything more than that? I open my eyes and look up at him.

'Sorry,' I say, as I wipe my eyes. 'For being a blubbering mess, I mean.'

'Don't apologise,' he says. 'It's what I'm here for.' And at that moment, I realise that I love him more than I ever thought it was possible to love someone. I tilt my head back and kiss him, the touch of his lips immediately numbing the pain, soothing and healing me. I imagine what it would be like to lie next to him. For his skin to be touching mine. For him to be inside me. I want that so badly. To be alone with him. Somewhere private. Where we don't have to hide from anyone.

'I can't do this any more,' I say, breaking off from the kiss in order to breathe.

He looks down at me, alarmed.

'Sorry,' I say. 'That came out wrong. I mean I want to be with you alone. Somewhere private.'

He nods.

'I want that too. Pretty badly, to be honest.'

'I don't suppose you've any mates with penthouse flats overlooking Leeds?'

'I wish.'

'My mum's working next Saturday. My dad'll be at football. If I can get my brother out, there might be an hour or so when there'll be no one home.'

Rachid nods. Kisses me again. I seriously think I'll either pass out or explode if we don't do something soon.

'I'll ask Lorraine if she'll have Sam round at hers. Maybe

even suggest she asks Mum to come in for a cuppa on her way home from work, to give us a bit longer.'

'Are you sure she won't say anything?'

'No. I think she likes us having a secret. She always wanted a daughter. She told me that once. She got Tyler instead, poor cow.'

'And your brother won't suspect?'

'He's too busy being a twat.'

'Yeah,' replies Rachid. 'Tell me about it.'

I frown at him, sensing he's holding something back.

'What?' I ask.

'Someone's been posting crap about Marcus on review sites. Saying he doesn't turn up to gigs and he's let people down at the last minute.'

I groan.

'Fucking hell. I'm so sorry. Has Marcus reported it?'

'He did the first time and the account got shut down but whoever was doing it started another one.'

'Jeez, I'm so sorry. It's obviously Sam. So gutless he can't say it to someone's face. I don't even get what his beef with Marcus is.'

'Apart from the obvious, you mean?'

'Yeah. Mind you, he also reckons Daniel our neighbour ran over Tibs on purpose, even though he practically totalled his brother's car by swerving to avoid him.'

'Why?'

'Because they're Polish and Sam and my dad swallowed all that Farage crap about Eastern Europeans being low-life scum after their jobs.'

Rachid shifts his feet uncomfortably. I worry again that he's going to decide to ditch me for a girl whose family are less trouble. Instead, he takes my hand.

'Let's go in,' he says, nodding towards the café. 'The old-lady cakes are calling you.'

'Yeah,' I say with a smile. 'I hear them.'

The café is busier than it usually is after college but our table for two in the corner has been reserved, as we'd asked. I can see Larry behind the counter, smiling and chatting to the lady he is serving. I take a quick look at the display case.

'I'll sit down,' I tell Rachid, aware that I don't want Larry to see my tear-stained face. 'And I'll have a Bakewell tart please.'

I walk over to the table and sit with my back to the counter. The single rose in our vase has had its water topped up since yesterday. I like the idea that Larry sees it as his duty to keep it blooming for us.

When Rachid puts my Bakewell tart down in front of me, he has a message.

'Larry says this is on him and he's very sorry about your cat.'

I look at him quizzically.

'He asked where your lovely smile was, so I had to tell him.'

I turn around. Larry gives me a little wave.

'That's very sweet of him,' I say.

Rachid sits down opposite me and takes my hand.

'Don't ever think you're on your own, because you're not,' he says.

'Will we ever be able to be together? Properly together, not lying to our families and hiding out in an old people's café?'

'Yeah,' he replies. 'It's not going to be easy but nothing that's worth doing is.'

'Does your sister still think you're up to summat?'

'Maybe. Not much gets past her. She's probably worked out what Dad did too.'

'What do you mean?' I ask.

Rachid looks down for a moment.

'He had an affair.'

'Jeez. When was this?'

'About ten years ago. I heard noises one night and got up to go into their room and Mum was screaming at Dad about him seeing another woman. There were tears pouring down her face. It was horrible.'

'What did you do?'

'Nothing. Ran back to my room. I don't think my dad even saw me. Mum came in afterwards, but I pretended to be asleep. She tried to talk to me the next day, but I made out I hadn't heard anything. We've never spoken about it since.'

'Oh God,' I reply. 'That's really sad. And your mum's stuck with him all that time.'

Rachid shrugs.

'She loves him way too much to kick him out. But she's not been the same since. It's like the light's gone out for her and they're just going through the motions for our benefit.'

'And you've never talked to your sister about it?'

'No. She was only four at the time and she worshipped Dad. I've never wanted to say anything to spoil that for her.'

'And now?'

'She's started asking questions. Challenging him on things. She might not know about the affair, but she must have picked up on the atmosphere between them. It's like they put on a happy front for us, but I don't think they're happy. Not really.'

I reach out and squeeze Rachid's hand. I hate to think of him growing up with that hanging over him. Dad might be a complete arse sometimes, but he would never cheat on Mum. He wouldn't dare.

'We won't end up like that, will we? I couldn't bear it.'

Rachid looks into my eyes. I think for a moment he's going to make a joke, but he doesn't. His expression is way too serious for that.

'There'll never be anyone else for me.'

I nod. It makes the longing inside of me even worse.

'I meant what I said. About you coming to my house.'

'I know,' he replies.

'Are you OK with that? You don't think I'm being—'

He shakes his head, squeezes my hand.

'Of course not. I want that more than anything.'

I glance down, unable to stop myself thinking about what we will be doing this time next week.

'There'll be no going back, then,' I say.

'Good. I don't want to go back. I only want to go forward.'

I lean over and kiss him.

'You taste of Bakewell tart,' he says.

I smile. The clock with the countdown until next Saturday starts ticking in my head.

19

SYLVIE

I busied myself on the train in the same way I had for the past few days; visiting the websites of the international music academy in Paris that had a course I thought Rachid would love, and the international school that sounded the perfect match for Amina. I couldn't work out whether it was me or them I needed to convince most. But I wanted to feel ready when the moment came.

We were biding our time, for now. Bilal had got in touch with some former colleagues who were now in senior positions at various hospitals in Paris. Nothing official, just an informal approach at this stage. If there were no suitable positions for him, it wouldn't be happening any time soon. But if there were, we would need to move swiftly, and I wanted to be ready with something concrete to offer the children. Something that might stand a chance of winning them over.

I'd checked the universities too, of course. Not that there was anything for me. Positions like mine came up very rarely. That wouldn't matter, though. If everyone else was happy to go, I would be too.

I texted Maman. Her response came pretty much instantly. She was fine, her bruising healing well, if she wasn't simply saying that to reassure me. It would be so nice to be able to see for myself. To hear her say it in person and know it was true. I reminded myself of that as the train pulled into Leeds. And as I walked through the entrance of the university building.

'What I still don't understand,' said Abbie, looking somewhat queasy after the childbirth and post-birth care films I had showed them, 'is why anyone would have a second baby. I mean, I get that you might want the first because you think it's not as bad as people make out, but once you know, once your body's gone through that and you're still bleeding and peeing your pants a few days later, why decide to do it again?'

I smiled. I usually had at least one student who voiced such a thought after watching the films, and I suspected there were always plenty more who thought it but didn't say it out loud.

'Women are equipped to deal with the pain,' I said.

'Is that because of the oxytocin?' asked Thomas.

'Absolutely. It helps both during the birth and afterwards in developing the mother–infant bond, especially through breastfeeding. It's also a factor in romantic attachment and sexual arousal.'

'Not after watching those films, it isn't,' said Abbie. 'Because

I'm telling you, if any guy tries it on with me, the oxytocin is going to be hammered by that film playing in my head.'

Everyone laughed.

'Glad to know I'm doing my bit to keep the birth rate down for overworked midwives,' I said.

'I wouldn't bet on it,' said Jess. 'She'd soon change her tune if it were Timothée Chalamet chatting her up.'

I laughed.

'I'd have been the same with George Michael at your age,' I said.

'You do know he was gay?' asked Abbie.

'Yes, but we didn't back then. I had photos all over my bedroom wall.'

'How many children have you got, Sylvie?' asked Halima, getting us vaguely back on topic.

'Two,' I replied, 'they're seventeen and fourteen.'

'And was the second birth easier?' asked Thomas.

'It was, but it doesn't always work like that. There can be unexpected complications with any birth, however many children the mother has had. And it's important that, as midwives, you are alert to that.'

'Have you been there when a baby's died?' Jess asked, serious now.

'Yes. I've dealt with quite a few stillbirths, and births where the baby died within a few hours or days.'

'I'm not sure I could cope with that,' said Abbie.

'You will. You'll be strong for the mother. Because losing a child is the worst thing that can happen to any woman.'

'How do you do that? How do you support them?' asked Thomas.

'You acknowledge their loss and let them know you understand that nothing will ever replace that baby, and you give them time and space to mourn.'

Silence descended on the classroom. It was Abbie who managed to speak first.

'It sounds like being a midwife is the toughest job in the world.'

'No,' I replied. 'That's being a mother.'

As I sat opposite Edwina later, looking at the collection of family photographs that lined the shelves of her front room, I couldn't help thinking about Feodor's parents, who had sent him to England for a better life, knowing they might never see him again.

'Did Feodor talk much about his parents?' I asked. 'About the sacrifice they made for him?'

Edwina put down her cup of tea and glanced at the photo of him on her mantelpiece before answering.

'He found it difficult,' she replied. 'I still remember the first time he described the moment his mother said goodbye to him. It was so painful for her she could barely speak. And he was shaking as he told me about it. He never forgot what she did, and I always felt a huge sense of responsibility to take care of him for her.'

'You did an incredible job of that,' I said, with a smile. 'She'd have been so grateful.'

'It's me who is grateful to her. She gave me the love of my life. So many times, I've thought about her sacrifice. Whenever I've felt sad about being apart from my children and grand-children, I've reminded myself how fortunate I am to be able to see them when I do.'

I nodded and remained quiet for a moment, mulling over her words.

'What's troubling you?' Edwina asked.

'Maman had another fall.'

'Oh, I'm sorry,' she said.

'It's nothing serious and she didn't have to stay in hospital overnight, but next time it could be different, and I could be too late again. That's what swayed me, really.'

'What do you mean?'

'Bilal wants us to go back to Paris.'

'I see.'

'He's angry about everything that's happened here in the last few years. The way we've been treated. Amina's unsettled too. It might simply be a tricky phase for her, but I can't help feeling it would be better for her to be growing up in Paris.'

'And what about you?' Edwina asked. 'What do you want?'

I hesitated before replying.

'I'm not sure that really matters.'

'Of course it does. Your happiness matters as much as anyone's.'

'I don't think I can ever be truly happy again. It's a case of making the best of it.'

Edwina knew, of course. I hadn't been able to hide it from her.

'You can't forgive or forget?'

'No. I've tried. I really have. But it torments me. I still imagine him with her and think I can smell her on him. Some things you simply can't erase.'

Edwina nodded.

'He's so lucky to have a wife like you,' she said. 'And I think he knows that. Even if he isn't very good at showing it.'

'He says Paris will be a fresh start for us. A chance to rekindle the old flame.'

'Perhaps he's got a point. It's the city where you first fell in love with him. Maybe you can fall in love with him all over again?'

I smiled at Edwina.

'I've never fallen out of love with him,' I replied. 'That's the problem.'

Bilal came into the kitchen later, not long after Rachid got home. I knew straight away that things were moving fast. Something about the lightness of his step, the light in his eyes.

'There's a job, isn't there?' I asked.

'Head of department at Hôpital Lariboisière,' he said.

'Have you applied?'

'Not yet. I wanted to discuss it with you first.'

I was grateful for that, while at the same time telling myself I shouldn't be.

'You should go for it,' I heard myself saying. 'It's too good an opportunity to pass up.'

'Are you sure? I want this to be a decision we take together.'

'I'm as sure as I can be.'

'Thank you,' he said. 'How about we look at some apartments when we're over during half-term? Just in case things move quickly.'

'OK.'

'Should we tell the children?' he asked.

'Let's wait and see if you get it first.'

He nodded and kissed me on the forehead. We both knew he'd get it. We both knew we'd be living in Paris by the new year.

R & J

WhatsApp

Are u sure this is going to be OK? I don't want you to get in trouble   21:06

It's sorted. Sam's going to Lorraine's and she's invited Mum round after work   21:06

Excellent. Are you sure she won't say anything to your mum?   21:06

No chance. She won't break a promise. She just told me to be careful   21:06

And you're still OK with it all? I don't want to put any pressure on you   21:06

You're not. This was my idea, remember. I want it more than anything   21:07

More than Bakewell tart?   21:07

          21:07

I can't wait to be with you. Just the two of us alone   21:07

Guess what I'm listening to 21:07

I Wanna Be Your Lover 21:07

🔥 21:07

See you on the train 21:07

Love you 21:07

20

DONNA

I was first downstairs as usual. It still felt strange, not having Tibs miaowing and rubbing around my legs in the kitchen, demanding to be fed. I'd put his bowl and litter tray in the shed for now. I wasn't sure if we'd get another cat but didn't want to throw them away, in case. The important thing was that they were out of Jodie's sight. Though, to be honest, she'd dealt with it better than I thought. Working on the musical costumes at college seemed to have distracted her. Or maybe someone had taken her mind off it. Either way, I wasn't going to complain.

The flowers Jakub and Daniel had left were still on the kitchen table. Neil had merely grunted when I'd told him who they were from. Though I hoped he had still appreciated the gesture.

He wandered into the kitchen as I put the mugs of tea on the table.

'Morning,' he said. 'What time does Sam have to be at this thing?'

'Two thirty. You need to pick him up from school at one thirty. I've sent you a text with postcode and phone number and that.'

'I still don't like idea of him being labelled.'

'He's labelled now, Neil. As a bloody troublemaker.'

'Well, let's see what she says. He might just be a chip off old block.'

'That's all I need. Another one of you.'

Neil pulled a face at me.

'Tell him to make sure he behaves and takes it seriously. You can always take him to cinema afterwards as well as Maccy D's if he does.'

'Bit of a pricey bribe.'

I shrugged.

'I don't want him to muck things up. Anyway, it'll be good for you two to spend some time together.'

'OK,' he replied. 'I'm not going to argue with an evening out. Long time since I've been to cinema. Is there owt good on?'

'Don't know, you choose. Nothing too violent, though.'

Jodie made it downstairs as I was about to leave. She looked stunning. She put the effort in every morning. Not that she needed to make much of an effort. It took me half an hour to disguise the 'old and knackered' look. She barely needed a slick of lipstick and some eyeliner to look like a supermodel.

'You look nice, love,' I said.

She started, as if she hadn't meant for me to notice, and mumbled 'thanks' under her breath.

'How are costumes going?'

'Good,' she said. 'We're getting there. I'll still be late every night for a while yet, mind.'

She looked down, avoiding eye contact. I decided not to say anything. She seemed happy, and if he was taking her mind off Tibs, that had to be a good thing, surely? I picked up my bag and headed for the door, hoping to God she wasn't going to get hurt.

It was strange, getting home to an empty house later. I should have planned ahead and arranged to see a friend or do something nice, but I'd been so busy sorting out everyone else, I hadn't thought about myself.

I couldn't be bothered cooking for one, so I got a pizza out of the freezer. I decided to crack open a bottle of wine too, knowing I could take the rest round to Lorraine's at the weekend. It was the nearest to a treat night I was going to get.

While the pizza was cooking, I stuck a Bon Jovi CD on, safe in the knowledge that no one was around to take the piss out of my taste in music, or the fact that I still listened to CDs. I even sang along to 'Livin' on a Prayer' at the top of my voice, without fear of being laughed at. Jon Bon Jovi had been my teenage heart-throb; posters plastered over my bedroom walls, nights spent gazing into his blue eyes, imagining a future where we were together. He was my first love, to all intents and purposes, and a lot safer than going out with any of the dickheads at school. The great thing about falling in love with someone you were never going to meet, let alone get together with, was that you didn't have to worry about being disappointed. About feeling let down and having all your hopes and dreams crushed. I'd picked a good 'un too. Still with his high school sweetheart after all this time. Still looking amazing for his age. I wasn't bitter or jealous that it hadn't been me. I'd been brought up understanding that fairy-tale romances didn't happen to girls from Low Moor. The thing that worried me was that Jodie didn't believe that. When we'd watched *Pretty Woman* together, she'd taken it as confirmation that if she could find a ticket out of this place, she could have an entirely different life. I didn't want to crush her dreams. All I could do was be there when she discovered that real life didn't work like that.

I was sitting on the sofa with my feet up, still listening to Bon Jovi, when Jodie arrived home. She smiled when she saw me. That was what love was doing to her, softening the edges.

'What's this then, eighties girls' night in?'

'Summat like that,' I replied. 'Thought I'd make most of it.'

'What time are Dad and Sam getting back?'

'In about half an hour. They went to cinema afterwards. You can join me if you like. You can play Prince stuff if you can't stomach Bon Jovi.'

She looked at me and for a moment I thought I saw her waver. Maybe even consider telling me about the boy who had got her into Prince. She thought better of it, though.

'Nah, you're all right. I've got things to do.'

I nodded, trying to hide my disappointment.

'Do you want owt to eat?'

'No thanks. I went to Greggs at station. Enjoy your eighties night.'

She headed upstairs, a lightness in her step. A lightness that I had never really known, but which I found myself wondering what it would be like to try on, even for one night.

It was about twenty minutes later when I heard Jodie shout 'little bastard' at the top of her voice from upstairs. I put my glass down and jumped up, immediately back on a war footing and trying to work out how the enemy could have done something to upset her when they weren't even in the house.

'What's happened?' I called out, arriving breathlessly at the top of the stairs.

The door to Sam's bedroom was open. Jodie was sitting there with his laptop open in front of her.

'He's in some private far-right group on Facebook. My brother's a fucking Nazi.'

'Let me have a look.'

I went in. She turned the screen around to face me and started scrolling down: a video of a bearded man talking in his bedroom, a swastika flag behind him; footage of a racist attack with comments below about how they deserved it; the St George's flag with 'Whites Only' written along the cross.

I sat down on the bed, unsure what to say or do.

'How did you even get into his account?' I asked.

Jodie looked at me. 'That's your first question? Really? It

doesn't matter, does it? Fact is he's not right bright when it comes to thinking up passwords. And the only reason I tried to get in, is because he's been posting bad reviews about Marcus, that DJ at my party.'

'Why didn't you tell me?'

'Because he'd only deny it, then delete it all to cover his arse. I needed proof.'

'Oh God,' I said, holding my head in my hands. 'What do I do now?'

'You take his phone and laptop away or turn him in to police. Choice is yours.'

'What if he's already done summat illegal?'

'Probably has. But if you let him carry on being mixed up with this lot,' she said, nodding towards the screen, 'God knows what he'll end up doing.'

I looked up at the ceiling and groaned. I felt stupid for not being more clued-up about this stuff. All that time I'd thought it was better him being shut in his room on his computer than hanging about on street corners. I was such a bloody fool.

The van pulled up outside. We heard two doors slamming.

'Hadn't you better put it down?' I asked Jodie. 'He'll go mad if he sees you on his laptop.'

'You haven't been listening, have you?' she said. 'We need to confront him with evidence, it's only way he'll admit to it.'

I knew she was right. I just wished my relaxing night at home didn't have to end with a full-blown family barney.

There were noises downstairs. I went to the top of the landing, my legs feeling wobbly, and for once, it wasn't the wine.

'We're up here,' I called.

Sam arrived first.

'What the fuck's she doing in my room?' he said. Before either of us had a chance to reply, he looked down and saw his open laptop on the bed.

'Hey, give me that.'

Jodie pulled it to her, Sam lunged forward, but I stepped between them.

'Not so fast,' I said. 'You've got some explaining to do.'

'She shouldn't be anywhere near my laptop.'

'Guilty conscience?' I asked.

Sam's cheeks flushed.

'What's going on?' asked Neil, arriving in the doorway.

'Sam's in a private far-right group on Facebook,' said Jodie. 'Bunch of fucking psychos.'

Sam lunged towards her again. Neil stepped in this time.

'Is this true?' he asked Sam.

'It's just some lads having a laugh. Bit of banter, like.'

'Nice lads like this one,' said Jodie, turning the laptop around to show Neil the photo of the guy with the swastika flag.

Neil looked at Sam.

'It's just a flag. It doesn't mean owt.'

'Have you met any of these people?' asked Neil.

'A few who are local.'

'Has Tyler met them too? Is he mixed up in this?' I asked.

'Once or twice. He's not in Facebook group, mind, so don't go grassing him up to Lorraine.'

'If you've got your cousin involved in this sort of stuff, I have to tell her, don't I?'

'They're not criminals. They're a right laugh. Ones I've met are United fans.'

'That doesn't make it OK,' Neil said.

'Nothing makes it OK,' shouted Jodie. 'You should turn him in to police.'

'And what about you coming into my room and hacking into my account?' said Sam.

Jodie snorted a laugh. 'A four-year-old could get into your account. And I only came in to look because of bad reviews you've been posting online about DJ from my party. Do you wanna tell Dad about that too, or shall I?'

'Fuck off,' shouted Sam. 'It's private and you had no right.'

'That's enough,' I said. 'Sam, we'll take your laptop and decide what we're going to do about this. And you can hand over your phone, too.'

Sam looked at Neil but, seeing he wasn't coming to his defence, rolled his eyes and grudgingly passed me his phone.

'Jodie, leave him alone now and we'll all go and cool down a bit.'

'With pleasure,' said Jodie, getting up and pushing past Sam as she left the room.

I turned to Sam.

'And you can spend some time thinking about how you need to get your life sorted.'

I left the room. Neil said something to Sam that I couldn't quite make out, then followed me downstairs. My almost empty wine glass was still on the kitchen counter. I was tempted to take the bottle out of the fridge and down the rest in one.

'That boy'll be death of me,' I said.

'At least we caught it early, before he's done owt,' said Neil. 'If it's just online stuff he hasn't done anyone any harm.'

I stared at him, unable to believe what I was hearing.

'Oh, so it's OK to hang out with Nazis, as long as you do it in private.'

'Don't twist things, Donna. You're as bad as Jodie.'

'We're not twisting owt. And if it weren't for Jodie, we wouldn't have found out what he were up to. He's not getting this back,' I said, holding up the laptop. 'Not when he can't be trusted.'

Neil sat down at the kitchen table, his head in his hands. I could see his shoulders shaking. It was unusual for Neil to let his emotions get the better of him.

'What is it?' I asked.

'Therapist said he's got this dysgraphia thing. Best option for him is to use computer instead of writing by hand. We've got to ask school to let him have a laptop for all his lessons and exams.'

I sat down opposite Neil. I felt bad now. In all the commotion, I'd forgotten about where they'd been.

'Jesus,' I said, with a deep sigh. 'How are we going to trust him with laptop?'

'Now he's been found out, he won't be stupid enough to carry on with it.'

'Do you want a bet?' I asked.

'Why don't we give him final warning? Stand over him and watch him delete that Facebook group. We tell him that we'll be checking it and his phone every week, so we'll know if he's been up to no good.'

'Will we? Don't they know how to hide any dodgy stuff?'

'Then we'll get Jodie to check it for us. That way, he'll have laptop for school stuff, but we keep an eye on what he's up to.'

I shrugged. I wasn't convinced, but under the circumstances, I didn't see what else we could do.

'I suppose so. I'm keeping his phone for a week, mind. That'll give him summat to think about.'

We sat for a while in silence. All I could think of was how the hell we'd screwed up so badly.

'What else did therapist say?' I asked.

'Not much. She's going to email a full report to us and school. They can use that to get some form he needs to qualify for special assistance.'

'He won't have to have someone sat next to him in class, will he?'

'Not that she said.'

'Mind you, it would probably have been a good thing to have someone looking over his shoulder, checking up on him.'

Neil sighed.

'He'll be all right,' he said. 'A lot of lads do stupid stuff at that age.'

I stared at him.

'I don't think you get how serious this is. Some of those

people could be terrorists. Remember what happened to that poor MP just before referendum?'

'Come on. This is hardly in same league.'

'We don't know what they get up to. That's what bloody scares me.'

There was a long silence on the other end of the phone, after I told Lorraine what we'd found.

'I'm sorry, sis,' I said. 'I know it's always our Sam who gets Tyler into trouble.'

'Don't make excuses for Tyler. He's fifteen, Don. Old enough to be able to tell right from wrong.'

'At least he had sense not to join that group.'

'We've only got Sam's word on that.'

'I'll send Jodie round to check his laptop if you like.'

'Nah, he's crap at lying to me. I'll ask him outright. And I'll tell him he's not to meet up with anyone from that group again.'

'I dunno,' I said. 'It were a lot easier in our day. At least when we were in our rooms, Mam knew we weren't up to no good.'

'Apart from that time you smuggled Andy Wright into your bedroom, you mean.'

I laughed. I could always rely on Lorraine to break the tension.

'Neil reckons there's no harm done but I hate to think about stuff he's been looking at.'

'What scares me is that if it wasn't for Jodie, we'd never have known.'

'And that were Sam's stupid fault too. He'd been posting bad reviews about that DJ at party. I bet that lad told her.' I paused before asking, 'She hasn't said owt to you, has she? About the lad?'

Lorraine hesitated before answering.

'You haven't got to worry about Jodie,' she said.

'I hope not,' I replied. 'It's bad enough worrying about what Sam's up to. If she's up to no good as well, it might send me over edge.'

21

RACHID

It's today. The best day of my life. At least it will be. I simply need to go through the motions of a normal Saturday morning, as if it's no different from any other. While all the time I'm counting down the clock in my head until I can be with her.

I stand in front of the bathroom mirror. Rub the styling clay between my fingers and carefully run it through my hair. I want to look my best. I have already put double deodorant on. And used two lots of mouthwash. If I smell any fresher than this, I may get myself arrested.

As I open the bathroom door, Amina is coming out of her room. She takes one look at me and says, 'You're not really going into college later, are you?'

There's no point in denying it. That will only rile her. She hates lying and I need to keep her onside. So I shake my head.

'Still think you can keep it a secret?' she asks.

'I can if you don't tell anyone.'

'And what's in it for me?'

She's smiling as she says it. Amina is the last person on earth who would try to blackmail anyone, least of all me.

'A big brother who'll stick up for you in family arguments.'

'You do that already. It still doesn't mean I win them.'

'When's this party you want to go to?'

'Next Saturday.'

'I could try to get you a pass out.'

'And how are you going to do that?'

'I don't know,' I reply. 'I'll think of something. Leave it with me.'

I turn to go downstairs.

'Would I like her?' Amina asks.

I hesitate before replying. 'Yeah,' I say, eventually. 'You would.'

'Good. Because I hope she's worth everything you're risking.'

'It's my life. It's up to me who I choose to live it with.'

'It won't just affect you, though, will it?' she says. 'If Dad finds out you're seeing a non-Muslim girl, he'll never let me live away from home at uni. He'll want to keep his eye on me to make sure I do the right thing.'

I'm about to deny that, but stop myself, because I know she is right.

'He won't find out,' I say.

'I hope not,' she says. 'For all our sakes.'

*

I'm kneeling on a prayer mat in the mosque, counting down the minutes until I can be with Jodie. I'm also crapping myself because I've never done this before. I'm assuming she'll realise that, but I'm still scared of not being any good.

I glance over at Dad, on the mat next to me, and wonder if he ever had even a moment's doubt about such things when he was my age. He always seems to ooze confidence when he's around women. I have no idea how many there were before Mum, or how many there have been since. Maybe he's simply got better at not getting caught. All I know is that he broke Mum's heart. I think it's still a bit broken now. I can see that sometimes when I look at her. Usually when she doesn't realise anyone is watching. I hate him for hurting her, I absolutely do. But I also can't help wishing I had some of his self-assurance. At least enough to get me through today.

When prayers are over, I watch how the other men swarm around Dad and how he loves it. Bilal Mastour: eminent eye surgeon, pillar of the community, respected family man. They look over at me and nod and smile. Some of them pat me on the back. Tell me how I look more like my father every day. That I'm lucky to have someone like him to teach me right from wrong. I smile and nod and say 'yes' and 'thank you' in the right places but it's all bullshit. And meanwhile the clock is ticking in my head, counting down the time until I can be with Jodie. He has no idea, of course, and I'm going to keep it like that. No one is going to tell me I cannot be with her. Least of all the man who betrayed Mum.

*

Dad drops me off near Victoria Gate. I start walking in the direction of college. I carry on for a couple of minutes because the one-way system will take him back past me. Only when I'm sure it's safe do I slip down a couple of side roads and head towards the station. He'll have picked Mum and Amina up from the shopping centre car park and they'll be on their way home by the time I get there. I'm getting used to the deceit. I don't even feel bad about it any more, because I know I'm doing it for a good reason. I'm protecting everyone from the truth. Mum would surely understand that.

Jodie messages me to say everything is set at her end and I tell her I'm on my way. I don't tell her I'm also bricking it. All I can think is that I don't want to let her down, to be a disappointment. I worry she'll expect me to know what I'm doing, and I'm not sure I do. She's probably way more experienced than me and I might end up fumbling around and making a mess of the whole thing and she'll have to say nice things to stop me feeling bad about it.

The train stops at Low Moor. I get off, do a search for Jodie's address on my phone and start walking. The houses here aren't like the ones where we live. It doesn't bother me but maybe it would bother her if she ever came to mine. I turn the corner into her road, check the first door numbers and see that I'm on the right side. I keep walking, trying to ignore the mix of fear and excitement bubbling away inside, until I'm standing outside her house. It looks like all the other houses in the road, except the wheelie bin has a large flowery sticker with the house number stuck on the lid. I suspect that Jodie hates it and that makes me smile. Something in my head tells me it would be wrong to ring the bell like an official visitor, instead of a secret one, so I message Jodie instead. Even though I know he's not there, I'm still terrified her dad will come to the door and the whole thing will go pear-shaped. He doesn't, though. Jodie answers. Her hair is still slightly damp where she hasn't finished drying it, and she smells just-stepped-out-of-the-shower fresh. She's wearing a long, flowing black skirt and a see-through green top with a black crop top underneath.

'Hey,' she says.

I can't begin to find the words to describe how amazing she looks, or how I know I will never forget this moment for the rest of my life, so I don't even try. I step inside, shutting the door behind me, and start kissing her. The sort of kisses we haven't been able to do in public, for fear of Larry chucking us out of the church café for offending his customers.

Within a few minutes, we're both so out of breath that neither of us can speak. She takes my hand and leads me upstairs. I can hear us both breathing heavily. I see the damp skin on the small of her back. I still taste her in my mouth. I didn't think it was possible to long for someone this much while you are holding their hand.

She opens the door opposite the top of the stairs and leads me inside. It's a small room, completely dominated by a metal four-poster bed with see-through curtains pulled across a white duvet and pillows. The walls are midnight blue, as are the blinds, which have been shut. The main light is off, but her bedside lamp is on. It's white, with little star shapes cut out, which throw bigger stars onto the walls. She's lit candles on a shelf next to her bed, I've no idea what the scent is but it's kind of intoxicating, or maybe that's just her. It's hard to tell. She reaches for her phone and Prince starts playing on her speakers. 'I Wanna Be Your Lover'.

She smiles at me, looking a bit nervous, awkward. The intensity of our greeting downstairs seems to have been momentarily put on hold. I worry for a second that she's got cold feet, just at the point where I've never felt more certain about anything in my life.

'Are you sure this is what you want?'

She nods enthusiastically. I remember my mum talking about that. Enthusiasm being a better word than consent.

I kiss her and it's like I've reconnected the circuit. Everything is live and buzzing again. She's kissing me while sliding my jacket off my shoulders. It drops to the floor. She starts unbuttoning my shirt.

'My turn,' I whisper, as I reach out to unbutton her top. They fall to the floor in unison. She slips off her shoes. I pull off my boots. We grin, daring each other with our eyes to go further. I struggle with the buckle on my belt. I should have worn joggers. I should have thought of this. By the time I release it and tug my trousers off the ends of my ankles and look up, she's standing there in nothing but her knickers and crop top. The ache inside me threatens to explode. I pull her into me, shutting my eyes for a second as the sensation of her skin touching mine ripples through me.

'I want you so much,' I whisper.

'Not as much as I want you,' she replies. Her lips part. My tongue is inside her mouth. Her hand reaches down inside my boxers and I groan. When she lets go and my eyes open, she is lifting her crop top over her head. The starlight from the lamp is flickering over her breasts.

I shake my head and sigh.

'What?' she asks.

'You. Being so beautiful,' I whisper. She smiles and playfully tugs at my boxers. I don't need any encouragement. I thought I would feel embarrassed standing there naked in front of her, but I don't. It feels like the most natural thing in the world. I pull her in close to me, kissing her neck, stroking the small of her back.

'I love you,' she says softly. It's the first time either of us have said it out loud.

'I love you too,' I reply, my hands cupping her face.

She smiles and I know that I will love her for the rest of my life.

The track changes to 'Raspberry Beret'.

'Sorry,' she says, reaching over to her phone on the bedside table, 'crap shuffle choice.'

'Cream' comes on instead. I raise an eyebrow. She smiles and holds back the curtain around the bed so we can slip inside.

'Hang on a sec,' I say. 'I've got something.'

I rummage in my jacket pocket for the packet of condoms I bought earlier and take one out of the box. It feels like a grown-up thing to do. Jodie gives me a little smile and I join her on the bed. A few seconds later I am lying next to her, barely able to look at her soft pale body because of what it does to me.

'I've never done this before,' I whisper.

'Me neither,' she replies. I'm surprised and more than a little relieved. 'And don't worry, I'm not going to be rating you on Tripadvisor afterwards.'

I laugh and start to kiss her, moving from her long, delicate neck slowly down to her perfectly flat belly. I look up at her to check once, then start to slide her knickers down. She rolls on to her back and lifts her hips to help me. And I know already that nothing in my life will ever feel as good as being inside her for the first time.

We lie there on the bed afterwards, our bodies wrapped together, our skin warm and damp against each other. Neither of us speak. We don't need to. We know we're connected now in a way that can never be broken. I can't stop smiling because I just had sex with the most beautiful girl in the world and it was fucking amazing. Plus, she gave the distinct impression that she enjoyed it too. Which makes me think it might happen again. It's all I can do to stop the smile sliding off my face, it's that big.

I stroke her back, plant little kisses on her neck and shoulder, watch the stars from her lamp dancing on the walls.

'I wish we could stay like this forever,' she says, eventually. 'It's like our secret little world behind these curtains.'

'Fine by me,' I reply, stroking her face. 'There's nothing outside that's better than what I've got in here.'

'Apart from pizza,' she says. 'I'm not sure I could live without pizza.'

'OK,' I say with a smile. 'We could order from Just Eat.'

'And I could grow my hair dead long and let it down out of the window for their delivery dude to tie it around box.'

I laugh.

'There, you see,' I say. 'All sorted.'

She's quiet for a moment. Her finger traces my spine.

'What'll we do if someone finds out?' she says.

'They won't.'

'Are you sure your sister won't say owt?'

'Yeah. She knows that if Dad finds out, it'll spoil things for her too.'

'How?'

'She wants to go away to uni but he won't let her if I've brought shame on the family.'

'What, by being with a white woman? Isn't that what your dad did?'

'Yeah. But he said that was accepted because Mum was a professional woman with a degree from a good family.'

She's quiet and I realise instantly what I've said.

'Sorry, that came out wrong. I didn't mean to diss you or your family. It's all kinds of wrong but that's how it is.'

'It's OK, I'm hardly going to defend my family when my brother's doing the Facebook equivalent of reading *Mein Kampf*.'

I stroke her face.

'It's you I'm choosing to be with, not your family. You're the one I've fallen in love with.'

She kisses me on the lips. Prince is interrupted by her phone pinging with a message. And another, a few seconds later.

She frowns, leans over, and picks it up.

'Shit,' she says. 'It's Lorraine. Mum's on her way home with Sam. There's a shopping delivery this afternoon we didn't know about.'

I'm out of the bed before she's finished speaking. Scrabbling for my clothes and pulling them on as fast as I can. Jodie isn't far behind me.

'Fucking hell,' she says. 'I'll be toast if she sees you.'

'She won't,' I say, grabbing my jacket from the floor. The condom box falls out as I do so. Jodie grabs it and stuffs it in her bedside cabinet.

'I'll keep them here,' she says. 'For next time.'

I kiss her goodbye.

'Go,' she says. 'Message me from station. And when you get home. And every hour. I love you.'

'Love you too.'

I turn and run down the stairs, out the door and along the street. Her words swirling through my head. Her scent in my nostrils and her taste on my lips. *Next time.* There will be a next time.

22

SYLVIE

Rachid arrived in the kitchen and gave me a hug. He'd been like this all week. Practically floating on air. Polite, attentive, eager to please. It was lovely but also disconcerting.

'What do you want?' I asked.

'Maybe I'm just being nice to my mum.'

'And maybe not.' I pulled away and looked at him, waiting.

'Have you thought any more about what I asked about?' he said.

'Amina's friend's party? I told you, it's your father you need to talk to.'

'He won't listen to me, but he does listen to you.'

'I'm not so sure about that,' I replied as I turned to pour Rachid a coffee. 'Anyway, what I don't get is why you're going to all this effort for your sister.'

He shrugged.

'She's treated differently to me because she's a girl and it's not fair. I thought you, of all people, would understand that.'

I turned to look at him and raised an eyebrow.

'What do you mean by that?'

'I'm simply pointing out that Amina isn't allowed to go to a party on Saturday night, but you let me.'

'That was different. You're older and you were working.'

'And she's going to be allowed to go to parties when she's seventeen, is she?'

I walked over to the fridge, keen that Rachid wouldn't see my face. He was right, of course. That was what made it so difficult.

'I'll talk to your father.'

'Thanks,' he said. 'You know what Amina's like. She's not going to get into any trouble, but it would mean so much to her to be like her friends for once. To feel accepted.'

I swallowed hard. I knew Bilal wouldn't see it that way. I wondered about telling him I was taking her to meet Leila, to make up for not going to the party. Although then I'd have to ask Fatima to lie for me, in case Bilal mentioned it to Fatima's husband at the mosque, and I didn't want to do that. It looked like I would have no option but to use my powers of persuasion.

'Thanks for sticking up for her,' I said. 'You're growing up to be the man I wanted you to be.'

Rachid looked at me. I could see the pride in his eyes.

'I don't have to follow the example I've been set. I'm going to be better than that.'

There was a sharpness in his voice. Bitterness, even. He knew, I was sure of that. Not everything, but enough to hate what Bilal had done to me. I wondered if he pitied me for staying with a man who had cheated on me. Perhaps I should defend Bilal to him. Say he'd apologised, that we'd put it all behind us and moved on. But that wasn't true, and I couldn't lie to Rachid the way that I'd been lied to for so long. I decided to let it go.

I squeezed his arm.

'I'll talk to your father.'

He looked at me, said nothing, picked up his coffee and left the kitchen. His phone pinged with a message. I heard him laughing as he read it. The lightness in the laugh sounded familiar. Like an old friend from long ago. One who no longer visited.

My students were quiet that morning. I suspected they were apprehensive about their first day out on placement with community midwives next week. The jump from textbooks and YouTube videos to real life was a big one and it was impossible to prepare them fully for it. All I could do was to try to equip them with the skills necessary to cope with whatever was thrown at them.

'This morning we're going to look at advocacy,' I told them. 'What's your understanding of what it means to be an advocate?'

Thomas raised his hand.

'Speaking up for someone who may not be able to speak for themselves.'

'Excellent,' I replied. 'The word "midwife" means "with woman", and it's your job to be with them during a hugely difficult and important time in their life and ensure their voice is heard.'

'So, is it basically about following what's on their birth plans?' asked Jess.

'Birth plans are just that – plans,' I replied. 'Ideally, everything will go smoothly, but if something unexpected happens, those women need a strong presence there advocating for them and ensuring their voice is heard. A senior male gynaecologist could be proposing one course of action, and you feel the woman's views aren't being listened to, that's where you step in to ensure they are.'

'Isn't that going against medical expertise?' asked Halima.

'You're not going against anything. You've advocating for the woman. She's in a vulnerable position, she's probably in a great deal of pain, she's worried about her baby. You need to ensure she still has a voice.'

'But what about her partner?' asked Jess. 'Wouldn't they speak up?'

I smiled, reminded of how young and idealistic they were.

'Not all women will have partners, or partners who attend the birth. And even if they do, it's possible that seeing someone they love in intense pain will mean they simply want the birth over with as quickly as possible and are therefore not best placed to ensure their partner's wishes are followed.'

The class fell silent, the reality and responsibility of their role clearly starting to sink in. And I found myself remembering how good Bilal had been during both my labours. Calm and attentive. Providing reassurance but never straying into patronising territory. I had never felt so loved and adored and appreciated. I was suddenly overcome with how much I missed that feeling. Missed what we used to have together. And how I would give anything to get it back again.

When I checked my phone at lunchtime, there was a message from Maman, asking me to give her a call.

'Maman, ça va?' I asked, as soon as she answered, her voice slight and frail.

'Isabelle?' she said. I frowned; she should have seen my name come up on her phone. And she always usually knew our voices apart.

'Non, c'est Sylvie.'

'Oui, bien sûr.'

She started to tell me slowly and uncertainly that she was fine, but she'd had another fall. Inside her apartment, this time. On her way to the bathroom during the night. Nothing broken, no real harm done, but she'd gone to see her doctor this morning as a precaution, and he'd recommended they run some tests. To try to establish if there was an underlying reason behind her falls.

I fought to keep my voice positive as I tried to reassure her that everything would be fine. That she must call me straight away if it happened again, even if it was the middle of the night. She promised, although I wasn't sure I believed her. I told her we'd be over at half-term. I didn't tell her about Bilal's job application, or the possibility of us moving back to Paris. I didn't want to get her hopes up when we couldn't be sure of anything. But I also knew that the reasons for us to return to Paris appeared to be increasing by the hour.

I could tell as soon as Bilal got home. His stature appeared to have grown since he'd left that morning. And the smile he gave me was unfeasibly large.

'You've got the job, haven't you?' I asked.

He nodded, allowing the smile to turn up its brightness still a notch further.

'They want me to start in January. New year, new beginning.'

I was unsure how to respond.

'Congratulations,' I said. It came out more uncertain than I had intended. For the first time, Bilal looked a little uncomfortable.

'I don't want you to feel pressurised into this,' he said. 'I know I'm the one who's been driving it. But I simply don't see a future for us in this country. I want better for our children.'

I nodded.

'Maman had another fall last night,' I said.

'Is she OK?'

'Yes, she's been checked over and she's fine, but the doctor wants to run some tests to try to find out if there's an underlying problem.'

'I'm glad they're doing that. It may well simply be her age, but it needs investigating properly. Have you told her? About us returning to Paris?'

'Not yet,' I said. 'I wanted to be sure it was happening.'

'Perhaps you should tell her now. It'll be a great weight off her shoulders, as well as yours. She'll be so happy to have us nearby. I've found some apartments online. I thought we could arrange viewings for when we're visiting.'

I held up my hand. He seemed to be getting ahead of himself.

'We haven't even told the children yet.'

'I think we should do it this evening.'

'Rachid's not going to be happy.'

'He's never happy.'

'He is,' I said. 'He's the happiest I've ever seen him right now.'

Bilal frowned, perhaps wondering how he had missed this, or realising that it could make his plans more difficult.

'Well, he'll just have to find something to make him happy in Paris.'

I sighed, knowing that wouldn't be easy. Which was when the idea came to me.

'It might help to offer them both sweeteners,' I said.

'Like what?'

'Maybe we could find an apartment with room for him to have his own little studio.'

'Fine, if you think it would help,' said Bilal.

'And what Amina wants most is more freedom,' I continued. 'Which at least comes free. You could start by letting her go to this party on Saturday.'

He looked at me.

'That sounds more like bribery than a sweetener.'

'It will help with Rachid too. He's been petitioning me, saying we're not treating her fairly. I want him to know that we appreciate him fighting for his sister like that.'

Bilal sighed.

'I suppose if that's what it takes. But we pick her up at eleven, no later.'

'Thank you,' I said, knowing how pleased she would be.

'We'll talk to them after Rachid gets home,' said Bilal.

I nodded, reluctantly, unable to stop the feeling that as one weight lifted off my shoulders, it was about to be replaced by another.

Rachid came home, as usual these days, practically bursting with the joys of life. I wasn't stupid. As much as I knew he was enjoying the course and his new-found independence at college, I suspected that there was a girl involved. He had a glow about him, a lightness in his step. The knowledge that we were about to burst his bubble made it painful to watch. I resolved to get it out of the way as quickly as I could.

'Hi,' I said. 'Come into the kitchen before you disappear upstairs. We've got something to tell you.'

He frowned at me. It was as if a dimmer switch had already been turned down inside him. I went to the bottom of the stairs to call Amina. She came straight down and saw her brother seated in the kitchen.

'What's happening?' she asked.

'We need to talk to you both,' I said.

She sat down next to Rachid, looking equally pensive. Bilal came in from his study, attempting to be bright and jovial, which only appeared to worry them even more. He glanced at me, appearing uncharacteristically nervous. I gave a little nod, barely noticeable but enough to set the whole thing in motion.

'I've been offered a job,' Bilal said, drawing himself up to his full height, as if this might help. 'At a hospital in Paris.'

I watched their faces intently. It was, predictably, Rachid who reacted first.

'What?' he said, his eyes ablaze.

'Head of the ophthalmology department at one of the country's finest hospitals. It's too good an opportunity to turn down.'

'You're going to Paris?' asked Amina, incredulously. 'When are we going to see you?'

Bilal looked at me again, but this had to come from him.

'I meant it's too good an opportunity for all of us,' he said. 'This country has made it quite clear that we're no longer welcome, so we're going to move to one where we will be.'

'No way,' said Rachid, leaping up out of his chair. 'You can go if you want to, but I'm staying here.'

'Don't be ridiculous,' said Bilal. 'We're moving as a family. We're not going to leave anyone behind.'

'I'm not going. This is my home. You can't do this to me.' Rachid jabbed his finger at Bilal as he spoke.

Bilal looked up at the ceiling before turning to me in desperation. The best I could offer was an explanation from my side of things.

'It's not just about your father's job offer,' I said. 'Grand-mère had another fall last night. The doctor wants to do some tests. She's not getting any younger, and I think it would be a huge help for her to have us around.'

Rachid was silent, my intervention having momentarily taken the wind out of his sails.

'Is she OK?' asked Amina.

'She's fine, sweetheart. But she might not be next time. If we're close by, we'll be able to keep an eye on her and move her in with us if necessary.'

Amina pondered this. You could almost hear her weighing everything up in her head.

'Where will I go to school?' she asked.

'I've found a wonderful international school which I think you'd love. You'd be taught in English. You'd be with teen-agers from all sorts of different backgrounds from all over the world.'

She looked momentarily interested, possibly even excited, before Rachid, who'd been standing silently listening to everything, spoke again.

'And what am I supposed to do?'

'There's an international music college,' I said. 'It has amazing facilities and a course that sounds similar to yours.'

'But I want to stay here. I've made friends, I've got a life outside this family, you know.'

'I understand that. It will be a wrench for all of us to leave.'

Rachid stared at me.

'You don't want to go, do you? This is all his idea.' He

gestured towards Bilal. There was a tone in his voice I hadn't heard before and it scared me. I struggled to think of something to say that he wouldn't see straight through.

'We think, in the long term, it'll be the best thing for all of us,' was all I could muster.

'So, he's making you give up your job as well?' asked Rachid. 'And we get no say in our futures?'

'You can choose the course you join,' said Bilal. 'And we can look for an apartment with enough room to set you up with a home studio. We'll get you the equipment you need too, if that helps.'

Rachid snorted a laugh and shook his head.

'So, you're resorting to bribery now? You seriously think that will work? Is that what you did to Mum to make her stay when she found out what you were up to?'

The kitchen descended into a stunned silence.

'Rachid,' said Bilal sharply.

'What? Don't like to hear the truth spoken out loud? Because you're not as perfect as you make out, are you? I know what you did. And I will not let you dictate my life the way you dictate hers.'

He pointed at me as he said it. Everyone turned in my direction. I was caught between trying to pretend he hadn't said it and denying the allegation.

'Rachid, this is not the time or the place.' I nodded towards Amina, who was looking between us, trying to make sense of it all.

'What's he talking about?' she asked. 'What happened?'

For a moment I didn't know which way it would go. But the initial adrenaline rush had subsided enough for Rachid's concern for Amina to override anything else.

'Take no notice of me,' he said. 'I'm just mad at him for not listening to us, as usual.'

'Will someone tell me what's been going on?' shrieked Amina. 'I'm sick of being treated like a kid.'

When no one replied, she stood up and fled from the kitchen.

I looked at Bilal. He was standing slumped and motionless. I waited for him to say something. Anything. When he didn't, I felt I had to step in.

'Why didn't you ever say anything if you knew?' I asked Rachid, my voice soft and low.

Rachid stared at the floor, looking for all the world like the seven-year-old boy standing in our doorway.

'You were pretending it hadn't happened, so I thought I should do that too.'

I squeezed my eyes shut for a second, trying to hold everything together.

'I stayed with your father for your and Amina's sakes. And because I still loved him. He didn't force me to stay and he's not forcing me to leave now.'

Rachid hesitated before replying.

'I would never treat anybody the way he's treated you. You deserve so much better than that. Go to Paris if you want to, but I won't be going with you.'

He walked from the kitchen without so much as a sideways

glance at Bilal. We stood in silence for a few seconds. Bilal took off his glasses, pressed his fingers against the bridge of his nose and blew out.

'How did he know?' he asked softly.

'The night I found out. He appeared in the doorway of our bedroom. I was never sure how much he heard. I tried to talk to him, but he didn't want to say anything.'

Bilal nodded.

'I'm sorry, I had no idea.'

Bilal looked at me, as if realising, perhaps for the first time, that the memory of that day was etched in excruciating detail inside my mind.

'At least I understand why he hates me now.'

'He doesn't hate you,' I replied.

'I think it's obvious he does. And now Amina is going to lose any respect she had for me too.'

'We don't have to tell her,' I said.

Bilal reached out and stroked my shoulder.

'I think we both know that we do.'

I sighed and walked a few steps closer to him.

'Why have you never talked about it since?'

'I was ashamed,' said Bilal. 'I still am. I suppose I thought that if we didn't talk about it, we could pretend it never happened. That wasn't fair on you, though. None of it was fair on you.'

We stood there for a few moments before anyone spoke again.

'Did you mean it?' he asked. 'About still loving me?'

'Yes,' I replied. 'I did then, and I do now.'

'Rachid was right,' Bilal said. 'You do deserve so much better than me.'

I walked over to the sink and stared out of the window into the darkness beyond.

'So, what do we do now?' I asked.

'I start by saying I'm sorry. To you. To our children. I know Rachid won't want to hear it. Clearly, I lost his respect a long time ago. But maybe I still have a chance with Amina. She deserves to know the truth and she should hear it from me.'

I turned around to face him.

'Thank you,' I said. 'I've been waiting a long time to hear that. But I think it's best if I talk to her first.'

'You shouldn't have to do that,' Bilal replied.

'I know. But I shouldn't have had to do a lot of things.'

I knocked on Amina's door and heard a mumble from inside. When I went in, Rachid was there, his arms around her, gently wiping the tears from her face.

'Thank you,' I said to him as he got up.

'I'm sorry she found out this way. But it's Dad who should tell her, not you.'

'He knows that. I asked to speak to her first.'

Rachid nodded and walked past; I squeezed his hand as he went. I sat down on the corner of Amina's bed, reached out to stroke her bare foot.

'The thing about loving someone, is that it leaves you open to getting hurt. Perhaps that's why I sound a little cynical when we talk about it. Because I've been hurt, and I don't want that to ever happen to you.'

'What did he do?' Amina asked, her eyes fixed on my face.

'Your father had an affair,' I said. 'A long time ago, when you were four years old. She worked at the same hospital as him, when I was at home, looking after you.'

I watched as Amina fought the words, not wanting them to penetrate her idealised world, where love lasted forever.

'I can't believe he'd do that to you.'

'I know. Nor could I.'

'How did you find out?'

I hesitated. I hadn't thought about how much I should tell her, which details were better left unsaid. But I did want to answer as many questions as I could.

'They went away for the weekend to the same conference. Only the hotel rang here to say they'd found an earring of mine in his room after he'd left. He'd stupidly written his home number on the form when he'd checked in.'

Amina wrinkled up her nose.

'That must have been horrible for you.'

'It was. Fortunately, I had you with me at the time. I don't know what I'd have done otherwise.'

'But you never told me.'

'You were too busy watching *Dora the Explorer*,' I said, managing a smile. 'And afterwards, well, I didn't see the point of hurting you unnecessarily.'

'But Rachid knew?'

'He overheard us arguing that night when your father came home. I wasn't sure how much he'd heard, but clearly enough, even at that age.'

'Why didn't you throw Papa out?'

I smiled again.

'Because I would never do anything to hurt you and your brother. And because I still loved him.'

'But how could you, when he'd cheated on you like that? I don't understand.'

'I hope you never do,' I said. 'But love isn't always perfect. It can be messy and complicated. You also need to understand that your father loves you very much and he feels bad about hurting us all. I want you to give him a chance to say sorry.'

'Why should I?'

It was a fair question and deserved an honest answer.

'Because the alternative is to live the rest of your life hating him, and that's going to hurt you even more.'

There was a knock on the door. When Bilal came in, he sat down on the floor, as if he felt the bed might be encroaching too far on her territory.

'Ma belle,' he said, reaching over to take her hand.

She looked at him, her big brown eyes desperately flashing between a whole gamut of emotions.

'I'm so sorry,' he began. 'I behaved appallingly and hurt the three people I love most in the world. That's unacceptable. I let you down and I'll never forgive myself for that. I don't expect you to forgive me either.'

Amina sniffed and wiped the tears from her face.

'So, how am I supposed to deal with all this? It's like I've discovered a whole family history that I knew nothing about.'

'Did you really not suspect?' I asked.

'I suspected you weren't happy,' she said. 'But not why.'

We both looked at Bilal. Clearly, thinking badly of him hadn't been something she had wanted to consider.

'I understand it will take time,' said Bilal. 'And that it changes how you feel. I think the best thing I can do is try to make your mother happy again.'

Amina nodded.

'That would be a good start,' she said. 'Also, I need to understand that you're growing up fast and demonstrate more trust in you,' he continued. 'Which is why we're letting you go to the party on Saturday.'

'Really?' she said, looking between me and Bilal.

'Yes,' he replied. 'You'll be dropped off, and we'll collect you at eleven, but you can go.'

For a moment, it was like the sun had risen over her face, but within seconds, a large cloud had obscured it again.

'Rachid won't come to Paris,' she said. 'None of this matters because we can't be a happy family without him.'

'He'll come,' I said, reaching over to take her hand. 'It's a shock, that's all. He doesn't mean it. He simply needs time to come around.'

'No,' she said. 'He's right, you don't know him. Not like you think you do. He won't change his mind. And I'm not going to Paris without him.'

She got up from the bed and ran into Rachid's bedroom, leaving Bilal sitting there, his head in his hands. And me wondering if by trying to bring our family together, we might just have broken it apart.

R & J

WhatsApp

Dad's got a job in Paris. He wants us all to move   21:12

WTF?   21:12

I know. I've told him I'm not going. There's no way I'm leaving you   21:12

You didn't tell him that?   21:12

Not about you, no. But I told him I'm not going. And I let slip about his affair, so there's been a huge scene and Amina's in a real state   21:13

Jeez. What did your dad say?   21:13

Came out with all this crap about going together as a family or not at all   21:13

He's going to make you go, isn't he?   21:13

He won't. I promise you. I'll do whatever it takes to get out of it   21:13

Fucking hell. I knew this was too good to last   21:13

Don't say that. I won't let anything or anyone come between us   21:13

But how can you stop it?   21:13

I'll think of something. Trust me   21:13

I can't believe this is happening. I'm shaking   21:13

I'll call you. Now   21:13

PART FOUR
11 October 2019

23

DONNA

Jodie looked a shadow of her normal self when she came into the kitchen. The skin around her eyes was puffy, her face downcast.

'What's up?' I asked.

'Nothing,' she said, before turning her back on me and walking over to the fridge.

'Doesn't look like nothing to me,' I replied.

She shrugged and poured herself a Diet Coke.

'For breakfast?' I asked.

'I didn't get much sleep.'

'Why's that then?'

She shrugged again. Jodie knew how to be awkward when she wanted to. And I knew not to push her too hard when she was being like this. It still didn't make it any easier, though.

Neil came into the kitchen and frowned as he saw her slumped over her Diet Coke at the kitchen table.

'What have I told you about late-night drinking on a school night?' he said, with a chuckle.

Jodie remained silent. I shook my head at Neil and mouthed, 'leave her'. He went to the fridge, poured himself a Diet Coke and sat down next to her.

'If you can't beat them, join them, eh?'

'For fuck's sake,' she said, her chair scraping on the floor as she stood up and fled upstairs.

'What's up with her?' Neil asked.

'She won't say but I did try to warn you.'

'I'd better keep out of her way till it blows over. She's worse than you when she's got a strop on.'

'Charming.'

'Too many hormones in this house, that's trouble.'

He had a point, I supposed.

'At least Sam seems a bit more with it the last few days,' I said.

We'd brought in a rule where he wasn't allowed his laptop or phone in his bedroom overnight. We had them on charge in our room, so he couldn't creep in and get them.

'Yeah. Wish we'd thought of that sooner.'

I resisted the temptation to point out that he hadn't thought of anything.

'Anyway, I'd better be off. Make sure he gets his arse in gear for school. And tell him to keep out of trouble.'

I texted Lorraine on the train and asked if she had any idea what Jodie was upset about. She rang straight back.

'No. What's happened?'

'She wouldn't say but she looked like she'd been crying, and she didn't eat any breakfast.'

'Is she going to college?'

'Yeah. I think so.'

'I'll message her. Try to find out what's wrong.'

'Let me know what she says.'

'Of course,' replied Lorraine. 'It'll probably be nowt, though. You know what they're like at this age. Turn every little thing into a drama.'

'I'm worried it's got summat to do with that lad. Though if they have split up, that's no bad thing, to be honest. It were never going to last.'

Lorraine said nothing.

'Right,' I said. 'Well, let me know.'

'Will do. And try not to fret.'

I ended the call and sat and drummed my fingers against the phone. I wished I had the sort of relationship with Jodie where she could tell me if she had a problem. The sort of relationship she seemed to have with Lorraine. Tyler had spent a lot of time at our house when he was younger. He'd shared a room with Sam when Lorraine had been working nights. He was so often at the breakfast table, he felt like a third child at times. And yet I had no meaningful relationship with him now. Other than as an auntie who sometimes gave him a hard time. I had no idea what made him tick, what he was into, what his hopes for the future were. And yet Lorraine seemed to know all these things about Jodie. Had the inside track on what was going on in her life. Clearly, somewhere along the line, I'd failed as an auntie, as well as a mum.

My phone beeped. I checked the message from Lorraine.

'*It's just a falling out with Zoe at college. She said some hurtful stuff online. Nowt to worry about.*'

'*Thanks,*' I replied, trying not to think about why Jodie hadn't felt able to tell me that.

As soon as I saw the school's name come up on my phone, I knew it was trouble. When the call came I was in the middle of trying to explain to Mrs Walker that there was nothing we could do about her neighbour's cat crapping in her garden, and it certainly didn't entitle her to a council tax rebate, so I couldn't answer it. Once she'd finally left, I asked Carole if I could take my break early. The staff kitchen was empty, so I nipped in there to make the call. I was put through to Sam's head of year, Mrs Hurd.

'Thanks for calling back,' she said. 'I just wanted to let you know I've passed the occupational therapist's report on Sam to our SENCo, Mr Davison, and please do send us the report from the doctor after Sam's appointment today.'

I hesitated, wondering if I had missed something. If there had been another appointment set up that Neil had forgotten to tell me about. But the moment of self-doubt was overtaken by the truth crashing down on me. He was playing us all for fools.

'Has Sam left?' I asked.

'Yes, I think his dad picked him up from reception.'

I couldn't speak for a moment.

'Right,' I said, eventually, not knowing what else to say but realising I needed to get off the line before she twigged that I didn't have a clue what was going on. 'I've got to get back to work, but I'll be in touch.'

I ended the call and rang Sam. Predictably, his phone went straight to voicemail.

'Let me know how your doctor's appointment goes,' I said. 'You'll be needing a visit to bloody A&E when I get hold of you.'

I stood there, my whole body shaking. Everything I'd done to try to help him, and this was how he'd repaid me: bunking off school and using his condition as an excuse. I was too embarrassed to ring Mrs Hurd back and tell her. And if I did, I knew it would mean him being transferred to another school, which nobody wanted to happen, me included.

But I did need to know where the hell he was and who he was with. I texted Lorraine and asked if she knew if Tyler was in school because Sam wasn't. Lorraine rang back five minutes later.

'Apparently not,' she said. 'Just had a message from his head of year.'

'She told me Sam's dad picked him up from reception for a doctor's appointment.'

'Shit. Who are they with then?'

'I don't know, but there's nowt we can do, is there? I'll keep trying them. I'll call you as soon as I hear owt.'

*

When I got home from work later, Sam was in the kitchen, emptying the dishwasher for probably the first time in his life, as if he thought that would make everything OK.

'Where the hell have you been?' I asked.

'School were doing my head in. I needed to get away.'

'So, you lied about having a doctor's appointment? Mrs Hurd's expecting us to send her the full report. How do you suggest we get around that one?'

He shrugged and started putting the cutlery in the drawer.

'Put that down and look at me. Do you take me for some kind of mug?'

'Yeah, this one,' he said, picking up the 'World's Best Mum' mug Jodie had bought me for Mother's Day years ago.

'I'm not laughing, Sam. And nor is Lorraine. You're going to tell me where you and Tyler were this afternoon. Or do you want me to phone Mrs Hurd back and tell her you didn't have a doctor's appointment?'

Sam put the mug down on the kitchen counter.

'We bunked off, it were no big deal.'

'Mrs Hurd said your dad picked you up from reception.'

For the first time, Sam looked worried.

'I lied.'

'So, who did pick you up?'

'No one.'

'I can tell her it wasn't your dad and ask her to run CCTV footage if you like.'

Sam sighed.

'He's just some guy I know.'

'Well, you can tell me who he is and what you were doing with him.'

The colour rose in Sam's cheeks. It was only then the penny dropped, and I realised, yet again, how stupid I'd been.

'It's someone off that Facebook group, isn't it?'

'So what if it is?'

'Right. I'm ringing Mrs Hurd.' I took my phone off the kitchen counter.

'No, don't.'

'I will unless you tell me exactly where you were and what you were doing.'

Sam hung his head, seemingly aware I meant it.

'We were outside a school in Halifax, trying to recruit new members.'

'You what?'

'Giving out leaflets and that. Telling them how the immigrants are taking away their jobs.'

I stared at him.

'Fucking hell, Sam, have you heard yoursen?'

'We have rights too, you know, only they're being taken away.'

'Who told you that?'

'Rob, from group. He says white lads like us are being ignored. That we need to rise up and make our voices heard.'

'Jesus Christ, wake up. They're trying to get you angry, so you'll cause a bit of aggro on their behalf. They're making you think everyone's against you when they're not.'

Sam stood shaking his head.

'They're telling truth when everyone else is too scared to. Nobody's bothered about me at school. And even if I do manage to get on some college course for thickos, I'm not going to get a job at end of it, am I? And yet all these immigrants get whatever they want.'

I shook my head.

'Sam, that's complete crap. Us and teachers have been doing everything we can to help you. That report we got cost money we didn't have, and you've repaid us by lying to me and school and bunking off to recruit kids into some crackpot group you're in.'

Sam was visibly shaking now.

'You see,' he said. 'This is why I lied about it, because I knew you wouldn't listen to me. Rob said you wouldn't. Well, fuck you, you're as bad as rest of them.'

He picked up my 'Best Mum in the World' mug and smashed it on the floor before storming out of the kitchen.

I stood there, staring at the fragments of mug on the floor. And knowing that 'Best Mum' had been a total lie.

24

JODIE

It's like the world is conspiring against me and Rachid being together. The whole Paris thing is doing my head in. I'm desperate to be alone with him, but now Sam's been grounded for bunking off school, Rachid can't come here today like we'd planned. And we can't go to his house because ALL THE REASONS. I did think about asking Lorraine if we could go to hers, but she'd have known what we were up to, and I didn't want to risk her telling Mum, so I didn't dare ask in the end.

Which is why I'm stuck here on my own thinking about last week when Rachid was lying next to me and wondering if it will ever happen again. If he goes to Paris with his family, that'll be the end of us, and I don't know if I can bear that. Having tasted something that good, how can I go back to what my life was like before?

I sigh and check my phone. It's time to go now. We're not

going to the café today. I've got something different planned. I take a final look in the mirror, pull a brush through my hair and do another spray of perfume, before picking up my bag and leaving the room.

Sam and Tyler are downstairs watching TV. It's all they can do as they've had their phones, laptops and games consoles taken away.

'So long, losers,' I say as I pass the open living-room door.

'Where you going?' asks Sam, turning to face me with a scowl.

'Out. Because, unlike you, I haven't been grounded for trying to sign kids up to join Hitler Youth.'

Sam sticks his middle finger up at me.

'You're going to see him, aren't you?' he asks.

'I have no idea what you're on about,' I reply, hoping he won't notice the tremor in my voice. 'I'm going to college to work on show costumes.'

'Yeah, right. You're going to see your boyfriend. The one who messages you five hundred times a day.'

I take my time and try to breathe, knowing that if I respond to what he said in the way I'd like to, it will make him even more suspicious, and I can't risk that.

'Newsflash: maybe I'm simply more popular than you,' I say.

Dad comes out of the kitchen, mug of tea in hand. He's had to stay home to make sure Sam and Tyler don't do a bunk.

'Everything all right?' he asks.

'It is now,' I reply, opening the front door, 'because I'm getting away from this place.'

*

I arrive outside the side entrance to the Playhouse in Leeds. It's opposite college, so if anyone does see us here, we have a ready-made excuse. Rachid messages to say he's five minutes away. My heart quickens. I don't ever want to lose this feeling. That is the one thing I am clear about amongst all this mess.

It's his hair I see first, flashes of black bobbing up and down as he climbs the flight of steps below. He smiles when he sees me and I'm hit by a wave of happiness, which crashes into the wave of despair released at the same time.

I practically run into his arms. I don't care who sees us, I simply need to be next to him. When I eventually prise myself from his chest to speak, it all spills out of me.

'I'm sorry you couldn't come to my house. I'm sorry my idiot brother screwed things up. I'm sorry that we have to meet in secret like this, I'm sorry I can't shout how I feel about you from top of Victoria Gate car park. I'm sorry your parents want to go to Paris, I'm sorry about Brexit and all the crap with your dad, and I'm sorry about all of it.'

Rachid looks down at me and smiles.

'That's a pretty comprehensive apology. Although you do know none of that stuff is your fault?'

'Even my brother joining Hitler Youth?'

'Even that. When they talk about grooming, they should talk about the groups targeting white lads in areas like yours. He's just swallowed all the poison they pump out online.'

'I know. I'm still ashamed of it, though. Not that there's owt I can do about it. It's too late for him. He's beyond saving.'

'The important thing is he's not going to come between us.'

I look down at my feet.

'What?' he asks.

'Before I left, he said summat about me going out to meet my boyfriend.'

Rachid's brow creases. I've hardly ever seen him look worried.

'You don't think he knows?'

'He can't do. He probably just suspects because of party. And he made some comment about me getting lots of messages.'

'We'd better be careful,' Rachid replies. 'Maybe turn our notifications off.'

'OK,' I say. 'Anyway, we're going somewhere to take our minds off all this crap.'

'Why does that worry me?' he says with a smile.

'Because you know me too well.'

'Yes,' he replies. 'Exactly that.'

I lead him around the front of the Playhouse and down the road to our left. He looks up at the BBC building.

'Hey, you've got me a gig on live radio.'

'Nope, sorry. That would have been a cool thing to do. But we're going there instead.'

I point to the red-brick converted warehouse opposite. Rachid frowns at me.

'It's Playhouse's costume hire department. I've been before and it's awesome. Any costume you could ever want is there.'

'I don't get it. Do you want me to play dressing up with you?'

'No. I've got an appointment. Musical theatre lot at college announced yesterday they're doing *West Side Story* next year and my course are making most of costumes and we've got to hire the rest.'

'What? That means our *Hairspray* cover story has been blown.'

'I know. But good news is I've been made chief wardrobe mistress, which is why I've made an appointment to check out *West Side Story* costumes here, to give me some ideas and find some pieces we can hire.'

'And we can tell our parents they had to change the show because of licence problems, which means we'll need to carry on staying late and coming in at weekends for months longer.'

'You're not just a pretty face, are you?' I reply with a smile. We cross over and I ring the bell on the door.

'Who am I supposed to be?' Rachid asks.

'My wardrobe assistant, of course.'

'But I know nothing about fashion design.'

'Then you'll have to wing it, darling,' I say, grinning at him.

We're buzzed through and climb two flights of steps to the costume hire floor, where a woman with wild pink hair lets us in.

'Hi, I'm Jodie and this is Rachid,' I say. 'I called about the *West Side Story* costumes.'

'Yes, come in, let me show you where you can find what you're looking for.'

We follow her down what looks like a period drama aisle and turn the corner to find ourselves amongst a sea of fifties-style costumes, with an entire rail of brightly coloured skirts.

'Here you are,' she says. 'We've got a full range of Sharks and Jets costumes and pretty much everything else you would need. Feel free to try anything on and if you need any help just shout.'

As soon as she's gone, I gaze along the aisle, a smile spreading across my face.

'Oh my God, these are amazing,' I say, running my fingers along an array of brightly coloured satin skirts, all with a shock of tulle netting underneath.

'Confession time,' says Rachid. 'I've never seen *West Side Story*, so I have no idea what I'm looking at.'

'They're costumes for "America", and this,' I say, spotting a white lacy dress with a red satin sash and pulling it out from the rail, 'is Maria's dress for a big dance scene where she meets Tony. I'm going to make my sash from velvet, because I fucking love velvet. I'd dress whole world in velvet if I could.'

I hold the dress up to me and spin around. Rachid is smiling, slowly shaking his head.

'What?' I ask.

'You, being in your element.'

'I'd love to work in a theatre doing costumes one day. That'd be so lush.'

'You should apply to Playhouse when you finish uni. Then we could meet for lunch when I'm in my final year at the College of Music.'

His mention of the future breaks the spell. I want to believe a future like that is possible. But the reality of our lives comes crashing in again.

'It won't work if you're in Paris, though, will it?' I say, hanging the dress back on the rail.

'I told you, I'm not going.'

'You won't have any choice. Your dad's not going to change his mind, is he?'

Rachid sighs and turns away for a second.

'He keeps saying we're not welcome here. That he wants better for us.'

'He's got a point. I'd get out of this shit-hole country if I could.'

Rachid turns back to face me.

'And I'd take you with me if I could. But neither of those things can happen.'

'We could go off together,' I say. 'Somewhere they won't find us.'

Rachid looks at me. I don't think he knows if I'm being serious or not.

'I mean it,' I say. 'I don't want to stay here if you go to Paris. You don't want to go to Paris without me. So, we need to stop it happening.'

'What, run away together?'

'It wouldn't even be that. I'm eighteen, I can live where I want. They can't stop us. Not really.'

I watch him thinking. Weighing things up in his head. I spot the veil Maria wears for her bridal-shop scene with Tony and put it on.

'Maybe,' he says slowly. 'That's not actually as crazy an idea as it sounds.'

'I mean, we'd need to get work,' I say, 'but there are enough branches of Greggs around for me to get a job.'

He shakes his head. Maybe he doesn't want to stop this happening after all, and he's simply pretending to make me feel better.

'No. I don't want you giving up your course, going to uni, your dreams of designing things like this,' he says, gesturing at the costumes around us.

The ache inside me releases. I feel bad for doubting him now. I don't know what I've done to deserve this guy, but I'm not going to let him go.

'Thank you,' I say. 'But what about your course?'

He shrugs.

'It's different. I've only just started. I'd rather be working, learning on the job.'

'OK,' I reply. 'So, we need to move to a big city but not Leeds. Someone would spot us, and my dad would try to drag me back home. What about Manchester? Easy enough for me to get to college on train, but far enough away from here to put some distance between me and my family.'

'I know this guy in Manchester,' says Rachid, his face brightening. 'He's a music producer, got his own studio and everything. Maybe he could get me some work, introduce me to people. I could help out with gigs, like I did with Marcus.'

I smile as I hear the rising excitement in his voice. He's making it sound like an actual plan. Something we're really going to do.

'So, let's do it,' I say, as I pull the veil back from my face.

He smiles, places his hands on my shoulders and kisses me.

'We'll need to plan it all out carefully,' he says, starting to pace up and down the aisle. 'Sort out a place to live and I'll put some feelers out about work.'

'Have we got time to do all that?'

'Dad's not due to start till January. I don't think they'll move until the Christmas holidays.'

'OK. But we need to be careful not to let on what's happening. I don't want either of our families screwing this up for us.'

'Sure. I'll start to soften a bit to throw them off the scent. Apologise to Dad for what I said. Pretend I'm coming around to the idea of Paris.'

'What about your sister? Will she buy that?'

'Don't worry, she's sweet. I got her a pass out to a party tonight. She won't say a word, not even if she suspects.'

'OK. I'll start trying the Greggs in Manchester for some weekend work after Christmas. I want to pay my way. A flat there isn't going to be cheap.'

Rachid looks at me and smiles as he shakes his head.

'What?' I ask.

'This is totally crazy. I can't believe we're actually going to be living together.'

'Just so you know, I'm crap at cooking and washing-up so we'll have to live on takeouts.'

'What do you mean? I can cook,' he replies. 'My mum taught me because she doesn't want me to be one of those guys who leaves it to women.'

'Jeez,' I say. 'I really have fallen on my feet, haven't I? Hot in bed and useful in kitchen. You're a keeper.'

Rachid laughs so much the wardrobe woman pops her head around the corner.

'Just checking you're OK?' she says.

I quickly take off the veil.

'Great, thanks. I think we've found what we were looking for.'

'Wonderful,' she says. 'If you want to reserve anything for specific dates, I can do that for you. Come and see me before you go.'

She disappears again. I turn back to Rachid, who's standing there looking at me.

'I love you, Jodie Cuthbert,' he says.

I choke up so much hearing him say it that I can't even reply. And by the time we've left the building, the moment has gone. But later, after I get off the train and wave to him from the platform as it pulls out, I send him 'Let's Pretend We're Married' by Prince on Spotify.

25

SYLVIE

Amina was coming out of the bathroom when I reached the landing, a white towel wrapped around her wet hair, her expression downbeat. She'd been quiet when I'd picked her up after the party last night, offering only vague, monosyllabic answers to my questions as I'd driven her home. She'd hardly said a word to me since finding out about Bilal's affair and the Paris announcement, but I'd hoped the party would perk her up a little. Now I was concerned it had made her worse.

'Are you OK, sweetheart?'

'I've got a stomach ache. I don't want any breakfast this morning.'

'Poor you,' I said, stroking her face. 'Do you want to talk about it? Sometimes it helps, you know.'

She looked down for a moment before gesturing with her head toward her room. I followed her in.

'I hate him,' she said, as soon as the door was closed. 'I can't forgive him for what he did to you.'

I hugged her to me, the towel damp against my face.

'I get that,' I said. 'I couldn't forgive him for a long time either. But it's not good for you, hating someone you also love. It messes with your head.'

She managed a watery smile.

'I can't even look at him, let alone speak to him. How could he be so cruel?'

'I haven't got a good answer to that,' I said. 'And believe me, I've spent a long time thinking about it. All I've come up with is to try to draw a line under it. Because I can either spend my whole life letting it eat away at me, or put it to one side and try to make things a little better.'

She nodded but didn't seem convinced.

'What I want you to remember,' I continued, 'is that none of this is about you. Your father loves you so much, I think he's more upset about having hurt you than anyone else.'

'I don't want him to be,' she said. 'I want him to feel bad about hurting you. That's how it should be.'

I shut my eyes for a second, took a couple of breaths.

'Remember once when you asked me about what romantic things we'd done together? The truth is I could remember so many, but it hurt too much to tell you about them. It was proper, big, romantic love and I thought I'd never feel anything stronger in my whole life. But the second I held Rachid in my arms, and a few years later you, I knew that was a whole new level of love I'd never expected. And we both still feel like that about you, so you can't blame him for that.'

'But I want you and Dad to be happy like a proper married couple.'

I squeezed her hand, not wanting to break it to her that there were plenty of married couples in a worse state than us.

'I think things will get better between us now,' I said. 'Not suddenly, but little by little. I think this coming out has actually been a good thing for all of us. It might not seem it now but in the long run it will be.'

Amina sighed. I had a sense that there were other things troubling her.

'Is it just that and the whole Paris thing, or did something happen at the party?'

She appeared relieved that I'd given her the opportunity to unload some more.

'Becky and Jasmine barely spoke to me. They were drinking and hanging out with their boyfriends. I may as well not have been there.'

I nodded, not wanting to show her how relieved I was that it was nothing worse than that.

'And you felt left out?'

'Yes. I wanted to go because I was desperate to fit in, but they were so mean to me, I'm not sure if I even want to be their friend any more.'

'I know you don't want to hear this,' I said, 'but I honestly do think things will be better for you in Paris. You'll have the chance to make new friends with girls from all sorts of cultures and backgrounds. I think the international school will suit you. People will accept you for who you are. And that's all I want, for you to be comfortable in your own skin.'

Amina looked up at me, her eyes betraying that she wanted what I had said to be true.

'Do you mean that or are you just trying to make me feel better?' she said.

'Both,' I replied. 'I wouldn't be going along with this whole Paris thing if I didn't think it was the best thing for you.'

She nodded slowly.

'You don't want to go either, do you?'

'It wasn't my idea, but I'm coming around to it. I think it will be good for me and your father. Give us the chance to make a fresh start. And I'm so pleased we'll be able to be close to Grand-mère.'

Amina nodded. I knew she liked the idea of that too. But then her face clouded again.

'But it doesn't matter, does it, because Rachid's not coming. And there's no point without him.'

'Leave Rachid to me,' I replied.

'He won't change his mind.'

There was something about the certainty in her voice that threw me.

'Why do you say that?'

She hesitated.

'He just won't. So there's no point any of us starting to get excited about Paris, because it's not going to happen.'

I knew better than to ask Rachid and Amina if they wanted to FaceTime Grand-mère to let her know the news about Paris. There would be nothing worse than me announcing the news with two morose teenagers in the background.

But when they were in their rooms and I was alone in the kitchen, I did FaceTime Maman rather than phone, because I wanted to see her reaction. I watched as the smile appeared on her lips, then spread out until it radiated across her entire face. Her eyes glistened with tears and her voice, when she was finally able to speak, was shot through with relief that, for once, she couldn't disguise. She asked if we were doing this because of her, as she was perfectly capable of looking after herself, thank you very much.

I told her that we were moving for a whole host of reasons, but primarily because we didn't feel welcome in the UK any longer. And that it was a decision we believed was the best thing for all of us.

She asked if Rachid and Amina were happy about it. I didn't give a direct answer. Simply said that they would adjust and make new friends quickly.

If she'd been with me, she would have patted me on the hand at this point, being wise enough to know how teenagers worked, and how difficult this must be for me. As it was, she let the matter drop and allowed her face to settle into an expression of contentment. I tried to commit it to memory for the next time I doubted the wisdom of our decision.

'How was your mother?' Bilal asked, when I slipped into bed next to him that night.

'Good, thanks. And delighted at the news, of course. I suspect she's been secretly hoping this would happen since Papa died.'

'Well, at least one person in the family is happy,' he said. Barely two words had been spoken between him, Rachid and Amina since he'd been 'outed'. I'd watched as he'd deflated before my eyes, his dignity trampled and squashed. The man who had always prided himself on being a pillar of the community, reduced to nothing in front of his children.

'You need to give it time,' I said. 'They're both in shock.'

'I know, and it's not fair that you're having to deal with that too.'

'They're my children,' I said. 'That's what I do.'

There was a long pause before he spoke.

'I want you to be more than simply their mother,' he said.

'What?' I asked, turning towards him.

'I miss the old Sylvie. The one I fell in love with.'

'So do I. I could do with her youth and energy.'

'I meant her confidence.'

'Yeah, well we know what happened to that.'

Bilal took the blow with a degree of dignity.

'You still have her beauty,' he said after a while.

'Don't say that.'

'What?'

'It's embarrassing, you pretending you still feel anything for me.' He stared at me without saying anything, so I continued. 'I'm the menopausal, middle-aged mother of your children. I suffer from night sweats and brain fog and there's a muffin top where my waist used to be. You pretending you still find me attractive is frankly quite insulting.'

'Is that really what you think?' he asked.

'It's what I know. What I see in the mirror.'

He shook his head.

'What?'

'Of course I still find you attractive. But you've lost so much confidence that you simply won't believe it. And you won't let me anywhere near you, not emotionally.'

'It's called self-preservation. I got my fingers badly burnt once. I don't want it to happen again.'

Bilal reached over and brushed a strand of hair from my face.

'I understand that. And I know it's all my fault. But if we're going to have any chance of making this work, you have to let me back in and let me love you.'

I blinked back the tears. He was right. I knew that. But I was still so very scared.

'I can try,' I said. 'You'll have to give me time, though. Just like with the children.'

'Of course. And Paris will help, I'm sure of it. In a few months' time things are going to be so much better.'

He smiled as he said it. It was the first smile I'd seen from him since it had all come out. I didn't have the heart to erase it by telling him what Amina had said about Rachid. So I simply nodded, kissed him gently on the lips and turned out the light.

*

When I arrived downstairs the next morning, there was already a coffee waiting for me.

A moment later Bilal came through from the study, put his arms around me and planted a kiss on my lips.

'What's that for?' I asked.

'We're going back to the city where we fell in love. That has to be a good thing for us.'

'Let's hope so,' I replied. 'For all our sakes.'

'I've emailed the estate agent who came for the valuation on Saturday to ask him to get the house on the market as quickly as possible. He says he's already got someone lined up who's keen to view it.'

He kissed me on the neck. Something he hadn't done for a long time. For a moment, I was transported back to an apartment in Paris, where every morning used to start this way. I wanted to allow myself to be swept away by him again. To become that confident, carefree woman he'd fallen in love with, forget about everyone else and surrender to it. I couldn't, though. Because I was still the mother of his children. And life wasn't that simple any more.

I was walking back to the station from the university, having finally summoned up the courage to hand my notice in, when Bilal texted me to say the estate agent would be coming the following morning to take photos and do the measurements. I said that was fine. There was nothing else I could say. Once something had been set in motion, it was pointless trying to jump off, even if it was going too fast for you. All I could hope was that somehow Rachid would scramble on board at the last moment and come with us as a willing passenger.

Maman texted me as I was on the way home to tell me she'd emailed a link to a nice rental apartment she'd found online. I smiled; she clearly couldn't contain her excitement at our imminent arrival, and I wasn't going to complain about her trying to find us somewhere nice to live. Besides, Maman had always had exemplary taste, and as I opened the link, I saw that this apartment was no exception. There were beautiful high ceilings and light, airy rooms. There was even a small basement with an en suite bedroom and second room that she said would be perfect for the children's friends coming to stay, but which I was already earmarking as a studio for Rachid. I checked back; it was not far from Montmartre, exactly the area of the 18th arrondissement we'd been looking at. Easily commutable for the hospital and Amina's school. Even the monthly rental, although right on our upper limit, was doable; particularly as we'd got a good valuation for our house. The obvious thing to do would be to submit an enquiry online to see whether we could view it while we were over during half-term. My finger hovered over my phone; I couldn't help feeling I was now the one speeding things up, when I'd been anxious about how quickly everything was happening. I glanced up to look out of the train window and check where we were. Someone had left a newspaper on the seat opposite me. The headline, above photos of those MPs who would be taking part in the Stop Brexit march in London on Saturday, was 'TRAITORS'.

I went back to my phone, filled in my details on the apartment enquiry form and pressed 'submit'.

Edwina was at her front gate when I arrived home, wrapped up as if it were December rather than October. Her face crinkled into a smile as soon as she saw me.

'Sylvie, dear, you're looking well. Have you had a good day?'

'Yes,' I replied. 'I think I have.'

'And how are those lovely children of yours?'

I hesitated, unwilling to lie to her, or even to be economical with the truth. Besides, I was aware that the estate agents would be putting up a *For Sale* sign in a day or two, and I didn't want her to find out like that.

'We have some news,' I said. 'Bilal has taken a head of department position in Paris. We'll be leaving around Christmas.'

'How wonderful,' she replied, doing a good job of hiding her disappointment, then, looking at me more closely, 'Is it wonderful?'

'It's the right thing to do,' I said. 'And it will be such a relief to be close to my mother.'

'And what about the children?' Edwina asked.

'That's where it gets more difficult.'

'They don't want to go?'

'Rachid's saying he won't come with us.'

'Oh dear.'

Edwina reached out and squeezed my hand. She was a mother first and foremost, and she understood that their pain was your pain.

'I'm hoping he'll come around. Although maybe not.'

'It's a difficult age to be moving,' said Edwina. 'He's just found his independence at college and no doubt made lots of new friends and now you come along and remind him that his parents are still in charge.'

I nodded; I hadn't really thought of it like that before.

'The frustrating thing is that I do think it would be an amazing opportunity for him and he'd love it once he got there.'

'Then you must remember that it's OK for your children to hate you for something, as long as they see you were acting out of love.'

I squeezed her hand in response.

'Where will I be without your words of wisdom?' I asked.

'I'll keep in touch with you like I do my family. I have Skype, you know. I'm really rather up with these modern technologies.'

I laughed.

'That will be lovely, and we'll be sure to come back for visits.'

Edwina smiled. It was a sad smile. One that suggested she had learnt that these promised visits rarely materialised.

I resorted to cooking leftover lasagne from the freezer for dinner, to give me as much time as possible to get the house ready for the photographer's visit the next day. I dispatched Bilal to organise his study and Amina to tidy her room. I was in the middle of attempting to squeeze as many pots as possible into the kitchen cupboard when Rachid arrived home.

'Hi,' I said. 'How are the rehearsals going?'

'Bit of a nightmare today, actually. They've had to change the show; they're doing *West Side Story* now, so I've got to start from scratch with the music,' he replied.

'That's a shame, after all your hard work. When's the show?'

'Er, May, I think.'

We would be gone by then, of course. I felt another pang of guilt.

'Perhaps we can arrange to come back to see it.'

Rachid looked at the floor.

'No need,' he said.

I went back to putting things in cupboards. 'They're coming to photograph the house tomorrow,' I said, as matter-of-factly as I could.

'Right.'

'I know this is difficult for you, but if you wouldn't mind tidying your bedroom a little, that would be a big help.'

He hesitated and for a moment I thought he was going to tell me again that he wasn't going to have any part in this.

'OK,' he said instead. I stopped what I was doing and turned to look at him, seizing on any hint of a breakthrough.

'Thank you,' I said. 'I know it's not easy. I didn't plan for it to turn out like this.'

'I know.'

'For what it's worth, there's an apartment available which

has a basement for you to have your own studio. We can view it when we're over at half-term if you like.'

I studied his face, trying to work out what was going on inside his head.

'You don't need to do that.'

'I do, though. I know this isn't what you want. The least we can do is to give you your own space and help you to pursue your dreams.'

If I didn't know better, I would have said that Rachid looked embarrassed by this, upset even.

'It's not your fault, Mum. I get that. My beef's with Dad.'

'Please try not to be too hard on him. You've seen what this is doing to him. He sees Paris as a chance to put everything that's happened behind us and make a fresh start.'

'Mum.' Rachid put his hands on my shoulders. 'It's OK. I get that it's a good opportunity. I'm cool with it.'

I swallowed hard. He turned and left the kitchen. I stood there, my hands shaking, my ears caressing the words I'd been so desperate to hear. Although my brain was still unsure as to whether I should accept them as the truth.

R & J

WhatsApp

Fuck, this is happening way too fast
21:28

What is???
21:28

Someone came to view the house early this evening and they've offered the asking price
21:28

What? I thought it were only going on market today
21:28

They asked to view it straight away. They need to move quickly
21:28

So will you have to leave before Christmas?
21:28

I don't know. Mum's talking about viewing an apartment when we go to Paris at half-term. Dad's asking if the hospital will release him from his notice earlier. It's all gone a bit crazy
21:29

Shit. What are we going to do? 21:29

We need to move fast. I'll start looking at
flats in Manchester 21:29

OK. You do still want to do this don't you?
I don't want to push you into it 21:29

Course I do. There's no way I'm going to
leave you. You're everything to me 21:29

Love you 🤍 21:29

26

DONNA

I lay staring at the ceiling, unable to get to sleep. It wasn't unusual these days; various menopausal symptoms vied for my attention during the night. But it wasn't insomnia or the itching that was keeping me awake, it was the sound of crying coming from Jodie's room. Something was up, but I no longer had a relationship with her where we talked about stuff like that. I wasn't sure when that had happened, but she seemed to have decided to lump me in with Sam and her father and be furious with her entire family. Apart from Lorraine, of course. Jodie never blamed Lorraine for anything Tyler did; it was his feckless father's fault for buggering off and leaving her as a single mum. But there was no such get-out-of-jail card for me, because those who parented pretty much single-handedly when they were still living with the other parent only got pity.

I wondered whether to get up and knock on her door, ask if she wanted to talk about whatever it was that was bothering her. But the thought that she would probably tell me it was none of my business stopped me doing so. I heard her phone beep with messages several times. It could be Zoe from college, I still wasn't sure if they'd made up or not after the falling-out. Or it could be the lad at her party.

I must have fallen asleep again, because the next time I opened my eyes the sun was streaming through the gap in the ready-made IKEA curtains that had never quite fitted. And when I turned over, I realised that Neil had already got up.

I went out onto the landing and stopped for a second outside Jodie's bedroom door. All was quiet. Not even the ping of her phone, which was usually what I heard from her room these days. I tried to take some comfort from the fact that at least she had got some sleep.

I headed downstairs for a cuppa. Neil was standing peering out of the front-room window.

'What are you looking at?' I asked.

'There's an ambulance outside next door.'

I went to the window as the paramedics emerged with a frail-looking Pawel in a wheelchair and loaded him into the back. Jakub and Daniel were standing either side of their mother, clearly distraught.

'We ought to go out and see if we can do anything to help,' I said.

'Why?'

I turned sharply to Neil. 'Because they're our neighbours.'

I waited till the ambulance had pulled away, then stepped outside. Daniel was helping his mother into the back of his new car.

I caught Jakub's eye and he came over to me.

'Is your dad OK?' I asked him.

'He's had a heart attack.'

'Oh, I'm so sorry to hear that. Is there owt we can do to help?'

Jakub shook his head.

'No thank you. We're going straight to the hospital now. The paramedics think he'll pull through.'

'I do hope so. Give your mother our love.'

He nodded and hurried over to the car. I went back inside the house.

'Pawel's had a heart attack,' I said to Neil.

'Poor bugger,' he said. I suspected it had dawned on him that we had never been good neighbours to them. And yet, despite that, they would still have been there for us in a similar crisis.

'I'll get summat for them to take into hospital for him on my way back from work.'

'Yeah,' he said. 'That'd be nice.'

Jodie arrived in the kitchen looking like she hadn't got much sleep.

'Can I get you some breakfast before I go?' I asked.

'No thanks.'

'Not hungry?'

She shook her head and walked out. I sighed.

'What's up with her?' asked Neil.

'I don't know. I heard her crying last night. She's right upset about summat.'

'Won't she say what?'

'Not to me. I'm going to see Lorraine after work tonight. I'm hoping she'll have spoken to her.'

'Why does she talk to her and not you?'

'That's a good question,' I replied.

Lorraine had her bright and jolly nurse face on when I arrived later.

'Hi sis,' she said, 'I've got wine out of fridge ready for you.'

I smiled at her, unable to muster the sufficiently cheery reply I knew she expected.

'You OK?' she asked, frowning.

'Worried sick, that's all.'

'About who?'

'Well, I never stop being worried about Sam but summat's up with Jodie, now.'

'What makes you say that?' she asked, pouring an indecent amount of wine into the already oversized glass.

'I heard her crying in her room last night.'

'Oh,' she said, pouring her own smaller measure and returning the bottle to the fridge.

'I were hoping she might have told you what were going on.'

Lorraine went to the cupboard and busied herself pouring

some snacks and nibbles into a bowl before returning to the table. She noisily munched through five pretzels then looked up at me.

'That lad's family are planning to move to Paris.'

'What? Why didn't you say owt?'

'She made me promise not to. I didn't want to lose her trust.'

'And what about me? Doesn't my trust count for owt? I'm your sister, or had you forgotten?'

Lorraine's face crumpled and she looked down at the table.

'I couldn't bear to lose the bond I have with Jodie. She's nearest thing I've got to a daughter. And she were only thing that kept me going after . . .'

I reached out my hand to squeeze hers. We never spoke about it. Because I knew it was still too painful for her, even eighteen years on.

'I'm sorry,' I said. 'I didn't mean to get you upset.'

'It's always there,' Lorraine replied. 'It's never gone away, and it never will. Having to say goodbye to her before I'd even had a chance to say hello.'

'I know. I saw way you managed to hold it together for Jodie's sake at her party, but I knew you'd be hurting underneath.'

'I had a little cry in ladies. When I were on my own. That's when Jodie came in. She knew I'd seen her with that lad when I'd gone out on top of stairs to have a breather. She begged me to keep it a secret. She were worried about Sam causing trouble again if you and Neil knew. And I've never been able to say no to her, because, well, you know why.'

I shut my eyes and nodded.

'I feel so bad,' I said.

'What for?'

'I love how close you two are. I really do. But I'd be lying if I said I didn't get a bit jealous of that sometimes.'

'Jealous? How can you be jealous of me? You have a daughter. You have what I lost weeks before Jodie arrived. What I longed for but had taken away from me.'

'I know, and that's why I feel so bad. It's just sometimes when I see how you two are together, I think you're more of a mum to her than I've ever been.'

We both started crying. Big, sloppy tears that only sisters can have together.

'You're a daft bat sometimes,' said Lorraine. 'Who were it who sat up all night with her when she were teething, who went into school when that little bastard were bullying her and got it to stop, who always put her first? Always.'

'I know,' I said. 'But I don't think she sees it like that.'

'I'm sure she knows it deep down. It's not cool, though, is it? To be mates with your mum. Which is why she talks to me.'

I wiped my face. Picked up my wine glass and took a slurp.

'Thank you,' I said. 'For being there for her. I'm glad she's got you. I really am. I just need you to let me know if she's ever in any kind of trouble.'

Lorraine looked at me.

'She's been seeing lad since party. It's got pretty serious. But he's going now and that's end of it. That's why she's upset.'

'OK,' I said. 'As long as that's all it is. I can deal with a broken heart. Or rather she can. Broken hearts can be mended. It's probably for best in long run. I don't see how it could ever have worked.'

Lorraine nodded, although she didn't say anything.

'Is it wrong of me to say that? Only it's true, isn't it? You've only got to look at what happened at party.'

'He seems a right nice lad from what she's told me. Worships her from sound of it.'

I felt a pang of guilt for being glad he was going now. I didn't even know what it felt like to be worshipped. Maybe I was jealous of Jodie too.

'You think I should have had it out with Sam and Neil? Made it clear to Jodie that she were welcome to see whoever she liked?'

Lorraine shrugged.

'I don't think it would have done any harm to tell her that. And to say it in front of Sam and Neil too, so everyone knew you meant it.'

I shut my eyes.

'Jesus, I ballsed that right up, didn't I? I were just trying to keep peace. Trying to smooth it all over and make it go away.'

'Well, he's leaving now,' said Lorraine. 'So I guess that puts an end to it.'

'Yeah. I'll do better next time, though. And if I don't, you give me a kick up arse, OK?'

Lorraine smiled. One of those smiles she did to hide the pain.

27

RACHID

Mum's on her laptop at the kitchen table when I walk in. She has her back to me, so I can see what she's looking at, which is probably why she doesn't snap the lid shut. She looks up instead, clearly embarrassed, like she's been caught watching porn or something.

'Morning, sweetheart,' she says, brushing her hair back from her face. The grey streaks in it are more visible than they used to be and the skin under her eyes has dark shadows. I know she doesn't want this any more than I do. She's simply trying to put on a brave face as usual.

'This is the apartment I told you about,' she says.

I look at the screen. It's stylish, but then I wouldn't expect anything less from her. When I don't say anything, she starts scrolling through the photos until she gets to the ones of the basement.

'This is the room which could be your studio. And the bed-room next to it is an en suite.'

I nod even though it's ridiculous of her to think that having my own toilet would in any way encourage me to go to Paris.

'Can we afford it?' I ask, catching sight of the price.

'We'll be fine,' she says with a smile. 'As long as you're both OK with it, that's all that matters.'

I want to tell her that I won't even be there with them, because I'll be in Manchester with Jodie. But I know if I give her any hint of that, our plans will fail before we've even got on the train.

'Looks good,' I say.

She gazes up at me with an expression that suggests she doesn't dare to believe what she's hearing.

'Really? Because if you like it, we might have to move fast. The agent said there's been a lot of interest and it may be gone by the time we view it at half-term. She suggested we put a deposit down straight away; that way we could stay there when we visit Grand-mère, maybe even start to get your studio set up. How does that sound? I know it's sudden, but sometimes doing things on the spur of the moment is a good thing. *Carpe diem*, as Robin Williams said.'

The words come out in an excited splurge. She's looking at me expectantly. Shit. I can't bear the thought of her renting it to please me when I know I will never live there. Because I will not even be in the same country as them.

'I don't know,' I say. 'I'm still trying to get my head around it all, to be honest. Maybe it would be better if we waited till half-term. It would be good to see it for ourselves first.'

'OK,' she says, unable to hide her disappointment. 'I'm sure there'll be other nice apartments, if this one's gone by then. Your father's asking the trust if they'll release him early from his notice. We'll have a clearer idea about timings later.'

I nod and say nothing. I know me leaving will break her heart and I hate myself for that already, but it's the only way I can avoid breaking Jodie's heart. And Jodie is everything to me now.

'Thank you,' she says, taking my hand. 'For coming around to the idea, I mean. I know it was a huge shock for you, and that you have your own life here, but I know you'll love it when you get there.'

I walk over to the fridge, unable to look her in the eyes and feeling like a complete bastard for doing this to her. I take out the orange juice and pour myself a glass before turning back to her.

'There's a Stop Brexit march in Leeds tomorrow. Loads of my friends from college are going. I want to go. It's the only way I can show my anger at what they've done to all of us. Are you OK with that?'

Mum smiles and nods. 'Sure. I don't see why not. Maybe don't mention it to your father, though. He'll be at that conference all day, so there's no reason for him to know.'

'Thanks, Mum,' I say, kissing her on the top of her head. 'I knew you'd understand.'

She goes back to her laptop, staring at the photos of the

apartment still on the screen. No doubt dreaming of the better life she thinks awaits all of us.

Jodie gets on the train and sits down next to me. Just the feel of her body next to mine, the scent of her, is enough to remind me why I'm doing this. She takes one look at my face and asks, 'What's happened?'

'Mum's on about putting a deposit down on an apartment in Paris. She's getting it just for me, so I can have my own studio and room in the basement. I told her not to do anything yet but if Dad gets released from his notice today, they might do. We're going to have to leave sooner.'

'How soon?'

I look at her. I feel bad doing this, but I know if I let it go any longer, I won't be able to get out of going to Paris.

'Tomorrow.'

'Fucking hell,' says Jodie.

'I know. It's crazy, but if we don't do it then, the whole thing could fall apart.'

'How are we going to get that one past them?'

'I've got a plan. We're not going to mosque. Dad's speaking at some medical conference. Mum and Amina are going shopping in Leeds. I've told Mum I'm going to the Stop Brexit march in Leeds. It'll give us time to get away without anyone noticing.'

'That's brilliant. My mum's working and Dad's going to United match. It's a lunchtime kick-off. I'll tell them I'm going on the march too. Sam's still grounded but he usually sleeps till twelve at weekends. He won't even know I've gone until it's too late. Oh my God, it's perfect timing.'

I can feel the excitement as she says it. We're going to do this. We're going to move to Manchester together before anyone can stop us. I lean over and kiss her.

'One more day,' I say.

'But where are we going to live?'

'I'll book an Airbnb, just till we can get somewhere permanent. I'll have it all sorted by the time I see you at the café after college. You haven't got to worry about a thing.'

She smiles at me. Her eyes are glistening.

'It's going to be OK,' I tell her. 'Everything's going to be fine.'

I get to the café first. When I go in, Larry is putting a fresh tray on the display.

'Cheese and chive scones, with home-grown herbs tended by yours truly,' he says, 'if you think your young lady would like one?'

I smile. 'I'm sure she would. And the usual tea and coffee please.'

I hold my card over the machine.

'Wonderful. I'll bring them over.'

I sit down at our table. When Larry arrives with the tray I am switching between the tabs on my phone, making sure I have everything lined up to show Jodie. I want her to be blown away by my plans.

'I was thinking,' says Larry. 'I don't even know your names.'

I hesitate. I'm so used to keeping everything secret between us. But this is Larry, and we're leaving tomorrow. There's no harm in telling him.

'Rachid and Jodie,' I say.

'Well, Rachid, I can't tell you how much it brightens my day to see you two young lovebirds together. Makes me forget about all that's bad in the world.'

I smile. He may be a cheesy dude sometimes, but I like him.

'Thanks. Glad to hear it.' I have to stop myself saying that we'll miss coming here as he walks away.

'Man, cheese scones,' says Jodie, when she arrives a few minutes later. 'I'm a sucker for a good cheese scone, my nan used to make them when I were a kid.'

'Well, these have Lozza's home-grown herbs in them.'

She takes a bite and wipes the butter from her lips, kissing the air.

'I tell you. If I were fifty years older, I'd be after him.'

'Thanks,' I say, laughing. 'What about me?'

'You need to learn to make cheese scones like these, if you want to be a keeper.'

'What if I told you I'd booked us a great Airbnb in Manchester?'

'I'd say show me and I'll decide if you're still a contender.'

I open the first tab on my phone, swiping through the pics of the leather sofa and TV in the lounge, and the little Juliet balcony with views over Manchester.

Jodie gives a little squeal and grabs my arm across the table.

'Seriously? Is this where we're going to live?'

'Yep. I've booked it for two weeks but if we can't find a flat to rent by then, we might be able to get it for longer.'

'But how can you afford it? That must have cost a bomb.'

'Think they'd had a late cancellation, so it was on cheaper than usual. And I had some money saved that my grandmother gave me last Christmas and birthday. We're her only grand-children, so she tends to spoil us a bit.'

'Oh my God, now I feel bad, like we're making her an accomplice to our crime.'

'I know. I don't feel brilliant about it myself. But she always tells us to follow our dreams and, well, my dream is to be with you.'

She leans over and kisses me on the lips. I can see her eyes glistening.

'Thank you, so much. I promise I'll get a weekend job as soon as I can to pay my share. I can't believe we'll be in our own place this time tomorrow.'

'I'll forward all the deets to you now. It's a ten-minute walk from Victoria, so it'll be easy for you to get to Leeds and back. It's got one of those key-safe boxes so we can let ourselves in.'

Jodie's phone beeps with my message. She checks it and bites her lip.

'It hasn't seemed real till now. It were like some game we were playing, but it's not a game, is it?'

'No. This is for real. The two of us. Our own place. We'll be in control of our own future.'

'Then I choose you above Larry,' she says, 'although if you can make cheese scones like his, you'll be a total keeper.'

I laugh and go through the rest of the plans, sending her the times of the trains we'll be getting, the whole itinerary for the day.

'This is amazing,' she says. 'It's like a master escape plan. All we need is tension-building background music.'

'I can send you some of that if you like.'

'Nah. I'll be crapping myself enough without it.'

'Why?'

'None of those great escape movies ever goes smoothly, does it? What if it all goes wrong and your family or mine twig what's going on?'

'They won't,' I say. 'You said it yourself, the timing couldn't be more perfect. No one's going to be at home to see us leaving. And this time tomorrow, we'll be in Manchester.'

She nods, though I can tell she's still worried.

When we stand up to go, Jodie seems reluctant to leave.

'It feels weird. This is the last time we'll be here together.'

'You can still visit.'

'Not without you. It won't be the same. This is our place.'

She fishes in her backpack, pulls out a pen, takes the unused serviette from under her plate and starts to write on it.

'What are you doing?' I ask.

She holds it up for my inspection. It reads:

You're a star, Larry. Thanks for making us so welcome – keep burning brightly! with a smiley face next to it.

'He won't find it till we're gone,' she says, laying it on top of the plate. 'I just want him to know.'

I reach out and take her hand.

'Come on,' I say. 'One more night.'

When I get home, Amina comes out of her room as I get to the top of the stairs.

'What are you looking so happy about?' she asks.

'Is it a crime to smile in this house?'

I regret my response immediately. Not just because it sounds like I'm picking a fight with Amina, but because she knows I am not usually so defensive.

'What's going on?' she asks.

'Nothing. I had a good day at college, that's all.'

'You've just seen her, haven't you?'

'I don't know what you're talking about.'

'What's going on? Mum says you're coming to Paris with us. That you've changed your mind.'

It cuts like a knife. Lying to Mum is bad enough but lying to my little sister kills me a bit inside.

'Yeah,' I say. 'It's not forever, is it? I can come back here in a couple of years.'

She looks at me for a long time, as if deciding whether she believes me, then turns and goes back into her room.

28

SYLVIE

Bilal was checking himself in the wardrobe mirror when I came back into the bedroom after my shower. He still looked good in a suit, always had done. I went up to him and adjusted his tie slightly. It was only as I did so that I realised how long it was since I'd last done that.

Bilal looked down at me, brushed a wet curl from my face before cupping it with his hands.

'This is the best thing for us, I've no doubt about that.'

He spoke in such an authoritative voice that it was hard to disbelieve him.

'It's the speed it's happening which has thrown me,' I said. 'I don't want to rush things now we've finally got Rachid on board.'

'I think it's better this way,' said Bilal. 'Get on with it before he changes his mind.'

I walked over to the window. I so wanted to believe he was right.

'Rachid said we should wait to view the apartment at half-term.'

'And we both know it will be gone by then,' replied Bilal. 'I'll put the deposit down on Monday. We don't need to tell the children until after they've seen it. We've got an amazing opportunity here and we need to move fast.'

I nodded. I'd been trying not to make Rachid feel bad when I'd said I was sure we'd be able to find something similar if this apartment went. We wouldn't. It was perfect and I really didn't want to lose it.

'OK,' I said. 'Monday it is. Will you be home in time for dinner tonight?'

I was aware as I said it that there was a slight edge to my voice. Sometimes the fear that there might be extracurricular temptations at these conferences came out unexpectedly. Bilal took his hands away from my face. Perhaps he'd detected it too.

'I should be. I'll text you when I'm leaving Leeds. What have you got planned today?'

We'd already agreed that the children wouldn't go to mosque without him, even though it was a Saturday.

'I'm taking Amina shopping. I told her I'd get her some new things for Paris.'

'That's good. Get her something nice from me. And Rachid?'

I hesitated. In the new spirit of honesty and openness, I really didn't want to lie. But neither did I want to risk Bilal trying to stop Rachid going on the Brexit march. And the desire to avoid more family conflict tipped the balance.

'He's going into college later, still working on this show.'

Bilal inspected himself for a final time in the mirror, brushed an imaginary speck of dust from his jacket and turned back to me.

'I'll see you later then,' he said, kissing me on the lips.

I sat down on the bed and listened to his footsteps on the stairs, the front door banging and the beep of his car alarm before he got in and pulled away. I picked up the hairdryer, telling myself over and over again that everything was going to be fine.

Rachid didn't make it down to the kitchen until just before Amina and I were due to leave. He seemed a little edgy. I wondered if going on his first political march was worrying him.

'You'll be fine, sweetheart,' I said, picking up my keys from the table. 'Just stick with your college friends and to the planned route. And try to avoid any television cameras, we don't want your father spotting you in the crowd when he watches the evening news.'

He bit his lip and went straight to the fridge. Amina eyed him from across the table.

'Have you made a placard?' she asked him.

'Sorry?' he replied.

'A placard. Like that one we saw the girl with before the last march.'

He appeared flummoxed by her question.

'Er, no. I think Leeds for Europe have got some placards we can carry.'

She nodded, still looking hard at him.

'Well, have a good time,' I said, grabbing my bag. 'Try to get home for dinner this evening. It will be nice to have the whole family together, we've got lots to discuss.'

Rachid walked over to the kitchen counter, again with his back to us.

'Are we going to get that apartment?' Amina asked.

'Maybe, we'll talk about it later. Right now, we need to go and catch a train. Bye, Rachid. Take care,' I said.

I went to give him a hug, but he picked up the coffee pot at the last moment, so I simply stroked his back and left him to it.

When we arrived at Halifax station, the platform was busier than usual. A mixture of Leeds United fans, people going to the Stop Brexit march and those, like us, who were simply planning a bit of Saturday morning shopping but seemed to have picked the wrong weekend for it.

I guided Amina to the far end of the platform, sensing that she was uneasy. When the train pulled in, we got in the end carriage and sat directly behind the driver's cab.

I talked about the apartment, about the international school she was now enrolled in for January, anything to try to distract her from the noises in the rest of the carriage. She remained tight-lipped. Pensive, even. It occurred to me that something else might be troubling her.

'Is everything OK?' I asked.

'Yeah,' she said. 'When did Rachid ask to go on the march?'

'Yesterday. It was a last-minute thing, I think. He said some of his friends from college were going.'

She nodded but said nothing.

'You don't mind him going, do you?'

'No, of course not. I'm surprised, that's all.'

'I told your father he was going into college. I didn't want any more arguments between them, so please don't mention it in front of him.'

'OK.'

She put her AirPods in and stared out of the window the rest of the way.

I could sense the atmosphere at Leeds station as soon as we stepped off the train. It was completely different to a weekday rush-hour commute. We didn't usually travel by train at the weekends, as Bilal always drove us to the mosque, so I wondered at first if I simply wasn't used to the Saturday football crowd. But when I saw the numbers of police at the ticket barriers and beyond, I suspected that wasn't the case. A group of young men pushed past us, chanting something about 'Tommy' and punching the air with their fists. One was wrapped in a St George's flag, another a Union Jack. A third was carrying a placard that read, TO DELAY IS TO BETRAY.

'What's going on?' asked Amina, grabbing my arm.

'I don't know, I think there must be some kind of counter-demonstration planned too. People who want the Brexit bill to go through. But don't worry, there are lots of police here, we'll be fine.'

It wasn't us I was worried about. It was Rachid. I was aware he could be a target while he was on his march. I had no idea what type of people his friends from college were. Whether they were the sort to avoid trouble. I thought again of the girl with the BOLLOCKS TO BREXIT banner. I gripped Amina's arm tighter.

The noise levels rose again as we got to the ticket barriers. People were jostling us from behind. Two elderly women in front of us were dressed in blue and yellow and carrying a GRANDMAS AGAINST BREXIT banner between them. No sooner had I noticed them than a man pushed through from the side and shouted 'Fucking traitors!' in their faces. I looked around, expecting police officers to rush forward and arrest him, but they stayed where they were, holding the line, presumably wanting to maintain a fractious peace, rather than risk a full-blown riot.

I stopped in front of the two women.

'Are you OK?' I asked. 'I'm so sorry that happened to you. Can I help at all?'

The white-haired one shook her head.

'Thanks, pet, but we're fine. They breed us girls tough in Bradford.'

I managed a little smile. Amina pulled at my arm.

'Come on,' she said. 'We need to get out of here.'

It was no better outside, though. If anything, it was worse. Police had tried to cordon off an area between the rival protestors, but bottles were being thrown towards the mass of blue-and-yellow-clad Remainers.

'I don't think it's safe,' said Amina. 'We should go home.'

'That's not a good idea right now. The last thing I want to do is head back through that station. Let's hurry straight to Trinity. It'll be fine in there.'

Getting to the shopping centre was easier said than done. The police cordons meant we had to take a detour. Anger was spilling over all around us: shouting, chanting, police ordering people to get back. Amina clung on to me. By the time we made it inside Trinity she was physically shaking.

'I'm sorry,' I said, pulling her to me. 'I had no idea it would be like this. I wouldn't have brought you if I'd known.'

'I want to go home.'

'I know, but we can't do that at the moment. We need to wait it out. I'm going to call Rachid, tell him not to come in for the march.'

Amina had tears in her eyes but said nothing. I wasn't sure if I'd catch Rachid in time as he'd said he was getting the train an hour after us.

It rang for a long time before he answered. It didn't sound like he was on the train.

'Mum?'

'Don't come over to Leeds. There's some kind of far-right rally going on as well as your march. The police have set up cordons outside the station but it's not a safe place to be.'

'Are you OK? Where are you?'

'We're in Trinity. Amina's pretty shaken up but we're going to wait here until it's all over.'

There were more police sirens outside. The sound of smashing glass. Amina screamed. Rachid was silent for a moment before saying, 'I'll come and get you.'

'No, it's not safe.'

'I know, that's why I'm coming to get you. I'll call you when I get to Trinity. We can meet outside the Apple Store.'

'Are you sure?'

'I don't want anything happening to you. Dad's not around, so I'm going to be the one to get you home safely.'

'Thank you, sweetheart,' I said, my own voice trembling. 'Come out of the station through the side entrance. It will be safer for you.'

'OK. But don't leave Trinity. Go in a shop or somewhere for a coffee if you can. Somewhere out the way, just in case.'

I ended the call and put my arm around Amina.

'Your brother's on his way to get us,' I said. 'Everything's going to be fine.'

R & J

WhatsApp

I've tried to call you but there's no reply.
I've got to go to Leeds now. Mum and
Amina are hiding in Trinity because
there's some far-right rally kicking
off. I'm going to get them, bring them
home on the train, then catch the train
back. I'll dump my case in left luggage
at the station, so I can pick it up later
without them knowing. Don't wait for
me. We can't risk it. You catch the trains
as planned and get to Manchester. Go
straight to the apartment. I'll meet
you there later. Let me know when you
arrive. I'll be as quick as I can. Love you

10:22

29

DONNA

Neil arrived in the kitchen wearing his Leeds United shirt. Sometimes I counted my blessings that he'd never slept in it, though I suspected he would if they ever actually won anything.

'Bit early for that, isn't it?' I said, pointing to the shirt.

'I'm leaving not long after you. Always like to get a few pints in before a lunchtime kick-off.'

'You'll be bloody comatose before final whistle.'

'May not be a bad thing, way they're playing at moment.'

I smiled and shook my head.

'Did you tell Sam last night that he's not to leave this house?'

'He won't do if Jodie's here, will he?'

'Were you not paying attention? She's going on this Stop Brexit march in Leeds.'

'When are they going to give up, eh? Talk about bad losers.'

'Don't you dare say that to her. I don't want another row before I go.'

'And you think Sam'll stay in when there's no one in house?' asked Neil.

'I forgot it were early kick-off. I thought I'd be back before you went, didn't I? Hopefully, he'll sleep in, and Tyler's supposed to be coming over later, which might help. Someone to remind him he'll be grounded forever if he steps foot outside house.'

'We need to put one of those bloody trackers on him,' said Neil. 'Like they do for people on tag.'

I would have laughed, but the thought of that one day happening to Sam for real prevented it.

Jodie came in. She was still in her dressing gown but managed a 'Morning' and a hint of a smile, which was something before nine.

'Who's this then?' said Neil. 'Not my daughter up so early on a Saturday, surely?'

I braced myself as I waited for Jodie's inevitable reaction, but it didn't come. Instead, she spent a ridiculously long time rummaging in the fridge.

'You OK?' I asked when she finally turned around. She nodded, although I could have sworn there was a tear in her eye when she straightened back up.

'Have you seen my phone?' she asked.

'No. Didn't you have it in your room?'

'I came down last night for a glass of water. I thought I must have left it in here.'

'No. And we'd know if you had because it would have been beeping like mad as usual.'

'Have you tried ringing it?' asked Neil.

Jodie rolled her eyes.

'Battery's dead by now, isn't it?' she replied, in barely more than a whisper. 'It were already at five per cent when I went to bed.'

I looked at Neil, who shrugged. I knew he'd long given up trying to second-guess Jodie's moods.

'Right. Well, it'll turn up somewhere,' I said. 'Dad's going to footie soon, so if your brother surfaces before you go, make sure you tell him he's not to leave house, OK?'

'Like he ever listens to owt I say.'

'Please, Jodie. I've had enough grief to last me all year.'

'OK,' she said.

'We're thinking of getting one of those trackers put on him,' said Neil. 'So he can't go AWOL without us knowing.'

Jodie didn't laugh. She didn't say anything. She went over to the sink and filled the kettle.

'Got time for another brew before you go?' she asked.

''Fraid not,' I said, 'but you can owe me that one for later.'

'And me,' said Neil. 'I'll have it when I'm sobering up after United get another pasting.'

I waited for the comeback but she said nothing.

'Right, I'm off, then,' I said.

Jodie came over and gave me a hug.

'Are you sure you're not after summat?' I asked.

'No. You put up with a lot of crap. Sometimes, I reckon you must need a hug.'

*

I called Lorraine as soon as I got on the train. At least I knew where I was when Jodie was being an arsey cow.

'Have you heard from Jodie? Summat's up. She were right nice to me this morning.'

'She texted me last night. Said she loved me.'

'Does she usually do that?'

'Sometimes.'

I couldn't remember her ever doing that to me but decided to say nothing.

'If you hear owt from her, will you let me know?'

'Will do. Probably just her hormones, mind. You remember what it's like at that age.'

'Not as bad as they are at my age!' I said.

Lorraine laughed.

'I'll be leaving for work just after Sam gets here at ten.'

'Eh? He won't be up before midday. And he told me Tyler were coming round to ours later.'

'Oh God,' said Lorraine. 'Sounds like they couldn't get their story straight. They'd better not be up to summat.'

'Send Tyler round to ours when you go. Jodie'll let him in, and I'll let Sam know they're both to stay put. Hope it's a quiet day at work for you. Give me a buzz when you get back.'

'Will do.'

I sent Sam a message. He would get it when he got up, at least. If Tyler hadn't arrived by then.

When I got to Leeds station and saw all the police I was tempted to take a photo and send it to Jodie with a caption saying, 'They're ready for you here,' but I was worried she'd take it the wrong way, especially with her being in a weird mood this morning.

It was only as I went through the ticket barriers and caught sight of the lines of police outside that I started to get worried. It seemed a bit heavy-handed for a bunch of middle-aged people waving EU flags. But then I saw the crowd being held back by the police on the other side of the street and heard the chants of 'Traitors' and I realised why they were here in such large numbers.

I hurried round the corner and walked far enough that I could no longer hear their chanting before I rang Jodie. It went straight to voicemail and I facepalmed my forehead as I remembered her missing phone was dead.

Sam's phone went straight to voicemail too. I left a message asking him to tell Jodie not to go to the march because there was trouble in town, but even as I said it, I knew she wouldn't take a blind bit of notice of anything Sam told her. I texted Tyler too, though I didn't hold out much hope that she'd take any more notice of him.

There was nothing more I could do. If she did make it to Leeds, all I could hope was that she had the good sense to turn around as soon as she saw what was happening and go straight back home again. And that was when the penny dropped, and I realised it was not Jodie I should be worrying about. It was Sam.

30

JODIE

I still can't find my phone. I search the kitchen for the hundredth time, even checking the fridge in case I somehow had one of what Mum calls her 'menopause moments' last night. Not there. I shouldn't have come downstairs, but I desperately needed to talk to Rachid without anyone overhearing. And though I was pretty sure that Mum and Dad were asleep, I could see the light on under Sam's door when I checked.

So, I'd crept down to the kitchen to call Rachid. I'd blubbered down the phone and said I was in a complete state about today, and he'd told me he loved me, that it would all be fine, that he had everything under control. All the things you want to hear when you're crapping yourself about running away together the next day.

But now I can't find my phone, and I'm crapping myself all over again. I hate the thought that Rachid can't get in touch.

He might think I've got cold feet. That I'm going to leave him hanging on platform 16 at Leeds station, like someone jilted at the altar.

I'm not, though. I would never do that. I'm going to go through with it. Even though saying goodbye to Mum and Dad without crying killed me a bit inside. At least I'm not bothered about leaving Sam. I can't wait to get away from him. But I'm running away from home and moving in with my boyfriend and it's kind of doing my head in right now. I need to speak to Rachid. I need him to calm me down. I need to find my fucking phone.

I glance up at the kitchen clock. Shit, this is getting ridiculous. I'll have to leave without it soon. I can't miss this train, Rachid will think I'm not coming. I run up to my bedroom and stuff the last few things into my suitcase, before starting to lug it down the stairs. It is too heavy to carry, so I bump it down one step at a time, hoping the noise doesn't wake Sam.

I'm almost at the bottom when there is a knock at the door. It's probably the postie, and if I don't answer it, he might knock louder. I yank my case down the last few steps, leave it at the bottom of the stairs and open the door. Tyler is standing there. He's wearing a baseball cap and a Union Jack T-shirt under his bomber jacket. He looks like a complete prick.

'What you doing here?' I ask.

'Hanging out with Sam, if that's OK with you? And your mum says not to go to Leeds for march because there's trouble brewing.'

'Yeah, right. Nice try to stop me going. I can't see Remainers smashing up Briggate.'

He smirks, pushes past me into the hall, heads for the stairs and finds my case in the way.

'Going somewhere?' he asks.

Before I can answer, Sam calls out from the top of the stairs. He's already dressed in a dark hoodie and jeans.

'She's running away with her boyfriend, isn't she?'

I stare up at him, aware that I'm starting to shake. I don't understand how he's rumbled us.

'His name begins with R,' he continues. 'Let's guess what it is, shall we? Like in *Rumpelstiltskin*.'

'Fuck off, Sam.'

'Maybe Ryan or Rhys? No, that's not right, is it? Only we've met your boyfriend, haven't we? You remember him from her party, don't you, Tyler? Looked like more of a Raheem or a Raj to me. Am I getting closer yet? Only I know it begins with an R because I saw a notification come up on your phone last night saying he'll see you on train. Shouldn't have left it in bathroom, should you? You really ought to be more careful.'

He pulls my phone out of the pocket of his joggers.

'You bastard,' I say, lunging forward to try to grab it.

'I've been waiting to get you back for snooping around on my laptop,' he says, holding the phone up in the air.

'I were trying to save you from your fascist friends.'

Sam looks at Tyler. They both laugh and shake their heads.

'Don't know what you mean. Because our friends are ones

protesting in Leeds today against a bunch of bad losers who think they can overturn referendum result.'

The penny drops. That's where he and Tyler are going. That must be the trouble Mum was warning me about. And these lying little sods are going to join in and pretend to be hard men.

'You make me sick,' I say. 'Wait till Mum hears about this.'

'Only she won't, will she? Because you haven't got a phone and if you call her on landline, I'll tell her that you're about to run off with your immigrant boyfriend.'

I want to smash his fucking face in, but I know he's not worth it. And he's right, he's got me over a barrel, and the most important thing right now is that I catch this train.

'Give me my phone,' I say. 'I know battery's dead anyway, so I can't call her.'

He considers this for a second.

'Only if you get charger out of your case and give it to me first.'

'You're such a devious little shit.'

He smiles at me, like it's a badge of honour. I have no choice, I know that. I can at least buy a new charger when I get to Manchester. But I can't leave without my phone. I unzip the outside pocket of my case, get out the charger and throw it to him. He drops my phone to the bottom of the stairs.

'You leave house first. We'll follow behind. Don't try borrowing anyone's phone on train. You'll regret it if you go back on your word.'

I shake my head. Tyler opens the door. I pick up my case,

turn back and take one last look at Sam. Although I can't see the soulful eyes of the little brother I used to have, because they're lost somewhere behind a lens of hate. No words pass between us. But there's an unspoken understanding. I walk out of the house for the last time.

I run down the ramp at the station, the case clipping my heels, and stand in my usual spot to wait for the train. Rachid will be in the first carriage. That is our arrangement. As I struggle to get my breath back, I tell myself that I'll see him soon, and everything will be OK. We can still do this. In two hours, we'll be in Manchester, in our flat, and none of this will matter.

Sam and Tyler arrive on the platform. They stand at the opposite end to me, but I can see the smirks on their faces, hear them laughing at whatever they're looking at on their phones. I worry they'll start hassling Rachid on the train, but if they do, I'll tell the guard and get them thrown off. There's no way I'm going to allow them to spoil this for us.

I hear the vibrations of the train on the tracks. He's coming to me, and once he's here, everything will be fine. The train comes to a halt, with a grinding of brakes. I look for Rachid's face in the window, but I can't see it. I get on, dragging the case up behind me, and look around the carriage, searching for him, but he's not there. I know instantly that something's wrong. He's never let me down before. Maybe he panicked when I didn't reply to his messages. Thought I wasn't going to show. My hand reaches for my phone by habit, and I groan as

I remember it's dead. There are no charging points on these trains, even if I did have mine or could borrow someone else's.

I walk through to the next carriage just in case, although I know he won't be there. My case catches a man's foot, and he tuts at me and shakes his head. When I get to the end, I peer through the window to the final carriage. Sam and Tyler are there, fortunately with their backs to me, but there's no sign of Rachid.

The plan's unravelling. It's coming apart at the seams. I walk back to the first carriage and sit down. My outstretched leg is trembling, and I can't seem to stop it. Perhaps he had to change his plans, catch an earlier train because someone in his family twigged what was going on. He's probably been calling and messaging me all morning. I tell myself he'll be on platform 16. That we'll laugh about this later. That all I have to do is get to Leeds and he'll be there waiting for me. And tonight we'll be in Manchester together.

PART FIVE
19 October 2019

31

SYLVIE

Amina pressed up against me as we waited for Rachid outside the Apple Store. He'd messaged a few minutes ago to say he was on his way from the station. We were doing exactly as he'd asked. Staying safe, out of trouble. I just wished I knew that he was.

The police sirens had stopped now, but I suspected that was because every available officer in West Yorkshire was already here. We could still hear the shouting and chanting from outside. I'd told Amina to put her phone away because she'd been looking at photos and footage of the trouble online and it had only made her more anxious.

We'd made it into a few shops, but she hadn't wanted to try anything on, and it was clear that shopping was very much off the agenda.

I pulled her closer to me and smoothed her hair.

'He'll be here any minute,' I said.

'But then we've got to go out there.'

'We'll have Rachid with us this time. He'll look after us.'

I tried to sound more confident than I felt. The truth was, I didn't want to go out there any more than she did, but I was hoping things had calmed down enough for us to get to the station.

My phone beeped with a message from Rachid.

'*I can see you.*'

I looked up and spotted the top of his dark, gelled hair bobbing along behind a couple of teenage girls. Relief flooded through me. Amina started to cry.

'Hey, it's OK,' he said, giving her a hug as soon as he got to us.

'I didn't think you'd come,' she replied.

He looked at her long and hard. I had no idea what was passing between them, but I loved how much they cared for each other.

'Let's go,' he said, taking us both by the arm. 'We'll head for the side entrance to the station, that's the way I came.'

'Were they all still there?' asked Amina. 'Were they throwing things?'

'The police have kettled them in. They can't get to anyone.'

I wasn't sure if it was true, or he was simply saying that to get Amina out of the shopping centre. But all I could do was go with him and hope for the best.

As we stepped outside onto the street, we were met with a sea of blue and yellow, as the Stop Brexit marchers made their way down Boar Lane. There were whistles and a few drums, even the distant sound of a brass band at the head of the march. Amina relaxed her grip on my arm a little. I told myself this was going to be OK. I even allowed myself a little smile at some of the slogans on the banners. As we edged further towards the station, the noise levels rose again, but it was a different type of sound. Like a pack of big cats hissing and spitting, pacing the outer corners of a cage, desperately looking for a way to escape.

'Just keep your heads down and don't react to whatever they shout,' said Rachid, his own grip tightening on my arm as I saw the whites of Amina's knuckles on his.

As we approached the police lines around the protestors, we could see they were struggling to contain them as they tried to push forward. A second later there was a roar from the direction of the station as a new group of protestors came rushing out and started charging towards the back of the march.

'They're heading straight for us,' shrieked Amina.

'Come with me,' shouted Rachid. 'Don't let go.'

He broke into a run. I was glad I wasn't wearing heels, as I struggled to keep up with him. The people leading the charge were getting closer. They were young, probably no older than Rachid, but I could see the hate in their eyes. They were like fight dogs who'd been unleashed. We weren't going to get past them in time. I think Rachid realised that at the same moment I did. One of them, wearing a hoodie, lunged at us and spat in our direction.

'In here,' Rachid shouted, pushing us through the door of a fast-food takeaway on the corner.

The young woman behind the counter screamed.

'It's OK,' he said, holding his hands up in an attempt to reassure her, while keeping his back firmly against the door. 'We're getting out of their way. We didn't mean to scare you.'

We all held our breath as they ran past, the march itself clearly their intended target.

'Sorry,' I said to the woman behind the counter. 'We thought they were going to attack us.'

She nodded and gave a tentative smile. Amina blew out. Her hand was shaking in mine. I felt we should probably order something, but I suspected I wasn't the only one who had lost their appetite.

'Would you like a drink of anything?' I asked Rachid and Amina. They both shook their heads.

'I just want to get home,' said Amina.

'She's right,' said Rachid. 'If we leave it too long, it could get worse. And they'll all have to go home at some point. We don't want to be stuck on the train with them. Let's give it a few minutes then make a move.'

I stared at Rachid and wondered when he'd become a trust-worthy adult. Someone who I could rely on in a crisis.

'Thank you,' I said, stroking his arm. 'For all of this. Your father will be so proud of you.'

Rachid's expression suggested he wasn't bothered about Bilal's approval. But I was sure somewhere in there, the little boy who doted on his father was brimming with pride.

'Can't we call Dad and see if he can drive us home?' asked Amina.

'I'm afraid not, sweetheart,' I replied. 'He'll have put his phone on silent for the conference and he's due to speak any time now. He wouldn't be able to drop everything and take us home in time, even if we could get a message to him.'

Amina started fiddling with the tassels on her scarf.

'I can't wait to go to Paris,' she said. And, somewhat surprisingly, I found myself agreeing with her. Rachid said nothing, busily messaging someone on his phone. Finally, he looked up.

'If we go now, we can get straight on the next train home.'

I nodded and we all stood up, Amina visibly tensing as she did so. When we ventured back out onto the street, the atmosphere, while far from calm, appeared less volatile than before. The far-right protestors within the police kettle seemed a little more subdued, shouting and chanting, but no longer attempting to break through the police lines. The breakaway group from the station had presumably been rounded up.

We walked silently with our heads down, linking arms as we had before, until we got inside the station. Once through the ticket barriers, Rachid led us over the footbridge to the platform for the Halifax train. There were a good number of people waiting, some with Remain banners who appeared to have left the march early, perhaps because of the trouble, but fortunately no sign of those who had caused it.

The train doors opened, and we got in the last carriage, which seemed quietest. I sat next to Amina, Rachid opposite us. He pulled his phone out of his pocket and checked for messages again. He seemed quieter now, distracted. Perhaps he was simply coming down from the adrenaline rush of earlier.

We waited for what seemed like ages. More people were getting into the carriage all the time, most of them groups of men. The noise levels rose, and I started to feel uneasy again. I could tell from the way she squeezed my arm that Amina did too. Just before the doors closed, three middle-aged men jumped into the carriage. The smell of alcohol came with them, as did a string of obscenities.

'Fucking Remainer scum,' said the biggest, bald-headed one. 'They're trying to overturn result, and we're ones who get kettled.'

I caught Rachid's eye. He had his back to them but had heard what was said. So had half the carriage, thanks to the man's booming voice. Rachid put his finger to his lips before popping his AirPods in. I nodded and whispered to Amina to listen to some music too, in the hope it would stop her hearing anything else they said.

She didn't, though. Just sat there holding tightly on to my arm as the train pulled away.

R & J

WhatsApp

Jodie, where are you? I'm worried something's happened. It's all kicking off in Leeds. We had to run away from a bunch of Fascists. One of them spat at us. I'm on the train now with my mum and sister. We were all shit scared. As soon as I get them home, I'll say I've got to go to college to work on the show. I'll have to go back to Leeds station to get my case first, but I'll jump straight on the next train to Manchester. Let me know as soon as you get in the apartment. If you're worried about anything, call me and we can talk about it. I'm hoping it's just a problem with your phone. Call or message me as soon as you see this. Love you   13:03

32

DONNA

I kept trying Sam whenever I had a free moment at work that morning. I suspected he'd either turned his phone off or was screening my calls. Neil was right, we should have got a bloody tag on him. I had no doubt he'd gone to the protest. That would explain why he and Tyler had told me and Lorraine different stories about what was happening. He'd taken me for a fool. And I'd played the part so bloody well.

I couldn't get out of the building fast enough when my shift was over. It took a moment for my eyes to adjust to the bright sunlight. The Headrow was normally packed with shoppers at this time, but when I turned the corner, it seemed far quieter than usual. I headed straight through town to the station, deciding against popping to the shops for the bits and pieces I'd been intending to pick up on my way home. As I turned onto Boar Street, I saw the police were still there in large numbers, some with helmets and riot shields. They appeared to be escorting some of the protestors towards the main entrance to the station. I prayed that Jodie had got herself home before this turned ugly. And that if Sam and Tyler were here, they hadn't been stupid enough to get themselves into trouble.

I took a detour and went into the station through the side entrance. It seemed calmer inside, but there were still pockets of men shouting and chanting. I checked the departure board and hurried over the footbridge to the Halifax train, running onto it just before three middle-aged men, who jumped on, breathing heavily but still shouting their mouths off. They stank of booze too. I decided to take a seat at the far end of the carriage away from them.

The train set off. The men, who were standing even though there were seats available, were saying something about immigrants ruining our country. I tried to ignore them and messaged Jodie again, just in case. I'd left Sam so many messages I didn't bother adding to the tally, as he was clearly ignoring them. I texted Lorraine instead, asking her to let me know if she heard from either of them. I didn't want to worry her by saying why. There was no immediate reply, and knowing how busy Saturday afternoons in A&E were usually, I didn't expect to get one before she'd finished her shift.

As we approached Bradford Interchange, the three men moved nearer to a family at their end of the carriage. I could see that the woman and daughter, who had slightly darker skin than her mother and a mass of brown curls, looked uncomfortable. The young man opposite them, who had his back to me, leant closer to them and said something, before they all looked down at their phones. The rest of the carriage did the same, clearly deciding it was safest not to get involved. But the men's voices became louder. I picked out odd words: 'home', 'jobs', 'country'. It wasn't hard to fill in the gaps.

When the doors opened at Bradford, I heard them shout out, 'Aren't you getting off here? Isn't this where you lot all live? Fucking Mosque City.'

I could see the girl clinging on to her mum's arm. She looked to be on the verge of tears. I shifted uncomfortably in my seat. As the train set off again, one of the men banged his hand against the Perspex partition next to the doors. The girl jumped. Someone would say something in a minute. There were plenty of blokes keeping their heads down. Younger guys, who could probably take them on with much more success than I could. I saw the lad opposite them go to stand up, but his mother shook her head and gestured to him to sit down again.

The train started to slow down. We would be pulling into Low Moor station in a minute. I looked around to see if there were any sign of the guard coming through to open the doors from our carriage, but there wasn't. Maybe the family would get off here too, although, as the men were standing in their way, I realised they might not think it was an option.

I waited until the last possible moment to stand up and move towards the doors. As I did so, my eyes met the woman's. She had her arm around her daughter, whose face was buried in her chest. I offered what I hoped was a sympathetic smile. It was pathetic, I knew that. But in the circumstances, I didn't see how I could do anything else. She looked back down at her lap and clasped her daughter's hand tighter. I turned away, pressed the button to open the doors, and stepped off the train.

33

RACHID

I can't do this much longer. Just sit here and let these fucking idiots insult Mum and Amina. Mum's telling me to ignore them, she keeps pushing me down and whispering to sit tight and say nothing until we get off at Halifax. And Amina's looking at me with eyes begging me not to say anything. I'm doing it because it's what they want, but I hate myself for staying silent. Dad wouldn't be allowing them to get away with this. He would have stood up to them, challenged what they're saying, got other people to back him. Because when he stands up and starts talking, people listen.

But I'm nothing compared to him. I don't command respect when I walk into a room. Maybe that's why everyone else in this carriage is just sitting here, minding their own business, pretending this isn't happening, while these twats spill out all this crap. They may think they're being funny, but I've heard every insult twenty times before. I've got my music on to try to drown it out, but it isn't working. Prince is singing 'Alphabet Street' and I'm wondering if these guys even know their alphabet because we're talking seriously impaired intellects here.

The smallest one puts his head down next to mine to try to hear what I'm playing on my AirPods.

'He's listening to fucking Prince,' he shouts to the others. 'They won't listen to white guys' music, see. We're not good enough for them.'

'They always look after their own,' the bald guy says. 'Cover up for their own too. All operating in gangs, aren't they? Like they do round here. Police turn a blind eye because they don't want to be accused of being racist.'

I glance up and catch Mum's eye. She mouths 'Leave it,' to me again. A second later her phone rings. She looks to see who's calling, then answers it. She holds the phone tight against her ear and talks quietly, putting her other hand up to try to muffle her voice. I know instantly that it must be Grand-mère; she wouldn't have taken the call unless she thought it was important. But Grand-mère obviously can't hear her because Mum is having to speak louder. The guys stop talking for a moment. They hear her speaking in French. We are done for.

The biggest one sticks his head around the screen towards her.

'We speak English here, love. If you can't speak our language, you ought to go home.'

Amina starts to cry. I lean over and take her hand, gesture to Mum to end the call, but she has a worried look on her face and shakes her head. Something must have happened to Grand-mère. Maybe she's had another fall.

I turn around and speak to them for the first time.

'She's talking to my grandmother, who's unwell. She lives in Paris, that's why she's talking French.'

The guy bends down towards me before responding.

'Well, we don't like hearing foreign languages on our trains. Because they're English trains, aren't they? For English people. So, I suggest that if you aren't English, you get her to shut the fuck up and get off.'

The train goes deathly quiet. I wait for another passenger to say something. To stand up and step forward to defend us. There's only silence. Eyes fixed on phones. Everyone telling themselves it's not them being attacked, so they don't need to get involved.

I think of Dad and what he would do in this situation. I'm going to make him proud. I'm not going to let them abuse my family like this. I stand up.

Amina shouts, 'No!' But I'm not listening any more. I'm staring into the eyes of a man who I now see has a small swastika tattoo on his neck.

'I'm English and so is my sister. We were born here just like you and we have every right to travel on this train without being abused, as does my mum.'

'Well, you don't look English, do you? Your dad's clearly not English, if your French whore mother even knows who he is.'

I feel everything inside me rising. I want to smash his face in so hard, but I'm not going to give in to it.

'Rachid, leave him.' It's Mum's voice from behind me. She's off the phone.

'So, you do speak English when it suits you,' says Swastika Man.

'Leave my son alone,' says Mum.

'Why don't you fuck off home where you belong and stop telling me what to do?'

He lunges towards Mum. I put my arms out to stop him. Amina screams. A second later the other two have joined in and thrown me to the floor. The first boot goes between my legs. I wince but don't cry out. They've done this before, I'm sure of that. Other people are yelling at them to stop now but it's too late. The boot goes into my side this time. Harder. The next one to my face. I taste warm liquid in my mouth. Hear Mum and Amina screaming at them to stop. I'm aware of someone trying to pull one of them off. It's Mum's hand on an arm I see. She's going to get hurt, I can't let them hurt her. I manage to kick out to distract them. The kicks rain in harder on me. The pain's starting to affect my vision. Or maybe it's the blood, it's hard to tell. I think of Jodie waiting at Leeds station for me. Or sitting in our apartment wondering where I am. Who will tell her? She'll think I wasn't going to come. She'll think I don't love her, and I do. I love her more than life itself. I try to say her name but only blood dribbles out of my mouth, no words. I'm slipping in and out of consciousness now. The screams are interrupted with silences. I'm vaguely aware of the train slowing down and then stopping with a jolt. The kicks stop. The boots are gone. It's just Mum kneeling down next to me, crying my name over and over again. And then nothing.

34

SYLVIE

I lay on top of him, unable to bear to look at the bloodied face of my boy. He was still breathing, the rise and fall of his chest providing my only source of comfort. Amina was pressed up against me, trembling like a frightened animal. I had let my children down so badly. And over in Paris in a hospital bed lay Maman, who had rung to tell me she had fallen and broken her hip. Only I had to end the call to try to stop her grandson being attacked.

His chest was still rising and falling, though. Rising and falling. There were voices around me. Someone telling me help was on its way, that everything was going to be OK. I wondered how they could think that, when I knew already that nothing would ever be OK again.

My phone rang. It would be Maman calling back. She had heard enough shouting to be worried. I didn't answer it because I couldn't bear to remove myself from Rachid. Or to tell her what had happened.

I was vaguely aware of people being told to leave the train. Some of them were crying too. I didn't know why, because it wasn't their son and they'd chosen to stay silent when I'd needed them to save mine.

Someone knelt at my side and spoke into my ear. He said his name was Paul, he was a paramedic, and he was here to help. He asked me my name and who was lying beneath me.

'I'm Sylvie, this is my son, Rachid,' I whispered.

He told me we were safe now; the police were here and he needed to move me so he could tend to Rachid. I lifted my head. The blood was everywhere; all down my mustard-yellow jacket and seeping from Rachid's head across the carriage floor.

An arm stretched around my back and lifted me up, supporting me when my knees buckled. Amina clung to me, still not daring to even raise her head. The need to keep her safe and protect her was overwhelming. I wished I had a pouch she could climb into. Where she could crawl inside and be shielded from everything that was bad in the world. It was too late for that, though. All I could do was let her cling to me and tell her not to open her eyes.

'Is he dead?' she sobbed faintly.

'No, sweetheart,' I said. 'He's still breathing.'

The arm supporting me lowered me onto a train seat with Amina still attached. A woman's face appeared in front of me.

'Hello, my name's Ghazala, I'm going to check you over, while my colleague attends your son,' she said softly.

She asked Amina's name and whether either of us had been injured at all or were in pain, before she said she needed to remove my jacket. I realised that she was looking to see if any of the blood was mine. She let Amina stay clinging to me as she checked her over. Amina whimpered but offered no resistance.

'That's good. No physical injuries,' she said.

I hated myself for that. I should have fought them with my bare hands. I should have been battered and bruised and have teeth missing and be covered in my own blood, like Rachid was. It was my fault. I was the one who'd been speaking French. Rachid was simply defending me. I'd tried to pull them off, but I hadn't been strong enough. I'd cried and shouted for help, but no one had come to our aid. I wished Bilal had been here. If Bilal hadn't gone to the conference, this would never have happened.

Other people got on the train. I heard their radios before I heard the first of their voices next to me. I looked up to see a young man, not much older than Rachid. I couldn't help feeling that he shouldn't have to be doing this. I should have stopped it. Should have got my family off the train at Bradford when we had the chance, instead of being too scared to try to get past the men.

He said his name was PC Sawyer, that he was sorry about what had happened and that they would do everything they could to help and to catch those responsible.

I nodded, still unable to sort my thoughts into coherent sentences.

'We're getting the CCTV evidence from the train and their descriptions will be sent out to my colleagues,' he said. I frowned as I tried to recall anything distinctive about them, wishing now that I had paid more attention instead of trying to avoid looking at them.

'The main one had a swastika tattoo on his neck.'

It was Amina's voice. The police officer appeared as surprised as I was. Amina still didn't open her eyes, but she spoke clearly and deliberately.

'The second was shorter than the other two, he had a black baseball cap on and wore a denim jacket with a St George's Cross on the back. The third one was wearing a grey Nike hoodie and had a scar on his forehead.'

'Thank you,' said the policeman, busily taking notes. 'Did they have any weapons at all? A knife?'

I hadn't even thought of that. I had only seen their boots. I turned to the paramedic still tending Rachid on the floor.

'They didn't stab him, did they? They didn't use a knife?'

'No knife wounds,' he replied.

The relief ran through me, although it was short-lived.

'Is he going to survive?' I asked.

'We'll do everything we can. I'm going to get him to hospital straight away now.'

'Can we come with him?'

He looked at the police officer, gave a little shake of his head.

'Not in the ambulance,' said PC Sawyer, 'but I'll drive you and we can follow it to the hospital, while I ask a few more questions on the way. My colleagues will stay here at the crime scene.'

That's what this was now. A crime scene. I was vaguely aware of more police officers arriving on the platform. I looked down at the blood on the floor. Oddly, I didn't want to leave it. It was like leaving a part of my son behind. But I knew we had to. Because the only thing that mattered now was that he survived.

I watched as the paramedics placed a neck collar on Rachid and slid him gently onto a spinal board to carry him off the train, before transferring him onto a waiting stretcher. PC Sawyer helped us to our feet, and we followed my son, who'd walked onto this train but was leaving the station on a stretcher. I'd forgotten for a moment where we even were until I saw the Halifax sign. Amina frowned as we stepped onto the empty platform.

'What happened to all the people?' she asked.

'They had to leave the train,' I replied. 'I think they've closed the station.'

'But how will they get home?'

'I don't know.'

I couldn't think about anyone else. All I cared about was whether my son would ever come home.

R & J

WhatsApp

I'm so sorry, I've only just got your messages. Where are you? Please let me know you're all OK. I'm worried about you. I'm at the apartment in Manchester. Sam took my phone last night and the battery was dead this morning. He saw your message so he knew we were going to run away. He made me give him my charger before he gave the phone back to me, which is why I couldn't call. I had to buy a charger when I got here and I've just seen your messages and I'm so sorry about what happened to you in Leeds. Sam and Tyler went to it. Fuck knows what they did. And now I'm crapping myself again that everything's ruined and you're not coming. Please call me. Love you ♡

13:24

35

DONNA

I thought about that woman every step of the way home. How I'd let her down. It was like she'd looked at me, mother to mother, and yet I'd walked straight past, not said a word. Not even checked if she and her family wanted to get off the train with me. I was sure I recognised her, that I'd seen her on the train in the mornings. We'd never spoken, but I must have made the same journey as her countless times. Maybe if she'd said something to me, asked me for help, I would have stepped up. But I wasn't even sure about that.

She'd be OK. Someone would have stopped it. There were plenty of blokes in the carriage who would have intervened if things got heavy. Or the guard would have come along and chucked the yobs off at Halifax. But I still felt bad for not having said something. And I still couldn't get that image of her and her daughter clinging to each other out of my mind.

My phone rang just as I got to the front door. I rummaged in my bag and pulled it out, desperately hoping it was Jodie. It was Sam.

'Mum, I've been arrested.'

I stood there, my head not wanting to believe what I had just heard, but at the same time I knew straight away that it was true and how it had happened. He'd probably been part of that mob I'd seen earlier. My best hope was that he'd given a mouthful to a copper, but I knew it could be far worse than that.

'What the hell have you done?'

'I didn't do owt but they're doing me for threatening behaviour and resisting arrest. Me and Tyler.'

I groaned and looked skywards, shaking my head. Lorraine was going to be furious. This was what I'd been dreading. This was why we should have been harder on him before. Much harder.

'Jesus, Sam. You weren't supposed to leave the house.'

'Sorry.'

'You went to that Brexit thing, didn't you?'

'Did Jodie tell you?'

'No, she didn't. I saw it all kicking off when I came home from work.'

'We didn't hurt anyone or smash owt.'

'Oh, well, that's all right, then.'

He chose to ignore my sarcasm.

'Police said you have to come down station so they can interview us. Tyler can't get hold of Lorraine.'

'No. That's because she's looking after people who get hurt by idiots like you.'

'I said we didn't hurt anyone.'

I sighed.

'Which police station?'

'Elland Road.'

The fact that he was so close to Neil and yet I was the one having to deal with it was not lost on me.

'Why didn't you ring Dad?'

'He's at game, isn't he?'

'Right,' I said, trying to compose myself. 'I'll try to get hold of your father and get him to come over but if I can't, I'll set off back to Leeds now, though it'll take me a while. Keep your mouth shut and behave until I get there.'

I ended the call and screwed up my face. This was basically my lot. Sorting out the mess my family caused. I called Neil. He didn't answer. I checked my watch. They'd be in the second half now. Maybe he couldn't hear me above the crowd. I texted him, asking him to call me urgently. I didn't tell him what had happened because I had a feeling he might not ring back if he knew. He could choose to avoid trouble. I couldn't.

I waited a moment, willing the phone to ring. Nothing. I didn't even bother going indoors, simply turned on my heel and marched back down the road, my fury propelling me all the way to the station.

When I got there, I caught the tail end of an announcement about a train being cancelled.

'Was that ours?' I asked a woman on the Leeds platform.

'No. Manchester train. Summat about long delays due to a train stuck at Halifax.'

I thanked her, relieved that I only had a fifteen-minute wait.

Lorraine's phone went straight to voicemail. I didn't want to freak her out if she couldn't ring me, so I simply asked her to call me as soon as she could.

I tried Jodie again, but still no answer. I sighed and put my phone back in my bag. They always said family would be there for you when you needed them. Except for mine, it seemed.

The last thing I wanted to be doing was going back into Leeds, after what had happened earlier. The station was still packed with police. One of them nodded at me as I passed. He wouldn't be doing that if he knew that my son was one of those who had been arrested. I ought to have a sign over my head, MOTHER OF THE TEENAGE HOOLIGAN, that should sort it.

I went out the front to get a cab, not wanting to keep the police waiting any longer than I already had. When I told the driver where I wanted to go, he seemed to look at me differently. I wanted to tell him we weren't the sort of family who were in and out of police stations. At least, we hadn't been until now.

The woman behind the desk at Elland Road greeted me with the air of someone who'd already had a long day.

'Hello, my son Sam Cuthbert is in custody here. He said I needed to come in. He's only fifteen.'

I couldn't work out if her expression were one of pity or disapproval. Either way, it wasn't good.

'Right, if you could take a seat. I'll get someone for you.'

'Thanks. His cousin Tyler Parkinson is here as well. His mum can't come because she's working. He's fifteen too.'

The look was definitely a disapproving one this time. I couldn't say I blamed her. She probably thought we were the sort of family who let our kids run riot and were used to picking them up from police stations.

'They've never been in trouble before,' I added, by way of a defence. This wasn't strictly true, of course. They'd been in trouble plenty of times at school and with us, but I was trying to point out the lack of police involvement.

She nodded at me without replying and picked up her phone. A few minutes later a policeman was standing in front of me, asking me to follow him to the juvenile detention rooms where Sam and Tyler were being held separately. He said very little on the way. Only that a duty solicitor would also be present, and I was allowed to speak during the interview, but not answer questions on his behalf.

I was shown into the first room. Sam was sitting there with his head down, looking for all the world like he was waiting outside the head teacher's office for a good dressing-down. Although this time it was much more serious. And when he lifted his head, there was none of the usual cockiness. He looked genuinely scared. His eyes were moist with tears. And instead of reading him the riot act, as I'd intended to, I went over and gave him a hug. Admittedly, there was an unsaid element of 'I'll deal with you when we get home' about it. But right now, he needed some support. And family, however much they did my head in at times, always came first.

36

JODIE

He's still not answering. I've lost count of how many times I've called. All I can think is that his mum has stopped him going back into Leeds. Has somehow realised what he was up to. Or maybe he broke down and told them. Maybe he couldn't go through with it. Maybe I'm the one who's been jilted.

I'm sitting on the leather sofa in the apartment. I don't think I've even seen a leather sofa in real life, let alone sat on one. The whole place is dead swanky. But I can't enjoy it without Rachid being here. Without him I'm just a girl, sitting in an Airbnb, waiting for a guy who probably isn't going to show up.

I shouldn't even be surprised. Why would the son of a hospital consultant and a university lecturer want to run away with me? I come from the sort of family who think dishing out sausage rolls and pasties is better than getting a degree.

The sort of family who voted Brexit because they were stupid enough to think foreigners must be to blame for their shitty little lives. The sort of family who raise teenage lads who go to far-right protests because they think immigrants have ruined their country. Great catch I am.

I look down at my phone, willing it to ring. For it to be Rachid telling me none of that is true and the past seven weeks have meant as much to him as they have to me. I know deep down this is true. He's told me so many times. But I need him to tell me now so I can stop torturing myself. I stand up and pace the room, my phone in my hand. I go through to the bedroom. The bedroom where I'm supposed to be spending the night with Rachid for the first time. I brought candles with me because I wanted to make it perfect. I wanted it to be the start of our lives together. And for it to feel grown-up and everything first nights together should be. It wasn't even the sex I was looking forward to the most. It was waking up with him tomorrow morning. Him holding me in his arms. Us not having to worry about being disturbed or found out or anything like that.

I start as my phone rings, but it's Mum again and I don't answer. She'll be home from work now and wondering where I am. I told her the march would go on for a long time, that I didn't know what time I'd be back, but she's a worrier. Always has been. I flick through to the news sites and see photos and videos of the trouble. The trouble that my twat of a brother were involved in. It looks bad. Much worse than I'd expected. There are police with riot shields and helmets and lots of angry, screaming men who really don't know what they're angry about.

I hate to think of Rachid and his family having to deal with all that. Of his mum and sister being so scared they called him. I love that he went to help them almost as much as I hate the fact that my brother and cousin were part of it. But they must be home by now. He must be on his way to me. There'll be a reason why he can't get in touch. Like there was a reason why I couldn't. I curl up in the centre of the bed, hugging my knees to me. Telling myself over and over again that he's on his way.

37

SYLVIE

There was an emergency team waiting to greet Rachid when he got to A&E. It was like watching a scene from a hospital drama, except it was my son on that trolley. My son whose face was barely recognisable. My son being hooked up to various monitors as doctors and nurses surrounded him.

I stood there, feeling utterly helpless. I was medically trained. I should have been able to do this. I should have been able to save my own son. But bringing new life into the world involved an entirely different skill set to keeping a grown life in it. All I could do was stand there feeling inadequate. Feeling like I'd failed Rachid and unable to countenance the thought that I might never get the chance to make it up to him.

Amina still clung to me, her eyes heavy with worry. I had failed her too, of course. She should never have had to witness what she had that afternoon. She was fifteen. She was his little sister. It was all so senseless.

'He's in good hands now,' I whispered to her. 'They'll do everything they can.' I was trying to convince myself as much as her.

PC Sawyer guided me to the reception desk where a woman apologised for the fact that she needed to ask me some questions about Rachid. Name, date of birth, next of kin, that sort of thing. Somehow, I managed to answer them all while on autopilot. When they had everything they needed, a nurse showed us to a curtained-off area of A&E where we could wait.

'Is he going to be OK?' I asked.

'We're doing everything we can,' she replied with a sympathetic smile. I knew she was doing the same thing I had in my response to Amina. Trying not to dash our hopes, while at the same time preparing us for the worst.

It was only after she left that I registered the fact that PC Sawyer was still here with us. He poked his head around the curtain and asked if he could come in. I nodded.

'Just so you know, Rachid's clothes and personal possessions have been handed over to us by the hospital. They're being sent on to our forensic team. I'm afraid we can't let you have them back until our investigations are complete.'

I hated to think that this was what it was now. An investigation. It would have a crime number attached to it. Detectives working on it. I was glad of that, of course. But also sad that Rachid didn't seem to be my son any more. That I had no say over what happened to him and his things.

'What about his phone?' asked Amina.

'That too, I'm afraid.'

'But someone might be trying to call him.'

I looked at her, not understanding why she was so bothered about his phone.

'We do have to keep hold of it for now, because it could be needed for evidence. Is there anyone you need to contact?'

'My husband,' I said, realising belatedly that I'd been so caught up in it all that I still hadn't called Bilal. 'I need to let my husband know but he's at a conference and his phone is switched off.'

'Where's the conference? We can get a message to him to call you.'

'It's at the Crowne Plaza Hotel in Leeds. His name is Bilal Mastour. It's a medical thing. Eye-related. I can't remember the name of it.'

'That's OK. We'll sort it. Can I get you both a drink of anything?'

'No thanks,' I said, seeing Amina shaking her head.

He left and a few minutes later a doctor came in to see us. He was silver-haired and wore thick-rimmed glasses. He also wore the expression of a man who had come to deliver bad news.

'Hello, I'm Dr Deakin. I'm afraid your son's critically ill. We've had to put him in an induced coma and we're taking him for a CT scan now. We're concerned he may have a fractured skull and possibly have suffered internal bleeding or brain swelling. As soon as we have the results, we can decide on the next step, but he may well need emergency surgery.'

I opened my mouth to say something but could only manage what sounded like a cross between a yelp and a howl of despair. Amina buried her head in my chest and started crying again. I was losing him. Losing my firstborn child. And there was nothing I could do about it.

The doctor appeared genuinely upset. I thought about the times Bilal had come home and said he'd been unable to save or restore someone's sight. How he had seen it as a personal failing on his part. I wondered if this doctor would be going home tonight and telling his wife about the young man he hadn't been able to save. The grief-stricken family he hadn't been able to comfort.

'I'm sorry not to have better news,' he said. 'I'll come back to speak to you as soon as we have the results.' He hurried away, no doubt keen to return to a patient, however ill they were, rather than have to deal with the relatives.

I wanted so much to run after him. To beat down the door to be with Rachid. Hold his hand. Tell him I loved him, and I was so, so sorry. But I couldn't do that. He didn't belong to me any more. His body belonged to the hospital and his clothes and possessions to the police. To all intents and purposes, it felt like I had lost my son already.

Bilal called about five minutes later. I answered, already hating myself for what I was about to do to him, wishing I could sugar-coat the pill in some way. But he was a consultant. He knew how these things worked. The only thing I could do was tell him the truth, however unpalatable it was.

'Hi,' I said, before I choked and gulped back tears. I could hear Bilal's voice saying my name, asking what had happened and if we were all OK. It was a few moments before I could reply.

'Rachid was attacked on the train. He's critically ill in hospital with head injuries. They've put him in an induced coma.'

I started sobbing. There was something about saying it out loud that made it irrefutably real.

There was a pause, a long one, before Bilal replied in a barely audible voice.

'Do they think he's going to survive?'

'They can't say. They're doing a scan now, but they might need to operate. We're at Calderdale Royal. Please come straight away. Amina's with me. We need you.'

There was no hesitation on Bilal's part this time.

'I'm on my way.'

The doctor returned with the results of the scan before Bilal arrived. I knew from his face that it was not good news.

'I'm afraid your son has suffered a basal skull fracture. There is also evidence of bleeding on the brain which is causing a rapid increase of the pressure inside his head. We're going to have to operate to try to relieve that pressure. We don't know if it will be successful, but we do know that without it he won't survive.'

He paused as if he was waiting for me to grant permission, although I knew they would go ahead and do it anyway, even without my blessing. It wasn't really a choice, but an uncomfortable truth.

'OK,' I whispered eventually, more to make him feel better than anything. Amina appeared to have run out of tears and simply stared into the distance. He at least did me the courtesy of looking me in the eye as he spoke.

'We'll do everything we can. I'll be back as soon as he's out of surgery.'

I watched him walk away, aggrieved that other people got to be with my son and yet I wasn't allowed. What I wanted more than anything was to be with Rachid. To lay myself across him, as I had after the attack. To replicate the skin-to-skin contact with him I'd had after his birth, when the midwife had put him on my chest and the wonder of his touch had left me speechless and in tears. Bilal had sat next to me, had stroked my hair, marvelled at the long fingers that had gripped me so tightly, been consumed by all the hopes and dreams he had for him. But he had also known that he could not compete with my new love. That the bond between mother and child was stronger than anything we had together as a couple. Because it was undemanding. Unconditional. Unbreakable.

I heard Bilal's footsteps approaching before PC Sawyer pulled back the curtain. I had always been able to recognise them, in the way some people know the sound of their husband's car as it pulls up outside. Perhaps it was the authority in his step, or the sense of stature his footsteps relayed. But when I saw Bilal standing there, it was hard to think it was the same man. The confidence, the authority, appeared to have drained out of the very soles of his shoes. Leaving only a weakened frame, struggling to support the heavy load.

Amina stood up and threw herself straight at him, as if the force would somehow get the hurt and fury from her system. He wrapped his arms tightly around her. Bent to kiss her forehead, then opened his arms to embrace me as well, trying to absorb all our pain, while it was clear he was saturated in his own.

'How is he?' he asked.

'They're operating on him now. The doctor said he has a basal skull fracture and bleeding on the brain.'

Bilal nodded. The look he gave me underpinned the gravity of the situation.

'What happened?' he asked.

'There was a far-right rally in Leeds because of the Stop Brexit march. It got nasty. Amina and I were scared. I called Rachid and he came to get us. Only a few of them were on the train home and started abusing us. Then Maman phoned from hospital, she'd fallen and fractured her hip, so I spoke to her in French . . .' My voice trailed off. I didn't need to explain the rest to Bilal.

'Did they catch the men who did it?'

'I don't know. They ran off at Halifax. We gave them a description. Or rather Amina did. She remembered everything. She was so good. And Rachid was so good defending us. You'd have been proud of him.'

Bilal held us both tightly again. I could feel the pride he had in his children. I wished Rachid could have felt it too.

'I need to call Maman back, now you're here,' I said. 'She'll be worried sick. She's been texting me asking what's going on.'

I left Amina being comforted by Bilal and stepped outside the curtained area. PC Sawyer was standing outside, with a woman in a suit. He looked at me, as if unsure what to say.

'Sorry to bother you at what I know is a difficult time,' he said. 'This is DC Sarah Abraham from the investigation team. She's just got a couple of questions she'd like to ask you, if that's OK?'

'Fine,' I said. 'Although I'm not sure what help I'll be.'

DC Abraham guided me over to a small room off the nearby corridor.

'I appreciate this is an incredibly difficult time for you,' she said. 'But we need to clarify a few things and bring you up to date on our investigation. The descriptions you gave have been a huge help. We've got a couple of leads already and we're gathering CCTV from the train and Halifax station. Can you confirm that the men who attacked your son got on the train at Leeds?'

'Yes,' I replied. 'They jumped into our carriage just before the train left.'

'OK, and you all got on the train together at Leeds, but your son had arrived on a separate train to you, is that right?'

'Yes. I came over earlier with my daughter. We didn't know there was going to be trouble. We were scared so we made our way to Trinity as quickly as possible, and I called my son. He said he'd come over and get us home safely.'

'I see. And can I ask if he brought an item of luggage with him?'

'Sorry?'

'There was a slip to collect an item of left luggage from Leeds station in his jacket pocket. I wondered if you knew what it was and whether you have any objections to us collecting it?'

I frowned at her. I had no idea what she was talking about. She must be mistaken, surely?

'I don't know about any luggage,' I said. 'Are you sure it was his?'

She nodded.

'It's got his name on the slip and we've got CCTV of him dropping it off. A large case of some kind.'

I suddenly wondered what she was getting at. What the agenda was here. A young Muslim man leaving a large case at a station while a far-right rally was taking place.

'It's not what you think,' I said. 'He wasn't involved in anything like that. He hated any form of violence.'

DC Abraham held up her hand and shook her head.

'It's OK,' she said. 'I'm not suggesting anything of the kind. It's simply that we'd like to collect it, so we can rule it out as having any part in the investigation.'

'That's fine, then,' I said, still thinking the whole thing would turn out to be a mistake.

'And your son's phone,' she continued. 'We have to check it in case there may have been any communication with your son from those involved in the attack. He hasn't suffered with any malicious calls or online abuse that you're aware of?'

'No.'

'One number has made repeated calls to him today. Left lots of messages about his whereabouts. It comes up as J on his phone. Does he have a girlfriend at all? Only I thought you might want to get in touch with her to let her know. And it may be that we will need to speak to her in due course.'

I stared at her. She didn't know my son at all. Had no idea of the sort of young man he was. Even if he had been in a relationship, I didn't see why that should have anything at all to do with the investigation.

'No,' I said. 'He hasn't got a girlfriend. We don't need to contact anyone else. All we want you to do it to catch his attackers. Do you understand that?'

'Of course,' she said, standing up and opening the door. 'Please be assured that we're doing everything we can.'

I shook my head. Everybody said they were doing everything they could. But when we'd needed people's help, everybody had done nothing. The woman who left the train at Low Moor. All those who sat silently while we were abused, presumably because they didn't want to get involved. Although we, of course, had no choice in the matter.

The detective hurried off towards the exit and I found a quiet area in the corridor to make the call to Maman. She listened, mostly silently, occasionally letting out little sobs and gasps. She said she was sorry, over and over again. I didn't tell her that it had been me speaking to her in French that had escalated things. Instead, I promised to let her know as soon as there was any news and told her to concentrate on getting better herself. She wouldn't, of course. Under normal circumstances, I would be on my way to Paris to visit her now. She would be the family member we were worrying about. But these weren't normal circumstances. Because my son was fighting for his life in an operating theatre. And the bond between us ran so deep that I felt every cut as if it was my own flesh. The blood lost was also my blood. And with every second that passed, I felt the life draining away from me, as well as Rachid.

It was only when I got back to Bilal and Amina that I realised I'd been away much longer than they would have expected.

'Is everything OK?' Bilal asked, seeing my frown.

'Yes. Maman was upset, obviously. And the police wanted to ask a few questions. I had to talk to a detective. She said they'd found a left-luggage receipt in Rachid's pocket. That they had CCTV pictures of him dropping a case off at Leeds.'

It was Bilal's turn to frown.

'I know. I told her it must be a mistake. They were going to try to collect it anyway. She also said they had some leads on the suspects.'

'Good,' said Bilal. 'That's what they should be doing.'

I glanced at Amina, worried this would be upsetting her further. She was frowning too, while fiddling with her scarf again.

'What will they do with the case?' she asked. 'If it is Rachid's.'

'I don't think it will be his, sweetheart. But I'm sure they'll give it back if it is.'

She looked down at the floor, rocking slightly to and fro.

'Do you know if he's got a friend at college whose name begins with J?' I asked her.

'Why?' she said, looking up.

'The detective mentioned someone had been calling him a lot this afternoon. Sending messages too. I wondered if there was a college friend he was due to meet. Someone we should let know what's happened.'

Amina looked at me and Bilal, then shrugged.

'I think he might do,' she replied. 'But I don't know their name or number.'

I nodded, squeezed her shoulder and we went back to waiting, each of us seemingly in our own little world.

I knew before they told us. A nurse took us all to a small private room. There were three easy chairs and a strategically placed box of tissues on a small table between them. We used to have somewhere similar in the maternity unit where we took couples who had lost their baby. It was a grief room. Or, at best, a waiting-to-be-told-the-worst room. Somewhere you could be spared the prying eyes of other people while you tried to take in the unimaginable. And a way of sparing other people from hearing your anguished cries. The primitive howl of a mother who has lost her offspring and who knows nothing will ever be able to take away that pain.

'Dr Deakin will be with you in a moment,' the nurse said, her voice thick with sympathy. She was in her forties. I caught sight of the badge she was wearing. *Hello, my name is*

Lorraine, Staff Nurse. Perhaps she had already told me her name, I couldn't remember. Maybe she was a mother too. Or had undergone loss of some kind. Understood something of what this was going to do to us. I resented the fact that she knew already but did not have the authority to tell us. She was only here to prepare the ground. By the time Dr Deakin walked in, I simply wanted to get it out of the way. To spare him the anguish of having to find the words to tell us.

'I know he's gone,' I said quietly. 'A mother feels these things.'

He looked at me, seemingly unable to speak at first, but undoubtedly grateful that his role was only to confirm what we already knew.

'I'm very sorry,' he said. 'He suffered further bleeding after the surgery. Unfortunately, there was nothing more we could do. But he was still under the general anaesthetic, so he wouldn't have been in any pain or been aware of anything.'

I nodded, taking a shred of comfort in the fact that he died while he was sleeping, but still hating that the damage had been done while on my watch, supposedly in my protective custody.

The first cry came from Amina. It was a sharp, pained noise, one that made me fear she might never recover from this. I pulled her tight against me, held her cheek against mine, skin to skin. The second cry was from Bilal. He dropped to his knees on the floor as if praying and called out to Allah. His whole body shook as he sobbed quietly and said the same words over and over again.

'I'm sorry, my son. I'm sorry I let you down.'

I let go of Amina for a second and slumped onto the floor next to him.

'You didn't let him down. He did it for you. He protected us because he wanted to make you proud of him.'

'I was proud of him. Prouder than he will ever know.'

The truth of this pierced through my pain to a new layer beneath, which I hadn't even known existed. Our son was gone now. It was too late to tell him of our love, our pride, our hopes, dreams and fears for him. Because the worst of those fears had come true. We had lost him. And our family would forever be incomplete.

R & J

WhatsApp

Please call me. I don't understand what's happened to you. If you're not coming just tell me and put me out of my misery. I forgive you. I understand how hard this must be for you. Your family is so much more important to you than mine is to me. If you've chosen them, I understand that. Or at least I'll try to in time. But I can't stand the waiting and the not knowing. The worrying. I love you so much. I need to know you're OK. And I need you to know that I will love you forever. No matter what

16:47

38

DONNA

There was a long wait for the train home. The delays from Leeds earlier meant the timetable had gone entirely to pot. I stood silently, still struggling to get my head around it all. Sam and Tyler had been charged and released pending further investigations. The duty solicitor had made it very clear that it was in their best interests to stay well clear of trouble and to leave the private groups and online chat rooms in which they had been associating with the rally's organisers. I tried to tell myself that they were just silly boys who'd fallen in with the wrong crowd. The trouble was that these days, it was clear that could be much more serious than it was in ours.

When the train finally arrived, Sam sat down and immediately got out his phone. I raised my eyebrows and held out my hand. He rolled his eyes but didn't argue with me. Tyler's phone remained firmly in his pocket. Lorraine still hadn't returned my message. I knew she must be having a busy shift, in which case this news would be even more unwelcome when it came. Going to the rally had been Sam's idea. He had already admitted that to me. And Tyler, as usual, had gone along with it unquestioningly. They really didn't have a functioning brain cell between them. But they were our boys, our responsibility. And somehow me and Lorraine would have to work out what the hell we were going to do with them.

I'd left a long voicemail for Neil when I'd been waiting for them to be released from police custody. Mainly so that when he finally rang me back, I wouldn't have to tell him what our son had done when I was on the train or somewhere else in public. Because I was ashamed. Utterly ashamed of what he had got himself involved in. And I also knew that our approach before hadn't been enough to put a stop to it, so we would need to do things differently now. Ask for help from school if necessary. If he still had a school to go to, that was. Sam and Tyler were already on final warnings and being charged with threatening behaviour and resisting arrest wasn't exactly going to help their case.

As we pulled out of Bradford Interchange, I thought of the woman on the train earlier. Of the yobs abusing her and her family. My son and nephew were in danger of becoming those men. They had already racially abused a kid at school. They had been arrested at a far-right rally, for fuck's sake. And these were only the things that I knew about. God knows what else they had got up to. The idea that I could in any way claim to be a 'good' mum, that we were a 'decent' family, seemed laughable. I had failed big time. And I had no excuse whatsoever.

We got off the train silently and the rage grew in me as we made our way up the ramp from the station and trudged back to our house in the rain. By the time we got inside, and I shut the front door behind me, it was pretty much ready to explode.

'You are in so much trouble,' I shouted.

'We've said we're sorry,' replied Sam.

'Yeah, well that won't wash in court, will it? Or with your head teacher? Do you think they're going to accept sorry? In which case, why the hell should I?'

Sam and Tyler both stared at the carpet in the hallway.

'Well, things are going to change around here, I can tell you. We are not going to put up with you bringing shame on the family like this.'

'That's a bit rich. Didn't Uncle Rob get done for thumping a copper during miners' strike?'

I looked at Sam and shook my head.

'That's all you do, isn't it? Point finger at other people. Say it's not your fault. Tell me someone else is worse than you. I don't care. You're my son and I'm not having you end up in prison, and that's what's going to happen unless you change your ways.'

I stopped to draw breath. Tyler at least managed to look remorseful, which was more than could be said for Sam. But I knew Lorraine would be no less furious than I was.

'And you can start trying to think for yoursen,' I said to

Tyler, 'instead of following this idiot's example, because your mum is going to be mad as hell when she finds out and she doesn't deserve this grief. She works so hard to keep a roof over your head. Always has done.'

'Have you finished?' asked Sam.

'Oh, I've only just started,' I replied.

It was another fifteen minutes before I let them go up to Sam's room, having first removed his laptop. I knocked on Jodie's door, surprised she hadn't come out amongst all the commotion. She never usually turned down the opportunity to pile in when her brother was in trouble. There was no reply, so I went in. The room was empty, although unusually messy for her, with clothes strewn all over the place and drawers open. If I didn't know better, I'd have thought we'd been burgled. Clearly, she had left the house this morning in a bit of a rush. I could only think she must still be in Leeds after the march. Or maybe she had gone into college to work on the costumes. I tried calling her, sure she would have found her phone and got it charged by now, but it still went straight to voicemail. I left another message anyway.

'Jodie, it's Mum. I'm home now. Call me when you get a chance and let me know you're OK.'

I looked down again at the mess on her floor. I knew I should leave it to her to tidy up, it was the only way she'd learn. But I spotted the silk shirt that we'd given her the previous Christmas on the floor, and, remembering how much it had cost me, decided to hang it up.

When I opened her wardrobe, I was still thinking about Sam, about what the hell we were going to do. It took me a moment to register that something wasn't right. The rail was virtually empty. And the clothes on the floor didn't nearly make up for those that were missing.

My hand tensed on the wardrobe handle. I shut the door, as if that would make the issue go away, and looked up on top of the wardrobe. Her case was gone. There was a twisting sensation inside me, and my eyes immediately flitted around the room to see what else was missing. The framed lyrics to 'The Most Beautiful Girl in the World'. Gone. Jodie. Gone.

I ran downstairs to check the shoe rack. Her boots, Converse and sandals were missing too. Her jackets had disappeared from the coat hooks above. Shit. How could I have missed this coming? How could I have been so fucking stupid?

I raced back upstairs and burst straight into Sam's room.

'Hey, you're supposed to knock,' he said.

'Jodie's gone. She's taken all her stuff. Did you see her this morning before you left?'

Sam and Tyler looked down at their hands simultaneously. It was Tyler who spoke first.

'Yeah, but she was on her way out.'

'For the march?'

He looked at Sam.

'If you know summat, Sam, you'd better bloody tell me. You're in enough trouble already.'

'I weren't supposed to say owt. We had an agreement.'

'What are you talking about?'

'I wouldn't grass on her, if she didn't grass on me.'

'Grass on her for what?'

'She's run off with her boyfriend, hasn't she?'

'Boyfriend?'

'Yeah, him you stopped me thumping at her party.'

My mind was racing. How had I not seen this coming? Why had I assumed she would tell Lorraine the truth? The whole truth. Not simply what suited her.

'What time did she leave?'

'Same train as us this morning. About eleven.'

'So, she went to Leeds?'

'I dunno. I didn't see where she got off. She were in different carriage.'

I shook my head, not believing I was hearing this.

'And were she with him?'

'He wasn't on platform.'

'Do you know his name? Where he lives? Anything about him?'

'Jeez, what is this? It's not my fault she's gone.'

'You didn't exactly try to stop her, did you?'

I turned and headed for the door.

'His name starts with an R,' he called after me.

'What?' I asked, turning around.

'On her phone. His number came up as "R". She left it in bathroom last night and I saw a notification.'

'So has she got her phone now?'

'Yeah. I gave it back to her.'

'So, it should be working?'

'Doubt it, I've got her charger,' he said, nodding to where it was lying on his desk.

I raised my hands to my head, unable to believe this day could possibly be getting worse. At that moment my phone rang. I ran downstairs, hoping it might be her now. That she had realised what a terrible mistake she had made and wanted to come home. It wasn't her, of course. It was Neil.

'Sorry, I've just got your message. Have they released him yet?'

'Yeah, I'm home with him and Tyler now. Only that's least of our worries, because Jodie's run off with her boyfriend.'

'You what?'

'She has a boyfriend. Lad she were dancing with at her party. Sam knew she were running away with him but didn't tell us.'

'Fucking hell.'

'Yeah, my thoughts exactly.'

'Have you tried ringing her?'

'No, Neil. I didn't want to bother her,' I replied, rolling my eyes even though he couldn't see. 'Of course I did. She's not bloody answering, is she?'

'OK, keep your hair on. I'll be home soon. I'm just waiting for a train at Leeds. There's lots of delays.'

'Yeah, I know. Because while you went to a footie match and had a drink with lads, I came home from work, found out our son and nephew had been arrested, went back to get them, brought them home, only to find our daughter's run off with some lad we know nowt about.'

'Look, I'm sorry. I didn't know what were going on, did I?'

'Only because you didn't bother checking your phone. Never mind, you'll be home soon, won't you? So you can sort it all out yoursen, because I am sick and tired of having to deal with crap this family leaves me to clear up.'

I ended the call. My hand was shaking. Should I ring the police? I really didn't want to get them involved, especially not as I had only just got my son back from them. Besides, Jodie was eighteen. An adult. There was nothing they could do about it. I told myself she could be back by tonight. Or tomorrow, at least. Maybe it was simply a weekend away she had packed for. She never had travelled light. But I knew in my heart that wasn't the case. And I felt so, so stupid for not seeing it coming.

I called her for the umpteenth time that day.

'Jodie, I know what's happened. Sam told me. Please let me know you're safe. You don't have to call me or come home if you don't want to, but I need to know you're safe.'

39

JODIE

My phone rings. It's Mum again. I let it go to voicemail. I know she'll have realised I'm gone by now and will be worried, but I can't risk answering it in case I miss Rachid calling. I should message her. I might do later. But right now, I don't even want to do that. Because she'll want to know that I'm OK, and the truth is I'm not OK. Not anywhere near it.

I'm sitting in a Manchester Airbnb, having run away from home to be with the love of my life, only he hasn't turned up or contacted me. This leaves me with only two possibilities. Either he's changed his mind and decided not to come, or something has happened to him to stop him coming. Both of these are crap. Both leave me worried sick and wondering what the hell I should do.

Stay here and wait, I guess. There's no way I could go home

now, even if I wanted to. I'll never live under the same roof as Sam again. So, I suppose I'm stuck here.

I wander through to the kitchen, all gleaming chrome surfaces and shiny splashbacks. I hate its brightness. Its optimism. I'm not going to be cooking because I haven't brought any food with me. We were planning to go out for a meal tonight to celebrate our new life together, then go shopping for food tomorrow, like other couples did. Because that's what we were supposed to be – a couple. Without him, none of those things are possible. Because one minus one is a big fat zero.

The lack of food doesn't matter anyway because I'm not hungry. The last thing I feel like doing is eating. The only supplies I've brought with me are a handful of teabags nicked from Mum's caddy at home. I didn't even pick up any milk on the way here, I was in such a rush to charge my phone. But I decide to make tea anyway because it's something to keep my hands occupied.

Once it's brewed for a few minutes, I fish out the teabag with a spoon and take the mug back through to the living room. It's hard because drinking Mum's Yorkshire Tea is something that reminds me of home. And I'm not home. I'm here alone in Manchester.

I turn on the TV to try to distract myself from what's happened. I pick up the remote and flick through the channels, but nothing is able to hold my attention for more than a few seconds. For some reason, I settle on the news. Probably because I don't want to watch anything silly or with a studio audience laughing inanely, which the rest of Saturday night

TV seems to involve. I see the 'Breaking news' banner across the bottom of the screen.

A 17-year-old boy has died following what police describe as a 'hate crime' attack on a train in Halifax.

Everything stops. I don't understand how I continue to breathe because everything inside me has shut down. It's as if someone reached down into this room and pressed the pause button on my entire life. I sit motionless, wishing I could grab the remote control and press 'rewind'. Because if I hadn't seen it, I would still be sitting here thinking Rachid might turn up at any moment. But now I'm thinking something far, far worse.

I gasp and clutch my stomach. It feels as if someone is wringing out my insides like a sponge, trying to squeeze every last drop of life out of me.

'No,' I say out loud, shaking my head as if to emphasise it. 'No, no, no.'

The newsreader is talking about it now. They go live to Halifax. A reporter is standing outside the station. I can see Eureka!, the children's museum, in the background. I used to love going there as a kid. My mind is whirring, jumbling everything up. I put the volume up so I can concentrate on what she's saying. About how the attack took place this afternoon on a busy train from Leeds following the Stop Brexit march and a counter far-right rally in the city. That police say witnesses have described racist language being used to the victim and his family before the attack. That the three men involved fled at the station and police were studying CCTV footage from the train and platforms at Halifax and Leeds.

It's when she says that the victim, who hasn't been named, had suffered critical head injuries, and had died later in hospital, that I start to cry. Not normal human crying, more like an animal caught in a trap, the pain searing through its body.

I pick up my phone and call him again. Keep calling back every time it goes to voicemail.

'No,' I say again, quieter this time. It's someone else, the person they are talking about on the news. I have never wished anyone dead before, but I do now. Every single person on that train. I don't care which one of them it is, as long as it's not Rachid. Because I can't contemplate life without him.

They are back with the reporter in Halifax. She says police are appealing for anyone who was on that train to come forward. She says it was the 13.02 Northern service from Leeds to Manchester Victoria. I go back to the WhatsApp messages on my phone. The last one, where Rachid said he was on the train to Halifax. The time is 13.03.

I throw my phone down and collapse in a heap on the floor, sobbing and gasping for breath. I know it's him. I know that's why he hasn't called me. He would never let me down, never leave me here on my own, not unless something awful had happened. Something so awful that I can't bring myself to say it out loud. But I know. Know he has taken his last breath. And with it, my life too. Because I can't bear to live without him. I want to be with him. Let my light go out while our love is still burning brightly. Fizzing across the sky, blazing a trail of fire behind it. We can show them. Show the world how much we meant to each other. We'll write it in the stars for all to see. So that no one can deny our love.

I stretch out and retrieve my phone, find 'I Would Die 4 U' by Prince and put it on repeat. I sob my way through it the first time around, then crawl across the floor and reach up to open the door to the balcony. The fresh air hits me, cold and sharp. My ears are assaulted by sirens as a police car and an ambulance tear past. I want to tell them they are too late to save him. That they should have been there when he needed them. When they could have made a difference.

I kneel for a moment, still unsure if my legs will be able to support me. It's raining. They say it always does in Manchester. I hold my face up to the sky, wanting it to rain harder, hard enough to sting my face. For the flesh of my cheeks to be torn by it. I want to be punished because this is my fault. If I hadn't suggested running away together, if I'd accepted him going to Paris. I would have lost him, but he would still be alive. Still be breathing the same air as me.

My hands grasp at the balustrade, and I haul myself up to standing, swaying slightly, the streetlights below dazzling my eyes. I look up instead. But there are no stars over Blackfriars Road tonight. No moon, even. Only thick grey clouds smothering everything.

'I'm so sorry,' I whisper into the night. 'Sorry I wasn't there with you. I should have been. I would've laid down my life for you. We could have died together, like we were supposed to. But I'm coming now, so we'll be together again.'

I lurch over the balcony. My head is spinning. I see the lights of the cars down below. I hear Rachid's voice calling me. And I let go.

40

SYLVIE

We arrived home from the hospital as a family of three, when only this morning we had departed, albeit at different times, as a family of four. There was a corner piece missing from the jigsaw. There would be no way to replace it and the picture would never be complete without it. Every day I would see an empty chair at the table. Walk past an empty bedroom. Feel an absence that would run through the house like the most severe of chills.

For he had taken the warmth with him. The light and the laughter. I could not see how they could ever return. How the coldness in my heart could ever be thawed.

It was dark as Bilal led us up the path to the front door. Somehow, the entire day had slipped away while we were in the hospital. I followed, my arm tightly around Amina, desperate to cling on to the only child I had left.

The silence inside our house hammered at my head, reminding me of what was missing. More than missing, gone for good. We stood in the hall and hugged each other as we cried, arms around waists or shoulders. A scaffold of support when all around us was unstable.

After a while, I slipped silently out of the hold and walked into the kitchen to make coffee, leaving Bilal supporting Amina. Still trying so hard to absorb her hurt. When the coffee was ready, we sat wordlessly around the table, grasping our mugs, glad of that tiny bit of warmth. And with every second, the silence grew louder. The kitchen clock the only thing breaking it. Reminding us that time would pass so slowly now, that the pain we were feeling was interminable.

I lay with Amina in bed, stroking her hair, planting kisses on her face, doing everything I could to get some love and warmth into her.

'I can't believe he's gone,' she whispered.

'I know. Neither can I.'

'I should have stopped him,' she said.

'No. You are utterly blameless, sweetheart. You mustn't tell yourself otherwise.'

She looked at me, doubt and regret criss-crossing her face.

'Never forget how much he loved you,' I said. 'He would have done anything for you.'

She managed a little nod.

'Why didn't anyone help?' she asked. 'Why didn't they try to stop them?'

'I don't know. It's like they tried to pretend it wasn't happening. Try to sleep now. Or at least get some rest. If you need me in the night, come straight through to our room. OK?'

She nodded again and turned away from me, pulling the duvet around her and cocooning herself inside. I stayed there until she fell asleep, as I had done sometimes when she was little. It was the most soothing thing in the world, listening to a small child breathing. Watching the rise and fall of their chest. I'd done the same with Rachid many a time. More so perhaps than with Amina, because I hadn't had a toddler to look after too. His chest was still now. No heart beating inside. It was the hardest thing in the world, knowing your child had stopped breathing, while you were continuing to do so.

I stopped on the landing in front of Rachid's bedroom door. The compulsion to go inside was too strong to ignore. But as my fingers groped for the handle, Bilal came out of our bedroom and stopped me.

'No,' he whispered into my ear as he removed my hand gently from the door. 'Don't do that to yourself. Not tonight. Come to bed with me. We'll deal with everything else in the morning.'

I didn't argue, just let him guide me to our room. We undressed in silence then slipped beneath the duvet, holding on to each other as if a storm was battering the bed, and our very life depended on it.

'I didn't protect him,' I whimpered.

'You didn't stand a chance. Not on your own. If I hadn't gone to the conference, none of you would have been on the train.'

'He wasn't going into college,' I said. 'He was going to the march. I didn't want to tell you in case you tried to stop him.'

Bilal sighed.

'It doesn't matter now, does it? Nothing matters any more.'

I pulled him in tighter to me. We lay there in the dark for a long time, not saying anything, both of us lost inside our hurt. But at some point, he fell asleep. His gentle snoring was strangely comforting, although I knew sleep would not be visiting me. Not for a long time to come.

I was gripped by a sudden need to be close to my son. I pulled my arm out from under Bilal and got up, crept out onto the landing, and pushed open his bedroom door. I expected to see the usual mess on the floor, everything how he'd left it. Only that wasn't what greeted me at all. The bedroom was spotlessly clean and tidy. Even the duvet was neatly across the bed. It was his desk I noticed first. Some of the tech stuff that was normally scattered across it was missing. There was a distinct lack of things charging and trailing USB leads. I felt a stabbing pain inside. Something was wrong. I immediately thought of the left-luggage receipt. I crouched to look under his bed. His case was gone. I stood up, my legs almost buckling beneath me, and staggered over to the wardrobe. I opened the door quickly, as if I expected to find a monster lurking behind it. But I was greeted by something far scarier. His clothes rails were empty.

The scream I let out brought Bilal running into the room.

'Sylvie?'

I gestured at the empty wardrobe as I sat down heavily on the bed.

'He'd taken his things. The police were right. He had his case with him. He was going somewhere.'

Bilal stared at the empty rails, clearly not understanding either. I heard a shuffling noise and looked around to find Amina standing in the doorway, tears streaming down her face.

'I'm sorry,' she sobbed.

I got up and went over to hug her.

'What for?' I asked.

She gulped back more tears before replying.

'I think he was planning to run away with her.'

'With who?'

'His girlfriend.'

My frown deepened. She wiped the tears from her face.

'She was the J on his phone.'

I shook my head, unable to take in what I was hearing.

'I don't understand. Why didn't he tell us?'

'She wasn't Muslim.'

'That wouldn't have mattered,' I replied.

Amina glanced at Bilal and pulled a face that suggested she didn't think that was true. And I knew in an instant that she was right. That he would not have wanted to risk his father's wrath.

'I think she was the girl with the Brexit placard we saw that time in Leeds.'

I looked at Bilal. His expression mirrored mine. My mind raced, trying to join all the dots.

'Was it because of Paris?'

She nodded.

'I don't think he could bear to leave her. He didn't tell me what he was going to do. I would have told you if I'd known for certain. But I kind of worked it out from how he was behaving, and I couldn't bring myself to tell you because I didn't want to stop him being happy and now look what's happened—'

Her voice broke off and I pulled her to me again.

'It's OK, sweetheart. It wasn't your fault. I just feel so stupid for not seeing it myself.'

The realisation hit me as I said it. All those nights he stayed late at college. There hadn't been any musical. It was all about the girl. She had been everything to him, and we had ploughed on with our plans to take him away from her without knowing it.

Bilal sat down on Rachid's bed and held his head in his hands.

'What have I done?' he said. 'Paris was all my idea. I drove him away. Drove him into the hands of those animals.'

It was Amina who took his hand. Who sat down and leant herself against his chest, the two of them united in guilt. I sat down on the bed next to them.

'It's no one's fault,' I said. 'Apart from the people who whipped up the hatred and those who killed him. They're the only ones to blame.'

'What about his girlfriend?' asked Amina.

'It's not her fault either,' I said.

'No. I mean we should let her know. She'll be worried.'

'Do you know where they were planning to go?' I asked.

Amina shook her head.

'We should tell the police,' I said. 'They'll have her number on Rachid's phone. They can get in touch with her.'

'No,' said Bilal. 'We're not having anything to do with her. She's already done enough damage.'

I gestured to Amina to go back to her room. When she'd left, I leant over and cradled Bilal's head in my hands as his body shook.

'If Rachid loved her,' I said, 'then we owe it to him to tell her. It's the one thing we can still do for him.'

We sat there for a long time like that, holding on to each other in the knowledge that the gaping hole in our family would never be filled, and we hadn't really known our son at all.

R & J

WhatsApp

I'm so sorry for not being there to save you. I Would Die 4 U. I hope you knew that. I will see you soon. Love you always

01:08

41

DONNA

I knew as soon as I heard it on the news. Knew that it was the son of the woman on the train. That nobody had intervened. That I had, effectively, left him to die.

Neil came into the living room carrying two mugs of tea, to find me crying on the sofa, staring at the TV screen.

'What's happened?' he said, putting the mugs down on the table.

It took a moment to compose myself before I could reply.

'A teenage lad has died after he were attacked on train in Halifax.'

'Bloody hell, is that why trains were delayed?'

I looked at him in disbelief.

'Is that all you care about? Why your fucking train home were late?'

'No, I didn't mean it like that. I were just working it out in my head.'

'The train they said he were on. It were my train. I saw him.'

'What?'

'When I came home from work, there were a group of blokes on train giving this family a hard time. Saying they should go back to where they were from. I didn't even see lad. He had his back to me. But I heard it all and I didn't do owt. I stood there waiting to get off and that woman, who must have been his mum, looked me right in the eyes. And do you know what I did? Fuck all, that's what.'

Neil leant over and put his arm around me.

'Come on, it's not your fault. You did right thing not to get involved. They might have turned on you.'

I shook my head.

'That's what I told mesen when I got off, but it's bollocks. Some woman saw her son beaten to death in front of her, because likes of me "didn't want to get involved".'

'You couldn't have done owt to stop it.'

'We don't know that. All we know is that I didn't bother trying because I'm so bloody English that I felt a bit awkward and tried to pretend it weren't happening. Like everyone else on that fucking train.'

I picked up my mobile.

'What you doing?'

'I'm phoning police. They're asking everyone on train to come forward. So I'm going to tell them what I saw, in case it helps.'

'You don't want to do that. You'll end up having to be a witness at court case or summat. Blokes like that are not to be messed with. Even if they go down, they'll have mates outside who could get nasty.'

'So, what do you suggest I do?'

'Let police do their job. They'll pick them up from CCTV. You don't have to get involved. We've got a son who's been arrested today and a daughter who's gone AWOL. I think we've got enough on our plate.'

I hesitated. He had a point. And what if Jodie or Lorraine tried to call while I was on the phone to the police? I put my phone back down.

Lorraine rang just before eight.

'Jesus, Don, I'm so sorry. I've only just got your message and seen loads of missed calls. Is Tyler with you?'

'Yeah. You'd better sit yoursen down while I fill you in.'

She listened silently as I told her what had happened. When I had finished, she simply said, 'I'm on my way.'

I did frozen pizzas from Farmfoods for the boys, telling Neil to take them upstairs and let Tyler know that his mum was on her way, and he'd better have an apology waiting for her.

As soon as Lorraine stepped into the hall, she threw her arms around me.

'I'm so sorry,' she said. 'I had no idea Jodie were going to do this. She hadn't said owt to me. I'd have told you if she had, you know that.'

I nodded.

'I know. She played us both. I can't believe I've been too damn stupid to realise what were going on.'

'You mustn't blame yourself. Where are boys?'

'In Sam's room,' I said. 'Do you want me to send Tyler down?'

'No, he can wait. I'll deal with him later. Right now, we need to find Jodie quickly before she finds out.'

I stared at her.

'Finds out what?'

Lorraine took my arm and guided me towards the kitchen. She sat me down at the table before taking a seat opposite.

'She's on her own. He's not with her.'

I stared at her, not understanding.

'How do you know? Has she messaged you?'

She reached across the table and took my hand.

'I helped to treat lad who were attacked on train in Halifax. I were with his family before they were told he'd died. It were him, Don. He were lad from party. Jodie's boyfriend.'

Her words ricocheted against my head. I refused to let them in. Refused to believe they were true. Because, if they were, I had left Jodie's boyfriend to be killed. I had walked away from him and his family because I didn't want to get involved. What I hadn't known, though, was that I already was. Because my daughter was in love with him.

'No,' I said, shaking my head vigorously. 'No, that's not true. It can't be.'

Lorraine squeezed my hand.

'I'm sorry, sis. I wish it wasn't true, but I thought I

recognised him as soon as they brought him in. Then when I had to hand over his possessions to police, I saw his student ID card. It was him.'

'But it could have been someone who just looked like him. You don't know for certain, do you? You only saw him once.'

Lorraine sighed and looked up at the ceiling before she replied.

'Jodie told me his name. The one on his card. Rachid Mastour.'

I stared at her, not wanting to believe it, but knowing it must be true.

'Oh Jesus,' I said. 'What have I done?'

'It's not your fault.'

'It is,' I replied. 'I were on train with him and his family. I heard blokes giving them some verbal. Right horrible stuff.'

Lorraine stared at me, her eyes wide.

'What did you do?'

'Fuck all,' I replied. 'I got off train at Low Moor. Told mesen someone else would sort it out. Guard would be along in a minute. Because I didn't know, did I? That he were Jodie's boyfriend.'

My head dropped down onto the table as I sobbed. Lorraine reached out and stroked my head. She didn't tell me it wasn't my fault again because she knew now it was. She was appalled by what I'd done. Sickened. As everyone else would be when they found out. And none more so than Jodie.

I sat up.

'We need to tell her,' I said. 'She'll be on her own, won-dering where the hell he is. She'll be worried sick.'

'I know,' said Lorraine. 'I'm worried she'll have heard about it on news. They might name him soon, if she hasn't worked it out already.'

'Ring her now,' I said. 'Tell her we know what's happened. You do it, because she won't answer my calls. And if she doesn't answer, leave a message.'

I hurried out into the hall, pulled on my jacket and picked up my bag. Neil came out of the living room and caught sight of my face.

'What's happened? Where you going?'

'To police station. That lad that died after attack on train. It were her boyfriend.'

'Fucking hell,' said Neil.

'Yeah. So that's going to go down well, isn't it? When I tell her I got off train and left her boyfriend to be beaten to death.'

'Come on, you weren't to know it were him.'

'It doesn't matter, does it? I left him there and least I can do now is tell police in case it helps them catch bastards who did it.'

Neil groaned and kicked the bottom step of the stairs.

'No,' he said. 'I don't want you to tell them.'

'Why on earth not?'

'Because I can't bear to see my family tearing itself apart like this. And you telling them is only going to make things worse. I just want her home. I want my little girl home. I want this all to go away.'

His voice broke. I could tell he was trying hard not to cry, and I loved him for that. I really did. But I also knew what I had to do. The one thing left I could still do for Jodie. I turned and walked out of the door.

42

JODIE

The sound of my phone ringing wakes me. I'm about to rush to get it in case it's Rachid, when I remember and the pain floods back in. I shift my body slightly. I'm wet and cold and ache all over. I can also hear traffic below me. I open my eyes. I'm lying on the balcony, covered with the rug from the sofa, my head resting on a cushion.

When I let go of the balustrade, I realised that Rachid would not want me to do it and toppled back onto the balcony floor. I'd lain there for a long time, gazing up at the clouds, knowing that somewhere beyond them the stars would be out. And wanting desperately to sleep under them. I'd grabbed the blanket and cushion from the sofa, wrapped myself up against the cold, and, at some point, must have drifted off to sleep.

And what now? I hadn't thought about that last night, hadn't seen how there could possibly be an 'after'. But now there was, I needed to find a way to get through it. The tears come again, sharp and bitter. I wish it had been me instead of him, and then I stop myself because I would not wish this grief on Rachid. Couldn't bear for him to suffer in the way I am now.

I shift my weight and try to sit up. My head spins. I can't remember the last time I ate, nor can I imagine ever wanting to eat again. I need to drink, though. My mouth is dry and rancid.

I unwrap the blanket, hold on to the balustrade and unsteadily get to my feet. The traffic is still going past below, people hurrying to wherever it is they are going. The world is still turning. It's only one person who has fallen off. It's simply that he took all my hopes and dreams with him.

I stagger inside, go through to the kitchen, and fill a glass with water from the tap. I sip it at first, unsure whether I'll be able to keep it down, but end up drinking it all. I go back into the living room. I left the door to the balcony open, and I decide not to close it, liking the jolt the cold air gives my body. I pick up my phone from the floor and check the messages. There's a voicemail from Lorraine.

'Jodie, please call me. I know what happened. I'm so, so sorry. Please let me or your mum know you're OK. We're worried sick about you. If you don't want to come home, we understand. But your mum wants you to know you're not in trouble. There'll be no questions. She just wants to give you a hug. She loves you, Jodie. We all do.'

Her voice breaks at the end. I wipe my eyes before I save

the message. I can't face talking to her right now, although I know I should. I want to speak to Mum too, for her to hold me like she used to when I was little and kiss me better to make everything OK, even though I know I'm too old for that now and that nothing will ever be OK again.

I decide to message them both when I'm on my way. There is somewhere I need to go first, once I have summoned up the courage. I look around the flat where I should have spent my first night with Rachid. I'm not quite ready to leave yet. I scroll through my Spotify list and put 'Sometimes It Snows in April' on repeat. And I lie there, tears pouring down my cheeks as I mouth the words that I can still hear him singing to me.

43

SYLVIE

Waking at dawn the next morning was, if anything, worse than the day before. Any slim possibility that it could have been a nightmare was dashed within a second of me opening my eyes. The silence was oppressive and the anguished, twisting sensation inside me stronger than ever. I knew instantly what had happened. Recalled every detail in my mind, just as it had played inside my head during the hours that I had lain awake last night. The only nightmare was a living one.

I crept out onto the landing and listened at Amina's door. Silence from within. I wanted to go in to see her, to reassure myself that my one remaining child was OK. But I resisted for fear of waking her, knowing she wouldn't have got much sleep either.

As I walked past Rachid's closed bedroom door, I averted my gaze, desperate to avoid thinking about the empty clothes rail.

The very idea that he had not been planning to come home to us last night tore at me, as did the fact that he'd been unable to confide in me about how he felt.

When I arrived downstairs, Bilal's study door was ajar and I could see him, head bowed on his prayer mat for a second, his bare feet pointing in my direction, as he completed Fajr. I was hit by a sudden pang of jealousy. I was glad he had his faith; I knew it was one of the few things that might provide some comfort in the days, weeks, and months ahead. I had nothing. I had put my faith in humanity and look how that had turned out.

When he'd finished, I gave him a moment in contemplation before I cleared my throat to let him know I was there. Bilal turned. There was a trace of something resembling peace in his eyes, but they were still clouded with pain.

'Sorry,' I said quietly. 'I didn't want to disturb you.'

'I didn't want to shut the door in case either of you needed me,' he replied, before he stepped forward to embrace me.

'I found it hard this morning,' he said. 'To perform Salah, I mean.'

I nodded and stroked his arm. 'At least you have your faith.'

He looked at me, appearing surprised.

'You have our family,' he replied.

'I don't,' I said. 'My family has been destroyed.'

The police rang soon after eight. It was DC Abraham, who I'd seen at the hospital. She said they would be sending a family liaison officer around, a woman who would be our main point of contact. She would also take us to the police station later to be interviewed and give formal witness statements.

My head was still spinning. I said yes to everything, not really taking it in. But I knew we had to help them catch the men who did this. That was the very least we could do for Rachid.

I wanted to wake Amina before the police arrived. I knocked on her door. She mumbled a 'yes', so I went in. She was lying on her bed, dark shadows under her eyes. I sat down next to her and took hold of her hand.

'I know you're hurting,' I said. 'I'm not sure how we're going to get through it either, but we will. We'll find a way.'

She stared out across my shoulder and said nothing, so I continued.

'The police are on their way. A family liaison officer is going to help support us and take us to the police station later to give our statements. You'll need to tell them everything, sweetheart. Everything you know.'

Amina nodded.

'I'm sorry. I should have told you, maybe you could have stopped him.'

'No,' I said. 'I doubt it. Anyway, I should have realised what was going on, that he wouldn't have changed his mind about Paris for no reason. I should have been the sort of mother he could talk to.'

We sat in silence for a moment.

'I think he really loved her,' said Amina.

I turned to look at her.

'Then I'd like to meet her,' I said. 'Because once she finds out, she'll be hurting too.'

Amina arrived downstairs while I was making coffee. I hugged her to me. She felt rigid and broken. She sat down next to Bilal. He put his arm around her shoulder, and I heard him whisper, 'Sorry.'

I offered them breakfast, which they both politely refused. I couldn't face anything to eat either. I wasn't sure I ever would again. When the doorbell rang, Bilal went to answer it, and reappeared in the kitchen a few minutes later with a tall, middle-aged woman with a sympathetic expression arranged on her face.

'Hello,' she said, looking at both of us in turn, 'I'm Gillian Hardcastle, your family liaison officer. I'm so very sorry for your loss.'

I didn't think I would ever get used to hearing that. It would never be anything other than a massively jarring shock. I nodded, still not being able to manage a 'thank you'.

'This is my wife, Sylvie, and our daughter, Amina,' Bilal said. Amina's gaze immediately fell to the floor.

'Please, sit down,' he went on, gesturing towards the table. 'Can we get you some tea or coffee?'

She glanced at the cafetière on the table.

'Coffee would be great, thanks,' she replied.

She waited until Bilal had poured it for her before she sat down and started talking.

'The first thing I need to tell you is that we made three arrests early this morning. We're as confident as we can be from the CCTV footage that they are the men responsible for your son's murder.'

The word hit me square between the eyes. It was the first time anyone had used it to our faces. But that was what Rachid was now. A murder victim. I was glad they had the men, although I also knew that meant there would be a trial, where we would have to relive the whole thing again.

'Good,' Bilal said. 'Thank you.'

Gillian nodded and continued.

'I also need to check if all family have now been informed?'

Bilal nodded. He'd made some calls from outside the hospital last night. His brother in Morocco; some extended family; the imam, who'd said he would notify everyone at the mosque. I'd managed to phone my sister. She'd offered to fly over from Belgium but I'd said I'd rather she went to Paris to be with Maman instead, because she was on her own in hospital and would need support. Her crying on the phone last night when I'd told her Rachid was dead would haunt me forever.

'And there's no one else you'd like us to contact?' asked Gillian.

Amina looked at me. I knew what she wanted me to do.

'There is one more person, actually,' I said. 'The detective I spoke to yesterday said someone had been ringing Rachid's phone; they were coming up as "J". I didn't know who it was at the time, but it turns out Rachid had a girlfriend we didn't know about. I'm afraid we don't even know her name, but I'd be very grateful if you could ring the number the calls have come from. Not on his phone, of course. I wouldn't want to get her hopes up if she hasn't worked it out by now.'

'Of course,' Gillian said, 'leave that with us and we'll give her whatever support she needs.'

I nodded and glanced at Bilal, who said nothing.

'Once we've spoken to her,' said Gillian, 'we will go ahead and release Rachid's name to the media.'

It would already be on the news, of course. I'd noticed that Bilal had not put Radio 4 on as usual this morning and had guessed why. But there would be no way we could shield Amina from the coverage once they'd released his name too.

'Do you have to?' I asked.

'I'm afraid so,' said Gillian. 'What we usually do at this point is ask the family if they have a photo of their loved one which they would like us to issue to the media. And perhaps a photo of you all together? It stops the papers from bothering you by trying to get pictures for themselves.'

Bilal looked at me. I shrugged.

'Can I send you photos from my phone?' I asked.

'Of course. Just reply to my text when you've had a chance to find something. We'll be holding a press conference this afternoon too, after he's been named. There's no need for you to be there now we've made the arrests, but if you'd like to put together a brief statement about Rachid, some families find it's helpful to be able to pay tribute to their loved one in that way.'

I stared at her. *Some families.* I'd forgotten that this happened to other people. That we weren't the first who had suffered such a loss, and sadly wouldn't be the last. Gillian must have sat at many kitchen tables, been with many families at their time of grief.

'We'll put something together,' Bilal said.

'Thank you. And I'm happy to help you with that if you're unsure about what to say. Do you have any questions, anything at all you want to ask?'

She looked between us. Amina looked as if she was about to speak, so I got in first to save her.

'About the suitcase,' I started.

'We have collected it. It did belong to your son. Mainly clothes and personal possessions. Some tech equipment.'

I nodded.

'We found out that he'd been planning to go away with his girlfriend. The one we didn't know about.'

I looked down at my hands, wondering what sort of parents she must think we were, that our son had kept something like that from us. That he had felt the need to run away with his girlfriend.

'I understand,' she said. 'It's really not something to worry about. We will speak to the girl as part of our enquiries and ensure that she is supported, but our investigation is focused on bringing your son's attackers to justice.'

'Thank you,' said Bilal, as if she had let us off a parenting misdemeanour. As if that was our biggest concern right now.

'Right,' said Gillian, looking at me and Amina. 'I'm going to let you get ready, then I'll take you to our Halifax station.

The senior investigating officer will meet you first and then you'll be interviewed by DC Abraham, who you met at the hospital. I'll talk you through everything and you can take as many breaks as you need.'

'We won't see them, will we?' asked Amina, looking up. 'The men who did it, I mean.'

'No,' said Gillian. 'You won't have to see them at all. They're being held at Bradford police station. That's where they're being questioned.'

Amina went back to fiddling with her fingers. I closed my eyes for a second, trying to steel myself for what was to come. One child dead. One emotionally scarred. And one failed mother left to try to hold it all together.

When we got to the police station, Gillian showed us into a room where a bald-headed man wearing a jacket a size too small for him was sitting behind a desk. He stood up and introduced himself in a subdued tone.

'Morning, I'm DCI Peter Whittaker, the senior investigating officer. I'm so sorry for your loss. I understand that this must be extremely difficult for you. Please know that we are doing everything possible to bring those who did this to justice.'

I was hit by the realisation that this was what our lives would consist of for the immediate future. People who had never met Rachid offering meaningless condolences. I nodded. Bilal shifted his feet. Gillian clearly understood that we wanted to get this over with. She showed us out and along the corridor into a smaller room, where DC Abraham was waiting for us.

She stood up and offered her hand, but Bilal didn't even give her the chance to start on how sorry she was.

'You've got them, haven't you?' he asked.

'We're pretty sure of it,' she replied, gesturing to us to take a seat. 'They're not contesting that it's them in the CCTV pictures. We suspect they'll try to say they were provoked and claim self-defence, but we have enough witnesses to be able to prove that's not true.'

'They didn't help, though,' said Bilal. 'These witnesses didn't help my family when they needed them.'

'No,' said DC Abraham. 'I appreciate that must be very hard. But we have gathered a significant number of statements from those on the train, including a woman who got off at Low Moor, shortly before the attack started.'

'I remember her,' I said. 'I think she's usually on my morning train. I looked at her. I was hoping she'd be able to alert the guard.'

'She came forward last night,' DC Abraham replied. 'She's given us a full statement and she's prepared to testify in court. It's fair to say she feels terrible about what happened.'

'Yes, well, it's a bit late for that,' said Bilal, stony-faced. 'They were all too late. All of them.'

Bilal stood up and walked over to the small window.

'If you need some more time before we go on,' said Gillian, 'you're very welcome to take it.'

'No,' said Bilal. 'We want to get this over with. We need my son back. When will he be returned to us? You understand that we need to bury him as soon as possible? Ideally within twenty-four hours.'

'We do,' DC Abraham replied. 'We take religious requirements very seriously, but I'm afraid there are some formalities we need to go through which mean that may not be possible.'

'What sort of formalities?' asked Bilal.

DC Abraham looked down at her hands for a second before replying.

'Unfortunately, the law requires that we carry out a post-mortem. We'll be doing that later today. We expect to charge these men within thirty-six hours, but I'm afraid they do have the right to ask for an independent post-mortem. We hope the coroner will release Rachid's body to you by tomorrow evening at the latest. Earlier, if at all possible.'

Bilal walked back over and stood in front of DC Abraham.

'You understand this goes against our beliefs? This is a dese-cration of his body. Is there no way you can avoid it?'

She shook her head.

'We need to bring the men who did this to your son to justice. And for that we need a post-mortem.'

I stared at her. The thought of Rachid being cut with a knife when he had already been through so much was too painful to bear. I'd been soaked in his blood. I'd had to see his face, battered and bruised beyond recognition, and now I was expected to let them cut him open. To scar his body too. His perfect skin that I had marvelled at when he was born. I stood up and asked to go to the toilet. Gillian accompanied me. She stood outside the cubicle while I retched into the bowl.

We sat silently in the car on the way home after we'd given our statements, my hand clutching Amina's. She had been brave, so brave. And she had again remembered far more than I had. Had been able to give so much detailed information that DC Abraham said she'd been a huge help.

Bilal had barely spoken since his outburst. He was hurting. I knew that was why he had lashed out. He considered that he had failed in his duty as a father to protect his family, even though he hadn't been there. And I understood that he was also angry that those who had been there had failed to help us.

Gillian saw us safely inside before saying she was going to give us some time on our own, but to call her if there was anything we needed. And then we were alone again. All three of us went to separate rooms, all needing time and space to try to come to terms with what had happened.

I was in the kitchen when the doorbell rang. I hesitated before opening it, worried it could be a reporter. I didn't really want to face anyone. But I did wonder if it might be Edwina, wanting to know if we were OK.

The young woman who stood on the doorstep had tears in her eyes, a suitcase by her side and a bunch of lilies in her hand. She looked at me and something passed between us. I knew instantly who she was.

'Are you Rachid's mum?' she asked. I nodded.

'I'm so sorry to disturb you,' she said, holding out the flowers as the wind whipped her red hair across her face. 'I got a call from police about Rachid.' She paused, clearly struggling to speak. 'I wanted to give you these and say how sorry I am for your loss.'

I took the flowers. She turned, as if to walk away. I stepped down onto the path and held out my arms to her.

'Thank you,' I said. 'For these, and for making my son so happy.'

She collapsed into my arms, and we stood there, holding tight to each other, our sobs and heaving chests combining to form one solid mass of grief and hurt and raw, unadulterated pain.

'I loved him,' she said. 'I loved him so much.'

I nodded.

'And I know he loved you. I only wish he'd told me.'

She sniffed. Tucked her hair behind her ear on one side. She looked how I felt: broken. I couldn't simply let her walk away.

'Please, come in,' I said. 'I want to meet you properly. I want to hear all about you and Rachid.'

She looked at me doubtfully. I gestured with my hand towards the open door behind me and she followed me into the hallway.

Bilal called out from the study.

'Who is it, Sylvie?'

I turned to the young woman.

'I'm sorry,' I said. 'I don't even know your name.'

'It's Jodie,' she replied, wiping her eyes with her fingertips.

Bilal stuck his head around the study door.

'This is Jodie,' I said. 'Rachid's girlfriend.'

He looked at her, at me and then shut the door without saying a word.

'I'm sorry,' I said to Jodie. 'He's finding this all very hard.'

'I should go,' she replied. 'I don't want to make things any worse than they already are.'

'No. You're part of our family now. Bilal may take a little time to get used to that, but he will come around. Please, come through.'

She left her case in the hallway and followed me into the kitchen. I picked up a vase from the windowsill and filled it with cold water before plunging the lilies in. I knew that Bilal would be riled by the flowers too; they were generally only given by Muslims after the burial, but she wasn't to know that. She wasn't to know a lot of things. I turned to face her. The girl who had captured my son's heart. Whom he loved more than anything. Whom he had been prepared to leave his family for. And I could see why. She had a luminous quality about her. She radiated light and warmth.

'Please, take a seat,' I said. 'Can I get you a drink of anything? Coffee or tea?'

She managed a thin smile.

'I'm fine, thanks. Rachid always drank coffee, and me tea. It kind of summed up differences between our families.'

I tried to imagine what their kitchen looked like. Her mother pouring from a teapot as they sat around the table. But

I suspected I had everything wrong. Because I knew nothing about them, nothing at all.

She sat down at the table. I gasped softly as she did so and she looked up at me, alarmed.

'I'm sorry,' I said. 'You chose Rachid's chair.'

She shut her eyes, reached her hand down and ran it across the grain of the wooden seat, as if she could somehow manage to connect with him through it, before putting her head down on the table and starting to cry.

'I miss him,' she sobbed. 'I miss him so much already; I can't imagine how much I'll miss him by this time next week.'

'I know,' I said, reaching out my hand to take hers. 'I still think he's going to walk through the door at any moment with his AirPods in, singing along to something by Prince.'

Jodie smiled and I sat down opposite her, each of us brushing the tears away from our eyes. There was so much about their relationship I wanted to know.

'Did you meet him at college?'

She nodded. 'Yes, on his first day. We weren't on the same course, though. I'm in my second year of fashion design. We used to get train back and forth together. I live at Low Moor.'

'And you saw him after college, and on Saturdays?'

She avoided my gaze for a second.

'Yeah. I'm sorry about that. He felt bad about lying to you, he really did. We met up at a café in an old church near college. We couldn't bear to be apart, see. From first time we met, we'd be messaging each other constantly. He used to call me at bedtime, and we'd sleep with our phones next to our pillows, so that if we woke in night, we could hear each other breathing.'

I stared at her, trying not to show my surprise. I had not expected this level of intensity. It made me feel even more stupid for not having realised what was going on.

'Where did you go yesterday?' I asked. 'The police found Rachid's suitcase at Leeds station. I wondered where you were heading to?'

'Manchester. An Airbnb. Rachid had booked it for a fortnight. You might be able to get a refund in circumstances. I've got all contact details if you want to try.'

I shook my head and looked down at the table.

'He were going to find us a flat,' she continued. 'Get some work doing music gigs and helping out in studios. I were going to get train over to Leeds to finish my course, he'd insisted on that.'

I nodded, feeling a sense of pride, and let her go on.

'And I was going to work in Greggs at weekends to help with money side. He had it all worked out. He'd thought of everything. Except this, of course.'

I sat there, trying to picture the life they would have had together. Imagining Rachid working hard to keep a roof over their heads while she continued her education. In so many ways the man Bilal had wanted him to be.

'I'm sorry,' I said. 'I should have asked him why he was so against going to Paris. We thought he was simply resentful of his parents deciding his future for him. That's what my husband thought, anyway. Rachid could be stubborn at times.

They both could. It's one of the things they had in common, if only they could have realised it.'

'We didn't see how we could tell anyone. My family, well, they're very different to yours. They come from a completely different background. See things in a different way. My brother were at rally in Leeds yesterday, with that nasty lot who caused trouble.'

She bowed her head. I frowned, remembering the contorted faces of the men behind the police lines. The hatred emanating from those who had run towards us.

'Oh,' I said.

'I know. He repulses me too. I've disowned him. My dad's not much better. I couldn't wait to get away from my family, to be honest.'

She looked at me and added quickly, 'Rachid didn't feel like that. He hated leaving you and his sister. He felt really bad about it.'

I looked up to see Amina standing in the doorway. Her gaze went to Jodie, then back to me. I nodded. Before I could say anything, she came in and threw her arms around Jodie. They stayed like that for a long time, hugging and crying together.

'He were so proud of you,' said Jodie. 'He loved you so much.'

'He loved you, too,' said Amina. 'I said to him once that I hoped you were special, and he said you were.'

They hugged again. It was a long time before they separated. When they did, it was as if a little of their own love for Rachid had rubbed off on each other.

'I'm sure he would have loved seeing you together like that,' I said.

Jodie started to cry again.

'I can't believe how nice you're being to me,' she said. 'You have every right to be mad at me for taking Rachid away from you.'

'You didn't take him away from us,' I replied. 'Those men did that. They've arrested them. Did you know that?'

She nodded.

'The police told me when they rang. I hope they rot in hell, I really do.'

She looked down and fiddled with the buttons on her jacket. I had a feeling she wanted to ask something.

'Go on,' I said. 'Whatever it is.'

'Where is he?' she asked, looking up at me.

I understood. I couldn't bring myself to use the word 'body' either.

'The police still have him. There's no nice way of saying this, but I'm afraid they have to do a post-mortem.'

Her expression was pained.

'I know,' I said, reaching out across the table to take her hand. 'I can't bear to think about it either. But we're hoping to get him back tomorrow and be able to hold his funeral on Monday evening or Tuesday morning at the latest.'

Jodie looked down. I knew it must be unbearable for her, the idea that she would never see him again.

'Would you like to see him? It's not normally done, and I

don't know how we'll arrange it, but I could ask if it's possible for you to see him before the funeral.'

'Yes, please,' she said, without hesitation. 'I just want to say goodbye.'

'I understand. I'll do my best. And you must join us for his funeral.'

Amina stared at me. I knew what she was thinking. But I would deal with Bilal. I would make it right with him.

Jodie appeared uncertain.

'I wouldn't want to make things any more difficult for you than they already are,' she said.

'It's what Rachid would have wanted, and we will honour that. Your family will be welcome too.'

She frowned at me.

'You don't want them there. I told you what they're like.'

'Even more reason for them to be there,' I said. 'Love is stronger than hate. You know that. I want them to know it too.'

She let out a big sigh, appearing to be weighing it up in her mind.

'OK,' she said eventually. 'If you're sure, I'll ask them. I don't know what they'll say, mind. They'll probably feel awkward about it.'

'If it would help for me to meet them beforehand, I'd happily do that.'

'Thank you,' she said. 'I'll ask that too. You could come to our house. I don't think we should intrude here. It wouldn't be fair on you.'

I nodded, knowing she was thinking about Bilal, not me. She was wise, as well as beautiful. But then, Rachid had always had good taste. I gave her my mobile number. She said she'd let me know what they said, though they might want to think about it overnight. I offered to drive her back home.

'No, thank you. I don't want to take you away from your family. I'll get the train. I left some flowers there earlier when I arrived. I want to go back and look at all the others, read some of the cards.'

I hadn't even thought about people laying flowers for Rachid. I couldn't bear the thought of going back to the station, right now, but I was touched to know that other people cared.

'Were there many?' I asked.

Jodie got her phone back out of her pocket and clicked on a photo, before holding it up for Amina and me to see. There were dozens, maybe hundreds of bunches of flowers outside the station. It was too late, of course, this outpouring of love, this show of human compassion. Too late to stop him being killed or bring him back from the dead. But it was something. A tiny glimmer of hope in the darkness. And right now, it was all I had to cling to.

R & J

WhatsApp

I went to your house today. Met your
mum and sister. You were right, they
are lovely. I only saw your dad briefly. I
get it, it's hard for him. He's still mad at
me. He's got every right to be, of course.
Maybe he'll come around. Maybe not. I
wanted to send you this photo too. It's of
the flowers that have been left for you at
Halifax station. I'm sitting here looking
at them now. It makes me feel close to
you. Although I still can't bear to think
about what happened to you here. It was
bad enough getting on train back from
Manchester. I kept imagining you lying
there on floor. And nobody helping you.
Nobody saying a word. I hope they feel
bad about it now. Hope they feel fucking
awful. They deserve to. Because although
it's nice that people have left flowers,
they can't bring you back. Nothing can.
And that's what really hurts. I miss you
so much. I'm going to miss you more

every single day. Some people say time heals but I reckon those people have never had a love like me and you had. Love you. Always 💔   18:37

44

DONNA

I wheeled the bin out to the front path. It was usually Neil's job on a Sunday night, but I wanted the excuse to get out of the house. I was anxious from the waiting. She was on her way. She had messaged to say that much, but she hadn't told me anything else. She would come in her own time. That's what Lorraine had said. I was desperate for the chance to comfort her, although I didn't know if she'd let me. And I was also desperate for the chance to say sorry, although I was aware my apology might not be accepted. Because some things can't be forgiven, however much you would like them to be.

I looked down the street, just in case, but nothing. I turned to go back in as Jakub pulled up next door.

'Are you OK, Mrs Cuthbert?' he asked, seeing the expression on my face as he got out of his car.

'Oh, yes, thanks. Just waiting for Jodie to come home.'

He nodded. He knew nothing about what had been going on, of course, but he still managed to appear concerned.

'How's your father doing?' I asked.

'He's much happier now he's home, thank you. He's going back to the hospital for some more tests soon.'

'Well, I hope he continues to make a good recovery,' I said.

Jakub thanked me and headed for his front door. He had a carrier bag of shopping from the Polish supermarket in each hand. He was a good lad. The sort of boy you'd have been proud to raise. I wondered what that must feel like. And what he'd think if Sam's court case was reported in the local paper.

I took one last look down the road and went back inside. Neil was in the living room, flicking through the channels on the TV, seemingly not able to watch anything for longer than ten seconds.

'Just remember what I told you,' I said sitting down next to him. 'Don't say owt to wind her up.'

'Do you think I try to do that on purpose?'

'I mean remember she's grieving. Tread carefully.'

'Are you still going to tell her?'

'I have to now, don't I? Police said I'll probably be called as a witness. I can't leave her to find out at court case.'

'Can't you at least give it a few days? Give her a chance to settle back in.'

'No,' I replied. 'We're going to do things differently from now on. No secrets in this family, so we don't get any nasty surprises. And that starts with me.'

Neil was quiet for a while, staring at the TV while clearly not watching it.

'She hates me,' he said, eventually.

'She doesn't. She just hates some of crap you come out with, that's all.'

'I don't know what to say to her. She's been going out with some Muslim lad behind our backs. What am I supposed to say about that?'

I turned to look at him, struggling to control my anger.

'You say you're sorry for her loss. It doesn't matter whether he were Muslim or not. He were her boyfriend and you need to tell her how sorry you are about what's happened, because that's what she needs to hear.'

'She hasn't needed me for years.'

'Well, she does now, so, you'd better step up to plate. I've probably lost her already, but you've still got a chance.'

I got up and walked out to the kitchen. I was back to pacing up and down, unable to sit still for two minutes, when I heard her key in the door. I froze, unsure whether I should rush out and greet her, or wait in here.

I poked my head around the kitchen doorway and saw her case in the hall. A case packed for a different life she never got to live. The tragedy of that hit me as she turned to face me. It was like the sadness was running off her face, making pools of grief in the spot she was standing in. I didn't stop to think about it any longer. I ran down the hall and threw my arms around her.

'I'm sorry,' I said. 'I'm so sorry that you've lost him.'

She let me hold her and I was so relieved that I could still provide some comfort, for now, at least.

'I loved him,' she said. 'I really did.'

Neil came out of the living room. He stood awkwardly in the hallway for a moment before the emotion of the moment got the better of him and he piled into us like it was a rugby scrum of grief.

'Sorry, pet,' he said. 'That were a horrible thing to happen to your lad. I'm glad you're home, though.'

She pulled away slightly.

'I don't know how long I'm staying,' she said.

'OK,' I replied, 'you take your time to sort things out, just so long as you know we're all relieved to have you back.'

There was a creak on the stairs. I looked up to see Sam at the top, seemingly uncertain as to whether he should come down. I'd told him it was Jodie's boyfriend who'd been killed, of course. He'd gone very quiet afterwards. We'd barely heard a word out of him since.

Jodie looked up at him. I knew from the expression on her face that any pretence that we were some kind of happy family was about to be shattered.

'I don't want you anywhere near me,' she said.

'All right. I were only coming down to say sorry.'

'Sorry? You were there. You were part of it all, so don't tell me you're sorry. I wish you'd died instead of him because I wouldn't miss you one bit.'

Sam turned and ran back to his room.

'That were out of order,' said Neil. Jodie took one look at him and ran straight upstairs, slamming her bedroom door behind her. And I stood there, knowing I had something far worse to admit.

I put it off as long as I could but the need to get it over with broke me in the end. I went upstairs with a mug of tea and a slice of Battenberg. She'd always loved what she called 'old-lady cakes'.

I knocked on her door. I wasn't completely sure what the grunt from inside meant, but I chanced it and went in anyway.

She was lying on her bed, her eyes red, looking at photos on her phone. I put the tray down on her bedside table without saying anything. She held up her phone screen to me.

'Look,' she said, showing me a photo of a young man with dark hair, shaved at the side, a little moustache and neat beard, with one arm draped casually around her shoulder. They were laughing. I don't think I had ever seen her looking happier. Apart from the night of her party, when she was dancing with him, perhaps.

'That's him. That's Rachid. He has a name. You all need to start using it. And I loved him more than anyone or anything else in the world and I will never love anyone as much as him, so don't start coming out with that crap about finding someone else one day because I am not interested, OK?'

I stood there and said nothing. She was furious before I'd even started. I didn't have a hope in hell of getting out of there alive, but I still felt compelled to tell her anyway. I sat down on the edge of her bed and reached out my arm to grasp her hand. I was surprised when she didn't push it away.

'I'm so sorry about Rachid, love. I wish we could have met him, but I get why you didn't tell us, of course I do. I'm ashamed of your brother's behaviour too.'

'Please don't call him my brother,' she said. 'I've disowned him.'

I nodded and bit my lip before I continued.

'I hate the fact that you felt you had to keep your relationship secret, that you thought running off like that were only way you could be together.'

'His family were moving to Paris. It all happened so quickly. We couldn't bear thought of being apart.'

'I can't imagine what she must be going through. His poor mum.'

She hesitated before replying.

'I met her today.'

'Sorry?'

'Rachid's mum. I went to their house, met his mum and sister.'

I looked down to try to cover up how much that hurt. The fact that she had been to see his family before her own.

'Oh, right.'

'She's lovely, his mum. Her name's Sylvie. She wants to meet you all. Said some good needs to come out of this, which is why she's invited me and all of you to Rachid's funeral.'

'Jesus, I don't know, love. I'm not sure that would be a good idea, given everything that's gone on.'

'She knows about Sam being at rally, but she still wants you there. She wanted to meet you all before funeral so I said she could come here tomorrow afternoon.'

I blew out heavily. The woman was certainly more forgiving than I would be. But I couldn't risk her turning up and recognising me from the train. I had to tell Jodie.

'Look, love, there's summat you need to know.'

Jodie propped herself up in bed. The change of tone in my voice had obviously got her worried. I decided to go on.

'When I came home from work yesterday, well, I didn't know it at time, but I were on same train as Rachid and his family.'

She stared at me, open-mouthed. There was no easy way to say it. I looked out of the window, because I was too much of a coward to say it to her face.

'I were sitting in same carriage. I only saw back of his head, mind. Not his face. But I saw his mum and sister. And the blokes who did it.'

'What do you mean? How do you know it were them?'

'Because they were giving his family verbal. Telling them to go back where they came from.'

'You heard them say that?'

I nodded.

'So, what did you do?'

I took a deep breath.

'Nowt. I'm not proud of it, love. But I did nowt. I got off train at Low Moor and I thought someone else on train would shut them up or guard would come along in a minute and throw them off. Only they didn't, of course.'

'Oh my God. I don't believe I'm hearing this. I thought you were better than other two.'

'I were scared they'd turn on me. They were big blokes, so I decided not to get involved. Like everyone else on train, as it turned out.'

'But you could have asked Rachid's mum if she were OK. You could have sat next to them. Or asked if they wanted to get off when you did.'

'I know,' I said. 'And for rest of my life I'll regret that I didn't do any of those things. I went to police station last night and gave them a statement. They said I might be called as a witness at trial, but I know that's all a bit late in day.'

Jodie stared at me; I could see the colour rising in her cheeks.

'You could have saved him,' she said. 'You could have saved Rachid's life.'

'If I'd known he were your fella—'

'No,' she said, shaking her head vigorously. 'It doesn't matter who he was. You should have saved him anyway. Because he was a fucking human being.'

'Jodie, I'm so sorry.'

'Get out,' she screamed. 'You're as bad as rest of them.'

45

JODIE

I thump my pillow repeatedly and scream in fury before curling into a ball on my bed. Turns out my family are my enemy. I no longer want to be a Cuthbert. The name fills me with disgust. I don't want to be here in their house. I want to be in our apartment in Manchester with Rachid. Lying in his arms, stroking his face, listening to Prince. But I can never have that now. He's been taken from me. And I'm so angry about it, I don't know how I'm going to survive.

I lie there for a long time, curled in a ball of fury, before I unclench my fists and reach for my phone to call the one member of my family I still trust. Lorraine picks up on the second ring.

'Jodie, are you OK? Where are you?'

'I'm at home but I can't stay here. I want to stay at yours, if that's OK. It's either that, or I go back to Manchester.'

She hesitates for only a second.

'Sure. Tell your mum, though. She needs to know where you're going.'

'Can you call her? I can't speak to her. Not now I know what she did.'

I hear Lorraine sigh. I guess Mum must have told her too.

'OK. Listen, I'll send Tyler around to yours, so we can be alone to talk things through.'

'Thanks,' I say. 'I'll see you soon.'

I leave it a few minutes, wait until I hear Mum's mobile ring. Until I know she won't try to stop me. And then I get off my bed, take a deep breath and head downstairs. My case is still in the hallway waiting for me. I pull on my jacket and take hold of it, trying not to think of the last time I did this, full of fear and anxiety, but desperate to start my new life together with Rachid. Now, there's nothing but an empty, aching hole inside me and a photo on my phone of some flowers left at a train station.

Mum says nothing as I open the front door. I can feel her gaze on me from the kitchen. I think she may be crying. But it's too late to be sorry now. We live and die by our actions. Or lack of them. I walk out of the door.

I see Tyler on the way to Lorraine's. I turn a corner and he's there. A holdall slung over his shoulder. I immediately cross the road, without saying so much as a word to him. He was there, he was part of it. He's the enemy too.

He has his head down as he passes me on the opposite side of the street. I hope he feels bad. I hope they all feel bad. All of them who were part of this.

When I get to Lorraine's house, I take a moment to try to compose myself and ring the bell. But when she opens the door, I collapse in her arms, sobbing.

'I'm so sorry, sweetie,' she whispers into my ear. 'I hate to see you hurting like this.'

She helps me inside and pulls the case in after me before shutting the door. I sink down onto the floor with my back against it. My body shaking.

'She left him to die,' I say. 'Mum got off that train and left him to die.'

'She didn't know who he was. She wouldn't have done that if she'd known.'

'But that's the whole point. It shouldn't matter.'

We sit there in silence for a long time, until my chest stops heaving and my breathing calms a little. That's when Lorraine tells me.

'I was there when Rachid was brought into hospital,' she says. 'I helped to treat him. We did everything we could. He died sleeping. He wouldn't have felt a thing.'

I stare at her and then grab hold of her hands. Because these were the hands that held Rachid, and through them I can feel close to him.

'Tell me everything,' I say. 'From the second you first saw Rachid till the last. I want to know it all.'

'Are you sure?' asks Lorraine. 'It's pretty tough stuff to hear.'

'I hate that I wasn't there for him at the end, but now I know you were, and I want to know everything.'

So she tells me. How there was an emergency team waiting

for him when he arrived. How they battled to stabilise him. How it was clear straight away that he had probably suffered massive bleeding on the brain, and the CT scan confirmed it, leaving them no option but to operate. How he was slipping in and out of consciousness during this time. There were no final words. No messages for loved ones. It was too late for any of that.

'Did you meet his family?'

Lorraine nods.

'It were horrible to see them so upset. They were all crying, even his dad.'

'I went to see them earlier. His dad didn't want to talk to me, not that I blame him. But his mum were lovely. She invited us all to funeral. Even when I'd told her about Sam being part of it all. Said some good needed to come of it and she wanted to meet my family. I said she could come round to ours tomorrow afternoon.'

'Wow. What did your mum say to that?'

'She doesn't think it's a good idea. Nor do I, now I know what she did.'

'And how do you think she feels about what happened?'

I stare up at the ceiling for a moment.

'Like a piece of shit.'

Lorraine nods.

'Couldn't have put it better mesen. So what happens now?'

'I can't take away what she did.'

'No. But you could forgive her for it.'

'And why would I do that?'

'Because maybe Rachid's mum is right. Maybe something good can come out of this. But you can't expect to bring two families together if you can't even forgive your mum.'

I bend my head, rub my eyes, which are still red with tears.

'What, so just cos my mum meets Rachid's mum, all of this crap's going to stop?'

'Nope. But you might change one mind. Maybe two. And change has got to start somewhere.'

46

SYLVIE

'I don't see how you can even be contemplating it,' said Bilal. 'We're making preparations for our son's funeral, and you want to invite the girl he was planning to run away with and her family to be part of it.'

I sighed and put down the mixing bowl in my hand. I had a lot of work to do, but there was nothing more important than this conversation right now.

'Yes, I do.'

'Are you deliberately trying to make things more difficult for me?'

'No, of course not. I'm trying to do what Rachid would have wanted.'

'Yes, well we can only guess at what he would have wanted, because he didn't tell us. Like he didn't tell us about his secret girlfriend or his plans to run away with her.'

I stared at Bilal.

'You're angry at him, aren't you?'

'Yes, I am. He lied to us, Sylvie.'

'And why do you think that was?'

Bilal walked over to the kitchen sink with his mug in his hand.

'Because he knew it was wrong and that we would try to stop him throwing away his future like that.'

'Not "we", "you". You were the one who fought with him over everything he wanted to do. You tried for months to stop him going on that college course, but he loved it. And he met a girl he fell madly in love with there. And just when he was having the time of his life, you decided to uproot us all and go back to Paris.'

Bilal stared at me. It was a long time since he'd seen me that angry. And no doubt he could remember what had caused my anger then.

'You wanted to go too. It was a family decision.'

'No. It was your decision, and I went along with it because I felt so guilty about Maman being on her own and I was worried about Amina. But you didn't stop to consult Rachid, you simply presented it as a fait accompli. What would have been the point in him telling us the truth? He knew you would simply have dismissed his wishes and gone ahead with it anyway. We've only got ourselves to blame for what he did. It's certainly not the fault of the girl he fell in love with.'

I took a breath, surprised at the ferocity of my comments. The expression on Bilal's face suggested he was too.

'Why didn't you say any of this before?'

'I tried, Bilal, but you didn't listen. You are always so certain you are right. And I think the whole Paris thing was your way of trying to make it up to us, for all the hurt you'd caused. I think the idea of drawing a line under everything appealed to you.'

He bowed his head. It was a long time before he spoke.

'We don't know anything about this girl.'

'You don't because you refused to meet her. I found out quite a lot. And I liked her very much. But the only thing that really matters is that our son was in love with her. That's all you need to know.'

When the bell rang later, I thought it must be Gillian, who had messaged to say she was on her way. But when I opened the door expecting to see her tall frame in front of me, I had to lower my gaze to meet the eyes of the diminutive figure that stood there instead.

Edwina was clutching a large ceramic dish with both hands and had an envelope sticking out of her coat pocket. A solitary tear trickled from the corner of her right eye and dispersed into tributaries along each wrinkle. I looked at her: so old, so precious. I knew exactly what she was thinking: that it should have been her, not the vibrant young man next door who she had watched growing up since he was a baby.

She held out the dish, her hands shaking.

'I didn't know what to bring. It seems such a paltry offering, but I remember Rachid enjoying my vegetable and potato bake. He helped me pipe the mashed potato on it once, I recall that very clearly. He was such a pleasure to have in our house, and Feo adored him, of course.'

I took it from her and put it down on the occasional table in the hallway, before stepping down onto the path and folding my arms around her.

'I would have come yesterday, but I didn't want to intrude on your grief,' she said. 'How are you holding up, Sylvie dear? I am so, so sorry for your terrible loss.'

I let her reach up and stroke my hair. She had a mother's touch. Tenderness and care in her fingers. And love. So much love in her heart.

'I'm feeling empty and broken inside,' I replied. 'It's as if they ripped him from my womb.'

'No mother should see her son die,' said Edwina. 'It is not the natural order of things. We bring life into the world. You have brought so many lives into this world. The loss of such a precious one is unbearable.'

She held me for a long time. Held me in her warmth and wisdom. Until, eventually, I stepped back, although I kept hold of her hands.

'I'm sorry, I should have invited you in,' I said.

'No, this is a time for family. I will leave you with them now, but I want you to know I will be here for you in the days and weeks and months ahead. And we will talk about your beautiful boy and what joy he brought to your life. Because their hate can't take that away from you. It can take a life, but not the memories. They are yours to keep and treasure.'

She squeezed my hands before passing me the envelope from her pocket and turning to walk slowly back down the path.

I opened it once I was inside. 'With Deepest Sympathies', the card said on the front, and inside, written in fountain pen in Edwina's elegant hand, it read, *Dearest Sylvie, Bilal and Amina, so very sorry for your loss. Hold each other tight. Rachid will always be part of your family. With Fondest Love, Edwina and Feo.*

Gillian arrived just after what would have been lunchtime, had we felt like eating. Although she greeted us warmly and asked how we were doing, she had a brisk, businesslike air about her, as if she was a woman with a lot to get through.

We gathered around the kitchen table, as had now become customary. She took out her notebook and phone, placed them in front of her, then looked up at us.

'Right, we've charged the three men we've been holding with murder. We'll be announcing it to the media shortly and they'll be appearing before a magistrate tomorrow morning. It's just a remand hearing at this stage, they won't be granted bail on such a serious charge, and you don't need to attend court, unless you want to, of course?'

She looked at each of us in turn. We shook our heads.

'The men's solicitor has confirmed that they are not requesting an independent post-mortem, so Rachid's body will be released to you very shortly and you're free to go ahead with the funeral this evening, as you've planned.'

Bilal's head dropped. I knew he was trying to hide the extent of his relief from Gillian.

'Thank you,' I whispered. It was all we wanted. We were getting our boy back. We could lay him to rest. Although it would be the hardest thing we had ever done in our lives.

Amina came downstairs shortly after Gillian left. She looked at our faces for clues. I nodded.

'We can go ahead with the funeral this evening,' I said. 'And they've charged the men.'

'Good,' she replied, solemnly. 'Can I invite somebody to the funeral, please?'

Bilal looked at her.

'Of course you can, although almost everyone from the mosque will be there. They have been wonderful, organising everything.'

Amina looked at me, then back to Bilal.

'I want to invite Jodie,' she said.

Bilal frowned.

'But you don't know her,' said Bilal.

'No, but Rachid did, and he loved her. And that's good enough for me.'

'And I'd like to invite her family,' I said. 'I'd like to go and do it in person now. It's what Rachid would have wanted. And that's what matters today. And when you have prepared Rachid, when he is washed and shrouded, I would like Jodie to have a few moments alone with him.'

'You know that's not allowed—' Bilal started.

I raised my hand.

'They had to conduct their relationship in secret. I don't

want to deny her the chance to say goodbye in private. Two minutes. That's all I ask.'

'Please, Papa,' said Amina.

She hadn't called him that to his face for a long time. Bilal stood deep in thought, before finally turning to face both of us.

'As you wish,' he said. 'I will be civil to them but can't promise any more than that.' He turned and walked away. I heard his study door shut behind him. I glanced at the clock. He would have gone to pray. I hoped he would find some comfort.

Amina ran over to me and gave me a hug.

'Thank you,' I said. 'For your bravery and your courage. Your brother would be very proud of you.'

R & J

WhatsApp

I'm going to come and see you later. Just for a few minutes on my own, your mum says. It means so much that they'll let me do it. Like they accept me. Accept our love. I ache to be with you again. And I know it won't be the same, but I want to be where you are. Even though you won't know and I can't touch you and it will hurt like hell. It'll be worth it. Because I will be with you and there's nowhere on earth I'd rather be

14:45

47

DONNA

I sat on the sofa with Neil, staring vacantly at whatever it was that we were supposed to be watching. Daytime TV hadn't got any better since the last time I'd seen it, but there really wasn't much else to do. I'd pulled a sickie this morning and, for once, allowed Sam to do the same. To be honest, it wasn't really pulling a sickie. I'd barely slept since Friday night and was pretty much at popping point. If I'd gone into work, I'd probably have lamped the first punter who complained about something, so it was more of a case of job preservation, really. Nor was I in any state to explain to Sam's head teacher why he'd have to take time off for a court case. That would have to wait for another day. And Neil hadn't had any work on anyway.

We still hadn't heard from Jodie. Clearly, she was in no mood to come back home. Lorraine had rung me late last night to say she was doing OK but needed some time to think.

I had no idea what was going to happen. Tyler would go back there after school this afternoon and I was quite sure Jodie wouldn't want to share a room with him. Maybe she'd go back to Manchester or move in with a friend. I suspected we'd lost her for good. There were some things you could apologise for, some rows that would blow over. But our family had done way too much harm for forgiveness. Which was why I was surprised to hear the key in the door a few minutes later. And even more surprised to see her standing in the hallway with her case. I gestured to Neil to turn the TV off.

'Right,' she said. 'Sylvie's on her way.'

'Who?' I asked.

'Sylvie. Rachid's mum.'

I frowned at her.

'Why's she coming here?'

'I told you. She wants to meet you. And she wants to invite you to Rachid's funeral later.'

'Don't be daft, pet,' said Neil. 'We can't go, can we? We're not Muslim.'

'It doesn't matter. She's not Muslim either.'

'Isn't she?' he asked.

'No. She's French. One of those bloody Europeans you wanted to send back home.'

I elbowed Neil in case he had any intention of rising to the bait. He said nothing. Jodie turned to look at me.

'I'm going upstairs to get myself ready for funeral. I want you to talk to her. To apologise properly for what you did. She'll forgive you. She's forgiven me and Sam, she's that sort of person. And she's reason I've come back here. Because I'm trying to be as big a person as she is and forgive you, though I'm not quite there yet.

'So, it's up to you. When she's finished here, she's taking me to see Rachid before funeral. I'll text you address of mosque and time it starts. You're either there or you're not. You decide what sort of people you are.'

She turned and left the room. I heard her footsteps go upstairs and the bump of her case behind her on each step. I looked at Neil. He shrugged. I couldn't have imagined how proud I would feel to be humbled by my own daughter.

The doorbell rang a few minutes later. Neil and I looked at each other without saying a word. I got up and opened the front door, having no idea what I was going to say. I recognised the woman who stood before me instantly. It was the eyes, of course. Although the panic and fear in them had been replaced by a sad, hollowed-out emptiness.

I saw a flicker of recognition on her face. A furrow of her brow. She knew. I was sure she knew. But I was going to tell her anyway.

'Hello,' I said. 'Jodie said you were coming. We're very sorry for your loss.'

She nodded. She was still looking at me. I was going to have to tell her. But not out here in the street.

'Please, come in,' I said, opening the door wider.

She stepped into the hallway. I was aware of not having hoovered since Friday. And then I remembered that her son had been brutally beaten in front of her, and that a few crumbs on the carpet were the least of her worries.

'Come through to kitchen,' I said. She followed me past the open living-room door, but Neil kept himself from view.

'Jodie's upstairs getting ready,' I said, and regretted it instantly. Like she needed reminding that her son was being buried later today. Did Muslims bury or cremate? I couldn't even remember that or bring myself to ask.

'Please, sit down,' I said, gesturing towards the table. She took a seat at the end. I sat down opposite her. We sat in silence for a moment as I desperately tried to form the right words in my head. But in the end, I cracked and blurted it out.

'You're right. It is me,' I said. 'From train on Saturday. I'm so sorry. I should never have left you like that. I've gone over and over it in my head. I were scared, see, though not as scared as you were, obviously. I've got no excuse. None whatsoever. If I'd known . . .' My voice trailed off as I realised how pathetic I sounded.

She sat staring at me for a long time. I half expected her to give me a mouthful, slap me across the face. Or simply stand up and walk out. Any of those would have been acceptable in the circumstances. She didn't, though. She extended her arm along the table towards me. I took her outstretched hand and she squeezed mine gently.

'Please don't feel bad about it,' she said.

'But I do. I'm nowt more than a coward.'

Sylvie shook her head.

'A coward would not have gone to the police and given a statement. Or agreed to be a witness in court.'

I frowned at her.

'You knew?'

'Not that it was you. But the police told me that the woman who got off the train had come forward.'

I shook my head.

'Still, Jodie will never forgive me for it, and I can't say I blame her.'

'Your daughter is hurting, like me. She will come around in time.'

I shrugged. We sat there, still holding hands but not saying anything for a while.

'Jodie is beautiful,' she said eventually. 'She radiates light and love.'

It was the nicest thing anyone had ever said to me.

'Thank you. Your son came to Jodie's eighteenth birthday party. He helped with music. We didn't know, of course. And it were a masked ball, so we didn't get a proper look at him. But I have never seen Jodie so happy as she were when she were dancing with him.'

Sylvie nodded.

'They must have made such a beautiful couple. I'm so sad I never saw them together.'

'Jodie's got photos of them together on her phone,' I said. 'Lots of them. I'm sure she'd send you some.'

'I'd like that,' she replied. 'I'm sure Rachid will have lots on his phone too, but it's still with the police.'

'I heard they arrested them,' I said. 'Bastards who did it, if you'll excuse my French.'

I realised as soon as I said it.

'Sorry, I shouldn't have said that, not with you being . . .'

I pulled a face. I was making such a pig's ear of this. Although she was kind enough not to say anything.

'Can I get you a drink — tea? Coffee?' I asked.

'No, thank you. I can't stop. I'm on my way to the mosque. That's why I came, really. Jodie is coming with me, but I wanted to invite you and your family to join us.'

'It's very kind of you,' I said. 'But I really don't think we should come. I wouldn't want to cause any more trouble.'

'My husband has agreed. My daughter wants you there too. Because it's what Rachid would have wanted.'

'I know, and we really appreciate it. But thing is, my son got arrested on Saturday. He were at that rally. He were one of them. Him and his cousin. I've read him bloody riot act about it too. But you don't want him at funeral. I can't bear to look at him, so I don't expect you to have to.'

'That's exactly why I want him there. Because if you lose him to these people, we've all lost. And Rachid's death will have been in vain. I want him to be there. I want him to see where this leads. To understand how futile it is. To see that we bleed and hurt and suffer just like you do.'

I bowed my head as I mulled over her words. She was right, of course. I could see that now. See it so clearly. I had no idea whether it would make a blind bit of difference to Sam, but I knew damn well I had to try. I looked at her and nodded.

'We'll be there,' I said. 'Can I bring his cousin too? One who were with him.'

'Of course,' she said.

'Good. That's sorted then. I'd better let you go.'

We both stood up. I held my arms out. She stepped forward and we embraced for a second or two.

'Your son did nowt to deserve this. Nowt at all. I'm so sorry.'

She looked at me and something passed between us. Perhaps a sense that we were not so different at all. A knowledge that in different circumstances we could have been making plans together for an altogether happier event. Instead of preparing for her son's funeral.

We walked out into the hall together just as Jodie appeared at the top of the stairs. She was wearing the dress she'd made for her birthday party. And over her head she'd placed a scarf of midnight blue with little stars on it. She looked every bit as beautiful as she had done that night. But as she walked down the stairs, I saw that her eyes were full of tears, her steps heavy. Every shred of light had departed from her.

She stopped at the bottom and looked at me.

'We'll see you there,' I said. 'All of us.'

She nodded and walked out of the house with Sylvie, pulling the door shut behind her.

I stood there for a moment, desperately trying to compose myself, to summon the strength I needed, and then I hollered at the top of my voice.

'Sam, get down here this minute. Neil, come out here too.'

Neil emerged from the living room. Sam descended the stairs slowly, still unable to look me in the eye.

'Right. We're going to Rachid's funeral. His mother has been kind enough to invite us, despite everything we have done. Jodie has gone with her now and I've told her we're all going to be there.'

'I don't want to go,' said Sam.

'Hard luck. Sylvie doesn't want to bury her son, but she's got to do it anyway.'

'What are we supposed to wear?' said Neil.

'It doesn't matter, does it?' I said. 'Same suit you wore to my dad's funeral, I'd imagine. Sam, you can put your school uniform on, if that's best you've got. And call Tyler and tell him to do same, because we're picking him up on the way.'

They both stared at me.

'Jodie needs her family to support her. This is going to be hardest day of her life and we're all going to be there for her, and I don't care how awkward you feel, because you won't feel one-hundredth as bad as she does right now.'

Neil caught my eye and gave a little nod. He turned to Sam.

'You heard your mother. Go and get yoursen ready and make sure you look smart when you come back down.'

Sam turned and headed upstairs without a word.

'Right,' I said, 'and you can order us a cab, because we're not turning up there in your work van.'

He nodded and went back into the living room. My phone beeped. I picked it up. It was a text from Jodie. It said simply, 'Thank you'. And for the first time in ages, I felt something vaguely resembling hope.

48

JODIE

I stand barefoot outside the room where Rachid lies. Sylvie had offered to come in with me but I told her what I tell myself now. That this is something I have to do on my own.

The door opens and Mr Mastour comes out. He looks older and shorter than I remember him from yesterday, almost as if he is ageing and stooping under the weight of his grief. We look at each other for a moment.

'Thank you for letting me do this,' I say. 'I'm so sorry for your loss. I loved your son very much.'

He nods in acknowledgement. I think he wants to say something but is unable to. In the end, he mouths 'Thank you,' to me, before standing to one side of the open door and turning his face away from me in an effort to hide his tears. I hesitate, unsure if I can do this, then summon up my courage and walk into the room, shutting the door behind me.

I'd tried to prepare myself for what would confront me, even googled it, as Lorraine had suggested. But still, seeing Rachid's body lying there is enough to stop me in my tracks. There's a smell of camphor in the air, and I don't know if it's that or simply the sight of his body that is making me feel sick and a little light-headed. I sink to my knees in front of him.

His entire body is wrapped in white cotton. There are four ties: one above his head, others across his forearms and legs, and the final one below his feet. I see only the outline of his body beneath the shroud. And yet somehow, it is unmistakably Rachid.

'Hey,' I say. 'I didn't recognise you without your AirPods.' I allow myself a tiny smile, knowing that, if he could, he would be smiling too.

'Your dad let me do this. Your mum and Amina persuaded him. If you could see him now, you'd know how much he loved you. I guess he didn't know how to say it to your face.

'My family are coming to your funeral. I apologise in advance. They'll probably show me up big time. But they'll be here, we've got your mum to thank for that. She really is awesome.

'Who'd have thought it, our families brought together by our love. I don't know how long it'll last. Maybe it'll be like that truce in First World War where they played a footie match together on Christmas Day and went back to killing each other day after. But at least it's happening. I just wish it could have happened when you were still alive.'

I pause to blow out hard. I'm trying so hard not to cry.

'At first, I thought maybe we were wrong, maybe they would

have accepted us. But, nah, they wouldn't have. Not without you getting killed. It's so stupid, isn't it? That someone's got to die before people can put aside their differences. So stupid and crap and pointless.

'And do you know what? I'd swap all this pretence of unity for one more day with you. One hour, one minute, one second. Just to look into your eyes, feel your breath on my face, hear you say my name. I nearly joined you, you know. When I heard. I went out onto the balcony of our Airbnb, and I were going to come straight to you. But you stopped me. Because I knew you wouldn't want that. And you're right. It would have been such a stupid waste.

'I don't have to die to prove how much I love you. I know and you know. That's all that matters. So, even though I can't imagine living without you, I'm going to try to live my life for you. For the things you believed in, the love we shared, the dreams you had for me. And I'll see your face every time I look up at the stars and hear your voice every time I listen to Prince. I've been playing "Sometimes It Snows in April" on repeat. Because it does, and things we don't expect to happen do. And people we love die. None of it makes any sense, and it's pointless trying to make sense of it. All that matters is what we had. And I'm so lucky and so privileged to have loved you. I may not have had you for long, but our star burned brightly. And I will never allow it to die.'

I shut my eyes for a second and hug my arms tightly around myself.

'All good things . . .' I whisper. And blow him a kiss.

49

SYLVIE

I stood there, Bilal one side of me, Amina the other. A wobbly tripod struggling to hold everything together as we said goodbye to the missing member of our family. The one who lay in front of us, at peace now. The son I had brought into this world, about to be returned to it. Too soon, of course. All deaths are too soon. But no mother should have to bury her own. To mourn the loss of a child so much a part of them that it feels like burying a limb.

Bilal gripped one arm, Amina the other. I had to support them now. That was my role in life. But I would always be Rachid's mother. No one could take that away from me. Would always be filled with love for him and regrets for the things I didn't say and do. My breath caught as I looked at him. My boy, who shone so brightly, now shrouded and still.

Behind me I heard the cries of the young woman he loved

so fiercely. Whose hopes and dreams had been shattered so cruelly. And who somehow, like me, needed to find a way through this. I turned; her mother and father were on either side of her, supporting her, looking lost and bewildered. And on the other side of her father stood her brother and cousin. Small and insignificant but with tears running down their faces. Tears that gave me a glimmer of hope.

Jodie looked up for a second, as if she could feel my gaze on her. Our eyes locked, united in grief. And forever connected in love.

Give me my Romeo, and when he shall die,
Take him and cut him out in little stars,
And he will make the face of heaven so fine
That all the world will be in love with night
And pay no worship to the garish sun.

Romeo and Juliet
by William Shakespeare,
Act III, Scene ii

Epilogue

DONNA

I always looked for her when I got on the train in the mornings. I still hadn't seen her since the funeral. Maybe she hadn't returned to work yet or had simply decided not to go back at all. Jodie wasn't sure, although she had said the family weren't going to Paris now, because Sylvie couldn't bear to leave Rachid.

It was probably just as well I hadn't seen her. I had no idea how to start that conversation. I imagined I would be the one who would find it difficult, because nothing I could say would make it better or take away her pain. I would probably keep a respectful distance. Let her get off the train first, so I didn't have to talk to her on the way to the ticket barriers. Try to avoid any chance of us walking side by side together along the platform, so I didn't have to look her in the eye and see the pools of grief that lay there. Didn't have to hear the pain in her voice. Or smell the sorrow that remained.

In truth, I wasn't worthy of her company. My family were not fit to walk the same streets as hers. I would carry that knowledge with me for the rest of my days. But she would carry something far heavier and far, far worse.

The train hurtled on towards Bradford. I played out the reverse journey in my mind, as I had done so many times. All the opportunities I had not taken to make a difference. To offer comfort or support. To maybe save a life.

At Bradford Interchange two young men got on, perhaps on their way to college or to work. They were loud. That was the first thing I noticed. Talking and playing music on their phone. Disrespecting the calm of the early-morning rush hour train. Whatever the track was, the words 'bitch' and 'hoe' seemed to feature prominently. People started to shift in their seats.

There was a young woman sitting opposite the men. She was wearing a hijab and was clearly uncomfortable in their presence. They noticed, of course. Smelt her fear. At which point they started to exploit it.

'Hey lady, you wanna sing along?' one asked. 'You wanna get up and shake your booty?'

The taller guy with stubble laughed.

'She can't do that, can she? It's against her religion. She gotta keep her assets hidden.'

I could see the young woman's body tense. I felt mine do the same. Every muscle straining against what I knew I had to do. Not to wait for someone else to intervene. Not to think it wasn't my problem simply because I wasn't the target. This woman needed help, now. And I was damned if I was going to make the same mistake twice.

I did nothing special or brave. Nothing that deserved praise, or in any way made up for what I hadn't done before. I simply did what every decent person should do for a fellow human being.

I stood up and stepped forward.

Afterword

I wish this novel hadn't been inspired by real-life events, but it was. The murder of Jo Cox MP, who represented the Batley and Spen constituency, not far from my home in West Yorkshire, affected me deeply. A few days later I went with my family and a friend to lay flowers near where she was murdered. We happened to arrive at the same time as her parents and I'll never forget the kind words her father had for my young son, his love and warmth such a contrast to the hate of the far-right activist who murdered his daughter.

My European friends and friends of colour, many born in this country, some who have made their home here, told me of the verbal abuse they had suffered during and after the Brexit campaign, much of it the worst racism they had ever encountered. Being told to 'go home' had become a regular occurrence in their lives.

I witnessed abuse and intimidation at Leeds station when I was on my way to a Stop Brexit march, and witnessed a black ticket inspector being told to 'go home' by an abusive football supporter at Manchester Piccadilly station.

And then a friend and her young son were racially abused by a group of men on their way home from Leeds station (one was later convicted). Only one person offered any support to them, asking if they wanted to get off the busy train at the same station as her. The initial lack of action from the police was troubling and the toll the crime and subsequent trial had on them deeply upsetting.

The divisions in our society had never seemed so deep. Hatred, much of it spouted by politicians and whipped up by the mainstream media, had spilt onto our streets. And yet I knew that many people were unaware of this, perhaps living in areas that weren't as divided or not having friends who were on the receiving end of such abuse. Or simply believing that such things couldn't happen in this country.

Leeds, which narrowly voted 50.3 per cent to Remain, against 49.7 per cent to Leave, seemed an obvious setting for the novel, and a reimagined version of *Romeo and Juliet* the obvious way to personalise these issues and make it a very human story of a young couple's love being beset by the hate of the divided families and communities around them. Telling it largely from the point of view of two mothers who (to quote from Jo Cox's maiden speech in the Commons) have far more in common than that which divides them was hugely important to me.

It is not a political book. It's simply about humanity. I hope it will open eyes and hearts because, sadly, the hate hasn't gone away. To that end, I will be making donations from the royalties of this novel to HOPE not hate, www.hopenothate.org.uk, who work to challenge all kinds of extremism and build local communities, and to the Jo Cox Foundation, www.jocoxfoundation.org, which works to build a positive legacy out of the tragedy of her murder. If you are able to join me in making a donation, however small, I'd be very grateful. Or you could simply visit their websites and learn about their work.

What we can all do is be better allies, to listen to, give space to and amplify the voices of those people affected. To ensure everyone in our country feels welcome. To call out racial abuse and hostility to immigrants, refugees and those born in different countries to us. In short, to stand up and step forward.

Acknowledgements

This is a novel written during the pandemic, which made it tougher than usual for everyone involved. Huge thanks to the following people: my editor Cassie Browne for helping me get the best out of my characters and their relationships, my initial editor Emma Capron, assistant editor Kat Burdon, Milly Reid, Hannah Winter, David Murphy and all the team at Quercus. My copy-editor Rachel Wright for her attention to detail and to Holly Ovenden for the wonderful cover design.

My agent Anthony Goff for his invaluable advice, wisdom and support, and all the team at David Higham Associates who help bring my books to readers across the world.

Hamza Jahanzeb for his authenticity report, Graham Bartlett, police procedural adviser, for his highly recommended service www.policeadviser.co.uk, and 'Harry' for his paramedic review (any inaccuracies are down to me exercising artistic licence!).

Vie Olivia for her French perspective and experience of the permanent residence application and British citizenship procedures. Christoph for his experiences of applying for British citizenship, settled status and the impact of the EU referendum. Mahalia for her cultural perspective and feedback. Donations have been made to In Limbo, www.inlimboproject.org, The 3 Million, www.the3million.org.uk, the Joint Council for the Welfare of Immigrants, www.jcwi.org.uk, and Leeds Baby Bank, www.leedsbabybank.org, as a thank you for their help.

The book *In Limbo: Brexit Testimonies from EU Citizens in the UK*, from an idea by Elena Remigi, was a valuable source of research into the experiences of EU citizens and is an excellent read available via www.inlimboproject.org.

Thanks to my family and friends for their ongoing support, particularly my husband Ian for the author photos, book trailers/promo videos and interminable plot walks, and my son Rohan for his 24/7 tech support, designing my amazing website www.lindagreenauthor.com and sharing his GCSE *Romeo and Juliet* revision guides and extensive Shakespeare knowledge with me – looking forward to you directing the stage version!

To booksellers, librarians, book bloggers, reviewers and fellow authors for their ongoing support and to my readers, for buying, borrowing, reviewing and recommending my books. You've had a long wait for this one and I very much hope you enjoy it. Please do let me know by getting in touch via email: contact@ lindagreenauthor.com, Twitter: @lindagreenisms, Facebook: Author Linda Green, and Instagram: lindagreenbooks. I love reading your comments and will respond to as many as possible!

READING GROUP GUIDE

1. What would you say the Cuthbert and Mastour families have in common?

2. How do Sylvie and Donna respond to the conflict they encounter at home and outside?

3. Does the idea of a modern-day *Romeo and Juliet* work with the Yorkshire backdrop and Brexit divisions?

4. How are love and hate explored in the novel?

5. How do Bilal and Neil respond to the challenges they face?

6. What do you learn from seeing the situation from Jodie and Rachid's point of view?

7. If you're familiar with *Romeo and Juliet*, did it enhance your enjoyment of the novel? Do you think you would respond in the same way if you weren't familiar with it?

8. What do you think Sylvie and Donna could learn from each other?

9. How do you think you would react in Donna's situation on the train when she sees Sylvie's family being racially abused?

10. What do you imagine happening to the two families after the epilogue?